PLAIN JAYNE

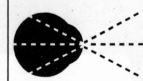

This Large Print Book carries the
Seal of Approval of N.A.V.H.

PLAIN JAYNE

HILLARY MANTON LODGE

THORNDIKE PRESS
A part of Gale, Cengage Learning

GALE
CENGAGE Learning™

Detroit • New York • San Francisco • New Haven, Conn • Waterville, Maine • London

GALE
CENGAGE Learning™

Copyright © 2010 by Hillary Manton Lodge.
Thorndike Press, a part of Gale, Cengage Learning.

Thorndike Press® Large Print Christian Fiction.
The text of this Large Print edition is unabridged.
Other aspects of the book may vary from the original edition.
Set in 16 pt. Plantin.

LIBRARY OF CONGRESS CATALOGING-IN-PUBLICATION DATA

Lodge, Hillary Manton.
  Plain Jayne / by Hillary Manton Lodge.
    p. cm. — (Thorndike press large print Christian fiction)
  ISBN-13: 978-1-4104-2464-8 (alk. paper)
  ISBN-10: 1-4104-2464-2 (alk. paper)
  1. Women journalists—Fiction. 2. Amish—Oregon—Fiction. 3.
Oregon—Fiction. 4. Large type books. I. Title.
PS3612.O335P53 2010b
813'.6—dc22
                                                2009053880

Published in 2010 by arrangement with Harvest House Publishers.

Printed in the United States of America
1 2 3 4 5 6 7 14 13 12 11 10

For Danny
I couldn't have done it without you.

While Amish believers do reside in western states such as Washington and Montana, the Amish community in this novel is purely a work of fiction. However, several Mennonite congregations make their home throughout Oregon and the Pacific Northwest.

CHAPTER 1

Sol called me at ten. Wanted to see me in five.

I couldn't tell if I was jittery with espresso or excitement.

"So, Brian." I propped my chin on the edge of our cubicle wall. "Who do you think he's gonna send to Miami?"

Brian sighed and didn't look up. "I have no idea."

"You don't want that story, do you?"

"Marisa would change the locks if I left that long."

"Are you talking about Cuba?" Laura stopped midstride as she nearly passed us. "Did Sol say anything?"

I masked a smirk. "I'll find out in five minutes."

Laura tapped her pencil on the ridge of Brian's cubicle. "*Such* a great story. Cuba, post-Fidel —"

"Miami, in April —" Brian drawled.

There was a moment of silence, out of respect for sunshine. Portland, Oregon, isn't known for its sunny springs.

Miami in April, a shot at an above-fold feature . . .

I wanted it. I wanted it bad.

"Have a seat, Tate," Sol said, stretching out in his chair, his cocoa brown arms tucked behind his head. All he needed was a stogie to top off his newspaper editor image, and a year ago that might have been the case. After twenty-five years of marriage, the missus finally got to him.

That, and the building's nonsmoking policy. Instead, Sol's arms lowered and he reached for his stress ball. A copy of yesterday's newspaper covered the immediately visible part of his desk. He tossed the ball from one hand to another.

I sat and crossed my legs.

"How's life?" he asked.

"Um . . ." Where was this going? "Life is good."

"Any major stresses going on?"

"Not really, no."

"Huh." He set aside the stress ball, adjusted his reading glasses, and leaned over his newspaper. " 'Henry Paul Tate of Lincoln City, OR, passed away Monday, March

20, of a heart attack,' " Sol looked up. "I'll skip a bit. 'Tate is survived by his wife, Kathy, daughters Beth Thompson, of Neotsu, OR, and Jayne Tate, of Portland, OR, and granddaughter Emilee Thompson, of Neotsu.' " He folded his hands. "I don't think I need to read the rest. There aren't any other Jayne Tates in Portland who grew up in Lincoln City, much less with a father named Henry."

"Are public records that amusing?"

"Were you going to tell me your father passed away?"

"That's my personal life." Such as it was. "I didn't think it mattered here."

And I didn't. Mom held the service on a Saturday, I drove to Lincoln City long enough to hear my uncle's very long eulogy, sing all three verses of "Blessed Redeemer," and hand wash the punch bowl set.

I did my duty. It wasn't as though I showed up in jeans and a Good Charlotte T-shirt and explained to everyone how my father could suck the joy out of a five-year-old. How he smiled about once a month, and usually to people other than his younger daughter. How my sister Beth married at eighteen to get out of the house, though I explained at the time how leaving for college accomplished the same goal.

11

No. I wore a nice black pantsuit with sensible heels, played the good daughter, drove home, and vacuumed my apartment.

Sol didn't say anything.

"Really, we weren't close."

He shrugged. "Whether you were close or not makes no difference to me, but I'll tell you this — your work is slipping."

"I'm your best features reporter!"

"Lanahan's my best features reporter. I keep you around for the day he digs too deep and they find him at the bottom of the Columbia River."

"Thanks." I was better than Lanahan and we both knew it, but Lanahan had staff seniority I couldn't accomplish without a fake ID.

"You're welcome. But you're not bad, your sources love you, and you can write your way out of a wet paper bag. That's why it's easy to tell when your work is slipping. Your leads are flabby and your descriptions are clichéd." He picked up a piece of paper and read from it. " 'Rain-soaked highway'?" He snorted in disgust. "Are you kidding me? What, you think you're writing for your college paper again?"

"I'll edit anything. You know that."

"But you've never had to edit this much. Look. You've always been the wonder kid

12

around here, but times haven't been kind to this business. We're laying off good reporters left and right and printing more AP celebrity fluff. If Bernstein and Woodward were trying to expose a presidency in this day and age . . . well, let's just say they wouldn't have gotten that far. Papers around the country are cutting their foreign correspondents and satellite offices or, worse, resorting to online editions only. People don't read newspapers anymore. Can you believe that? I'd be suicidal if my wife didn't have me doing tai chi. Does wonders for my nerves." He set his reading glasses on his desk and massaged the bridge of his nose. "Basically, the way things are going, you need to get yourself back together or look for a job elsewhere. Except, there really aren't jobs elsewhere. When was the last time you took some time off?"

"Aside from weekends . . ." Not that I ever really relaxed, per se, even on weekends. Either way, my relaxation techniques or lack thereof weren't Sol's business.

"According to your file, you have a lot of PTO time built up. I think you should use it."

Every muscle in my body tightened up. "How long? Is this a forced leave?"

"It's you getting a chance to save your job.

13

I'm doing society a favor — you'd make a lousy waitress. You've got three weeks saved. Use a week and a half, and I'll make up the rest."

"Sol —"

"You might think about some tai chi while you're out."

"What about . . . Miami?"

Sol sighed. "I'm sending Laura."

The words hit like a blow to my stomach. I could barely breathe. "She can't write a lead."

"Right now, neither can you."

My trip to Miami. My shot at an above-fold feature, all gone because I'd probably slipped too many passive verbs into first lines of my articles.

"It's for the best," he said. "There will be other big stories, Jayne."

I agreed with him out loud, but in my head I was shouting like mad.

I finished up my last projects and left work early. No sense in sticking around if anything I turned in was going to be thrown right back at me.

I wrestled into my motorcycle gear and hopped on my bike, thinking I might calm my nerves with a ride.

I didn't get past Powell's Books. I guess

that's the curse of being bookish. I got lost inside every time I visited, but there are worse places to be lost. Each of the rooms is color coded, but I always got the red room and the rose room mixed up. Not that it mattered — I was still surrounded by hundreds of volumes.

Even as I fingered through shelves of books promising to teach me about fine paper folding, I couldn't get the scene with Sol out of my mind. Ever since I'd started work at the paper, I'd continued to work at ninety miles an hour. I couldn't slow down. I didn't know how to slow down. At this particular moment, I felt as though my insides were tearing me in forty different directions.

What would I do if I had to take a vacation? I didn't want to see my family. My sister would show me which wall she had just painted and what item she had ordered from the Pottery Barn catalogue.

Maybe I'd be okay with that life at some later date, but at twenty-six I wasn't there yet. I didn't know how I'd fit a car seat onto my motorcycle.

Probably couldn't.

One magazine cover caught my eye. A long line of laundry fluttered in the breeze, and a little girl in a dark dress was either hanging it up or taking it down. She faced away from the camera.

I flipped through the pages until I found the article. The journalist — who wasn't half bad — wrote a portrait of a people apart. They forgave when faced with searing hatred. They often provided for other members of the community. They called themselves Amish after Jacob Amman, a man who set his group of followers into motion before fading into obscurity.

My mind starting ticking, even as my insides seemed to quiet down. I couldn't take my eyes off the picture of the girl hanging laundry. What would cause people to live like that, when there are electric dryers with de-wrinkle cycles?

I bought the magazine and started home.

A little internet research revealed an Amish community just outside of Albany. Yet more research reminded me of Harrison Ford's role in *Witness*, Jodi Picoult's *Plain Truth,* and a small army of other books about the Amish. They certainly didn't lack media representation.

I wondered how they felt about that representation. Nothing I'd read made this group seem as if they particularly enjoyed the limelight. I wondered how accurate that representation really was. The idea of a utopian society, working off the land and truly caring for each other — frankly, I had a hard time buying into it. Even if it did work, what was their secret?

I read a little more and learned that the Amish were similar to the Mennonites in their pursuit of a simpler lifestyle. Both were pacifists and against infant baptism, but the Mennonites connected to city electricity and drove cars. The Amish who left the community often became Mennonite.

My mind started whirring again. A column the paper occasionally picked up was written by a Mennonite woman — could she have connections to the Amish? Probably. I chewed my lip as I considered the possibilities.

A story was in here, and I had three weeks all to myself.

Shane frowned at me. "You're going to do what?"

I suddenly regretted my need to share the plan with my boyfriend. "I've got it all worked out," I said, a little defensive. "I'm off work for three weeks. There's an Amish community outside Albany. I'll stay in Albany for the first week or so. I'm hoping I can board at one of the farms after that."

Shane leveled his serious brown eyes on

me. "You're going to knock on doors and ask if anyone has room in the hayloft?"

I straightened my shoulders. "We occasionally print the column of a Mennonite woman —"

"What?"

"Don't interrupt. Ethel Beiler's the name of the columnist. I already talked to her. She knows a couple families in that area, and she's going to talk to them about me staying with them."

"That's crazy."

"That's journalism."

"Jayne." Shane released a frustrated breath. "Your dad just died."

"We weren't close. I told you that."

"But he was your dad. It doesn't matter if you were close or not."

We weren't getting anywhere. "Do you have anything interesting in your fridge? And when I say interesting, I don't mean, 'it's changed color since last month.' "

"There's some Mongolian chicken. Tell me again how long you're planning on being gone."

"About three weeks."

"Are you . . . ." he hesitated. "Are you still serious about us?"

My eyes widened. "Of course I am! Are you?"

"We've been together six months. You've met my parents, my brothers, everybody."

I sat down beside him. "And I think they're great, really."

"But you don't want me to meet your family."

"You don't want to."

"Yes, I do."

"No, really, you don't. I'm trying to save you the mind games, the guilt trips — you don't need that. *We* don't need that."

"Your sister? Your sister's like that?"

"My sister is brainwashed, and anything we say gets parroted back to the parents."

"Parent. Your dad's dead."

I cupped his face with my hands and planted a kiss on his unresponsive lips. "Trust me? Please?"

He sighed. "Three weeks?"

"Three tiny, little baby weeks. I'll be back before you know it. I do have a favor to ask . . ."

"Yeah?"

"Pick up my mail?"

"For you? Anything. Just make sure you come back."

I knew I couldn't head out of town without clearing it with Joely, Kim, and Gemma, so I called them all and set up lunch for the following day.

Joely Davis, Kim Keiser, and Gemma Di-Grassi were, for all intents and purposes, my best friends in the world. Kim and Gemma I knew through the paper. Kim was on city beat — and the only writer I knew who can make a highway construction piece read like an acetic social commentary.

Gemma worked in food, which meant she ate at fabulous restaurants and criticized the staff. Despite her job, she was one of the sweetest people I knew. And she made amazing *pots de crème*.

Joely and I met when I was on the crime beat — she was usually the only cop on scene with a sense of humor. I introduced her to Kim and Gemma, and we've all lived in each other's pockets ever since.

Joely shook her head as I approached the table. "Such a sweet bike. It's a Triumph, right?"

"We saw you through the window," Kim added. "Sit. Order. I'm hungry."

I glanced over the menu and picked everything I might not be able to eat while I was gone.

Kim lifted an eyebrow after the waitress left. "Giving up food for Lent and eating while you can?"

I shook my head. "I'm headed to Amish

country for a couple weeks."

"As punishment for what?" Joely asked.

Gemma swatted her arm. "Shut up. You'll have fun, Jayne. My aunt did that — went on a buggy ride and everything."

"Where did your aunt go?"

"Ohio."

"I'm actually heading to a community near Albany."

"What about the Miami story?" Kim asked, swishing the ice around in her water glass.

"Laura got it. I'm actually on leave for a bit."

Gemma nodded. "Because of your dad? That's probably a good idea."

"Laura can't write a lead to save her life," Kim said. "What are you going to do?"

"I'm using the time to get a story on my own."

I received three blank looks.

"Freelance," I clarified.

"Let me get this straight." Kim leaned forward. "You're taking leave to get this story? Did Sol not want it?"

"Sol doesn't know anything about it. The break was his idea."

"He wants you to take time off, and you're using it to get a story in Amish country?"

"Yes." I looked down and unrolled my

21

napkin, setting my utensils aside and placing the napkin in my lap.

I could feel the exchange of looks crisscrossing the table.

"Look," I said, "I don't do vacations. I'm a reporter — so I'm reporting. It's what I do."

Joely shrugged. "Hey, if you want to spend your time off writing about riding in a buggy, knock yourself out."

"Wow. Three weeks," Kim said with a chuckle. "You'll love that. The simple life, no BlackBerry —"

"Who said I had to give up my Black-Berry?"

"Are you positive you'll have reception?" Gemma asked.

"Then I'll drive to town."

"Tell me how it all goes," Joely said, leaning forward. "My cousin — the one in Pennsylvania — says he busts Amish kids all the time."

Somehow, that didn't seem to jive with my mental image from what I'd read. "Busts? Use your civilian words, please."

"Do you have any family members who aren't cops?" Kim asked.

"Just my grandmother — on my mom's side."

I snorted. "So what do these kids do? Use

unkind words when cow tipping?"

Joely shrugged. "The teen boys drive like they're not aware they're mortal, they throw huge parties with kids coming in from several other states . . . Tim says they hand out MIPs like candy canes at Christmas."

"Minor in Possession," Kim translated before anyone asked.

"Amish kids will do that?"

"With enthusiasm. Hey, it's the conservative kids who can rebel the hardest. Last month, my brother arrested two home-school kids for dealing meth. It can happen anywhere."

"So." Kim grabbed my hand. "What are you doing with your bike while you're gone?"

"I've got to get there somehow."

"You're going to drive a bike to an Amish community?" Kim laughed. "What about your car?"

"In the shop. If I leave a key with one of you guys, can you pick it up?"

They all nodded. "No problem," Kim assured me. "So . . . what does Shane think about all this?"

"He thinks I'm crazy. Nothing new."

"I still think it's weird that you guys have rhyming names," Joely said.

The waitress came with a tray full of food.

Joely, Kim, and Gemma received their respective plates . . .

And I got my four.

"Have enough to eat there?" Kim asked, poking at my sushi with her fork.

"I think it'd be clever," said Joely, "if you freeze-dried your leftovers."

Gemma nodded. "Then you could reconstitute them at your leisure. You know . . . a little water, some sleight of hand with a camp stove . . ."

"I hope you're all enjoying this. Maybe I'll learn to cook while I'm there."

"You're afraid of ovens," Kim lifted an eyebrow. "Remember?"

"It's not a fear, per se. It's apprehension," I shot back. "Over a heat source. Joely's afraid of clowns."

Joely crossed her arms. "Lots of people hate clowns. Fear of ovens — that's odd."

"You'll have to tell me what the food's like," Gemma said before taking a bite and chewing thoughtfully. "I've heard it's mainly German. A lot of carbs, a lot of meat . . ." Her voice turned thoughtful. "You know what I think? I think this trip will surprise you."

"I wanted Miami to surprise me."

"You hate flying," Kim pointed out.

I shrugged. "You may have a point there."

CHAPTER 2

After packing for five minutes that evening, I realized that maybe taking my bike wasn't the best idea. I had no idea what to bring with me.

Normally, I'm the girl who could travel the world with a shoulder bag. I wad, I roll, and when necessary I do without.

But this time I had no idea if I was dressing to fit in with a church service or a barn raising.

I'm not like most girls. I'm not given to fits of indecision over what to wear on a Saturday night. My sister, Beth, was always the pretty one — I never felt the need to dress up. Jeans and a T-shirt, slacks and a blouse — my wardrobe pretty much ended there. If it was cold, I'd throw on a hoodie or a blazer.

How did the Amish feel about pants, though? None of the women wore pants. Would they be offended if I did? Would I be exempt?

I sighed and dug through my closet. Somewhere at the back I had a skirt my mom made me wear to band concerts in high school.

It was in the back, clipped on a skirt hanger to a cloth I used as a photography drape. I held it up and sighed again.

My hips had grown a bit since I was seventeen.

Defeated, I picked up my phone and called Gemma.

I skipped the preliminary greetings. "I need clothes," I said in lieu of hello.

"Are you ill?"

"Really, I need at least one skirt or something if I have to —"

"You have to be running a fever if the word 'skirt' came out of your mouth."

"Do you want me to call Kim?"

"I'll be there in twenty-five minutes."

Sure enough, she was, with a garment bag in tow. "You weren't specific, so I brought a selection," she said, giving me an awkward one-armed hug that ended with a hand on my forehead. "You don't feel warm."

I rolled my eyes. "I wore a dress to my sister's wedding."

"Right," she said, heading down the hall. "But, see, I wasn't there to see it. And if I didn't see it — did it really happen?"

I didn't honor that with a comeback. Gemma's lips settled into a smile. "Okay, then. I know you've got a lot of black, and frankly, you can wear black slacks with a black blouse and a colored scarf. You'll be dressed like an average Frenchwoman."

"Dressed like your mother, you mean."

Gemma pointed a finger in the air. "And her friends!"

"I need something skirt-ish. I don't know how they feel about women in pants."

She laid the bag on the bed and tugged on the zipper. "You didn't say what length you wanted, so I brought all of them. What size are you, anyway?"

"Larger than I was in high school."

"Helpful. Try this one," she said, giving me a handful of black skirt. "We're about the same size."

I didn't even have the skirt zipped when Gemma began shaking her head. "Nope, not that one. Here —"

"What's wrong with it?"

"It doesn't hit your hips right. Try this." She handed me another.

"It looks just the same."

"It's not."

"But —"

"Kim's on speed dial."

27

I yanked the second skirt out of her hands and then shimmied until the first fell to my ankles.

"Now . . ." Gemma's brow furrowed, "remind me why you're going to investigate the Amish?"

"Look at them. They can't be that perfect."

"I don't think anyone believes they're perfect. If I remember right, the kids are only educated to the eighth grade level."

I shrugged. "It's an instinct thing. I always know when I'll find something."

Gemma opened her mouth, closed it, and turned her attention to skirt number two. "That's the skirt."

We studied my reflection in the mirror. Gemma tilted her head. "I think you're ready to be Amish."

With Gemma's help, I managed to pack up the panniers and fit my electronic equipment into my laptop backpack. I didn't pack everything, figuring I could always go home if I wanted my extra memory card for my camera. Either way, I needed room for my copy of John Hostetler's *Amish Society*.

I left early the next morning.

The cold April air whispered around my collar as I rode south on I-5. The busyness of Portland disappeared, office buildings giving way to hills and trees.

I missed the buildings. A part of me never felt comfortable outside the city. I forced myself to brush off the feeling and ride on. I was a reporter. I had work to do.

After what felt like forever, I finally parked my bike outside Albany's Comfort Inn on the south end of town.

The room was nice enough, not that I was paying attention. I unloaded the panniers, stuck my digital recorder in my jacket pocket, and headed back out.

The whirring of saws and other limb-severing equipment could be heard from the street. I parked my bike and proceeded with caution.

More internet research had revealed an abundance of Amish carpentry businesses. And while I did not close my eyes and point to one in the phonebook, I did pick the one whose owner's name sounded the nicest.

Levi Burkholder. Good man name.

The scent of sawdust filled my nose. The door I'd chosen led directly into the shop. Men fed pieces of wood through huge saws; others sanded assembled pieces with electric sanders. Strains of the Blue Man Group melded with the din of the machinery.

One of the workers noticed me. "The customer area is through those doors," he said, pointing.

"I'm looking for Levi Burkholder. I'm a reporter."

"A what?"

"A reporter!" I yelled.

"Reporter. Right. I'll tell Levi. I'll have him meet you in the customer service area."

"The what?"

"Customer service area!" he shouted before turning around. I hoped he was going to look for Levi, but shop culture wasn't my realm of expertise.

As instructed, I waited in the customer service area, where I found outdated copies of *American Woodworking, Modern Woodworking,* and a *Woodcraft* catalogue. I flipped through one and read about wood garage doors making a comeback.

Fascinating stuff.

The door opened and a man stepped in. He was about my height and broad shouldered, although younger than I'd pictured. I put the garage doors down. "Are you Levi?"

"Hmm," he said, seeming to consider the idea. "What if I were to tell you that I was?"

Then I would ask to see ID. "Then I

would have a couple questions for you."

He leaned against the counter. "Really."

"If you really were Levi."

"What makes you think I'm not?" His expression turned injured.

I wasn't born yesterday. "We'll call it gut instinct."

"Yes, let's."

"Let's what?"

"Call it gut instinct. You have a very interesting gut, what with its instincts and all. I always thought guts were for digesting. Glad yours can multitask."

I suddenly remembered why I hated small towns; weird people lived there. "It's a gift."

"A very special gift," he said, and probably would have continued if the door hadn't opened. "Hi, Levi. You're just in time. We were talking about her multitasking gut."

The real Levi stood a head taller than the first guy, his wiry body and ruffled dark hair covered in sawdust. He rolled his eyes and looked to me. "Is he bothering you?"

"Not yet," I answered. Close, though.

"I apologize, really. Spencer was just getting back to work."

"I was?"

Levi didn't break his gaze. "He distracts easily. Spence? Go file something."

31

"Right, boss," Spence answered with a salute.

"Sorry about that." Levi stuck out a callused hand. "Levi Burkholder."

I shook it. "Jayne Tate."

"You're a reporter?"

"Yes. I'm writing a piece on the Amish community, and I was wondering if I could interview you at some point."

"Come on back to my office." He gestured down the hallway, and I followed.

Levi opened the door; I could see Spencer beside the desk.

"Are you trying to be in the way?" Levi asked.

"You told me to file. I'm filing."

"Go help Grady."

"She looks nice. You should ask her out."

"Spence!"

Spencer hustled out the door. "Finding Grady."

Levi turned back to me. "Have a seat. Did I already apologize for him?"

"Yes, you did."

"Well, I apologize again." He tented his fingers. "Have you ever had your own business?"

"No, I haven't."

"If you do, don't hire your friends."

"Point taken."

"They are very hard to fire. I've tried several times. It doesn't help that Spencer is one of the best carpenters in town. And his mother would skin me alive." He shook his head. "What were we talking about?"

"The Amish."

"Why did you want to talk to me?"

"You run an Amish furniture business."

"What do you want to know?"

"How many Amish workers are in your employ? Do you come from an Amish background? How does the Amish lifestyle and work ethic affect your business, if at all?"

He nodded and glanced at his watch. "Those are a lot of questions. Unfortunately, I don't have much time today. I can tell you that I have eight Amish teenagers under my employ. Six of them are carpenters, the young men. Two young ladies come after hours to clean up the shop."

I raised an eyebrow.

"Not that they couldn't make a chair as well as their brothers," he added. "Their families prefer for them to have more . . . domestic jobs."

I held up a finger. "Do you mind if I record this?"

He shook his head. "Not at all."

I retrieved my digital recorder from my

bag, pressed the record button, and set it on his desk. "Thanks."

"No problem. So that's eight Amish teens. I pay all of them what they're worth — a lot of businesses who hire them don't."

"Why don't they?"

"These kids are raised to work hard and expect little in return. It doesn't occur to them to complain."

"Why not?" When I was a teen, it had occurred to me all the time, to my parents' chagrin.

"Their group culture centers around a strong work ethic, and their personal identities center around that group culture."

"What's your personal connection to the Amish?"

"Pardon?"

"You sound like you have more than a passing knowledge of them."

He checked his watch. "An interesting question for another day. What's your schedule like tomorrow?"

I made the pretense of pulling my date book out of my bag.

Tomorrow's page was blank.

"I have time in the morning and later in the afternoon," I said.

"Do you want to come back by in the morning, then?"

"That works." I began to pencil it in. *Levi, woodshop.* "What time?"

"Ten thirty?"

"Ten thirty." I wrote it in before looking up. "Thanks for your time today."

He smiled. "You're welcome. I'll walk you out."

"That's all right. I'm sure I can find my way."

"I don't know where Spencer is."

I hoisted my bag over my shoulder. "Lead the way."

Spencer was indeed lying in wait at the front counter. "Very nice to meet you. Come back again."

I waved a goodbye.

Levi followed me out the door. "He's stupid but harmless."

"I'll take your word for it."

"That your bike?"

I allowed myself a smile. "It is."

"2007 Triumph Bonneville?"

"2008."

"What's the capacity?"

"About 865 ccs."

Levi let out a low whistle. "She's pretty."

I smiled. "I think so." I reached for my helmet.

"Drive safe."

"I will," I said, before turning the ignition

switch and revving the motor. When I turned the corner, I noticed Levi still stood near the curb.

CHAPTER 3

I stopped for lunch, picked up some groceries, and took a long ride through the back roads of Albany before returning to the hotel that afternoon. Once I was settled in there, I checked my messages.

Joely wanted to know if I'd been run over by a horse yet.

Gemma left a voice mail with care instructions for the black skirt.

Kim let me know that Laura emailed the paper, informing them that, in less than twenty-four hours in Miami, she'd managed to wind up in the ER with sunstroke.

Nothing from Shane.

And nothing from Ethel the Mennonite columnist, who had sounded optimistic about finding an Amish host family for me.

I thought about calling Shane but then changed my mind. With me gone, he was probably stationed in front of the TV, and a conversation punctuated with "How could he miss that shot?" wasn't my idea of fun.

Instead, I typed out my notes from my interview with Levi and settled in for an evening watching *Little House on the Prairie* reruns.

I parked my bike in front of Levi's shop at ten thirty the next morning. I entered through the customer service office, a little electronic *ding* signaling my presence. Footsteps sounded down the hall. As they approached, they seemed to slow until the person stepped cautiously around the corner.

"Are you the, um, the reporter?" the man asked, his face turning brick red.

"Yes, I am," I said slowly, not wanting to scare him.

His head bobbed a couple times. "Okay. Okay, good, that's good. Um, Levi told me if you came that he'd be back in just five, maybe six minutes."

"Oh. That's fine."

"I'm Grady," he said, holding out his hand like a peace offering.

"Nice to meet you, Grady."

"Did you, um, go to high school in Lincoln City?"

Oh, no. His face did look a little familiar. "Taft?"

A tentative smile touched his lips. "Yeah. Are you Beth's sister?"

I sighed on the inside. More than sixty miles away, and I still couldn't run incognito. "Yes. My older sister."

"We graduated the same year. I moved here a couple years ago," he said, giving a sheepish smile. "Too many carpenters in Lincoln City."

"True, very true." As in, you could throw a rock in any direction and hit a contractor.

"I was sorry to hear about your dad," he added. "My mom told me."

My inward sigh deepened. I hugged my arms to myself. "Thanks," I said, not knowing what else to say.

Levi chose that moment to step through the shop door. "Good, you're here." He closed the door behind him. "Hope you haven't been waiting long, Jayne."

I shook my head. "Grady and I have been catching up."

"We went to the same high school," Grady told Levi.

Levi's eyebrows lifted. "Really? In Lincoln City?"

"Her dad was an elder in the church I grew up in."

Ah. No wonder he knew. "He passed away recently," I blurted out, wanting to get that in the open before Grady could.

Levi's face softened. "I'm sorry to hear that."

I hiked my bag higher up my shoulder and nodded.

"I'm ready to go when you are," he said.

"Go?" I'd anticipated another interview in his office.

"I'm desperate for coffee."

"There's coffee in the kitchen . . ." Grady offered.

"Spencer made it."

Grady winced. "Oh."

Levi turned back to me. "Are you game? There's a coffee shop within walking distance."

"Ah . . . sure. That sounds fine."

"Excellent." He brushed off the few remaining wood shavings from his shirt. "If Mrs. Van Gerbig calls, tell her the walnut came in and she'll be very pleased."

Grady nodded and then Levi and I set off.

"Tell me how you decided to write about the Amish," Levi said about six steps into our walk. "I gather you're not on assignment."

"I'm a staff reporter for the *Oregonian*," I answered, fighting the indignation welling inside me. "But I also write freelance on the side."

"No offense to your professionalism. I just figured there's no breaking story around here — didn't think a newspaper would pay for you to come down unless someone was dead. You're at the *Oregonian*? I think I've read some of the pieces you've written."

I must have heard him wrong. "Really?"

"Didn't you write that article on children in foster care?"

Officially impressed. The indignation died down. "Yes, that was me."

Granted, he very well could have googled my name. Most of my stories live on in on-line archives.

"I remember reading that story. You made the children and their foster parents seem so . . . real."

"They are real."

"A lot of people don't like to observe the reality. They record the surface and pat themselves on the back. You didn't." He shot me a look. "A lot of writers do that with the Amish."

"I noticed that."

"Will you be different?"

"I'll try. From what I've read, the Amish hold the rest of the world at arm's length. I can only observe so much from the outside."

"That piece you wrote about the gubernatorial scandal — that wasn't bad either."

I suppressed a grin. "That was actually a whole series. I was the one who discovered the diverted funds."

"I'll bet you're popular in Salem."

"I'm fairly certain there's a picture of me with some darts in the middle. I had good sources, though. Something I need for this story too."

He seemed to process that thought for the rest of the walk.

The café featured small, uncomfortable-looking booths, cranky baristas, and coffee so strong I felt my tooth enamel cringe.

"Much better," Levi said after a sip. "Spencer makes the office coffee much too strong."

"Spencer's is too strong?" Stronger than the cup o' joe eating away at my stomach lining? "Does he brew it to float a horse-shoe?"

"Hand planer."

"Ah." How appropriate.

"Are you going to answer my question?"

I furrowed my brow. "What question?"

"Why are you interested in the Amish?"

Cute. "Maybe. But yesterday I asked you about your personal involvement with them. I asked first. I win."

"Touché." He shrugged. "My best friends growing up were Amish. We played a lot of volleyball, spent all of our time together."

"Amish kids play volleyball?"

"Like there's no tomorrow. Baseball and soccer too. And they can be very competitive."

"Huh." I fished my digital recorder from my bag again. "Do you mind?"

"Go ahead."

"Why an Amish-style carpentry shop? What made you want to start a business?"

"I have an economics degree from the University of Oregon. Worked in corporate land for a few years, made money. At the end of the day, I wanted to be closer to my family."

"Why?"

"You like the tough questions, don't you? My parents are getting older, and I'm the oldest. I suppose I feel a certain amount of responsibility. I have different . . . resources, I guess, than they do. As for the shop . . . well, like I said, I wanted to move closer and I'd always liked working with my hands. There's a market for the Amish woodcraft, as well as a steady supply of labor."

"How many siblings?"

"A lot."

" 'A lot' being code for . . ."

"Seven," he answered, before downing the last of his coffee. "Okay, your turn. Why the

Amish?"

I thought about turning off the recorder but decided against it. I never knew when he might say something interesting.

"Hard to say," I told him truthfully. "There's something very simple and beautiful about the Amish, yet also very confusing."

I watched Levi's expression but couldn't read the emotions behind his eyes. "Confusing?" he asked.

"It seems like such a difficult lifestyle. The rest of America is so driven by technology and information that the fact the Amish aren't in school after eighth grade astounds me."

"Technology and the Amish aren't necessarily mutually exclusive."

"No?"

He checked his watch. "I know an Amish family in the community outside town. They'll serve lunch soon, and I'm sure we could invite ourselves over."

"Really?"

"You can observe firsthand."

"My goal is to spend some time in an Amish household," I admitted. "In fact, I'm waiting to hear back from one of the columnists I know from the paper. She promised to look into that for me."

Again, the face I couldn't read. "I may be able to help you with that," he answered after a moment. "But lunch first. If you walk with me back to the shop, we can take my truck."

I hesitated. Driving to a place I'd never been with a man I didn't know to a location with spotty cell phone reception did not rank high on the list of good ideas.

"Or you can follow on your bike," he added. "I have four younger sisters. I wouldn't want any of them riding with strange men."

That was the thing; Levi wasn't strange. There was something about him that was completely trustworthy.

And I had pepper spray in my bag. Just in case.

I watched the landscape change as we drove by. Once we were out of town, we passed neighborhoods with houses perforated by a dozen wires. Satellite dishes served as lawn ornaments.

I hated small towns.

And I grew up in one, so I was allowed to say so with experience.

After a while, the neighborhoods thinned out and cattle ruled the open spaces. A few sheep.

I remembered my earlier conversation with Joely. "Do Amish kids cow tip?"

Levi laughed, an easy laugh that made me remind myself I had a boyfriend. "None of the kids I knew did — they were busy dating. Can't say about some of the Pennsylvania kids."

Twenty minutes later occasional clusters of homes came into view. They sat in a small valley, homes surrounded by pastures and farmland. There were no wires, but if I wasn't mistaken, a sprinkling of wind-power generators.

Interesting.

It started to rain as Levi turned the truck down a long gravel road. A large white farmhouse sat at the end, with a barnlike building on either side for moral support. A woman hurriedly removed several pairs of pants from the laundry line as the raindrops grew larger. Levi raised a hand in greeting.

She waved back, yanking the last pair of trousers off and carrying the basket inside. By the time we made it to the covered porch, she was waiting for us at the door.

"Levi!" she said, standing on her tiptoes to cup his face and kiss his cheek. "What are you doing here?"

"Do you have extra for lunch?"

"I always have extra for lunch," she answered, her eyes on me.

"This is Jayne Tate. Jayne, this is Martha."

Martha looked from me to Levi, her eyes searching but guarded. "You are welcome in our home."

I tried not to stare. She was dressed as I'd seen Amish women in photos — a long dark blue dress, black apron, and white kapp. Her feet were encased in black, lace-up shoes. Dark, itchy-looking stockings covered the visible part of her legs.

A small storm of footfalls thundered from the upper floor, and two little girls, an almost adolescent boy, and a teen girl descended the stairs. The youngest girls squealed Levi's name and ran for his legs. He hugged them both, calling them by name. The older two followed at a more dignified pace. That they knew him well was obvious.

"Jayne," Levi said, continuing the introductions. "This is Sara —" he started with the teenager, "Samuel, Leah, and," he picked up the littlest girl, "this is the oldest, Elizabeth."

"I'm not the oldest!" Elizabeth squealed, revealing a missing front tooth. "I'm only five!"

"And they're all playing hooky from school today."

Another round of giggles and disagreement. "It's grading day," Leah said. "No school."

"Oh, right," he said. "They're all out of school and they're all having lunch with us."

"You're staying for lunch!" Elizabeth wrapped her arms around his shoulders, preventing him from putting her down.

But she had to get down anyway, because Martha ordered a group hand washing. Each child, except Sara, had a surprising amount of grime coating their fingers.

Lunch consisted of chicken potpies, cooked cabbage, rolls, stewed tomatoes, and sliced apples hidden under layers of brown sugar and oatmeal.

I enjoyed the potpie and decided that if I didn't think about the calories, they didn't count.

I ate a sparing amount of cabbage.

And avoided the tomatoes.

The rolls and apple dessert were divine — I knew Gemma would want the recipes.

I asked some questions about the farm and how the family spent their day. Martha gave simple, short answers. They began working at dawn and retired for the day around nine. The younger children attended school during the day while the older ones worked. Amos helped his father on the farm

48

while Elam worked as a bricklayer in town. Sara made most of the family's clothes and mended on demand.

I tried to scribble down notes as I ate.

After the plates were cleared away, Martha showed me around the farm with the children following like ducklings. They ignored the rain and I tried to follow suit, even as the raindrops seeped into my clothing.

Once inside the barn, Samuel, Leah, and Elizabeth showed me the animals they took care of. Samuel had a pig, while Leah and Elizabeth watched over a pair of lambs. I could hear Levi mentioning something to Martha, but I couldn't make out the words.

We trudged back a few moments later. Levi hugged them all around. I shook Martha's hand and waved at the kids. Then Levi opened the truck door for me, and I climbed in. Samuel and Leah ran after the truck for a little while, feet bare in the mud. Levi relaxed when they turned back to the farmhouse.

"I hate it when they do that," he said with a sigh. "I don't think they really understand how dangerous cars can be."

"Your truck is probably one of the only motorized vehicles that comes on their property."

49

"Buggy accidents happen every year. They should know better."

"How many accidents? I remember seeing reflectors and lights on the buggy in the . . ." Buggy barn? Garage? What did they call the buggy-storing shelter?

Levi didn't seem to notice my terminological confusion. "Lights and reflectors don't negate the fact that they're still unprotected on the road. Even motorcyclists wear helmets, and the wood buggies leave the Amish every bit as exposed as a biker. They may as well be walking down the highways."

I didn't know what to say. "They seem to like you."

Levi's hands began to fidget on the steering wheel. "I've known them for a long time."

"Through your business?"

"No, before that. They're . . . my family."

CHAPTER 4

As Levi's words sank in, I felt myself stiffen. "Wow. Okay. Your family. Right. You see, in journalism school they teach us to begin with the most important information."

"I know I should have explained earlier —"

"I don't know. Do you think that would have been helpful?"

I replayed scenes from lunch over and over in my head. Everything made sense now. I couldn't believe I hadn't picked up on it before now.

"I don't know why I didn't say anything."

"Hey, your call. By the way, I'm actually a European royal. Sorry I didn't mention it earlier."

"It took me years to get over the stigma of being 'the Amish boy.' "

"I was the elder's daughter. Didn't slow me down."

I looked into his eyes. Levi had very nice

eyes; I tried to remember if I'd noticed his eyes before. I caught myself before I continued down that mental road. He had lied to me. Well, he hadn't exactly lied to me, but he had deceived me, and I didn't much appreciate it.

Frankly, being a reporter, it was fairly embarrassing. That's what I got for not asking the right questions.

At Levi's suggestion, he and Grady grabbed some wood for a ramp and rolled my bike into the back of the pickup. I sat and waited for them, teeth chattering. My clothes had refused to dry, despite the fact that Levi turned the heat on until it felt like inner Qatar inside the cab.

Levi never complained.

He dropped me off at my hotel and helped me unload my bike. "I could arrange a time for you to interview my parents, if you're interested."

I chewed on my lip. "I'll let you know." Frankly, I was feeling pretty forgiving at the moment and I couldn't trust myself to be rational.

Inside my hotel room, I stripped off my work clothes and wished I'd brought my sweatpants. Instead, I made do with the softer clothes that I had, rolled up my pant legs and soaked my feet in the bathtub.

I called Shane while my toes turned lobster red.

"Jayne?" He sounded surprised. "Where are you?"

I was surprised to hear the amount of noise surrounding him. "In my hotel room. Where are you? It sounds like you're at a club."

"Something like that. How's the story coming?"

I'm spending a lot of time with a guy you probably wouldn't like. "Fine. Taking some interesting turns. I miss you."

"Yeah. Good. Good for you."

Okay . . . "Can you hear me?"

"It's pretty loud in here. Can I call you back later tonight?"

"Okay," I said, trying not to feel blown off.

He never called back.

I considered my options the next morning.

First, my absence from the paper was limited. I really did need to manage my time well, which meant I needed to use the resources I had instead of wasting time finding new ones.

And second, if I was going to use my existing resources, I needed to forgive Levi.

What a pain.

I took a shower and checked my phone afterward. Still no call from Shane. Where had he been the previous afternoon, anyway? He'd never been that much into the club scene . . . and usually when I called, I very nearly had his complete attention.

Unless he was watching a game. At that point, my only chances for conversation came at commercial breaks. Maybe.

Shane aside, I put away my pride and called Levi's shop.

Spencer answered the phone. "Albany Amish Woodcraft, how may I direct your call?"

"May I speak with Mr. Burkholder?" I asked, trying not to sound like myself.

"I can see if he's available," Spencer replied. "May I tell him who's calling?"

I sighed on the inside. There was no avoiding it. "Jayne Tate."

"Jayne?" The tone of his voice switched from phone automaton to best buddy. "When are you coming down here?"

"If you transfer me to Levi I'll be able to find out."

"I can ask him for you. Wouldn't want to add to your stress level."

"I'll live."

Spencer gave a dramatic sigh and I heard

a click before being transported into harpsichord land.

When Levi picked up, I heaved a sigh of relief. "I hate harpsichord."

"Who is this?"

"This is Jayne. Tate. Sorry — you have harpsichord music playing while your listener is on hold. I hate harpsichord. Makes me want to jump off of things. Tall things. I'm rambling. I didn't mean to call and ramble."

"Why did you call?" He didn't sound annoyed, only curious.

"I had a couple more questions for you. For the story."

"Oh. Does that mean you accept my apology?"

I wanted to find a way to skirt around answering that and came up blank. "Yes."

"Thank you," he said, his voice softening. "In that case, I can tell you that my mother called me this morning. Said she and my dad talked it over, and they've agreed to let you stay with them while you're working on your story."

"Really?"

"I assured them that you wouldn't be bringing drugs or alcohol into their home. They're prepared to keep your bike in their shed, and when you need to charge your

55

laptop — I'm assuming you have a laptop — you can bring it here."

"I don't know what to say."

" 'Thank you' should do it."

"How much should I pay them? I mean, I'm not expecting free room and board."

"My mom said something along the lines of thirty dollars a day."

"I'm sorry . . . thirty?"

"Yes. They're very thrifty."

I shrugged, not that he could tell over the phone. "Could I pad that a little more?"

"If you want. I wouldn't worry too much about it."

My mind reeled. I'd never thought this trip would be saving me money. "Thirty?"

He chuckled. "Do you want me to tell them you'll come?"

"Yes, before they change their mind!" I said, and then I caught myself. I never meant to be so relaxed around Levi. It just happened.

"How soon do you want to go down? I'll drive. We can load your bike in the truck again."

Was I ready? A part of me balked at leaving civilization behind. I knew journalists who had survived the difficulties of the Afghan desert, but while I stayed within American borders I expected a certain

56

standard of living.

Electrical outlets. Wireless connections. That sort of thing.

"Do they have indoor plumbing?"

Levi laughed. "Some Amish families don't, but my parents do."

"You think I'm a wuss."

"I think you're normal."

"I guess I should pack and check out . . ."

"Do you want me to drive you down?"

"Probably better that way."

"Meet me at the shop?"

"Okay."

"What time should I expect you?"

I checked my watch. "Half an hour? An hour? Something like that."

"Looking forward to it," he said.

And I believed him.

My hands shook with nervous excitement as Levi drove me toward the farmhouse for the second time. I was going behind the closed doors of one of America's most introverted societies.

And I couldn't stop worrying about the fact that Shane hadn't called me back. The concern kept me quiet through most of the drive until Levi commented on it. "You seem distracted," he said.

Understatement.

I tried to remember if I'd mentioned the presence of Shane to him or not, and then I berated myself for caring.

It's not as though I were *interested* in Levi. I was with Shane, right?

"I tried to call my boyfriend last night," I said, and found myself watching Levi's reaction.

His grip on the steering wheel shifted. "Unsuccessful?"

I shrugged. "I don't know. It sounded like he was out. At a bar or something . . . who knows. He said he'd call me back, but he didn't."

"Does he usually?"

"Usually what?"

"Call you back."

"I think so. It's not something that's been a problem before."

"How long have you been together?"

"Six months."

His grip shifted again. "Is he a social guy?"

"Not really. We are more of a coffeehouse couple, I guess. It's nothing."

"Hmm."

"Hmm?"

"I don't know what to tell you."

"Oh."

Yet another change in grip. "I suppose you could call him."

I scratched my neck. "I suppose."

"You don't want to?"

"I want him to call me back. I don't want to be the girlfriend who has to call constantly to get her boyfriend to return a call."

"I don't think two calls equals *constantly.*"

"You know what I mean."

"It's up to you."

"Is there much cell service at your parents' place?"

"Sometimes. Sometimes not."

"Serves him right."

As we pulled into the long drive toward the farmhouse, Levi pointed ahead. "Look."

I squinted. "What is that?"

"Your welcoming committee."

As we approached the house, I could see what he'd been pointing at. A row of children stood like sentries outside, facing us. "Those aren't all your siblings, are they?"

He laughed. "No. Some neighbor kids are mixed in there. They're all going to be very curious about you."

"Hence the lineup and the stare down?"

"Exactly."

I smiled at the kids as Levi pulled the truck around to the side. Martha came around to meet us, a cautious smile on her lips.

"Thanks for doing this, Mom," Levi said

after he climbed down from the cab.

"Your father believes this will be a good experience for everybody."

"Is he home yet?"

"Soon." She turned to me. "Come along inside, Jayne. I will show you around the house."

"Go ahead," Levi said. "I'll put your bike in the shed and bring in your bags."

"Are you sure you don't need a hand?" I asked.

"If I do I'll find Samuel or Amos. Don't worry. I'll catch up."

I followed Martha into the house and tried not to pay attention to the small herd of children who followed us.

The farmhouse smelled like baking bread and cedar, with a faint tinge of body odor. Martha led me through the dining room to the kitchen and front rooms, down the hallway to my bedroom.

A brightly patterned Amish quilt covered the bed. There was a small flashlight on the bedside table, and a large armoire rested against the opposite wall. I smiled. "It looks very nice."

Martha brushed aside the compliment. "The toilet and shower are across the hall."

I heard Levi's heavy footfalls a second

before he came around the corner with my bags.

Martha frowned. "Your father will be home at any moment."

Levi hoisted the bags over his shoulder. "I'll be gone in seconds."

"Your father . . ." my voice trailed off as I followed him.

"Isn't all that happy with me." He set my bags on the bed. "There, I'm done." He kissed Martha on the cheek. "I'm out."

I looked from Levi to Martha, trying to read their faces. "Can I walk out with you?" I asked, stalling. I wasn't quite ready to be left behind, deposited into another family's personal drama.

If I'd really wanted drama, I would have gone home.

But then, my family's not Amish, and therefore not newsworthy.

"Absolutely," Levi said, even as he patted heads and said goodbyes to the younger children.

I waited until we were well into the yard. "Why doesn't your mom want you home when your dad gets back?"

Levi reached for his car keys. "I left the community. My father doesn't talk to me."

"You mean, you're . . . shunned?"

Levi shrugged. "Not formally. I never

joined the church," he said, sighing. "Come by the shop tomorrow or give me a call. Sorry to dump you here like this, but I really should leave. Don't mention my name to him, okay?"

"Okay," I agreed as he climbed into the truck. "Bye!"

He paused and threw me a smile. "I'll see you later."

I watched him drive away.

CHAPTER 5

Martha found me upon my return to the house and finished the tour. Afterward I asked about the possibility of borrowing some clothes. In my jeans and sweater, I felt like a visiting alien.

I also hoped that the children might stare at me less if I looked like them.

Martha considered my idea, eyed me up and down, and called for Sara.

Sara and I are, apparently, about the same size.

She caught the vision, enthusiastically going through her own clothing collection and creating a pile of garments for me to try. She gave me two dresses of varying dark blue, a black apron, long black socks, a white kapp, and a black bonnet for outdoor wear. "If these don't fit," she said, "I'll make you new ones."

"I don't know that I'll be here that long . . ."

"I sew fast." It wasn't a boast, just a statement.

"Let me try these first," I said, carrying the pile back to my room.

There were no mirrors inside, but I had a small compact mirror stuffed into one of my bags. When I'd finished dressing, I held my arm as far from my body as I could. The glimpse I caught caused me to physically flinch.

Breathe, I told myself. *Clothes don't change who you are. While you might appear to the casual passerby to be a cautious, conservative farmwife, you know that underneath you are a liberated, talented, tough biker babe.*

I did not recognize the woman in the mirror. I'd known Jayne Tate for a while, and Jayne Tate didn't wear dark dresses — or any dresses at all, for that matter. And yet, when I moved, so did the simply-clad woman.

There was something oddly Marx Brothers about the whole thing.

I found Martha in the kitchen. She didn't say anything about my change of attire. Instead, she handed me a sack of potatoes and a paring knife. "If you would like to help with dinner," she said, "you may peel these."

Gideon walked through the door when I

was halfway through my first potato.

After my conversation with Levi, I expected Gideon to resemble a haggard, ugly old miser.

He looked more like a moustache-less Santa Claus, his beard to his chest, cheeks rosy from outdoor work. His eyes lit up when he saw me. "You are Jayne?" he asked, his voice tinged with a Germanic accent.

"Yes, I am." I offered my hand, which he studied for a moment before shaking.

He turned abruptly from me toward Martha. "Is dinner ready? I'm starved."

"Almost. I'll call the children in —" she started to say, but the sound of children's feet on wood floors drowned her out.

"Grandma!" they cried in unison, joy marking every face.

I peered out the window to see a tiny old woman emerge from a car. A dress like Martha's hung on her thin frame, although the older woman's had a floral print.

Martha removed her kitchen apron and joined her children outside.

"That is Martha's mother, Ida Gingerich," Gideon said, but he offered no further explanation.

Martha and her children led Ida into the house. "This is my mother, Jayne. She's staying for dinner," Martha said as she entered. "Mother, this is Jayne Tate. She is our guest for the time being."

I wanted to ask what Martha's mother was doing with a car, but I refrained. "Pleased to meet you, Mrs. Gingerich."

"Very nice to meet you, Jayne," she said, casting a shrewd glance over my person. I got the feeling she knew something I didn't. "Call me Ida."

Martha and I finished preparing dinner while Ida sat in the kitchen. They spoke in Pennsylvania Dutch, as far as I could tell, and I really didn't mind. Their world made no sense to me, and my brain had had about all it could take. Trying to decipher a conversation might push me over the brink.

Me and the potatoes, we were good.

"Let us give thanks," Gideon said, his voice soft with a rumble. Nine heads bowed in unison.

I used the moment to stare without being noticed. The men sat on one side of the table, the women on the other. We were surrounded by bowls and platters filled with food, tall glasses of thick, white milk, and a conspicuous lack of fresh vegetables.

After the moment of silence, I watched in fascination as this large family calmly, methodically downed huge quantities of food, with the men serving themselves first. Dinner conversation revolved around household chores and retellings of the workday. Samuel, Leah, and Elizabeth still attended school, while Amos, Elam, and Sara worked.

Gideon discussed with his sons which cattle needed to be moved, when to butcher the pigs, and the fact that some of the fence needed repair. Martha commented to Sara which garments were wearing out beyond use and which could be mended. Sara promised to start work on a new pair of pants for Samuel.

Not what I was doing at seventeen. My teen years consisted less of housework and family than of daydreaming about faraway colleges.

"Tell us about yourself," Ida said, interrupting my thoughts. "Where are you from?"

I shoved my hair out of my face. "I live in Portland, but I grew up on the coast."

Squeals of delight erupted around the table. "Where on the coast?" Sara asked.

"Lincoln City."

Leah leaned forward. "Did you go to the beach every day?"

"No . . . not every day. The weather's pretty nasty."

"Jayne, would you like more potatoes?"

Martha interrupted.

I declined.

Ida pressed forward. "What is your family like?"

I told them about my married sister, Beth, and her little girl. How my mother still lived in Lincoln City. Alluded to the fact that we didn't talk often. Work, you know.

"Only one sister?" Elizabeth's brow furrowed.

I smiled, realizing how strange that must sound to her. "Only one sister. Sometimes it got lonely."

I offered to do the dishes after dinner. Nine faces looked at me, aghast, but Gideon said yes.

After I'd finished scrubbing the last baking dish, albeit with Sara and Leah's help, Gideon offered to give me a tour of the farm.

"Whatever I can help with, put me to work," I said as we stepped out of the house. "Milking, whatever."

Gideon howled in laughter, but when we got into the stalls I saw why. The milking machinery towered over us both. "Many people think we Amish are against technology," he said, "and that's not true. We believe in three things." He held up three fingers. "We believe in serving God by being Plain. We believe in living outside the world. And we believe in hard work. Life should never be too easy for us. Milking equipment —" he gestured at the stainless steel tanks — "makes the milking easy, but it also makes it so we can work at other things even harder. We run the machinery on diesel and wind generators. We do not bring in outside electricity."

"I stand corrected."

Gideon led me to the corral next. "Our horses are not for riding, they are for pulling. Sugar and Shoe pull the buggy —"

"Shoe?"

He gave a rueful smile. "Elizabeth named him when she was tiny."

"Good choice."

"Balsam pulls the tractor."

"What do you grow?"

"Mainly sorghum and oats. Maybe next year, though, I will take out the sorghum and put in solar panels." He shrugged. "Maybe. The families living here in Oregon came because we wanted to follow the old ways *and* use technology. Many groups in Ohio use the technology, but their children run wild and the *Ordnung* became less important. There was too much compromise."

I tried to look as if I understood.

Ida drove herself home shortly after dinner. Even before the sky quite darkened, the children quieted, and before I knew it, everyone headed for bed.

At nine thirty.

Hadn't gone to bed so early since middle school.

After an unsuccessful attempt at sleep, I booted up my laptop. A message bubble informed me that no wireless networks were in range.

Somehow, I was not surprised.

I transcribed a few of the day's conversations and events for use in the future article. Played a couple hands of solitaire. Moved on to Minesweeper when it was time to relax, and then powered down the machine.

I burrowed under layers of quilts. Wished I had an electric blanket.

Sat up straight when a light flashed into my room.

Several irrational explanations fought for first place.

Maybe Ida had left something, and the lights were her car's headlights.

Maybe Levi was coming to tell me something. I dismissed that idea as soon as I'd thought of it — for Pete's sake, I wasn't fifteen anymore.

There could be robbers of some sort, but unless they were after the giant milking equipment or Martha's cast-iron cookware, I couldn't think of anything worth stealing.

And I doubted the resale value on cast-iron cookware made the effort financially viable. Cattle? Were cattle rustlers outside my window?

The light flashed again. I rolled out of bed, staying close to the ground. Glad I was a brunette and not a light-reflective blonde, I raised my head until I could just see out.

A man was outside with a flashlight. Okay, an Amish man, but an Amish man hanging around outside with a flashlight didn't seem that safe, either.

My heart stopped when I saw him reach toward the window next to mine.

Sara's window.

I pulled a quilt around my shoulders and whipped out to the hallway, the protective moves I'd learned in Joely's self-defense class playing through my mind.

I could have at least brought a heavy shoe as a weapon, I thought before turning the knob on Sara's door.

The opening door revealed the young woman, sitting at the window. "Get down!"

I ordered, all but tackling her to the ground. "There's a man outside!"

"No," Sara said, her voice hushed but firm. "There's none but David Zook outside."

I tilted my head to see David Zook peering at us through the window.

The "male lurker" was about seventeen, confused, frightened, and in need of a good haircut.

"What's he doing skulking around?" I asked, gesturing wildly at the window while vaguely aware of my fleeting dignity. "And pointing his flashlights at people's windows in the dead of night?"

Oh yeah, and never mind that this particular "dead of night" landed two hours before I usually went to bed.

"David is my . . ." Sara's eyes darted to the window and back at me. "He's my, um . . ."

"Gentleman caller?"

"Boyfriend," she spat the word out. "He's picking me up for a date."

I felt a headache coming on. "You knew he was coming?"

She nodded.

"Okay, whatever." I turned around and walked to the door. "Just remember," I said before making it out the room, "ninety-two percent of female murder victims were killed by men they knew."

I doubted this kind of thing ever happened to Seymour Hersh.

I dreamed about aliens that night. They landed in front of the farmhouse, their flashing saucer lights causing everyone concern. Shane captained the ship, although the aliens had trouble communicating with him. Instead of the helm, Shane stayed in the party area of the ship, where the aliens served orange fizzy drinks and made *Star Wars* references.

They clapped to an odd kind of rhythm with their webbed alien hands. At some point, I realized I wasn't listening to the clapping of extraterrestrials but someone knocking at my door. I sat up and reevaluated my surroundings. The tiniest hint of morning light was peeking through the windows.

The knock sounded at my door again. I shook my head to clear it. "Come in."

Sara poked her head in. "Could I come sit?"

I waved her in. "Sit." My mouth tasted awful. I yearned for an orange Tic Tac. "What's up?"

"I told David to be more careful with his

flashlight," she said, pulling lint off her apron. "The boys always come to the girls' windows after everyone goes to bed. That's how we have dates. That's how my parents had dates."

"Your parents are perfectly fine with you crawling out of windows with boys they don't know?" My parents would have had joint hernias, and before this conversation I would have considered them *less* conservative than Gideon and Martha.

"Oh, they know David."

"Do they know you're together?"

"No."

"How many girls come home pregnant?"

Sara's eyes widened. "None that I know."

I wondered how many she didn't know about, but I kept that question to myself. "I'm sorry if I startled you last night."

She giggled. "David might not come back."

"I'm truly sorry," I repeated.

"There are other boys," she said, with a shrug that was almost coy.

I played along. "Oh?"

"There is Milo Stutzman. And Henry Mullet."

I pressed my lips together to ensure a serious response. "You have choices."

"Yes."

"Tell me about your grandmother," I said, swinging my feet around. The floor was freezing. "Why does she have a car?"

"Grandma is Mennonite."

"Oh."

"She joined the Mennonite church when I was little, she and my grandfather."

"And your family still has contact with them?" I didn't say, "unlike Levi," but she caught my meaning.

"They joined a Mennonite church. Because they did that, we could still see them. Not Grandpa anymore, though. He passed on. But Levi joined a Baptist church. Our bishop didn't accept it."

"But the Mennonite church is acceptable?"

She nodded.

"Do you miss your brother?"

Sara nodded again. "Very much. Everyone thought he would marry Rachel Yoder. I heard that she wouldn't leave with him. Levi wouldn't talk about it."

"How often do you see him?"

She shrugged. "When my dad's not home, he'll come visit. Sometimes . . ." she leaned in closer, "I visit him in town."

"Really?" I couldn't hide my surprise. "At the shop?"

Sara gave a secret smile. "Grandma takes me."

Ida was more of a rebel than I'd given her credit for. "So he's stayed in touch with your grandmother too?"

"Oh, yes. Everyone but Dad."

"Your dad's angry?"

"Hurt, I think. But it's not my place to question."

At that moment my stomach gave a long, loud commentary on the state of its condition.

Empty.

"I think I'm ready for breakfast. You?"

Sara grinned, and the rest of the day began.

CHAPTER 6

I called Levi after breakfast, using the cell number he'd given me earlier. "Your grandmother drives a car and your sister sneaks out at night," I said. "There's so much you didn't tell me."

"Is everything okay? Are they treating you well?"

"They're fine so far. Why didn't you warn me that things between you and your dad were weird?"

"If I tried to warn you about every family struggle, we'd be talking for a very long time."

"Oh. Well, then. Anything else you want to fill me in on while you've got me on the phone?"

He sighed. "My mother is wary of outsiders. Amos and Elam rarely speak to me if they have a choice."

"Why the tension between you and your dad?"

"It's complicated."

"Try."

"Cutting me off is the Amish version of tough love. The reasoning is that if I'm separated from everybody, I'll eventually relent and return."

"But you aren't separated from everybody. Your mom and your sisters talk to you. Ida too."

"They figured out I had no intention of returning, ever. I think my mom decided she still wanted me as a son."

"That's good, I suppose."

"And as for Sara sneaking out, that's how they date."

"She told me. Still doesn't make sense to me."

"Imagine having seven or more siblings teasing you about the guy you're dating."

I winced. "Good point."

After breakfast, the younger children went to school, the men went to work, and I shadowed Sara with her chores. The Burkholder household attained a level of clean I doubted I could ever aspire to. We scrubbed the floors before moving on to the laundry.

Never again would I take washing clothes for granted — Sara and I had to start their washer using the gas generator. To dry the clothes, we pinned them to a line of twine strung across the washroom. "If we hang them outside in the wet, they'll turn colors and smell bad."

"I'll bet," I said, pinning the shoulder of one of the boys' shirts. "Mildew is gross."

"Mildew?"

"They get greenish-grayish patches?"

"Yes."

"That's mildew."

"What is it?"

A part of me wondered how on earth she didn't know about mildew, and then I reminded myself that she'd stopped attending school at fourteen. "Like mold. It's a fungus — it starts out with spores and it likes to grow in warm, damp environments."

"Spores?"

I bit my lip, thinking of how to phrase it in a way she'd understand. "Fungus seeds."

"Fungus seeds," she repeated, mulling over the concept. "I understand."

"And they're nasty to get out of clothes. I lost a load of towels that way — left them in the washer. Stank so bad."

She pinned up a dark dress. "You talk like Levi."

"How so?"

"You both seem to understand the world

better. You've learned things. Gone to school."

I wanted to tell her she could go to school too. I mean, there had to be some sort of program that would help her catch up, wouldn't there?

But I didn't think today was a good day to make waves in the family. "You can learn things outside of school."

"I've learned everything I can here," she said.

The bitterness in her voice took me aback. "Do you want to learn more?"

She seemed to catch herself. "I want to learn how to be a better person. To serve my community, to serve God."

I shrugged. "I'm probably not the best person to talk to when it comes to God, but my guess is that it's possible to learn and serve at the same time."

"Maybe in the English world," Sara said, pinning the last pair of pants to the line with a kind of sad finality. "In the Amish world, there is only serving."

"We're going to Grandma's," Sara told me that afternoon. "There is room for you to come if you like."

"I'd love to." I put down the laundry I'd been folding. "What's going on at Ida's?"

Martha secured a bolt of purple cloth beneath her arm. "Quilting."

I almost froze in place. "Quilting? You mean, like actually making quilts?"

The women gave me twin blank looks.

"Yes," Sara said. "Don't some English women quilt?"

"They do, some of them. Just not any of the women I know."

I dropped my cell phone into my apron pocket, on the off chance that Shane got through. Reception had been spotty during the day.

Martha hitched the horse to the buggy, and then we set off bumpily down the road. People waved at us as we drove by; Martha nodded, Sara waved back. I probably looked as though I had missed my calling as home-coming queen.

Along the way, Sara told me about the quilts. Friends and family members often gave quilts as wedding gifts, but the market for Amish-made quilts in the last ten years had skyrocketed to the point where the women felt no qualms about meeting during planting season and working on quilts to supplement the family income.

I fingered the bolts of cloth as I listened. There was the purple cloth Martha had carried, which reminded me of a Sunday school lesson about Lydia. I couldn't remember who Lydia was or what she did, only that she dealt in purple textiles. She was probably a believer — most of the women in the Bible were.

A second bolt shimmered yellow in the pale afternoon sun. "You don't wear yellow, do you?" I asked Sara.

She shrugged. "Sometimes the younger children do. Why?"

I pointed to the fabric.

"Oh," she said. "English women like light colors in their quilts. The lighter quilts sell faster than the darker ones."

"Makes sense." That also accounted for the pale blue fabric that reminded me of the last robin's egg I'd found as a child. "How far is it to Ida's?"

"She lives on the outside of town, on the other side."

"So . . . we have to drive through town?"

Sara nodded.

Martha remained stoic.

As we neared town, the other drivers' stress levels rose. Some passed us in a swoosh of metal and air, honking as though they were auditioning to be New York cabbies. The buggy shuddered each time.

Others just sat behind us as if we were leading a procession. I suppressed the urge to repeat my homecoming wave.

Once we got into town, people stared. Some stared openly, others used techniques usually reserved for checking out members of the opposite sex. A few people whipped out their cell phones to take pictures. Sara ducked her head. Martha's gaze remained fixed on the road ahead of her.

Suddenly it occurred to me that people were also taking *my* picture. A giggle started deep inside and grew to a laugh. Sara turned around. "What?"

"They're taking pictures of us," I said, another peal of laughter threatening to break loose.

Sara's expressions darkened. "It's hard to stop them."

"But they're taking pictures of me too! Me! And I'm not even Amish!" Another cackle escaped. "The joke's on them!"

She smiled. "I suppose so. But you're giving them something to photograph: a laughing Amish woman."

"Sorry." I sobered. "I'm just not used to dealing with the paparazzi."

Except for the cars in the driveway, Ida's house and the Burkholder home could have been one and the same. A couple other buggies were parked in an adjoining field, attended by bored-looking horses. Martha pulled up next to them.

I saw that hitching posts were actually in the field and watched as Martha tied up the horse.

It answered my question about how one parked a buggy without an emergency brake.

The sound of women's voices met us on the porch before we even made it into the house. Once we were inside, I paused.

How did so many women fit in here? It was like the circus Volkswagen with the clowns. And not only were the women packed in like sardines, they had quilts pulled taut in giant frames.

Crazy. I assumed the fire marshall had no idea what went on in normally quiet Mennonite homes.

I watched from a safe spot near the wall as Martha and Sara moved into the crowd. They greeted, they hugged, they commented on fabric. After a few moments, Sara stopped, her eyes searching. When she found me, she wove through the masses toward me and grabbed my hand. "Come and sit with us! You can cut squares."

"You don't want me cutting squares," I said, shaking my head and trying to free myself.

But Sara had a farm girl's grip. "Anyone can cut squares."

"I tried making a nine-patch in fourth grade. I was the only kid whose project looked less like a quilt and more like Jackson Pollock. And I really mean Jackson Pollock — not one of his paintings."

"You're not in fourth grade anymore," Sara retorted, all but shoving me into a chair. I received a few calm smiles, as if reporters got harnessed into sweatshop labor all the time. "Here are your scissors," she said, giving them to me handles first, "a template, and fabric." She set the purple bolt in my lap. "Make sure the corners are nice and crisp."

And with that she left.

I struggled through the first few squares. I couldn't get the fabric to cut without it folding oddly on the scissors, resulting in a less-than-straight edge of the square.

Or rectangle. I began to think that maybe Sara needed to be more open minded when it came to the desired shape of the quilt pieces. What was the template but a constraint against creativity? She might think she wanted squares, but had she really considered rectangles? Rectangles opened up so many possibilities. They were easier on the eyes, visually.

At least, that's what the guy at Video Only said when he wanted me to spend the money on a widescreen TV.

"You need to use the edges of the scissors," a voice said to my right.

I jumped and turned. With the complete commotion all around me, I hadn't noticed Ida taking a seat next to me. "Sorry . . ."

She waved a hand. "Didn't mean to startle you. You might try moving the fabric down so it's closer to the tip of the scissors. I think that pair has a dull spot in the middle."

I obeyed, moving the fabric down the blade before making the snip. A clean-cut piece dropped into my lap. "Thank you!" I said, picking up the fabric and eyeing its perfection. "That's much better."

"You've never sewn before," she observed.

"Never."

"It's useful. Even in your world, there's wisdom in knowing how to sew a button back on."

I couldn't tell her I usually chucked clothes once they began to shed their buttons or grow holes.

I cut another square. This time it actually looked like a square. "This is fun, though. And I enjoy learning new things."

"How is my grandson doing?"

Okay, that was a serious change in subject,

although I suspected this line of questioning to be her original intention. "Fine, I guess. I talked to him this morning."

"He's a good boy, Levi. He had a lot of opportunities to do other things, but he chose to stay near the family that rejected him."

I hid my surprise that she would discuss such a personal subject in such a crowded room. Although you could barely hear your own thoughts, much less another conversation. "Why did he leave the community?"

"I don't know how he stayed so long. He was so curious, so smart. He wanted to know how the world worked, and he couldn't understand why no one else did. The teacher at the school used corporal punishment, at the time, and Levi was strapped for asking too many questions. He read better than many adults, and he would read the family Bible. He asked the bishop once if King David got into heaven even though he led armies."

"What happened?"

"The bishop told Gideon, and Gideon had to discipline Levi, or else the community would have looked down on him for being a lax father."

"Is the community that involved?"

"Everyone has to keep up appearances.

Watch the squares — you don't want them too small. There needs to be seam allowances."

"Seam allowances?"

"About half an inch, since they'll be sewn together."

"I get it." No, I didn't.

"After Levi left he went to school and got himself a fancy education on scholarship money. Worked for a big company in California before he came back here and opened his shop. He's been here ever since."

"Why do you think he came back?"

Ida arched an eyebrow. "To be close. To be available."

"Available in case . . ." I followed Ida's gaze to where Sara stood, overseeing one of the frames and examining the seams.

Of course.

He wanted to be close to help his siblings get out, if they wanted.

I looked around at the Amish women filling the room. They weren't highly educated, but these women appeared happy. Industrious. Savvy in their craft. Aside from the overzealous watchdog community, why would anyone ever leave?

I asked Ida as much.

"I left because my husband left, and I didn't want to be apart from him. Not everyone is cut out to be Amish. Still . . ."

I waited.

"Well, I was a little surprised about Levi's leaving, at least concerning Rachel."

Rachel?

Ida pointed to another woman.

This woman looked around my age, and resembled what the rest of the world would consider the ideal paragon of Amish beauty.

There wasn't a trace of makeup on her face, but she didn't need it. Her skin was clear, her cheeks, rosy. Her teeth were white and straight, her hair a rich chestnut. She looked like the sort of woman who followed the rules and always did the right thing.

"Were she and Levi . . ."

"They were never engaged, though everyone thought they would be." Ida shook her head. "But I don't know that Rachel would have been able to leave."

My chest tightened as I looked at Rachel and realized she was everything I wasn't.

CHAPTER 7

The buzz of my phone interrupted my jealousy of Rachel. "Excuse me," I said to Ida. I disentangled myself from the pile of squares before picking up the phone.

The caller ID read "Shane Colvin."

About time. I snapped the phone open, even though I couldn't hear a thing. "Let me get outside," I said, hoping he could at least hear me, even if I couldn't hear him.

Come to think of it, the last time we talked he couldn't hear me because he was in some kind of club. This time, I couldn't hear him because I was off quilting.

Oh, the irony.

"Hi," I said, then stalled. "Um, how are you?" Why haven't you called me? What have you been doing?

"Fine," he answered, as if he hadn't been putting off calling me at all. "How's the story?"

"Interesting, very interesting."

"Did you find someone to stay with?"

"I did, actually."

"Yeah?"

"Yeah."

Ladies and Gentlemen, the world's stupidest conversation.

"Who with?"

I sighed. "An Amish family outside of town. I found them through a contact."

"The Mennonite lady?"

"You know, call me old-fashioned, but I always thought that 'I'll call you back tonight' meant that the caller would call back that same night. Maybe it's supposed to be a different night. Maybe that's what all the cool kids are doing now. Or is it code? Because I left my secret agent decoder ring back at my apartment, thank you."

"I'm sorry I didn't call you back . . ."

"You're calling me back now, and it's not even sunset. Not at all nighttime, so now I'm really confused."

"Jayne . . ."

"The cool kids must really hate you."

"I'm sorry. I went to a talk at the university with my brother; you caught me just as it let out. Then Jordan wanted to go out for a drink, and I got distracted."

"You got drunk?"

"I was the designated driver. Jordan was

singing sea shanties by the time I took him back to his dorm."

I winced. "He can't sing."

"No, and his pitch gets worse after a couple brewskies. And he forgot words . . . I don't know why I'm telling you all this."

"Is it true?"

"Why wouldn't it be?"

I wrapped my nonphone arm around myself. "Sorry. I'm feeling very vulnerable right now. Must be the bonnet."

"You're dressed like one of them?"

"Down to the kneesocks."

"I bet you look cute."

"Shut up," I told him, but in truth a smile sneaked out. He always had that effect on me.

"You're doing okay?" he asked.

"I'm doing okay. What's going on in the world out there?"

"Oh, you know. Death, destruction, political upheaval. The usual."

"There's something comforting about not getting a newspaper." I paused. "Don't tell anyone I work with I said that."

He chuckled. "Don't worry, I won't. I don't think Kim would ever talk to you again."

"She wouldn't. Ever." Kim. I missed Kim. And Joely and Gemma . . . "I miss you."

"I miss you too."

I met Shane when I covered the construction of the new Civic Center. Shane, being near the bottom of his architecture firm's food chain, was the most accessible source. I asked him about the design process and inspiration; he asked me to dinner.

Being with Shane excited me. For the first time I was in a grown-up relationship involving dinners at nice restaurants and intellectual conversation.

There wasn't a beach bonfire to be found, no sad high-school dances with wilted helium balloons, no furtive make out sessions in dorm hallways. I felt as though I'd finally broken free of my past.

Shane took me home to meet his parents and two younger brothers. I think a part of him waited for me to return the gesture.

Scratch that. I *knew* he wanted me to. But I just couldn't do it.

How could I explain that he represented my separation from home? I liked Shane for a lot of reasons, one of which was that he knew nothing about my life before I came to Portland. If I took him home, it could ruin everything.

But another part of me wondered how long I could continue to run.

■ ■ ■ ■

After I hung up with Shane, I brushed Rachel from my mind.

Jealous? I wasn't jealous. I had handsome, urbane Shane waiting for me at home.

Urbane Shane. That was funny. I would have to call him that in passing some time.

Levi was just a guy. A complicated guy, but a guy nonetheless. I was, perhaps, a bit attracted to him, mainly because he was here and Shane wasn't.

I was bigger than that, stronger than that. Levi certainly had his own baggage as well, and I didn't need to go near that with a ten-foot pole.

Although professionally, it could help with the story.

Being a journalist was complicated sometimes.

I cut a total of fifty squares that afternoon. Sara examined my work on the way back. "Good," she said. "I should be able to use these."

Don't know how she could tell, with the buggy bouncing the way it was.

Martha made a beeline for the kitchen when we returned. A pot of stew bubbled on the stove. Baking sheets of yeasty dinner rolls rose in the oven. "Is there anything I can help with?" I asked.

She wiped her hands on her apron. "I don't think so. All that needs doing is baking the rolls. Why don't you see if Sara needs help with the mending?"

They were awfully eager to arm me with a needle, first with the quilting and then with the mending.

I didn't mention my concerns. Sara sat in the family room beside the glow of a propane lantern. "Your mother told me to help you if you needed it."

She cocked an eyebrow. "You can sew?"

"No."

"Okay." She took a critical look of my Amish ensemble. "If you would like," she said, "I can make you a new dress."

I sat down next to her. "I'm not going to be here that long . . ."

"I'm quick. I could have a dress for you in a couple of days."

"Only if you want to . . ."

"May I measure you?" She didn't stop for an answer. "I'll get my tape."

"Shouldn't we . . ." Was it proper to be fitted in the family room? But then, I didn't suppose the Amish were all that concerned with the finer points of tailoring. I waited. If she wanted to make me a dress, who was I to stop her?

I started writing in my head — *Within a few days, Sara wanted to sew for me. But why?*

She returned a moment later, arms laden with fabric, a tape measure, and a pincushion shaped like a cupcake. "I ain't opposed to taking in the dress you're wearing."

"Do whatever you want. Do you enjoy sewing?"

"I do."

"When did you learn?"

"I started when I was eight," she answered, pinning my dress along the sides. "This dress was made for someone larger than you. You're also wearing a real bra."

As opposed to fake ones?

Sara must have read my expression. "We usually make undergarments to hold and . . . flatten." She began to blush.

"Oh." No lift and separate here, then. I stuck my hands on my hips. "Well, what do you need me to do?"

She regained her composure. "To start, I need the length of your torso, arms, and legs from the waist."

I held out my arms. "Should I stand like this?"

"You could, but I left my notepad in the

kitchen."

"Ah." I put my arms down.

For all of her quiet Amishness, Sara possessed a surprisingly acerbic wit. There was a real teenager struggling to get out.

Heaven help us.

She came back from retrieving her notepad and started with measuring my arm. I stood very still. "Do you sew all the family clothes?"

Sara scribbled a number. "Most of them. Sometimes Mother and Leah help with the hemming."

"Leah sews?"

"Elizabeth is learning. All Amish women sew."

But Leah and Elizabeth were so young. I couldn't imagine wielding a needle and thread at that age.

Nor could I imagine feeding cows, but the children took care of the livestock on a regular basis.

"You're going to be here tomorrow?" Sara asked, after measuring my torso.

"Yes."

Sara looked over her shoulder toward the kitchen. "Could you take me to town?"

"What?"

"I need to take mending back to Levi."

"You do Levi's mending?"

"Shh!" She waved her hand at me. "Not so loud."

I lowered my voice. "Why are we whispering?"

"Normally Grandma takes me to town, but she can't for a week and suggested you take me."

"Why are we whispering?"

Sara glanced again at the kitchen. "I don't want my mother to hear and tell anything to Father."

"Doesn't your father wonder why you have normal clothes in your mending pile?"

"I mend them in my room. Can we take your motorcycle?"

"What?" I forgot to whisper.

"Shh!"

"Sorry," I spoke in a hush again. "I don't have a second helmet."

"That's okay."

"No, it's not okay. It's illegal, and even if you had a helmet, I don't think you could ride and keep your skirt free."

"What if you borrowed Grandma's car?"

"I thought she was busy."

"She might not need her car."

"Well, let me know."

Truth be told, being jarred by the buggy all the way to Levi's didn't appeal to me.

Apparently Sara was a skilled negotiator, because I found myself driving Ida's Buick to town the following afternoon.

Ida held my bike as collateral.

"Remind me what you told your mother?" I said as we zipped down the highway at fifty-five beautiful miles per hour.

"I told her Grandma needed us to take some things to a neighbor, and they were too heavy for her to lift, so she asked us to help."

"And then didn't come along?"

"She's busy today."

"With what?"

Sara shrugged.

If there was anything I remembered from my teen days, it was the necessity of details in a good parental lie. Not that Sara needed to know that . . . although she seemed a bit proud of her subterfuge.

She had also insisted that I stay in my Amish clothes, lest anyone suspect we were headed to the outside world. But being a reporter, and a darn good one, I didn't mind the fact that I was driving a Buick older than my older sister and wearing a bonnet.

The Buick? The bonnet? All prime material.

As was Spencer's face when we walked in.

"Ms. Tate!" he said, and that was all.

Nothing makes a man speechless faster than a grown woman in a pinafore.

"I have mended clothes for Levi," Sara said, full of noble purpose.

Spencer nodded, still silent, before retreating down the hall toward Levi's office.

Sara frowned. "He's usually more talkative than that."

I restrained a smirk. "It's been a tough day for him."

"Jayne! Sara!" Levi grinned like a boy receiving a dirt bike. "What are you ladies doing?"

Sara pulled the bundle out from under her arm. "I have your clothes."

"Oh. Good. Come back to my office."

Sara all but skipped after him. I lagged behind, watching.

They belonged with one another, brother and sister. Seeing them together, studying their faces, I could see the family resemblance. Granted, Levi's hair was dark and Sara's blond, but the slight upturn of the nose and the shape of the eyes identified them as siblings. The way they both seemed to smile with their whole face. Not that I'd seen Sara smile very often. Was she simply more serious in disposition, or unhappy? I'd had friends in high school with permanent rain clouds over their heads. Somehow, Sara didn't strike me as being one of them.

Levi turned at the threshold of his office door. "Coming?"

I nodded and quickened my steps.

"You know," Levi said, closing the door after I'd stepped through, "I haven't seen Spencer speechless since his mother announced that she was 'down with new bling.'"

I winced. "I hate the word 'bling.' It came and went and yet it's still printed in the media."

"And uttered by mothers."

"I'm sure Spencer was glad to know how hip his mother was."

"He couldn't talk for five minutes."

"That must be a record."

"Levi!" Sara tugged on his sleeve. I quieted and let her have a moment with her brother.

With painstaking care, she pulled out each garment and showed him how she had tended to each piece of fabric.

"They all look perfect," Levi told her.

Sara smiled and tried on the humble-Amish expression, but she didn't quite make it. They chatted for a few minutes before she excused herself to the ladies' room.

Leaving Levi and me alone together.

"She's starting to talk like you," he said.

"What?"

"Your mannerisms, your patterns of speech. She admires you."

I snorted. "You wouldn't think it."

"She's seventeen," he said with a laugh. "It's her prerogative."

"I met Ida."

"How is she?"

"Fine, although I have no previous experience to compare it with. I can't tell you if she looks worn or has lost weight, but I can say she likes personal questions."

"She is fine then."

"And she likes to talk about you."

Was it my imagination, or was that a blush forming near his collar?

"She has always been very good to me."

"That's nice."

"She's also sad I'm single."

"Most grandmothers are, I guess. Mine passed away a long time ago, but that seems right."

"Have you heard anything from your boyfriend?"

I ducked my head. "Yeah. He called yesterday."

The expression on his face turned plastic. "Glad to hear that."

I flushed. My heart raced. My mouth grew dry — all in all, my body is very good at impersonating a high school crush.

And if I didn't know better, I'd think he was looking at my lips.

Or was I looking at his?

I had to get out of that office. Without any sort of verbal warning, I stood, turned, and headed toward the door.

At least that was my intention. Next thing I knew, my foot caught, the world spun, and I had carpet lint between my teeth.

CHAPTER 8

In an instant Levi crouched next to me on his hands and knees. "Jayne? Are you okay?"

I blinked from my position on the floor. "How did that happen?"

"I think it was the garbage can."

I lifted my body enough to look. Sure enough, there was an ankle-biter garbage can, overturned and looking guilty.

Sara peered over me, having returned in time to see my appointment with gravity. "What happened?"

"I'm a moron, that's what happened." I put my wrist down to push myself up, and then I yelped in pain.

"What's wrong?" Levi's gaze focused on my hand. "Did you break something?"

Was it me, or did my left wrist look larger than it used to be?

The X-ray tech squinted at me. "Looks bad."

I stopped myself from rolling my eyes. My wrist, by now, was three times its normal size.

The woman positioned me on the table, laying a lead apron over my torso. "So, are you Amish?"

I winced. Levi had driven us straight to the hospital ER, no matter how many times I begged for him to take me back to the farm so I could change clothes. I mean I wasn't going to die. Really, just the quickest of clothing changes . . .

But he didn't, and here I was on the X-ray table feeling like a kid who got caught playing dress-up.

"Sure, yeah, I'm Amish," I said. I was embarrassed enough without having to explain that I was undercover reporter Amish.

I mean, really.

The glow of the streetlights reflected on the bright white compression brace. "It's just a sprain," I groused as we drove back to the shop. "Don't know why I need this thing. It's not very Amish."

"I could make a black sleeve for it," Sara suggested.

"More punk rock than Amish." I sighed. "And I can't ride my bike with this."

Levi shot me a quick glance as he drove. "What did the doctor say about you riding?"

"The swelling should be down in a week or two, but I shouldn't ride until I get my full range of movement back." I sighed again. "That part may be a while."

"At least the sling's navy!" Sara chirped.

"Yes, the sling is appropriately Amish looking."

"Don't worry about your bike," Levi said. "I can take it back to the farm if you can drive the truck."

"That's all well and good, but that leaves me with only a buggy."

"Buggies are good enough for a lot of people."

"Hmm, yes, but I need to have a motor of some sort around." I looked him in the eye. "And the tractor doesn't count."

His mouth snapped shut. "Fine. I won't suggest that, then."

"Don't." I thought out loud, "My car's probably out of the shop by now . . ."

"Do you want me to pick it up for you?"

"No. Kim probably has by now."

"I could drive it down."

"It's in southeast Portland."

"I need to make a delivery in Portland anyway."

"How are you going to get there if you're

driving the car back?"

"I could take your bike."

Like that was going to happen. "Nobody rides my bike but me."

"Really?"

I would have crossed my arms if the action hadn't shot sparks of pain to my shoulder. "Yes. Really."

"You're getting cranky. Do you need another pain pill?"

"No, I don't need another pain pill. And how would you make a delivery using my bike?"

"It's a box. I could easily put it into a well-padded backpack."

"You own a furniture store."

"Yes."

"And you're delivering a box?"

"If there's one thing they teach you in business, it's diversification."

"Do you even have your motorcycle endorsement?"

"I do. I've got my own helmet and everything."

"Good, 'cause you're not wearing mine."

"Why not?"

"You'd get man cooties on it."

Sara giggled from the backseat.

"That's enough from you, young lady," I said. "Man cooties are very serious. They cause all kinds of problems."

The girlish giggling continued, and I couldn't help but join in. I sobered when I looked at Levi's earnest face.

Yes, man cooties could do all sorts of things. They could make you forget about your boyfriend.

"So," Sara said, interrupting the moment, "what are we going to tell my parents?"

I shrugged my right shoulder. "I don't know. What are you going to tell them?"

"You're not going to help me?"

"I'm not going to lie to them."

Sara opened her mouth, shut it, and then crossed her arms.

"She's right, Sara," Levi said. "Mom can smell a lie twenty feet away. Lies and rock music."

"She's got a good nose, your mother."

"Woman's got eight kids," Levi said. "By now I think she's telepathic. Don't worry about it. I'll come in with you — that'll be distraction enough."

"How are you going to get back?" I asked. "I mean, after you take Ida's car back to her."

"I can take your bike, or Ida can drive me home."

Sara snorted. "And send you with two loaves of bread and a batch of cookies."

"Oh," I said with a nod. "Such sacrifice."

In the end, my wrist brace stole the show. Gideon roundly ignored Levi, Martha hovered around my arm, asking if the brace came off so she could put a poultice on it, but then suggesting maybe putting it on my fingers might help.

Sara all but ducked away to her room. Smart kid.

I sent Levi out with the keys to the bike, telling him I'd call him about it later. Then I headed to my room to see if the magical phenomenon of cell service happened to be functioning.

For once it was. I dialed Kim's number. "Do you know if anyone's picked up my car yet?"

Kim snorted. "You leave for Amish country, and you're worried about your car?"

"I sprained my wrist —"

"And here I am being a jerk. Bet you can't ride like that. Sorry. Do you need me to drive your car to you?"

"Actually, a friend of mine is going to pick it up."

"Someone Amish? That's original. I thought they didn't drive."

"They don't, and no, he's not Amish."

"*He?* Who is he? How did you meet him?

Have you told Shane about him?"

There are disadvantages to being friends with investigative journalists.

"He is the owner of a local Amish-style woodcraft store. It's complicated. His family is Amish and they're the ones I'm staying with."

"Interesting. And Shane?"

"No."

"Even more interesting. Why haven't you told Shane?"

"Haven't really had the opportunity," I hedged. As in, Shane hadn't directly asked about him.

Not that Shane had a reason to, but never mind.

"Anyway, he's going to drive my bike up and I need someone to give him the car. Who picked it up?"

"Joely was going to, but she got called out. It's sitting in my driveway."

"Can I send him to your place, then?"

"What's his name?"

"Levi Burkholder."

"Nice strong man name."

"Whatever. Flirt with him all you like — just let him take the car."

"So you're not interested?"

"I'm with Shane."

"Right. Are you leaving the bike here?"

110

"Hmm." I thought for a moment. "Would it put you out too much to meet him at my place with my car? That way he could leave the bike there."

"Good enough for me. Is he cute?"

"I'm not answering that."

"He is, then."

"Kim —"

"I know, I know. You're with Shane. I can flirt all I want, and I'm looking forward to it."

I called Levi moments after, using my window of airtime before the airwaves shifted and I lost reception.

"So she's expecting me?" he asked after I gave him directions to my apartment.

"Expecting" seemed so . . . subtle. "Yes."

Next thing I knew, the call dropped. No service.

Part of me wondered if I should have warned him. I mean, if we were golfing, and there was a golf ball headed for his cranium, I would yell "fore" or "heads" or whatever you're supposed to say to warn people on a golf course.

But on the other hand, Kim was single, Levi was single, and they'd probably have lovely sandy-haired children. Bully for them. I had Shane.

■ ■ ■ ■

There's something about sleeping in an Amish house. Aside from the sound of teenagers skulking in the night, it's silent. I couldn't even hear the traffic from the highway. And the stars? Impossibly bright. I'd forgotten how bright stars could be.

When I was a teen, I'd hike to Cascade Head at night just to look at the stars. They reminded me how little I was, and how big the rest of the world was. Sometimes I would pray, back when I did such things. I thought I could hear God better when I was under the stars.

Is that why the Amish lived so far from the city lights? Could they hear God better?

After the demise of my arm, I found myself in strictly observation mode. When the children were home, I followed them around with my notepad in hand.

I had avoided children in my old life. But the children I had interacted with, including my niece, were nothing like the youngest Burkholder children.

There were moments when they laughed like normal children. When Levi appeared, you'd think they were promised a trip to the circus.

Were children still into the circus? Or did they prefer to stay home with their Wii? I wouldn't know.

Either way, these children spent the bulk of their time in a state of soberness I'd never observed in any other American children. They attended to their chores without Martha harping on them.

And yet they still had very individual personalities. Samuel had a penchant for practical jokes; I'd actually heard some of the family members refer to him as "Joker Sam." Permanent nickname? I hoped not for his sake. But when he wasn't tending to the cows or doing his homework, he seemed to enjoy removing key items and putting them somewhere else. Martha found half of her kitchen pots on the seat of the tractor once. Elizabeth's faceless doll was in the pantry, next to the flour.

Samuel at least had sense enough to leave Gideon's things alone, though I wondered if in the past he had tried something and paid the consequences.

Leah, by contrast, was shy and reserved. She probably paid the most attention to her schoolwork, and she seemed to be constantly cataloging information.

Elizabeth was the dreamer. If I was sitting

in the living room with my notepad, she would occasionally curl up next to me with her doll, telling me what "Mary" had done that day while she was away at school.

The older boys remained a mystery to me. I knew Amos helped his father with the heavy manual labor around the farm. I asked Sara once if he were planning on marrying soon; she answered that marrying season wasn't till November. Whether there would be a family wedding in the autumn or not remained anyone's guess.

Elam worked in town, often coming home covered in concrete dust. At least, I guessed it was concrete. He resembled Levi in face but not expression. Whereas Levi's face was usually open and friendly, Elam's was wary and often creased in a frown.

Then there was Sara.

Sara tired of my brace within days. "You're going to have to learn to sew a button sometime," she said. "Your left hand doesn't do *that* much. Don't you think you could try?"

So I did.

If I held my injured left arm just right, I could manage to hang onto the fabric while my uninjured right arm maneuvered the needle. Sara helped with the threading for humanitarian reasons. A needle through my finger didn't help anyone.

"You insert the needle here," she said, pointing at a spot in the fabric scrap.

"Why there?"

"Because that's where the button's going."

"What if I wanted to put the button somewhere else?"

"You don't."

"I don't?"

"No."

"Okay." I followed her directions. "Like that?"

"Yes."

"Shouldn't I have a thimble or something?"

"For just sewing a button, you'll do."

Five minutes and two thread knots later, I held up my button-laden fabric scrap with pride. "There!"

Sara nodded. "That will do."

"Are you ever proud of your work?" I asked.

"No. It is not Amish to be proud. To be prideful, arrogant — *hochmut* — is a sin."

"You're not rubbing your work in other people's noses, though. It's pride of a job well done."

"It can become arrogance."

"But what if it doesn't?"

Sara opened her mouth to answer when

Gideon stomped in the door, fresh from the fields.

And I do mean fresh. I could smell him eight feet away.

"The Colblentzes' barn caught fire," he announced with a wheeze.

Martha left the kitchen. "Is anyone hurt? Did the fire spread?"

"None's hurt. Jacob's Billy got the animals out. Titus said bad wiring's to blame."

"And the Colblentzes' house?"

"Fit and fine."

By this time Samuel, Leah, and Elizabeth were down the stairs and full of questions.

"Billy's barn? Did he get burned?" Samuel asked.

Leah tugged on Gideon's shirt. "Is Susie okay?"

Martha held a hand to her chest. "Was there damage to the house or fields?"

Gideon shook his head. "They said it was the wires, so it burned from the inside. The fields are fine, the house is fine. We'll have the barn raisin' on Friday."

I stifled an excited gasp. A real, live Amish barn raising? How lucky could I get!

CHAPTER 9

I couldn't have planned for a barn raising better myself, unless I'd personally set fire to the Colblentzes' barn.

Which, of course, I didn't. I'm afraid of matches. And it's unethical journalism.

The day before, Martha's baking and cooking kicked into a gear I'd never seen. With impossible speed she produced three pies, a baked custard, a side of roasted pork, and four loaves of bread.

The woman's a machine.

I worked in the garden that day, as best I could. Without using my left arm, I sat on the ground in the dirt, pulling weeds and neatening rows of beans and vegetables that the family would can for the next year. Leah kept me company, commenting on the state of the plants and the likelihood of rain.

We'd counted our third water droplet when my phone rang in my apron pocket. "I'll be right back," I told Leah.

She watched as I walked back toward the house. It occurred to me that she didn't watch people answer cell phones very often.

Shane's name flashed on the caller ID. "The rain must help the reception. How are you?"

He exhaled hard into the phone. "Feeling pretty stupid."

"Why?"

"I went to pick up your mail like you asked. Who was the guy at your apartment with your bike?"

Uh-oh. "I sprained my wrist pretty bad. Levi's a friend of mine, and he offered to take my bike back and get my car."

"He did."

"Yes."

"Why didn't you call me? I would have taken care of everything."

I sighed. "Shane, you're up to your eyebrows in work, and it's not like your office is anywhere near the repair place or my apartment. You would have been driving all day."

"I wish you'd asked."

"Service cut out. Aside from smoke signals, there was nothing I could do. And you don't really have any south-facing windows."

"Glad this is all a joke to you. Is your wrist okay?"

"It's fine, and I'm joking because you're overreacting. There's nothing for you to worry about."

"Sorry. You're a beautiful woman —"

"Yeah, well, so is Kim, and she sounded single and motivated when I talked to her."

"The guy looked like a real rube."

I bristled. "That was uncalled for."

"He does!"

"He worked hard to catch up with his peers and is the first member of his family to attend, much less graduate from, college. He left a corporate job to be near his family. I think you can cut him some slack."

I guessed it was a corporate job. Ida had said "big company." Either way, Levi had achieved more in his lifetime than most of us, Shane included.

"I just don't like him," Shane said, his voice weighted with resentment.

"Couldn't tell."

"Look, if you say it was nothing, I'll believe you."

"Nothing," I said, hoping the slight shake to my voice didn't travel over the cellular frequency.

"Sorry I got upset. You said your arm's fine?"

"It is."

"Tell me if you break a leg?"

"If I have cell service, you'll be the first to know."

When Leah and I finished in the garden, I took my notepad and sat in the kitchen while Martha toiled away. I didn't think that many pies existed outside of a Shari's.

She worked uninterrupted until Elizabeth ran in squealing that the pig was in the garden.

"Jayne?" she said.

I looked up from my notes.

"Could you remove the pie from the oven if I'm not back in five minutes?"

"Of course," I heard myself agree.

Maybe she'd be back in five minutes and be able to remove the pie herself. I mean, how hard is it to chase a pig?

Five minutes rolled by. No Martha.

I set my notes down and approached the oven. The familiar coil of discomfort tightened in my stomach. I hated ovens. Always had.

Martha had left a hot pad by the stove. I used it to open the heavy door. I peered in — a lemon meringue number sat inside, looking lightly browned, innocuous, and yet menacing at the same time. It *knew* I had to deal with it. And it might be lightly browned now, but if I just left it there, that nice golden color would be a thing of the past.

Gingerly, I reached in, greeted by waves of oppressive heat. Were there any other hot pads? I backed away, looked around, and eventually located a few more in a drawer.

Two per hand. Except that my left arm ached. Armed with two pads in my right hand I reached in again toward the lemon meringue with its caramel-tinted peaks. I grasped each side of the pie and lifted it from the rack. The contents swished; I froze.

Seriously, it was a pig in the garden, not a yeti. What was taking so long? It seemed safer to leave the pie in the oven than risk coating the floor with it, but I heard no sound of approaching footsteps.

Breathe, I told myself. *You're an adult. Adults remove things from ovens. They seldom die from the experience.*

My hands were growing warm, even through the double layer of protection. Now or never. With careful movements, I raised the pie in my grasp and placed it on the stovetop. Finally. I closed the oven door and backed away with a jump.

Done. I had survived. No burns. The pie looked beautiful, and a part of me felt proud that I had had a hand in it. Maybe I could try baking.

Then I smelled it. The tiniest whiff of smoke. I looked at the pie — not a burnt or charred spot on the thing. Where else could it be coming from?

The scent grew stronger. "Sara!" I called, hopeful. Nothing.

Logically, it had to be coming from the oven. Now that I thought about it, it should probably be turned off, right?

I turned the knob all the way to the left. Maybe the smell came from something that fell to the bottom of the oven. Martha *had* been cooking all day, so I supposed that something dropping or dripping wasn't a stretch of the imagination.

I opened the door to the oven; at the sight of flames, I jumped back. But even as I saw the flames, I saw the source.

Hot pad one of two.

Probably should have counted when I was done.

With the new influx of air, the flames experienced a growth spurt. I yelped and made a mad grab for the water faucet in the kitchen sink.

Martha had to have tongs somewhere . . . When I found them (located oddly near the canned goods), I snatched the blazing hot pad from the oven and flicked it to the sink.

It landed with a satisfying hiss. I poured more water over the smoldering ruins before closing the now flameless oven. As I closed it I saw a figure in the kitchen entryway.

I'd come through the pie and the following emergency with a certain grace, but seeing Levi caused my heart to pound.

"How long have you been there?" I demanded.

"Long enough," he said, his smirk answering my question.

"Do you make a habit of sneaking up on people?"

"I didn't want to startle you while you were firefighting."

"Thanks."

"Where's my mom?"

"Chasing a pig and taking too long."

"She likes you," he said, replacing the smirk with a smile.

"How can you tell?"

"She trusts you with pie."

"Good to know. So you came down to give me a hard time?"

"Yes. And I have your car."

"As long as you've done something useful."

"Keys?" He held out a familiar-looking set of car keys.

I took them and dropped them in my

apron pocket. "Thanks. Everything go okay with Kim?"

"Yes," he said, but another answer flashed in his eyes.

"What happened?"

"Your boyfriend is Shane?"

I chewed my lip. "Yes . . ."

"He came for your mail. That's what he told Kim."

"Okay."

"I don't think he was happy to see me."

Not really, no. "I wouldn't take it personally. How's Kim?"

He shrugged. "Fine, I guess."

Huh. "She's one of my best friends," I said. "She's brilliant. Great instincts."

"Good for her."

"And she's pretty. Don't you think she's pretty?"

Levi sighed and leaned against the wall. "I'm not interested in Kim, if that's what you're hinting at."

"Well, you should be. She's a catch."

"I'm sure she is."

"You should be so lucky."

"Jayne —" He opened his mouth as if to say something, but he must have changed his mind. "Never mind."

"Thanks for getting my car. It was a huge help."

He gave a small smile. "You're welcome. Anytime."

There are buffet restaurants with less food than at an Amish barn raising. Tables had been set up thirty feet from the charred barn. Pies upon pies stretched nearly as far as the eye could see. The sky threatened rain, but this group seemed to hold back the emptying of the heavens out of sheer will.

"How often do you guys do this?" I asked Sara as we carried food items to the tables.

She shrugged. "As often as we need to. Usually not till summer. We don't get many fires this time of year."

"Makes sense. Thanks for my dress, by the way."

Her face lit up. "Do you like it?"

"I do. It seems like it hangs really well."

"It's because I cut it on a bias. That's why there's a seam down the middle — if you look at the weave, it forms a V-shape when it's sewn together."

"Clever." I set the pork down on the table. "How's that?"

"Fine."

"Do we have to carve it?"

"The men will."

"You really like sewing, don't you."

Her face grew still, and she looked as though she chose her words carefully. "I understand fabric and the way it covers people. I understand it the way Levi understands wood."

"Do you think you would ever want to work with fabric outside the community, the way Levi does?"

"I think there's another pie in the buggy — I'll go get it," she said, her words coming out in a panicked jumble.

She all but ran back to the field of parked buggies.

I felt like Kelly McGillis in *Witness,* walking around and watching men sweat, move beams, and pound nails.

Except there was no Harrison Ford or that other blond guy vying for my attention. And that was okay with me, because I'd come to the conclusion that there were too many men in my life right now.

Personal life aside, I focused my attention on the structure taking shape before my eyes. What would it be like to live in a community where everyone took care of each other? When my dad died, my mom had the reception catered. I had the feeling that here, she would have been swimming in custard and cobbler.

One year a coastal storm blew a tree into our kitchen. We had to leave it until the insurance man came out; contractors arrived two weeks later. What would it have been like if the neighbors had come over with their tools and gotten the job done?

On the other hand, the din was incredible. Aside from the gaggle of men constructing the new barn, another group tore the old one down, piling the burnt and damaged wood near the road. The scene looked and sounded like a battle, builders versus breakers.

I tracked down Leah and Elizabeth, who were playing with the other children mercifully far away from the noise. Two sets of sticks had been driven into the ground, turning an otherwise ordinary field into a soccer stadium for the kids. Leah and Samuel, in particular, could boast of FIFA-worthy feet. I'd never seen kids move like that.

Not that I was a soccer aficionado of any kind, but I'd watched enough with Shane to know what did and didn't constitute ability. If these were any other kids, they'd be recruited out of high school to play nationally. Not these children, though. At some point, they would put down the soccer ball and turn to adult responsibilities full-time.

But wasn't it better that way? I'd known scores of people from school who dreamt of the rock star or pro-baseball player life, but whose careers never made it further than the video rental store. These kids were realistic, or at least their parents were.

Were they losing anything by having fewer opportunities? Or did their lessened options serve their purpose?

I mulled the thought in my head as I watched the ball travel up and down the field.

"Jayne?"

I jumped, nearly dropping my laptop. I looked up at Sara. "You have very quiet feet."

"Can I show you something?"

"Of course."

"In my room?"

"Okay." I closed the lid to my laptop and followed her.

When we were inside her room, she shut the door and spent another moment with her ear pressed to the doorframe. Once she decided the coast was clear, she walked across the room and stamped her heel.

At least it looked like a heel stamp, but her foot went right through the floor, revealing a loose board. She got on her hands and knees before retrieving what looked like a stack of magazines.

"Yes," she said, laying the pile on the bed.

I took a closer look. There were catalogs for JCrew and Anthropologie, as well as copies of *InStyle* and *Vogue.*

"Yes to what?" I asked.

"Your question."

"Which one?"

"The one about me and Levi being the same."

CHAPTER 10

I lowered my voice, not wanting my questions or Sara's revelations to be overheard. "You would leave?"

Sara clasped her hands around her knees. "I would think about it."

"What would you do?"

"Go to school. Become a clothing designer."

"Really." I sat back on the bed. "Where do you get these?"

She looked down. "Sometimes I get them when I go to town. Sometimes Levi gets them for me."

I tried to picture builder Levi, motorcycle-riding Levi, purchasing a copy of *Vogue.*

Nope. Couldn't get there.

But Sara as a fashion designer? Couldn't get there, either. "When did you start getting interested in —"

"We would go into town, and the women would be wearing such beautiful colors. Not just blues and greens and purples, but reds and pinks and yellows. I could tell by the cut of their clothes which ones were more flattering and why. And," she said, reaching to the bottom of the stack, "I have these."

She held a sketchpad.

"May I look?"

She nodded.

The sketches were very well done. Even I could tell that. Sara's designs showed a creative use of lines and a good eye for color. I would have expected an Amish girl to design dresses with high necklines and low hemlines, but these weren't. "I can see Gemma in this one."

"Gemma?"

I lowered the sketchbook. "Friend of mine, back home."

Sara pulled her legs up and hugged her knees to herself. "What's it like choosing what to wear from a hundred options every day?"

"I don't have a hundred, although Gemma probably does. I don't know. It's hard sometimes to choose."

Sara looked skeptical. "Really?"

"Usually I throw things on and don't think about them much, but I've known Gemma to be twenty minutes late because she couldn't decide on an outfit."

"But you don't?"

"Well, most of my clothes are black. Matching isn't hard at that point. Gemma has shoes that match sweaters, and bags that match pants, and skirts that match earrings. Dressing like Gemma is complicated."

"I want to meet her."

I smiled. "Maybe I can get her to come down."

"I hate wearing black. I don't like blue, either."

"What do you like?"

"Yellow. Purple. Orange. Bright green. Pink."

"Hopefully not together."

She laughed at that. "No, not together. I like white too. Everything looks cleaner with white."

"How would you leave?"

Sara bit her lip. "Levi would help me. I'd live with him for a while. Get my GED. Try to get into design school." She shrugged. "I don't know. Maybe I'll stay and be baptized here. My parents stayed."

"Your grandparents left."

"I don't know. Do you think it's possible to go to heaven, even if you're not baptized?"

"I — I'm not really the person to ask," I

stammered. "I haven't been to church in years."

"But you went to church?"

"My dad was an elder."

"You left the church?"

"I stopped going, yeah."

"Do you worry about going to hell?"

"Do you?" I found it safer to deflect the question.

"Our bishop says the English don't go to heaven. I don't think Jesus was Amish, though, and I don't think His disciples were. I think His disciples went to heaven."

"I think so. So . . . do you think you could live apart from your family? You seem so connected."

"I'd have Levi. And Grandma."

"I don't see my mom and sister. Sometimes, I wish things were better."

"Why don't you make them better?"

"It's complicated."

"You should try to make things better."

"Sometimes, people just get stuck. Why don't Levi and your dad talk?"

Before she could answer, footsteps sounded down the hallway. Before you could say "Spring Collection," Sara snatched up her pile of contraband and stashed it safely under the flooring.

■ ■ ■ ■

I really did wish things were better with my family. The early nights at the Burkholder farm gave me lots of time to think about how much in my life I wanted to change.

But when it came to my mom and sister . . . what could I do? I couldn't be the daughter my mom wanted. She wanted the traditional good girl. I couldn't be that girl. She nearly had a heart attack when I drew on my Converse sneakers in ballpoint pen as a teen. My shoes didn't look like the other daughters' shoes. At least, they didn't look like the shoes worn by her friends' daughters.

I didn't care what they thought. Her friends' daughters smirked at me and whispered behind my back about the streak of purple in my hair and the band T-shirts I wore as they strutted around in their Tommy Hilfiger outfits.

Even though I grew out of the Converse-sketching, hair-dying phase, I don't know that my mom ever noticed.

And Beth . . .

I didn't know how to reach her. I didn't know how to be her sister.

What would it be like to live in a family

like the Burkholders? To have my family mean so much to me that I changed careers to be near them, like Levi?

I dreamed about pie that night.

Odd, considering my fear of ovens and accidental pyromaniac tendencies. But the pie looked really good. I think it was a nectarine raspberry pie. I don't know where that came from. I don't think it's possible to have nectarines *and* raspberries together in a pie. Either way, it sounded really good. It sounded good as breakfast food. Pie was pretty close to toast and jam, wasn't it? Maybe more like toast, jam, and some fruit chunks, but it still sounded good.

Really good.

To my disappointment, Martha had not read my mind that morning. There were potatoes, sausages, and a steaming mound of cheese-topped scrambled eggs, but no pie.

I couldn't blame her, though. She'd made, like, a billion pies the day before. Maybe she had pie elbow, or whatever you call a pie-induced injury.

I helped clean up the breakfast dishes after the men left for work. "I was wondering," I said, as I scrubbed plates, "if you could teach me how to bake."

"What kind of baking?"

"I don't know. Bread — I've never made bread. The cobbler you made the other day was really good. Or," I paused artfully as I removed a stubborn bit of cheese, "there's pie. I don't know how to make pie."

Martha stopped drying dishes. "You don't know how to make pie?"

I shook my head.

"Your mother never taught you to make pie?"

"I wasn't much interested in baking when I lived with my mother."

To say the least. I couldn't be bothered to make toast at the time.

"The most important thing about the crust is not to make the shortening bits too fine."

And so it began.

When the last dishes were put away, Martha insisted that I measure out the flour myself, even with my injury. I dipped the cup measure into the flour bag, filled it, and then clumsily tried to scrape off the excess mound of flour on the top with my sore arm.

Martha shook her head. "You can't scoop like that. Dump it out."

Startled, I obeyed.

She removed a spoon from a drawer. "If you scoop, you may get air bubbles and your amounts won't be right. Use a teaspoon to add a little in at a time."

I tried to follow her instructions, but maneuvering the spoon and cup measure with my brace proved too difficult. Martha stepped in and offered to fill it, now that I knew the correct method.

After all the flour made it successfully to the mixing bowl, Martha taught me how to cut in shortening using two butter knives, drawing them across the bowl in opposite directions. "Many recipes tell you to continue until the mixture resembles coarse sand, but they're wrong. Only mix until it looks like little peas. Your piecrust will come out flakier that way."

After she rolled out the crust — another task I couldn't complete with a brace — she turned back to me. "What sort of pie do you want to bake?"

I bit my lip. "A fruit pie?"

"What fruit? We have apples, canned apricots, frozen berries . . ."

Apricots were kind of like nectarines. "Apricot? And raspberry?"

Martha lifted an eyebrow. "Never done that before."

We rinsed the apricots and let them dry a bit in a strainer. The raspberries remained frozen when we stirred them with the apricots, some flour, a little sugar, a half-teaspoon of cinnamon, and a pinch of nutmeg. After we poured the filling into the pie pan, Martha showed me how to fold over the top sheet of pie pastry and crimp the edges shut.

"Now you have to cut vents," she said, handing me the knife. "You could cut slits or make a design. You can also use your scrap crust as decoration."

I cut two hearts out of the leftover piecrust, and then I cut a heart in the crust itself as a vent. "How's that?"

"Good. Now put it in the oven."

Uh-oh. "Is the oven on?"

Martha gave me a blank look. "Yes. The oven must be hot when you put the pie in, or the pastry won't bake right."

Hot oven, hot oven. Oh, dear. "Um . . ."

"*Ja?*"

"Er . . . I don't think I can do it."

"You can't . . ."

"Lift. I can't lift the pie pan with one hand." I let out a forced chuckle. "Too heavy. Lot of fruit in there."

Never mind I removed the meringue the day before. But wasn't meringue lighter because of all that air?

"Oh." Martha grasped the pie with one hand and yanked the oven door open with the other. A wave of hot air greeted my face. She set it perfunctorily on the rack, closed the oven, and eyed me up and down. "You should eat more. Strengthen you up."

Leah wrinkled her nose. "What kind of pie is it?"

I tapped her kapp. "Apricot raspberry. Doesn't that sound good?"

"I ain't never had apricot raspberry pie."

"There's a first time for everything."

"It smells good," Elizabeth said.

"It smells like pie," Samuel corrected decisively.

"Who wants a slice?" I asked.

The pie had waited, uneaten, untasted, until the children returned from school. They greeted it with the enthusiasm reserved for strange things like sweetmeats and marzipan.

I cut into the pie with a knife, the crust still slightly warm under my fingers. After cutting the first wedge, I tried to lift it out with the flat edge of the knife.

What landed on the pie plate looked less like pie than it did a fruity train wreck.

Leah squinted at the plate. "I think you need a pie server."

"Oh. Right." I started fumbling through the drawers in front of me, but Leah pulled one out from a drawer across the kitchen.

"Here you go."

"Thanks." The next slices came out much prettier. I passed out forks and led the troops to the kitchen table.

My first bite melted in my mouth with an explosion of flavors. The tartness of the raspberries contrasted with the muskiness of the apricots.

Did everyone's first pie come out like this? I hadn't baked since I was in middle school home economics, and even then my muffins had collapsed like my mother's dreams for my future.

But the pie? The pie was special. Even as I devoured the rest of my slice and scraped the last bits of goo and crust from the plate, I wondered what other things I could learn to do while I was here.

Gideon took me aside after dinner that night.

Your daughter wants to leave your family to become a fashion designer, I thought.

"We'll be going to church at the Lapps' home, day after tomorrow," he said.

Clearly, he couldn't read minds. I had to think for a moment and shift gears. Was it Friday already? I'd completely lost track of days since my arrival.

"Sunday. Church. Okay," I said after I'd oriented myself in space and time.

"We don't allow outsiders into our church services."

"Not ever? I mean, observing the service would show me a lot about your culture. And I wouldn't talk. I could sit in the back —"

Gideon held up his hand. "No outsiders. I don't want to bring trouble to my door."

Trouble? What would that look like? Images of Amish men carrying pitchforks flashed through my mind.

"We follow the *Ordnung*," Gideon said.

I nodded. "I've heard the term."

"We must follow the *Ordnung* at all times. And we must never give anyone cause to be thinking that we're not."

"Okay . . ."

"Some people don't much like that you're here, is all. We see nothing wrong with it, but we don't need the bishop at our door for anything but a friendly dinner."

"I understand. That's fine," I said.

But inside I was disappointed.

Sunday dawned cold and drizzly. While the woodstove in the living room emitted a fair amount of heat, my feet still ached with cold. I put serious thought into turning on the oven in the kitchen, pulling up a chair, and reading a good book.

Maybe not my most brilliant idea, but thinking is tough when your feet are blue.

While I contemplated the state of my chill, the Burkholder family prepared for church. Their preparing for church resembled in no way my family's preparation for church.

In my family, there was a lot of rushing, arguments over bathroom space, and encouragement to finish breakfast quickly.

The Burkholder process resembled clockwork. Each child dressed and prepared himself or herself. The boys, including Amos and Elam, wore newer-looking pants and crisply pressed shirts. All the girls wore dresses I hadn't seen yet, in lighter colors and nicer fabrics. Where bedlam reigned in the Tate household every Sunday morning, the Burkholders moved with a peaceful sense of routine.

The routine continued until the family filed out the door, looking a bit like the von Trapp family.

From inside, I could hear their steps halt and the tension heighten.

"Daddy," Elizabeth asked, "where's the buggy?"

I stood up from the rocking chair and peered out the door, over the children's shoulders. The shed doors were open and the buggy was nowhere to be seen.

CHAPTER 11

"The buggy may be gone," Gideon said, with a nearly undetectable tightening of the jaw, "but we will still get to church. We will walk."

"How far away are the Lapps?" I asked.

"Two miles from here."

"I have my car now. I could drive you."

The entire family perked up like daisies in fresh water.

"I mean, I'd have to take two trips. You wouldn't all fit . . ."

Two minutes later Gideon, Amos, Elam, and Samuel were buckled in. I'd pulled an old University of Oregon sweatshirt from the trunk of my car over my Amish ensemble so I looked less like a driving Amish woman and more Mennonite, perhaps. It was just too much work to take off the organza kapp. The ride over was silent, and when I unloaded my passengers outside the Lapp residence, I turned around to pick up Martha and the girls.

"There is something I must show you in your room," Martha announced when I returned. Without pause, she marched me back to my bedroom and closed the door. "Take off your sweatshirt and kapp," she said.

I stopped myself from frowning, shrugged out of the warm garment, and dutifully began the kapp removal process.

From her pocket she retrieved a handful of hairpins. With quick movements, she pinned my short strands of hair up and fastened the kapp on top.

"Keep your eyes down. Stay in the back. Move your mouth during the songs. Don't let anyone notice you."

Before I could say a word of protest or thanks, Martha whirled out of the room and gathered the girls like chicks. "We're late," she said. "Thank Jayne for driving us."

Sara, Leah, and Elizabeth chorused their gratitude.

Martha instructed me to park a bit behind the buggies. I didn't know how it looked, an Amish woman behind the wheel, but then who was I to care how things looked?

For the first time in a long time, I realized I did care. I didn't care what people thought of me, but I did care what they thought of the Burkholders.

"Martha," I said just before she climbed out of the car. "I don't want people to talk. You've been very kind to me. I don't want you to have any trouble on my account."

"Keep your eyes down. You look Amish," she replied.

And with that she walked away.

I knew she was trying to give me a gift. A gift I didn't know if I could, or should, receive.

From what I remembered in my research, the men sat on one side of the room and the women on the other. So if Gideon sat on the men's side, and I sat in the back and didn't say a word . . .

If he sat toward the front, this could work. People slipped in and out of church unnoticed all the time, didn't they?

Come to think of it, "people" was me. I recalled slipping in less and slipping out more . . . at least when my dad wasn't looking.

So if I could sneak out of church without my dad knowing, chances were I could do it without Levi's dad noticing, either.

I followed the path to the door Martha had taken earlier. The sound of singing voices filled the air. When I cracked the door open, I could see that even the minister —

pastor? preacher? — was facing away from the congregation. I slid into the back with the stealth of a cold war operative, minus the cyanide pill.

Benches served as the seating of choice. Old men, young women, small boys — every member of the community sat in this room, singing their hearts out. In German.

Even the children sat still and sang. I couldn't remember ever sitting that still in church, although I did remember singing.

The sermon began after the singing, not that I understood a word. It too was in the same dialect.

I remembered having a hard time as a teen staying awake and involved in the service. Here, everyone was bright eyed. I didn't see a single yawn, even though this minister didn't appear to be telling any family stories or funny moral anecdotes. He spoke firmly and directly, and everyone paid attention.

At least I thought he spoke seriously. He was stoic enough that he could be doing stand-up comedy and I wouldn't be able to tell.

I stayed through the service, hands folded, eyes cast down every time the minister looked in my direction. There was a recited prayer and another song, during which I stepped out and cut a trail for my car and the warmth of my sweatshirt.

My sweatshirt was firmly in place when Gideon returned. I searched his face for evidence of suspicion and found none.

Martha nodded at me. "Thank you for waiting, Jayne. We hope we haven't kept you from your work."

Tricky, this one. I denied inconvenience and watched as the men loaded up for the return home.

I sought Gideon out when we returned to the Burkholder farm. "What do you think happened to your buggy?"

"Probably stolen," he said with a shrug. "We will buy another."

"Shouldn't you contact the police?"

"It's Sunday."

"Okay. Tomorrow, then?"

"We can afford to buy another buggy. We don't got a need to seek revenge."

I shook my head. "I'm not talking about revenge, I'm talking about justice. Either way, eighty percent of stolen vehicles are found and returned. I don't know why a buggy would be different."

"Jayne —"

"By filing it with the police, you're at least doing what you can to protect your neighbors from the same thing happening to them."

I watched Gideon hear my words, watched his mind process while varying emotions crossed his face.

"*Ja,*" he said. "I think you are right."

"I have a cell phone. You're welcome to call the police with it."

He shook his head. "It's Sunday. It can wait until tomorrow."

I had a bicycle stolen once, when I was a student. Well, maybe not stolen as much as swapped. I came out of History of Ancient Greek Art to find that my bike was gone and replaced with an older, less gently used one than my own.

Same lock. Different bike.

I even looped around the bike racks a few times to make sure I wasn't crazy.

I all but sprained my thumb, dialing the police. Or rather, 411 to get to the police. But either way, I wasn't letting moss grow under the worn tires of the bike in front of me.

I couldn't imagine not immediately reporting the theft of my primary mode of transportation. In an odd way, I kind of respected it.

The thief (or thieves) who removed the buggy from the yard may have complicated the Burkholders' morning, but Gideon refused to give him (or her) the power to disrupt their day.

Admirable. And oddly empowering.

Since my original bike was covered by my parents' insurance, I was able to replace it with ease.

I kept the swapped-out bike for two more years (with the police's permission) before selling it to help fund a proper motorcycle jacket with Kevlar.

Maybe I hadn't needed to dial so fast.

The police, as I had suspected, treated the buggy theft pretty seriously. Although in monetary value the buggy was far less expensive than, say, a car, the theft carried the air of a religious hate crime. Officers came out and questioned Gideon and Martha, as well as the neighbors down the road.

Conversations were conducted outside, despite the light drizzle. I joined Sara, Leah, Elizabeth, and Samuel at the window, peeking from behind the curtain. When the cops finally drove away, Gideon and Martha returned to the house and behaved as though a valuable personal possession hadn't been snatched in the dark of night. They didn't seem at all bothered or stressed.

They may as well have had a PTA meeting.

Although the Amish probably didn't have PTA meetings.

Elam rode with his Mennonite buddy into town for work and didn't require my taxi services. Life returned to a fairly normal schedule, until Sara informed me that she was babysitting that afternoon and wanted me to come too.

"You've got to be kidding."

Sara shook her head. "Why do you think I'm kidding?"

"Well, I, um . . . I mean . . . me? Babysit? I don't trust myself around Leah and Elizabeth as it is."

Granted, I had no idea what to do with children. Whenever I saw Beth's daughter, I froze up. I mean, I was messed up enough. It wasn't as though I needed to share that with my little niece. Emilee was only five years old, and I wasn't the sort of person a five-year-old ought to be with.

When I was fifteen, the woman in charge of the church nursery called my mother and asked if I would volunteer. I showed up under protest with no idea what to do and no desire to find out. The other ladies, as far as I could tell, took one look at me, with my purple hair, Smashing Pumpkins T-shirt, and perpetual scowl . . .

Let's just say I was never invited back.

And that was fine with me. Baby poop was never my thing, anyway.

Not that I would show up for childcare duty looking like a roadie these days. I had grown up in the last ten years. But children remained a mystery to me, and I'd always assumed it was for their own good.

Now Sara wanted me to babysit. And she wasn't taking no for an answer. "They're good children," she said. "Because of the baby, I could use an extra set of hands."

"Baby?" My panic grew. "I don't do babies."

"What's wrong with babies?"

"They're little. They're breakable. They don't use toilets."

Sara just rolled her eyes.

We showed up at Naomi Zook's home shortly after lunch. She pulled Sara into a hug and introduced herself and the children to me.

Mary Ellen was the oldest at four years old, followed minutes later by her twin, Becky. The little boy, Doyle, had celebrated his third birthday a few weeks before. I shuddered at the thought of giving birth — again — a year after having twins. Not that I could imagine giving birth at all.

Baby Ruby was, naturally, the baby of the house, a scant three months old. Naomi placed Baby Ruby into Sara's arms the same way she might have transferred a much-loved bag of flour. Transfer completed, Naomi waved goodbye and left for errands in town.

"Okay," I said when she was gone. "What do we do now?"

"You should play with the kids."

"How?"

She shrugged. "They're kids. They don't care much."

"That's not going to work. You're going to have to give me something else."

"What did you like to do when you were four?"

I stuck my hands on my hips. "Listen to rock and roll."

Okay, maybe not rock and roll. But I bet Raffi sounds a lot like rock and roll to the Amish.

"You don't remember doing anything else?"

"I try not to think too hard about my childhood."

"Why not?"

"Just because. Now that I'm remembering, though, I seem to recall a few games of follow the leader." I turned to Mary Ellen,

Becky, and Doyle. "Follow the leader?" I said, my voice loud and clear. "Does that sound like fun?"

"They're young, Jayne, not deaf. But they might be if you keep yelling."

"Sorry." I lowered my voice and gestured with my good arm. "Follow me!"

We trailed around the farmhouse while acting like airplanes, elephants, football mascots, and newspaper editors, the latter two involving a lot of jumping and waving of arms. When that burst of energy, well, burst, I collapsed into a handy rocking chair.

As I rested, Mary Ellen whispered into Becky's ear, cast a furtive glance at me, and ran behind a corner. Becky followed. They stayed back there, giggling, peeking, and whispering.

"What are they doing?" I asked Doyle.

He looked away, shy.

"What are you doing, Mary Ellen?"

"We're sneaking!"

Amish children snuck? I had no idea. I turned to Doyle. "Do you like to sneak?"

He nodded without making eye contact.

The whispering continued. "Would you like to sneak with me?"

A pause . . . and a nod.

So we snuck. And after a successful campaign, Doyle, Becky, Mary Ellen, and I decided to turn our attention on Sara, who looked as though she had the easier time of it. She held the baby, and the baby was fine with the state of the union. But then, Sara had been around babies all her life. She probably knew exactly what to do.

We started behind the chair, then sprinted across the room to the stairwell, followed by a covert jaunt to the kitchen doorway and a shorter distance to where Sara stood, bouncing the baby and looking out the window.

"Oh good, there you are," she said, not at all startled by the children tugging at her skirts. "Can you hold Baby Ruby? I need to start dinner."

"Me?"

"Yes." She held Baby Ruby out.

I stepped back as if Baby Ruby were a smallpox blanket. Maybe "jumped" would be more accurate.

"I don't know what to do with babies. I've never been around babies."

"I thought you said your sister has a little girl."

"Yes, but —"

"And you saw her when she was tiny?"

"I did, but —"

"Baby Ruby is a baby too. And she's a real easy baby."

"You mean she doesn't poop? Or cry?

Because that's my definition of an easy baby."

The children behind me giggled at my use of the word "poop." I guess such things are humorous to children across all walks of life.

Sara rolled her eyes. Teen eye rolls, I guess, are also the same. "Of course she has . . . movements . . . and sometimes she cries, but she's a real good baby and I need to start dinner."

"But —"

"She doesn't bite. She doesn't even have teeth yet."

Baby Ruby gave a smiley, toothless giggle, proving Sara's point.

"I don't think —"

Sara didn't give me a chance to think. She placed Baby Ruby in my arms in such a way that if I didn't take the baby, she would have fallen to the floor.

To my credit, I knew enough about babies to know that the whole floor thing would be bad.

Baby Ruby looked at me and blinked. Then burped.

"You need to hold her so her head is supported." Sara moved my arm until Baby Ruby rested just under my collarbone, with my hand propping up her lolling head.

"Is she okay?"

"She's fine."

"Are you sure?"

"Very. Can you take the children to the living room?"

"I have the baby!"

"They can entertain themselves."

And they did. They played happily, resuming their game of sneak while I held Baby Ruby.

Then the unthinkable happened. Baby Ruby urped and released a tiny cry. "Sara!"

Sara poked her head out of the kitchen. "What do you need?"

"She's not happy!"

"Bounce her up and down. Take her to look out the window."

"Can she see that far? I mean, is her vision that good?"

"If it makes her happy, does it matter?"

She had a point. I followed her instructions, and to my surprise it worked. Baby Ruby quieted instantly, her head nestling against me.

This wasn't so bad. In fact, it was rather nice.

Baby Ruby yawned. I agreed.

CHAPTER 12

Baby Ruby grew heavy, so I sat in the rocking chair. Mary Ellen and Becky herded Doyle into a game of house. Doyle found himself instructed to check on the cows. Often.

These were happy kids. Were all kids this happy? All Amish kids? I suddenly found myself beginning to rethink my previous opinions on the short end of the human race. Maybe they weren't so bad or difficult.

Corruptible, probably, but I'd been watching over this brood for thirty minutes and none of them had tried to wield knives or leap from windows. Perhaps I wasn't the terrible influence I thought I was.

Perhaps.

I might have sat in that rocking chair forever if Sara hadn't finished starting dinner.

"She hasn't bitten you yet, has she?"

"Not yet."

Sara leaned over my shoulder to look at the baby. "She's asleep."

"Really?" I craned my neck to see. Baby Ruby's soft eyelashes rested against her cheeks, just as Sara said.

No wonder she'd become so heavy. Had to say, Baby Ruby was awfully trusting. She didn't know me from Eve. How did she know I wasn't going to kidnap her once she lost consciousness?

I touched her head gingerly. "I can't believe she fell asleep."

Sara shrugged. "She'll wake up hungry at some point. Did she try to root?"

"Root?"

"Try to nurse?"

"You mean, on my —"

"I don't think she's nursed anywhere else."

I could feel my cheeks turning pink. "But I, um, I don't . . . have any . . . you know."

"Babies don't know that. Don't worry. Naomi should be back from town soon."

A part of me felt disappointed inside. As disturbed as I was about the whole nursing thing, I was liking the sleeping baby, contented children experience.

Was it like this for Beth? Had my niece been anything like Baby Ruby?

How much had I missed?

■ ■ ■ ■

I asked Gideon over dinner if he'd heard anything from the police.

"No," he said with a shake of his head. "There has been no call."

I didn't point out that the phone, such as it was, was in an exterior shed ten feet from the house and didn't have an answering machine.

But then, the police probably guessed that the Burkholder residence wasn't much of a telecommunications hub. I'd wished at the time that Gideon would have given them Levi's number, but that would have meant acknowledging Levi as a son, and Gideon didn't seem too keen on that.

Sara and I finished the dishes while Leah and Samuel finished their nightly school assignments. Elam and Amos still seldom spoke to me, although it seemed they avoided me less since the car ride to church.

Meaning that they didn't necessarily leave the room when I walked in.

I wrote in my journal on my computer that night, wanting to get the details of my time with the kids and the soccer team of conflicting emotions that kicked my thoughts in circles around my head.

Seriously. I was conflicted to the point that my internal metaphors were getting weird. I rolled my head around to the side, willing my tense neck muscles to relax. I remembered my Tylenol PM. And my melatonin. Seemed like a good idea — I could use a good night's sleep.

The household noises subsided as everyone went to bed. I continued typing until the warning bubble on my desktop advised me to save all my documents lest anything be lost when my computer died. That was fine with me; I could barely see straight.

I tucked my laptop into its case, resolving to drive to Levi's shop sometime the next day to recharge the computer batteries.

I yawned, burrowed under the layers of quilts, closed my eyes, and let the over-the-counter sleeping pills carry me away.

Noises outside reached my ears just before I fell asleep.

I burrowed deeper. Probably another one of Sara's many admirers. I'd been through this before, and tonight didn't strike me as being a good night to fly around in my nightdress.

The amount of clatter increased. For Pete's sake, this particular boy wasn't very good at the whole courting-in-secret thing. I heard a horse whinny, and then I heard another sound.

A word. Followed by several more, and not the kind I heard out here. The Amish weren't much for colorful language.

My eyes opened. Who would talk like that? I could hear the rumble of a motor. I knew some of the boys drove cars before they were baptized into the church, but it's not as though you'd drive to a girl's house, impress her with your command of expletives, and bring a horse along for kicks.

I edged out of bed and peeked out the window. Boys with backward-facing baseball caps and saggy pants were leading Shoe out of the barn and away from the house.

I racked my brain for any reason how this could be construed as something harmless. Came up empty. It's not as though horses need midnight walks when they can't sleep, and even if that were the case, I don't think saggy pants are high on the list of horse-wrangling wear.

Before I could talk myself into a different course of action, I shoved my feet into my shoes and pulled on my armored motorcycle jacket.

I don't know why it hadn't occurred to me last time to wear my jacket. Maybe I was getting better at the whole Amish-defense thing.

I burst out onto the porch and assessed the scene. Three boys in hooded sweatshirts skulked in the driveway. One of them held Shoe's reins.

"What do you think you're doing?" I yelled, deliberately making as much noise as possible.

Shouts of "Dude!" and "Get out, man!" broke out. They began to scatter, but the boy holding Shoe's reins made a mistake. In his panic, he tugged Shoe closer to him while extending his foot. Shoe's hoof landed solidly on the kid's thin Converse sneaker.

The boy cried out and yanked his foot back, the force of which sent him sprawling on his backside. He tried to get up but yelped when he put weight on that foot.

The other hoodlums didn't wait for him — they jumped into a beat-up Datsun and sped away, scattering gravel in their wake. The kid on the ground shouted obscenities at them, ending in a whimper.

"What is going on?" Gideon stepped out onto the porch. Behind him I could see Martha, a quilt wrapped around her shoulders.

"Three boys were trying to take Shoe," I said. "This one got stepped on."

The kid's eyes widened at the sight of Gideon, whose sleep-mussed beard gave him a fearsome expression. In desperation, the boy backed away in a sort of crab-walk.

"If you are hurt, you should let us help," Gideon said. "It's fifteen miles to town."

"Do you want me to call the police?" I asked.

"Not yet." Gideon stepped off the porch and approached the boy. "What is your name?"

The kid looked sideways and back. "Drew."

I didn't believe him, and I could tell Gideon didn't, either. "Oh. What is your real name, Drew?"

This time "Drew" didn't break eye contact. "Mike."

"How is your foot, Mike?"

"It hurts."

"Can you take off your shoe?"

Mike looked from me to Gideon to Martha.

"If your foot is broken," I said, "it may swell to the point that you can't get your shoe off and they'll have to cut it off. Your shoe, not your foot."

"Oh." He fumbled with the laces, which were halfway untied as it was. When he removed his sock, the dark purple of the spreading bruise could already be seen.

"Shoe has big feet," Gideon said.

164

"Shoe?" Mike shot a confused glance at the sneaker in his hand.

"The horse," I answered. "The horse's name is Shoe."

"He has big feet," Gideon continued. "He's a draft horse, used for pulling, not for riding. Did you have something you needed pulled?"

"Huh?"

"Were you taking our horse because you needed to use him for something? A plow or a cart?"

Mike didn't answer.

"If you needed to borrow him, you only needed to ask. Though, daytime's the best time for asking. I can understand if you didn't want to wake us. If there's something real important that needs pulling, I can wake one of my sons to help you. Is there?"

Mike shook his head.

"Someone borrowed our buggy a day or two ago. Do you know where'n it might be?"

The boy looked away.

"Your foot does look like it's swelling. Do you want us to call someone for you? Take you to the clinic in town?"

"We took your buggy," Mike blurted.

"Oh?"

"We hooked it up to Nate's truck hitch."

Creative.

"Why did you take it?" Gideon sat on the ground.

Mike looked down, shame covering his features.

In that moment I was able to see him the way Gideon clearly did — not as a punk kid with an agenda of hate crime, but as a lost kid. A kid not beyond reach.

"It was just a joke," Mike said in a small voice.

"Hmm." Gideon thought on that. "Maybe it will be a funny one when we get it back. Do you know where it is?"

"Haight Street," Mike mumbled.

Gideon nodded. "That is a good joke. Would you like us to call someone for you?"

The boy fidgeted. He had to be awfully cold down there, considering the whole saggy-pant thing. "My sister."

I retrieved my cell phone from the house and gave it to Mike to make the call. While we waited for her, Martha and Gideon helped Mike into the house and set him up by the stove. Martha clucked over his foot and wrapped it up with ice and a salve that smelled like the inside of the ton-ton from the Star Wars movie *The Empire Strikes Back*.

Mike's sister showed up about a half hour later, looking as though she wanted to kill her brother with a pair of dull hedge trimmers. "You were out with Nate and Sean again, weren't you."

Mike looked down. "They left."

"Of course they did. How bad is it?" She gestured toward his purple, swollen foot.

"Probably broken," Martha offered.

The sister reached for her purse. "Did he break, damage, or steal anything? Do you people take checks?"

Gideon held up a hand. "No need. He ain't hurt nothing but himself. Take him to a doctor — it'll be all right."

She tried to argue, but Gideon wouldn't budge. They helped Mike to the waiting car.

I think Martha gave them a loaf of zucchini bread on the way out.

When the headlights disappeared down the road, the three of us went back to our respective rooms.

Sara, Elam, and Amos stood in the hallway, concern covering their faces. Gideon spoke a few words in Dutch; everyone returned to bed.

I lay in bed, trying to sleep, not able to get the evening's events out of my head.

How could Gideon be so gentle, so gracious, so *forgiving* of Mike the hoodlum and yet refuse to have a relationship with his law-abiding, talented son? Levi's only crime was to leave the community and join a church with instruments. Mike had taken the family's main form of transportation and was caught removing one of their horses, and still he had received patience and kindness.

Why was Levi held to such a different standard? Wasn't he, as Gideon's son, worthy of a certain amount of grace?

I drove into town the next morning, citing the deadness of my laptop and cell batteries. Truth be told, it felt good to put on normal clothes and head toward civilization. I picked up Starbucks on the way in, filling a tray with an assortment of drinks and carbohydrates.

"Jayne!" Spencer's eyes lit up when I entered the office. "Nice of you to drop by."

"Hi, Spencer. I brought coffee for everybody. Did I bring enough?"

"More than. I think Levi's here somewhere — want me to get him?"

"Yes, please. I need to plug in my computer and phone — all my batteries are dead. This," I gave the tray a tap, "is my thank-you present."

"We feel thanked. Hold on."

He disappeared behind the shop door. Levi stepped through a moment later, followed by Grady.

"Hi, Jayne. How are things?"

"They're fine," I said, wondering what Spencer had told him. Knowing Spencer, it could be anything. "I really need to charge my laptop batteries. Do you mind if I plug in and hang around a while?"

Was it me or did the three of them brighten? "I brought coffee for everyone," I added.

"You're our new favorite person," Levi said. "Everyone's been dragging today. Do you want to come back to my office?"

"Sure," I said, not particularly wanting to be Spencer's verbal sparring partner while I worked. "If I'm not in your way."

Spencer didn't say a word as I headed down the hall with Levi. A quick glance revealed his face stuffed with scone.

Which was, in fact, the root of my intentions with the Starbucks trip.

"How are things with my family?" Levi asked, sorting through some papers and desk bric-a-brac to make space for me.

I sighed and relayed the events from the previous night.

"Have they said how they are planning to bring the buggy back?" he asked when I finished.

"No."

169

"I have a hitch on my truck. If it worked for the boys, I don't see any reason why it wouldn't work for me."

"Wouldn't you have to drive awfully slow?"

"I learned to drive a buggy before I learned to drive a car. I'm not a complete stranger to driving slow."

I narrowed my eyes. "How many speeding tickets did you get after you left?"

"Don't ask."

"What made you leave the community?"

"I wanted to go to school."

"That was all?"

He shrugged. "It was time."

"You know Sara wants to leave."

"Did she tell you?"

"She showed me her sketches."

"Do you mind taking back some contraband? I've got a stack for her."

"What are you going to do if she decides to leave?"

"Help."

"You don't think she should stay?"

"I think it's up to her. If she makes the decision to leave, I'll support her."

"And if she decides not to go back?"

"That's up to her too."

"Will your dad cut her off as well?"

"I don't know. Probably. I don't know how

many children he'd have to lose before he changed." Levi shrugged. "It's who he is, who he was raised to be."

"You were raised the same way."

"Mostly. Everyone's different. Is this enough space for you?" He pointed at the tidy desktop.

"I'm game."

"I'll let you work, then. Want to try to get the buggy with me afterward?"

"Sure."

He grinned. It was such an engaging grin, I didn't mind the prospect of driving at fifteen miles per hour, towing a buggy behind us.

CHAPTER 13

I checked my email in the quiet of Levi's office. There were the usual memos about sundry office happenings but nothing life altering. Then I poked around online, catching up on current events.

Bombings, earthquakes, corporate shenanigans . . . life seemed so much easier on the Burkholder farm.

Granted, the previous evening's events with Mike weren't exactly a picnic. But in relation to world destruction, the attempted horse theft didn't amount to much.

I pulled up my word processor, discovering that if I was careful I could still type with my left hand. I wrote about life at the Burkholders', learning to bake and sew, and my experience with Naomi's children.

Then there was my confusion over how to deal with Sara.

The part of me that grew up in the English world wanted to support her to be all that she could be, to believe in herself, dream big, stretch her horizons, reach for the stars — all of those cheesy sayings found on motivational posters.

But another part of me recoiled at the thought. I wanted to remind her she was Amish and, because of that, above the English desire to live life in the fast lane. Sara had a family who loved her, who would surround her with strength and love and food for the rest of her life.

Maybe that was it — the idea that being Amish set Sara and her family at a different standard. They were the last bastions of a nonconsumer existence so foreign to those of us who complained of being sucked into the rat race.

I don't think I was alone in that belief. The Amish clearly held themselves to a very high standard of behavioral expectations. Leaving their way of life was not included.

Gideon could forgive Mike because he expected Mike to behave badly, being English. It was his nature. But Levi . . . Levi was raised to join the church and follow in the footsteps of his father and grandfather.

A knock interrupted my thoughts. "Do you have a moment?" Levi's head appeared in the doorway.

My hands froze on the keyboard.

It really is awkward when the person you're writing about walks in. "What's up?"

"I need an opinion in the shop."

I closed the lid to my laptop. "Yeah?"

"There's a sideboard I'm working on and . . . well, you'll see. Put these on." He handed me a pair of safety glasses.

"I don't know why you'd want my opinion," I said as I followed him. "Design isn't really my thing."

"Do you own a Star Trek uniform?"

"No . . ."

"Then you're more qualified than one of the people I would have asked."

"Grady?"

"Spencer."

I squeezed my eyes shut as the visual flooded my imagination. "Wow."

"He goes to the conventions and everything."

"May he live long and prosper."

The shop was just as loud as I remembered. Bits of dismembered — or preassembled, I supposed — furniture littered the expanse of the space. A heavy layer of sawdust coated the floor.

"It's over here," Levi said, pointing toward the corner.

The sideboard stood six feet tall, and though it was clearly unfinished, the wood gleamed. "It's beautiful."

"It's a commission piece," Levi said, running his hand over the side. "The client was specific about some parts, but not the side shelves."

I examined the side shelves. The ones in the center were long, with short rows of shelves on either side. "Okay."

"I want to put a glass cabinet-cover over the side shelves."

"Can you do that?"

He arched an eyebrow. "Yes . . ."

"I mean, is that Amish? Do the Amish do glass?" I tried to think of instances of glass in the Burkholder furniture.

"Sometimes they do. Our customers aren't exactly Amish purists, though."

"No?"

"People read 'Amish' as code for 'quality wood furniture of simple construction.' "

"I think people read 'Amish' as a lot of things."

"You're probably right."

"So what did you need my advice for?"

"You agree that the glass would look nice?"

My hand stroked the smooth wood. "Yeah. I think it would look great."

"I've got a few kinds of glass over here . . ."

"Aside from the breakable kind?"

He rolled his eyes. "Different patterns. Some with a bit of tint to them."

I tilted my head. "I don't think you'd want color. The wood is so pretty, you wouldn't want to take away from that."

"It is good wood."

"What kind is it?"

"Walnut with a hand-oiled finish."

"It's beautiful."

"Thank you. Want to see the glass?"

He showed me panes of glass, and we talked about the merits and detractions of each one. In the end we picked water glass for the rim of the cabinet, with plain glass on the inside. Levi explained how he would use silver solder and place the glass insets into the finished piece. "Want to help?"

I jumped back a foot. "No, no, that's fine."

He laughed. "Why not?"

One of the other guys in the shop started a saw and I jumped again. "You know . . . saws . . . blades . . . death . . . not really my thing. Besides, I have a sprained wrist."

"It's your left wrist, and the swelling's going down. You still have your right wrist. I'll help."

"I don't think so . . . ."

"You ride a motorcycle but won't try carpentry?"

My back stiffened. I knew what he was

doing, and I wouldn't let him win. "I know how to ride a motorcycle. I don't know how to use power tools."

"I do. I'll help."

"I'm wearing safety gear when I ride."

"I wear safety gear when I work. You're wearing safety gear right now," he said, pointing at my goggles.

"Building isn't my thing."

"But you're a reporter. Reporters try new things. Weren't you baking something last week?"

"Baking is different."

"How?"

"It's hard to lose a finger while baking."

"I won't let you lose a finger."

"What if I suddenly spaz out toward the moving blade? How would you stop that?"

"Why would you?"

"Seizure."

"Do you have a history of seizures?"

I straightened. "Not yet. I might."

"You might develop a history of seizures?"

"You never know."

He shrugged. "It's okay if you don't want to. I just thought you might want to try something new, you know, being a reporter."

He was good. He was very good.

"You wouldn't let me lose a finger?"

"Nope."

I tucked a piece of hair behind my ear. "If anything happens, I'm blaming you."

"I would be surprised if it were otherwise." He smiled. "I have sisters. Are you ready?"

"Sure." I exhaled.

As patient as if I were ten, Levi helped me pick an appropriate piece of wood to cut into frame pieces. After I chose a piece, he helped me line it up under the table saw.

My face was in a permanent flinch as I made the cuts, but all of my digits remained in their original locations. They even remained after I cut the angles and finished the matching pieces for the opposite door.

I had to admit that the pieces didn't look half bad.

After a while, Levi checked his watch. "Want to go get the buggy soon?"

"Let me swap out the batteries I'm recharging, then yes."

I walked past Spencer's desk on the way back to the office. "How's it going, Number One?" I called over my shoulder.

Spencer scowled. "Who told?"

I gave what I hoped looked like a mysterious shrug and kept walking. Just as I'd expected, the first battery was completely charged. I switched batteries and closed the lid again.

"Did you bring a jacket?" Levi asked from

the doorway.

"I'm an Oregonian," I said. "I'm impervious to rain."

"It might take some work getting the buggy hitched to my truck. You're welcome to borrow one of mine."

"You have more than one jacket at your workplace?"

"I don't like to be wet."

"And yet you live in the Pacific Northwest?"

"Do you want the jacket or not?"

I squared my shoulders. "I'll take a jacket."

"Smart." He tossed me a crispy-feeling parka.

"I wouldn't be smart without Gor-tex?"

"Just put it on."

"I'm not outside yet."

"You're exhausting."

"You invited me."

Two tarps covered the Burkholder buggy parked on Haight Street.

"Teen boys, you said?" Levi asked as he tugged the tarps to the ground.

"Yup."

"At least they didn't damage it much." He ran his hand over the front, examining where the boys had towed it before. "There are a few scuffs, but nothing that can't be fixed or repainted."

"That's good."

"Let's get going, then."

Ten minutes later, Levi had his family's buggy attached securely to his pickup. I climbed in the cab, just short of drenched. The rain was really coming down, and I was truly glad I'd taken Levi up on his offer of water-repellent gear.

"Now the long road home," Levi said when he joined me in the cab. "I'm going to put my safety lights on. Thanks for coming with me."

"Thanks for dragging the buggy back to the farm."

"I help my family out when I can."

"Why?"

"Why what?"

"They're so awful to you sometimes. Why are you so good to them?"

"It's the right thing to do."

"That seems so simplistic."

He shrugged. "Things might not always be the way they are. I don't want to have regrets."

"Everyone has regrets."

"I don't."

"Must be nice to be perfect."

"I'm not. I've learned from the times when I've messed up. Maybe someday my

180

family will come around. Families are complicated."

"Believe me, I know." I shifted in my seat. "I don't want to talk about this any more."

"That's fine." He drummed on the steering wheel. "How did you get into journalism?"

"I applied to the University of Oregon School of Journalism."

"No, I mean what got you interested?"

"I grew up in a very small, very touristy town."

"Lincoln City?"

"Right. I wanted to learn about other places, other people. I needed to be reassured that the world was bigger than my hometown."

"You lived on the coast. All you needed to do was look out on the ocean."

"But that was just one edge. I wanted to know about the other side. I read the *New York Times,* the *Washington Post,* the *San Francisco Chronicle,* the *Wall Street Journal* — everything I could get my hands on. I decided I wanted to work for a big newspaper."

"You stayed in Oregon?"

"I like the Pacific Northwest, but people in Washington don't know how to drive. That left Oregon, and Portland if I wanted a big city."

"Very logical."

"I got an internship at the *Oregonian* —"

"And the rest was history?"

"Pretty much."

"I get that. Let's see how this goes . . . ." He released the parking brake and eased on the gas. The buggy creaked and then lurched forward with the truck.

I checked over my shoulder. "Looks good."

"All right, then. Buckle up. This will be a bumpy ride."

"Really?"

"No. We won't top twenty-five miles an hour."

I laughed. "We should probably call and let the police know we've recovered the buggy."

"Better to have my dad call. That way you have owner verification."

"I've ridden in that buggy."

"You're not the owner."

"What happens if we get pulled over?"

"We make a run for it."

"What?"

"Kidding. We explain and hope for the best."

"You're funny."

■ ■ ■ ■

Despite the downpour Martha, Sara, Samuel, Leah, and Elizabeth met us outside as we pulled up with the buggy in tow.

Levi slowed the truck. "Do you mind jumping out and herding the kids back?"

"No problem." I unbuckled my seat belt and swung my door open, despite the fact that the truck wasn't exactly stopped. "Step back, guys," I said, "you don't want to get run over."

"You found it!" Elizabeth exclaimed, hanging on my leg. "You found the buggy!"

I started to pick her up and stopped myself. Stupid arm. I hugged her close, bending awkwardly. "We did and brought it back home for you."

Levi parked the truck and got out. "It's been scratched a bit, but otherwise it's in perfect shape."

"Where was it?" Martha asked, her voice carefully measured.

"Exactly where Mike said it would be," I answered.

Martha took Levi's hand. "Thank you."

He beamed. I wished his father had been there to thank him also.

CHAPTER 14

Levi and I drove back to the shop in relative silence. He turned to me after he pulled into his parking space. "Okay, Jayne. What's eating you?"

I sighed. "It just kills me."

"What does?"

"The way your family treats you. It's entirely unfair."

"Life isn't fair."

"I know, but . . ." I frowned. "I just wish things weren't the way they are."

"And I pray every day that they won't be."

"It's not right! Families shouldn't behave that way. They shouldn't decide who you should be and then turn around and punish you when it becomes clear that you cannot, will not be that person."

"Jayne?"

"What?"

"Are we talking about your family or mine?"

"I —" My mouth snapped shut. I paused. I couldn't think of when I'd said much on that subject to Levi. "What do you know about my family?"

"Not much. You hardly talk about them, and when you do, it's rarely pleasant."

I fixed him with a stare.

He ducked his head. "Grady may have said something."

"Grady?" My eyes widened in surprise. "What did he say?"

"You guys went to school and church together and knew a lot of the same people. He mentioned something along the lines of you being treated like the black sheep of the family."

I sat back in my seat, my head resting on the glass of the rear window of the cab. Grady knew. Surprising, considering the importance of image to my family. I tucked a bit of hair behind my ear. "I wasn't completely bad. That's what they'd have everyone think."

"Grady didn't say you were."

"I was a good student. I organized all of my scholarship and financial aid for college. I never went to my parents for a cent."

"I'm not accusing you, Jayne."

"Just because I listened to rock music and dyed my hair black my junior year, I was

185

the bad daughter."

"You don't have to explain anything to me."

I ran a hand over my face. "I don't like talking about this."

"Have you ever tried to make things better with them? Your family, I mean."

"I hardly see them. Not since I left home for school."

"People change."

"Do they? Have your parents changed?"

"I've changed. I'm people."

"You're different. My mother has worn the same perfume for the past twenty years — Calvin Klein's Obsession. It doesn't matter what I've accomplished in my life — that I put myself though school, graduated, found gainful employment in a field that's not easy to break into — it doesn't matter. I'm not married. I don't have babies. I don't matter."

Then, to my embarrassment, I felt tears prick my eyes. I tried taking deep breaths, tried to calm myself, but it wasn't any use. It hurt too much.

Levi put an arm around my shoulders and I leaned into him, sobbing. I think he stroked my hair, but it was hard to tell. All I could think about were the times I'd been hurt by my family.

After a few moments the tears slowed and my breathing regulated. I swiped at the dampness on my face and tried to reclaim my dignity. "I'm sorry."

"Don't be."

"But I really am. I don't know why I got so . . ."

"It happens."

"But I —"

"Do you want some ice cream?"

I scooted back, aware that his arm was still resting around my shoulders. "Ice cream?"

"You've heard of it?"

"I'm not one of those hysterical women who have to be slapped and then placated with bonbons."

I'll admit that when I spoke, it came out a little high pitched and, well, hysterical sounding.

"I didn't say you were. I just thought that you had a very busy afternoon and might appreciate a scoop of chocolate brownie ice cream."

"I'm also not one of those women who has fits until she gets her chocolate fix."

"Didn't say you were."

"I'm not really a chocolate brownie ice cream kind of girl."

"No?"

"No. I think I'm more of a fudge mint."

We walked from the shop to the ice cream parlor under the gigantic umbrella Levi kept in his truck.

Some people might question the consumption of ice cream in fifty-degree weather, and that's their prerogative. I'm just not one of them.

We ate our ice cream at a corner table, me with fudge mint, Levi with cookies and cream.

"When do you return to work?" he asked.

"A week and a half." I took another lick around the edge of my cone. "A week and a half, and it's back to business as usual."

"Are you looking forward to it?"

"I don't know . . . parts of it. I miss riding my bike around town and being stopped by all the old men who used to ride Triumphs."

"What?"

"Triumph is one of the oldest motorcycle companies."

"I knew that."

"Well, there are a lot of old men with fond memories of Triumph bikes from their past. They like to tell stories."

"It doesn't hurt that you're cute."

My cheeks turned pink. "It happens to the owner of the motorcycle shop I buy my gear from, and he's in his sixties. Anyway, I miss that."

"But you can't ride right now anyway."

"Rub it in, why don't you?"

"What else do you miss?"

"Oh, I don't know. Good coffee. Noah's Bagel. Central heating . . ."

"It can get pretty chilly at my parents' house."

"No kidding. But, I have to say, there are a lot of things I'll miss when I leave the farm."

"Like what?"

"The sense of family. Getting to do new things."

"Such as working with wood?"

"Such as baking. Spending time with children. Doing things by hand and feeling that I've accomplished something concrete, you know?"

"I do. They're good kids, aren't they."

"Your siblings? The younger ones, anyway. Amos and Elam still think I'm weird. But Samuel and the girls are terrific. I used to think I never wanted kids of my own. Now . . ." I shrugged. "I think I could live with it."

"That's a vote of confidence you don't hear every day." Levi rolled his eyes before attacking another bite of ice cream.

"Listen. I never thought I'd want kids. But now, I don't know. I guess I'm open to it."

"Raising kids isn't easy."

"You think I don't know that? My parents reminded me on a daily basis. Probably why I wasn't wild about the idea in the first place."

"You have a sister, right?"

"Beth. She's older."

"What's she like?"

"Imagine the good kid."

"Okay."

"That's Beth."

"Ah. You're not close?"

"We can't relate. She listens to Sandi Patty, I listen to Sam Phillips. I went to school, and she got her MRS degree."

He laughed at my joke.

"Seriously," I said. "It's not like I've really tried with Beth. I need to be better about that. She's the only sister I've got." I caught a melted drip with my tongue and pondered that thought.

When I finished my cone and Levi finished his dish, we walked back to the shop.

"Thanks," I said, swinging my purse, feeling happy and full of ice cream. "That was fun."

"Thank you for joining me."

By the time we'd returned, Spencer and

Grady were nowhere to be seen. Levi followed me back to his office where my laptop sat, as satiated of power as I was of sugar.

"I'll be praying for you and your family," he said as I wound up the laptop cord.

"I appreciate it," I said honestly.

He held my computer bag open as I slid the computer inside. "I know how much rejection can hurt," he said softly.

I felt myself grow teary again, but tilted my head downward so Levi wouldn't notice. "Yeah."

"Know that you're talented, funny, and a hard worker. You've earned my parents' trust, and that's not easy. Don't base your self-worth on what your family has told you over the years."

Levi's speech didn't help the impending waterworks, and this time I couldn't hide it. He frowned. "I'm sorry. Did I say something wrong?"

I shook my head. "No. You said everything right, and it was one of the nicest things someone's ever said to me. I'm sorry . . ."

And the tears fell, despite the fact I'd apologized in advance.

I slung my laptop bag over my shoulder. "I should go."

"Jayne —"

Levi reached for my arm. The feel of his hand stopped me in my tracks. "Everything will be all right," he said, and with the utmost care he caught one of my tears with his finger.

And then, as far as I can tell, I kissed him. On the lips.

It was just a little kiss, more like a brush. At least it started that way. It started as the tiniest nothing, but Levi wrapped his arm around my shoulder and the kiss deepened. I responded; he tasted like cookies and cream and smelled like cedar. My hands dug into his hair

This is nice, I thought. I had stopped crying, focusing my attention on Levi and that moment until a single thought entered my consciousness.

Shane.

I stepped back, ending the kiss and disentangling myself from Levi's inviting hold.

I couldn't make excuses — I had started it. Couldn't apologize, because a kiss that good shouldn't be apologized for.

Levi looked at me, flushed and slightly stunned.

There was nothing to say. I left as quickly as my feet could move.

Hormones. I chalked it all up to hormones.

If I thought about it, I remembered my monthly happiness should arrive next week, which would at least partially explain my erratic emotions and inexplicable behavior.

I dug through my bag until I found my phone. I plugged in my headset and then pressed buttons until I found Gemma's number.

"How's Amish country?" she asked when she picked up.

"Not there yet. Driving. If I get there and I still have reception, I'll tell you."

"You sound upset."

"I kissed someone."

"Oh." She paused. "Really?"

"Yes."

"Who? I'm guessing it wasn't Shane, or it wouldn't be newsworthy."

I winced. "Levi."

"The guy who drove your bike back?"

"That one."

"Kim said he was cute."

"Gemma!"

"What?"

"You're not supposed to encourage me!" I braked behind a slow truck. Why did trucks drive so slow when I was in crisis?

"If he was ugly, I wouldn't know what to say."

"It doesn't matter if he's ugly or cute, the

problem is that he's not Shane."

"True. Are you guys still together?"

"Yes!"

"Do you want to be together?"

"Of course I do!"

"Then why did you kiss Levi?"

"I was emotional. He bought me ice cream ... ."

"Right. That makes complete sense. I always kiss men after they buy me ice cream."

"Gemma!"

"Our eyes lock over the mocha ripple, and I just can't help myself."

"Be serious."

"No," Gemma said, her voice turning serious, "you need to be serious with yourself. If you really like Levi, then maybe you should do something about it."

"But Shane —"

"Probably doesn't want to be with someone who's into someone else."

"I'm a horrible person."

"Yes, you are."

"Thanks."

"I'm a horrible person too. That's the story of being a sinner."

"Yeah, I know. I was at that church service too. I got the memo."

"You'll make the right decision. Either

way, you need to talk to Shane."

I sighed. "I know."

After the crazy afternoon I didn't feel like a verbal sparring match with Shane. I drove back to the Burkholder farm, parking the car next to the buggy.

A light drizzle coated my head and shoulders as I crossed the driveway to the small porch. When I opened the front door, I found the family in the living room, gathered around Gideon.

Gideon looked pale. Martha looked worried.

"Is everything all right?" I asked.

"He's having trouble breathing," Sara answered.

All my senses jumped to alertness. "Has this happened before?"

Martha shook her head.

"Gideon?" I asked. "Does your chest feel tight?"

He shook his head. "It feels like Shoe is sitting on it."

"Same difference." I looked at Martha. "We need to get him to a hospital. Now."

CHAPTER 15

They say cell phones are best for emergencies, right? I reached for mine and flipped it open. No service. "Why! Of all times — where is the phone?"

Martha looked at me blankly. "The phone?"

"We need to call an ambulance, Martha. Gideon needs medical assistance."

Gideon shook his head. "I'm certain . . . I'm certain it will pass."

Martha ignored her husband. "Couldn't you just drive him in your car?"

"They have access to equipment I don't keep in my trunk. Where is the phone?"

"In the shed," Amos said, speaking up for the first time. "I'll take you there."

I followed him out the door, around the house, and behind the barn. I felt as though I should pray. Hadn't prayed for a while. Was I still allowed? Would God laugh at me?

For the sake of Gideon's life, I took the

chance and asked for guidance and protection for the Burkholder family.

The shed sat adjacent to the barn, looking more like a place for an outhouse than a place to chat, which is probably why they didn't. I lifted the receiver, relieved to hear a dial tone in my ear.

Amos started walking back to the house. "Don't go!" I said, as I dialed 9-1-1. "I need the address, and they may ask me things I don't know."

He stayed, and it was a good thing. He gave me the street address, as well as Gideon's age. The operator advised giving Gideon a tablet of aspirin to chew. I looked at Amos. "Does your family keep any aspirin?"

He shook his head.

"I have some in my bags —"

Amos' expression turned bewildered. I spoke again into the receiver, asking if it was necessary that I stay on the line.

The operator asked a couple more questions about Gideon's general health before clearing me to end the call. After hanging up, I strode back to the house, trying to remember where in my bags I'd packed the aspirin.

"Why does he need aspirin?" Amos asked. "He doesn't have a headache."

"Aspirin also thins the blood," I said, not

slowing. "I think your dad is having a heart attack, which means his blood is blocked and can't get to his heart properly. Aspirin makes it easier for blood to reach the heart."

I quickly found a plastic bag of miscellaneous vitamins and painkillers in my room and fished out an aspirin. I took it downstairs and gave it to Gideon, telling him the 9-1-1 operator said to chew it.

He must have started feeling worse, because he took the aspirin without an argument.

The EMTs arrived in a blaze of flashing lights; Elizabeth began to whimper. Sara pulled her up into her arms and spoke softly to her in Dutch. We watched as the EMTs loaded Gideon onto a stretcher and fitted an oxygen mask over his face. After the ambulance doors closed, the driver told Martha she could follow them to the hospital.

She turned to me. "Could you drive me?'

Amos stepped forward. "Us. Could you drive us?"

"Of course," I said, pulling my keys from my pocket.

Following the ambulance was easy at first, but after a while — and several red lights I couldn't run through — it disappeared into the darkness.

I realized I had no idea where the hospital was. "Martha?" I asked. "Do you know how to get to the ER?"

She nodded and proceeded to give me directions via landmarks.

I really hate when women do this. Men give street names, direction, mileage, and everything short of GPS coordinates. Women tell you to turn left at the second garden gnome. But Martha's husband was heading toward the hospital, fighting for his life, so I told my irritated self to hush up.

As I had this conversation with myself, Amos interrupted. "Take Queen and turn left on Elm."

I thanked him.

I pulled into the ER parking lot and performed what was not likely to be the best parking job of my life.

Inside, the administrative staff informed us that Gideon was having tests done and we would be informed when we could see him, and that we could take a seat and the coffee dispensers were around the corner to the right.

I stepped back. "That was a lot of hurry up and wait."

Martha frowned. "Hurry up and what?"

"Don't worry about it. Do either of you want coffee?"

Amos nodded, and I offered to go and discover exactly how awful the hospital coffee was.

Martha sagged against her son. "I need to sit down," she said.

"You both sit down," I said. "I'll find the coffee."

I followed the instructions and walked around the corner to the right. But the farther I walked the more I knew I needed to make a phone call.

I needed to call Levi. He deserved to know his father was in the hospital.

I passed the coffee station, not pulling out my phone until I'd walked down the hallway and found a second seating area.

"Levi?" I said when he picked up.

Oh, this was awkward . . .

"Jayne? Are you all right? I'm sorry things got . . . out of hand —"

"Your dad's in the hospital," I interrupted. "He had a heart attack."

"Is . . . is he okay?"

"They're running tests. We don't know anything."

"Where are you?"

"Past the coffee machines."

"At the hospital?"

"Yes. Your mom and Amos are here."

"I'll be over in ten minutes."

My eyes slid shut. I knew he would, but it didn't make my life any easier.

Just as he'd said, Levi rushed in like a windstorm ten minutes later. "Have they told you anything?" he asked, giving his mom a hug.

She melted into him. "Tests. We know nothing but tests."

He gave her a squeeze and strode to the front desk. "I need to know how my father is doing."

"Name of patient?" The receptionist looked peeved. But then, maybe her face was just stuck that way.

"Gideon Burkholder."

"He's having tests."

"I know he's having tests. I want to know if he's stable or if he isn't."

"I'll need you to wait, sir." She stood and disappeared behind a door.

Levi sighed. "I should call Rebecca."

I frowned. "Who's Rebecca?"

"My sister. She and her husband live in Washington." He reached for his cell phone. "She may not even answer. The phone is twenty feet from the house."

"Older? Younger?"

"Younger. She's between me and Amos." He winced. "Come on, Bex, pick up. You could hear when any of us were in trouble. I don't think your hearing's changed." He stood, leaning against the desk, head bent, clearly focused on the steady ring of the other line.

After several moments he straightened so fast you'd think the receptionist had returned and zapped him. "Karl? It's Levi — please don't hang up. My father's in the hospital, and I thought Rebecca would want to know. Thank you. I —" Levi sighed and closed the phone. "I should have had Amos call."

"Karl won't talk to you?"

"No. Rebecca will, but Karl . . . he's just trying to protect his family."

"You did the right thing, letting her know."

"She has my number if she wants to call." He shook his head as if trying to clear it.

The receptionist chose that moment to return. "Your father is in stable but critical condition."

I tilted my head closer. "What does that mean?"

The receptionist's voice softened. "It means he's not out of the woods just yet."

I finally went to get Amos his coffee. Retreated to the coffee is more like it. Now that I had — I shuddered to admit it —

kissed Levi, a part of me worried that if I were in too close of a proximity to him, I might do it again.

And that would be bad.

First, because I was still in a relationship with Shane.

Second, because we were in the hospital waiting to see if his father would live through the night. Not wildly appropriate timing.

Around eleven, a person clad in hospital scrubs came and found us. I managed to tag along, pretending to be family. No one asked. I didn't tell.

A doctor met us in the hallway. "You're Gideon's family?"

Again, I said nothing as Martha, Levi, and Amos nodded.

"He's currently stable," the doctor said, "but he'll need surgery. I put a call into the cardio unit in Corvallis, but they're full. I recommend transport to OHSU. He needs a good cardiothoracic surgeon."

"Wait. What is this 'OHSU'?" Martha's face tightened in confusion.

The doctor took a breath. "It's the Oregon Health and Science University, ma'am."

"It's a school?"

"It's a teaching hospital."

"What kind of surgery?" Levi interrupted.

"Your father has severe coronary artery disease. That means there has been a significant buildup of plaque inside three of his arteries, blocking blood to his heart. I recommend a procedure called a coronary artery bypass graft, in which veins from his leg would be grafted to repair the damaged ones. It's a kind of bypass procedure."

Levi shoved his hands in his pockets. "His chances without it?"

"Difficult to speculate, but likely very poor. Medications can buy him time, but his chances of a second heart attack are greatly increased."

Martha's face showed her anguish. "Is he comfortable?"

The doctor nodded. "He is."

"Can we see him?"

"Yes. He's resting now, but it's fine if he wakes up."

We all filed into the room.

Gideon looked so small in the hospital bed. I'd heard people say that of their loved ones when they were unwell, but I had never witnessed it to be so true.

Levi patted his mother on the back. "I'll be outside," he said.

I followed a moment later.

"Why did you leave?"

Levi snorted. "Did you hear the doctor?

He's still at risk for a second attack. Heaven knows that if he woke up and saw me in the room, it could happen right here."

"He might want to see you. Near-death experiences change people. Things could be different."

He gave a rueful smile. "They might. But I want him to be healthy before I find out."

"Does your mom have the money for the surgery? It can't be cheap."

"The Amish take care of their own. My parents have savings, and if that's not enough, the community chips in. They'll be fine."

"That's nice."

"It is."

Martha stepped out a few minutes later. "He'll be taken in an ambulance to the hospital in Portland. Tonight." She wrung her hands. "I want to go with him, but . . ."

"You can stay with me," I said, a little surprised even as I offered. "My apartment isn't that far from the OHSU campus."

"Amos needs to help maintain the farm," she said, clearly thinking out loud. "My mother can come and stay with the younger ones for a few days."

"Did the doctor say how long his recovery time would be?" Levi asked.

Martha shrugged. "Three days? Five?

They don't know exactly."

"Amos needs to get back, and you need to pack some clothes. We'll drive to the house and go from there." Levi pulled his keys from his pocket. "Would Sara want to go with you to Portland?"

Martha considered it. "Yes, I'm sure she would."

I frowned. "Won't Ida need Sara's help with the children?"

"My mother can handle the younger ones just fine. Naomi is nearby if she needs anything."

I wondered at Levi's suggestion of taking Sara to Portland. Was he trying to encourage Sara to leave by giving her a taste of outside life?

Martha took a deep breath. "I will say goodbye to Gideon and then we'll go back to the house."

Her eyes looked watery, but her face was stoic. She knew as well as we did that if Gideon didn't pull through the surgery, this could be the last time she saw him. I felt myself tear up too. I couldn't comprehend what that must have been like for her. To be married to someone for as long as she'd been married to Gideon, and then to have everything change so quickly.

A light squeeze on my arm redirected my

thoughts. "How many people can your apartment hold?"

I looked up at Levi, trying to figure out where his question led. "It's only two bedrooms, but it's fairly spacious. I was planning on giving Martha and Sara my room and taking the couch."

"I was just wondering," he said. "I'd like to be there too, but I can always find a room somewhere."

An argument raged inside my head. Being with Levi could be . . . dangerous. Having him stay in my apartment could be . . . more dangerous. A part of me enjoyed having him near, hearing his opinion on things, having someone else around to be strong and practical. I worried I'd enjoy it *too* much.

On the other hand, I did have room, and Martha and Sara would be there as well.

His father was in the hospital. And it would only be a few days, max. Surely he couldn't stay away from the shop for very long.

"No, it's fine," I heard myself say even before I had made up my mind.

"I can bring a sleeping bag and an air mattress."

I nodded. "You can sleep in the study."

Levi nodded back. "We'd best be going then."

■ ■ ■ ■

I drove Martha and Amos back to the farm that night. I packed up what I would need while Martha packed for herself.

Sara had greeted us at the door, desperate for word. Martha explained the trip to Portland, and Sara began to pack.

I think that if her father weren't going in for triple bypass surgery, she would have been completely delighted.

An hour later we left for Portland. Sara sat in the front seat next to me, her nose pressed to the glass as the farmhouses disappeared. I began to relax when the streets became truly familiar and my apartment complex came into view.

We woke up Martha, who had fallen asleep in the backseat during the drive. Sara and I carried the bags up the stairs, I unlocked the door, and everyone walked in.

My apartment seemed colder than I remembered. Granted, I hadn't had the heat on for more than a week, but it was colder in a different way. It didn't feel like home.

Levi called a few moments later, telling us he'd be there shortly.

I had Martha and Sara sit on the couch while I tried to get my room ready for their use. Not that it was *bad,* per se, but certainly not the standard of cleanliness I'd experienced at the Burkholder farm.

You wouldn't want to eat off my floor. And maybe not the table, either.

I remade my bed with fresh sheets and checked the floor for stray underwear. I especially looked through the study before turning it over to a certain carpenter.

A knock sounded at the door, and I knew Levi had arrived.

He had a backpack over his shoulder, a sleeping bag under one arm, and a pillow under the other. "I really appreciate this, Jayne."

I gave a crooked smile. "You're welcome."

"Sorry I was running late. I didn't want to keep you up — you'll get little enough sleep as it is — but I figured you didn't have a whole lot in the way of groceries."

Hadn't gotten that far. "No . . . not really."

"I stopped by the grocery store to pick up some staples."

"You didn't have to do that."

"You didn't have to take care of my family."

"So where are they? Did you fit them in that backpack?"

"In the truck. I'll get them in a moment."

"I can do that —"

He tossed me the keys. "Thanks. I'll be out in a minute."

Didn't know quite why he said that. How much food did he buy?

I understood once I saw the bags piled atop each other in the cab. I unlocked the door to find milk, eggs, flour, sugar, shortening, butter, sausage, ground beef, baking soda, baking powder, deli meat, sandwich rolls, an assortment of condiments, and a lot of other things I'd have to dig through the bags to discover.

"I didn't know what you had," he said, coming up behind me.

"A little more than stale Pop-Tarts and beef jerky." Although not much more.

"Like I said, I didn't know what you had. And knowing my mom, she'll want to cook."

I'd give him that. "It's fine. I really appreciate it. Truly."

Between the two of us, we managed to haul all of it up the stairs in one trip. "Did you leave any food at the store?"

"The day-old sushi. I turned that down."

"Right." I set the bags on the kitchen counter and began loading appropriate items into the fridge.

"I'll finish this," he said, stacking boxes and cans. "You go to bed."

"Bed's over there," I said, pointing at the

couch not ten feet from the kitchen. "I have trouble sleeping when someone's rummaging in my kitchen."

"Doesn't look like you've gotten yourself any blankets. I'm okay here. Go take care of yourself."

I was too tired to argue. I grabbed my college-era comforter from my closet as well as an extra pillow.

Sara and Martha were already fast asleep in my room, two in the morning being far past their bedtimes. I snuck in quietly and found what I hoped were matching pajamas.

As soon as I was in the bathroom, I discovered I had a cupcake-print top with Harley-Davidson logo bottoms.

Oh, well. I washed my face and brushed my teeth, and then I looked at myself in the mirror. Circles were already under my eyes, yet I was still completely keyed up. I found some sleeping pills — I would need them if I was going to be able to sleep with Levi around.

I made up my makeshift bed while he puttered in the kitchen, finding homes for baking items I'd never used and likely never would.

"Almost done," he said, wadding up empty plastic sacks.

"Not a problem."

"Does it feel good to be home?"

"Mmm." I climbed into my couch bed and snuggled against my pillow. The sleeping pill was kicking in.

"Thanks again for letting me stay."

"You bet."

And with that, I fell asleep.

CHAPTER 16

I blinked a few times, confused. Where was I?

Couch. Home. Gideon. Surgery . . . the last 24 hours filed into my memory like little marching soldiers.

I heard the clink of metal in the kitchen. Was Levi still putting groceries away? How long did it take?

My eyes opened a bit wider, wide enough to read the time on the wall clock. Half-past eight. I hadn't slept this late in more than a week.

I sat up and peered into the kitchen.

Martha, not Levi, stood in the kitchen. A collection of apple peels sat in a pile to her left; her forearms flexed as she rolled out what had to be dough.

Curious, because I didn't think I owned a rolling pin.

I swung my legs to the floor. "Good morning," I said.

Martha nodded. "Morning."

"What are you making?"

"Apple dumplings, hash browns, and sausage. For breakfast."

As I came closer, I saw that she was using two aluminum cans duct-taped together as a rolling pin. "I'm sorry. My kitchen isn't very well equipped."

"Most English kitchens aren't."

"Well, my friend Gemma has about every kitchen tool known to man . . ." She'd probably be willing to loan some of them out, at least for a few days.

"Have you heard anything from the hospital?"

"My phone hasn't rung. They said they'd call when he's out of surgery."

Martha nodded. I watched her. Her movements were jerky, her muscles taut. Dark circles had taken up residence beneath her eyes. In a moment, I understood. Making breakfast — a breakfast for nine that would be eaten by four — was her coping method.

And far be it for me to get in her way.

I heard a rustling from the direction of the study. I turned in time to see the door open and Levi emerge, face stubbled and hair mussed.

He gave a crooked smile. "Mornin'."

"Hey."

I was suddenly very aware that my pajamas didn't match.

Martha turned. "Levi."

"How'd you sleep, Mom?"

"Well enough."

"Is Sara still sleeping?"

"She is."

Levi turned back to me. "Mind if I use your shower?"

"Go right ahead," I said, even as I considered my towel situation.

"I brought my own towel."

"I wasn't worried," I lied. I could only hope I had two other clean towels for Martha and Sara. Even if I tried to run a quick load of laundry, my dryer took a good two hours to finish drying even a single towel.

Everyone froze when my phone rang. I dove for it, nearly tripping on my shag carpet. "Hello?" I was embarrassed to hear my voice shake as I answered.

The nurse on the other end of the line asked for Martha. I passed the phone over.

Martha held the cell phone awkwardly in her hand, but the awkwardness faded as she paid complete attention to the words coming from the tiny speaker.

"I will be right there," she said, before ending the call.

Or trying to end the call. Levi reached

215

over and helped her close the phone.

"He is just out of surgery," she said, reaching for her apron strings and untying them. "He is well, the surgery went well. He is not awake, but we can see him." She looked from me to Levi. "We can see him!"

Clearly, breakfast was forgotten.

I looked at Levi, hoping he wouldn't miss the fact that I was unwashed, clad in mismatched pajamas, and not ready to be taken seriously by hospital staff.

"I'll shower really quick, Mom, and drive you down."

"And Sara?"

"Sara's not awake yet."

"She needs to be woken."

"Even then, she'll need to get dressed and put together. Jayne can drive her down."

"Yes," I chimed in. "I'll drive her down shortly."

"Okay." Martha brushed the flour from her hands and walked back down the hall.

"Cereal?" Levi said.

"Cereal," I agreed.

Levi showered while Martha woke Sara up, and then he took his mother to the hospital. I showered and dressed in clothes that matched.

"Is that what you're wearing?" Sara asked

when she saw me.

"Yes," I said warily, suddenly understanding what it would be like to have a teenager in the house.

"But it's so . . ."

I raised my eyebrows.

". . . dark."

"You're wearing a blue dress and a black apron."

"Because I *have* to. You can wear anything you want, and you're wearing a black sweater with jeans?"

"Gemma helped me pick out this sweater. It's one of the most stylish things I own."

Oops. Shouldn't have said that. Sara's eyes narrowed. "But . . . you're English."

"Yeah, well, just because someone's English doesn't mean they dress like they do in magazines."

"But you live in Portland."

"The Portland uniform is jeans, a sweatshirt, and Chacos."

"What are Chacos?"

"They're sandals . . . and beside the point. We need to meet up with your mom and Levi."

Sara looked down. "I'm sorry."

"I know you're excited about being in the city, but your dad's not out of the woods yet."

"People have bypasses all the time, right?"

"Yes, but it's still major surgery."

"Do you think he'll be okay?"

"If the doctors say the surgery went well, that's a very good sign."

"Okay." She cast one more look toward me. "You don't even have a printed scarf you could wear with that?"

I put my arm around her shoulders. "If your dad's fine and we have time at some point, I'll take you to Gemma's closet. The two of you will be very happy together."

I was afraid Sara would fall out of the car, her nosed pressed so hard to the glass as we drove up Terwilliger to get to the hospital.

"Do you want to stop by the gift shop on the way up?" I asked her. "We could pick up some flowers or a card or something."

Sara shook her head. "Flowers? He wouldn't know what to do with them."

Okay, then. "When we get inside," I said, deciding to broach the subject, "you need to tell the receptionist who you are."

Sara frowned. "I have to talk to them?"

"Yes, you do. Tell them you're Gideon's daughter and ask to see him."

"Can't you ask?"

"I'm not a relative."

"Oh."

"Technically, I should wait in the sitting area for you."

"I'm not going alone!"

"I didn't think so. That's why you have to talk."

Sara sulked for a little while, but when we reached the desk, she gave a concise speech to the receptionist that included the importance of my presence.

The receptionist nodded and directed us to Gideon's room. Our feet quickened when we saw Levi waiting outside.

"Is Martha inside?" I asked, pulling off my jacket.

He nodded. "Sorry," he said in a whisper. "I'm trying to keep a low profile."

I pressed my lips shut and followed Sara into the room.

Martha sat beside the bed, holding Gideon's hand. His eyes opened wider when he saw me.

"Ah," he said. "Jayne's here."

Martha patted his hand. "She's been very kind, letting us stay with her."

"Sit down, Jayne," he said, gesturing to the chair on the other side of the bed.

I sat.

"The doctors tell me that if I had gotten to the hospital just a little later, my heart would have died. But it was not God's will that I die yet. He sent you to call the ambulance. Thank you."

I nodded, a stab of guilt piercing my heart. He might have had even more time, had I not been eating ice cream and kissing his son. "I'm glad you're feeling better."

Gideon rolled his eyes. "I don't know that I'm feeling better. I'm full of needles. But at least I can breathe, right?"

"We're glad you can breathe," Martha echoed.

I checked her grip on his hand — her knuckles were white. It must have terrified her, seeing her husband so close to death.

I thought of Levi outside the door. "I'm glad you're still here with your family." I tried to think of something clever I might say about second chances and reconciliation, but everything sounded as though it belonged on an inspirational billboard.

A shadow passed over Gideon's face. Maybe I hadn't needed to say anything after all.

While Sara and Martha kept Gideon company and Levi brooded outside, I excused myself to make a phone call.

The mention of Gemma's closet had made me think of Gemma's other talents. Namely, completing meal preparation without setting the kitchen on fire. At some point, members of the Burkholder clan would have to eat, and I didn't know how they would respond to Chinese takeout or the concept of beef-a-roni.

"Wow," Gemma said when we connected. "This is the clearest the line has been since you've been gone. I don't know what part of the field you're in, but remember it, will you?"

"Um, well, I'm not in Albany any more."

"Oh? Where are you?"

"OHSU."

"What! Why? Are you okay?"

"It's not me. Gideon had a heart attack, but listen. He had to come up here to have bypass surgery, and now I have three people staying in my apartment who can't live off crackers."

"Any vegetarians?"

"No. Definitely not."

"Any food allergies?"

"None that I'm aware of."

"How many people?"

"Four, including me."

"Four?" Gemma checked.

"Martha, Sara, me . . . and Levi."

"Levi's there?"

"Gem —"

"Levi, you kissed him, Levi?"

"There just aren't a whole lot of Levis in this world. Yes, same one."

"He's staying in your apartment?"

"In the study."

"Oh, that's kind of cute."

"Not helping!"

"Right. How about if I bring over some food from the restaurant?"

My shoulders relaxed. "Have I told you you're fantastic?"

"Not in the last ten minutes."

"Feel free to invite yourself over. Sara will want to analyze your outfit."

"I would, but I have study tonight."

"Oh." Study as in Bible study. "Well, have fun with that."

"I will. Have you talked to Shane recently?"

"I haven't."

"Just wondering. See you tonight?"

"Tonight," I agreed, and hung up.

Shane. Shane, Shane, Shane. Didn't know what to do with Shane. Didn't know what to do about Shane. I wanted to talk to him — well, catch up at least. But I didn't particularly want him to know I was back in town or to know I had houseguests.

If only I hadn't kissed Levi.

If only I could kiss him again.

■ ■ ■ ■

"Everything okay?" Levi asked when I returned.

"Yeah. I just secured us food for tonight."

"You didn't need to do that. I can cook."

"You can cook? Like what, toast?"

"Pasta. Jambalaya. Chicken Cordon Bleu."

"I'm impressed. I thought most bachelors ate noodles with butter and salt."

"I do that too."

"No poor-person pasta tonight. My friend Gemma is either cooking or bringing food from her family's restaurant. Either way, we'll eat well."

"You have good friends."

"I do."

"Holding up okay? It was a late night."

"You're asking me? It's your dad hooked up to the machines in there. How are you?"

Levi sighed.

I gave him a sad smile. "It's okay. You don't have to say anything."

Gemma arrived promptly at six thirty that night, and I wondered if she'd kicked up her wardrobe a bit to make up for not staying. Despite the fact that she was carrying an armload of casserole dishes, Sara studied her ensemble from head to toe.

It doesn't hurt that Gemma's half-French, half-Italian, and wholly striking.

"Whatcha got there?"

"Rosemary chicken lasagna, rolls, salad, soup from the restaurant —"

"What kind?"

"Italian Wedding, I think. Maybe potato and leek."

"I confuse the two all the time."

"I just had Niko throw some into a container. I wasn't involved in the soup choosing."

"If it's good enough for your brother, it's good enough for the rest of us." I turned to my houseguests, assembled as they were in the dining alcove. "This is my dear friend Gemma. Gemma, this is Martha, her daughter Sara, and her son Levi."

"Good to meet you," she said, possibly paying more attention to Levi than Martha or Sara. "Let me get the food and get out of your way."

"Positive you can't stay?"

"Sorry. Bible study, and I'm bringing the snack."

Knowing Gem, the snack involved something wrapped in prosciutto or stuffed with candied marscapone. Being on the receiving end of Gemma's cuisine was a happy place to be.

"What kind of Bible study?" Levi asked, out of the blue.

Gemma paused, a funny little smile on her face. "We're going through Isaiah."

I shoved my hands into my pockets, not particularly interested in the ritual Christians go through to identify each other.

"I like Isaiah. Are you going through the whole book?"

"And studying the historical context, yes."

"That must be fascinating."

"Completely fascinating," I said. "Want us to transfer the food out of these containers?"

"No, that's fine. The study is also interesting because we're reading the Scripture out of four translations, including Amplified."

"You can get some remarkable insights from the Amplified."

"It just takes a while to read through."

They shared a laugh. I fought the urge to roll my eyes.

"I do need to go, though," Gemma said. "Jayne? Didn't you leave your scarf in my car?"

"Scarf?" I wasn't much of a scarf wearer, and I couldn't remember the last time I'd ridden in Gemma's car.

But then I read the look on Gemma's face.

"Right. Scarf. I'll follow you out." I turned to my guests. "Feel free to start without me. I'll be right back."

Gemma waved goodbye to everyone, and then I shut the door behind us.

"I don't wear scarves," I said when we were halfway down the stairs. "You couldn't think of anything else?"

"Nope. So, that's Levi?"

"Yes, Gem, that's Levi."

"I like him."

"Fine. He's all yours."

She glared at me. "No. I mean I like him for you. Jayne, why on earth are you still in a relationship with Shane?"

CHAPTER 17

I sighed. "Why am I with Shane? He's smart. He makes me laugh. I enjoy spending time with him. We vote the same way, believe in the same things."

But on the inside, I knew the honest answer.

Shane was safe. He knew nothing about my past, and I liked it that way. He didn't pry into my life, at least not usually.

More than that, he was the first clean-cut, non-hick guy to notice me, to want to spend time with me. A part of me felt that I owed him for that.

I had a pretty good handle on Levi. He wouldn't let me shut him out of my life. Because of that, I couldn't afford a relationship with him. He would want too much.

I didn't tell Gemma that.

"Believing the same things doesn't make a great relationship. I mean, think of Meg Ryan and Greg Kinnear in *You've Got Mail,*"

I said instead.

"You do realize they were playing scripted characters."

"Fine," I said with a calculated shrug. "It's unprofessional to get involved with someone while I'm working on a story."

"You're not working on it for the newspaper."

"Still, I'm working on it. I'm on the job. I can't get involved."

"That's why half the family is staying in your apartment."

"Not half. Six, no, seven other members aren't here. Only thirty percent of the family are here."

"I stand corrected. You might just . . . think about it."

"Okay. I will. Here's your car," I said, as if, after three years of ownership, Gemma struggled with automobile identification. "Thanks so much for the food!"

"Are you getting rid of me?"

"Don't want you to be late for study."

Her mouth twisted into a wry smile. "That would break your heart, wouldn't it. You'll keep me posted on Gideon and everything?"

"Absolutely."

"You're not just saying that?"

"Absolutely not." I gave her a hug to make myself feel less guilty.

I watched Levi during dinner for signs that he was suddenly interested in marriage.

Not to me. To Gemma. Her cooking had that effect on men sometimes. They would envision themselves happy and well fed and that would be the end of that.

That Gemma was still single astounded us all, especially considering the quality of her meatloaf.

After dinner I found myself thinking that I was home, in possession of a TV, and wouldn't it be nice to watch Bill Moyers? I knew I had recorded shows on my DVR . . . but what was the protocol on television viewing when the Amish were about?

I could go with the strict interpretation and say I couldn't do anything they wouldn't, but then, I wouldn't be able to turn the lights on.

In the end I decided that using basic necessities was permissible (seeing as how I didn't own a Coleman lantern), but Bill Moyers was pushing it.

Martha beat the boredom by attacking my apartment with a vengeance. The dinner dishes were washed and put away into locations they had only ever dreamed of. After that, she swept the floor with a broom I didn't know I had before proceeding to hand wash the floor on her hands and knees. She used paper towels because I didn't own rags, a fact that completely amazed her.

I was completely amazed that I had a broom, so we were even.

"Thanks for letting her do that," Levi said in a voice quiet enough for Martha not to hear. "I think it's cathartic for her."

"I just keep feeling like I should tip her or something," I said, wrapping my arms around myself. "I'm not quite a slob, but I don't think this apartment was this clean when I moved in."

"It probably wasn't. The Amish have a standard for interior cleanliness that outsiders can only aspire to."

"I didn't say I aspired. I don't enjoy scrubbing on my hands and knees."

"The irony is that they'll walk barefoot through mud and wash less than we might have them wash, but the houses are always very clean."

"And the rest of us are the other way around."

"Like I said, thanks for doing this."

I shrugged, remembering the sight of Gideon nearly lifeless in his hospital bed.

"You're welcome."

I walked the halls of a ward in a daze. There were doors on either side of me; they stretched as far as I could see. Some of the doors were open, some were closed. Some had people inside, others had puppies.

One had a green iguana.

I continued until I found the right door. I don't know *how* I knew it was the right one, because the name on the whiteboard to the side read "Artemus X," and I didn't know anyone named Artemus X.

I knew the person inside. People, rather. My father was on the bed, wires and tubes entering and exiting through his nose, his ears, his feet, his fingers. I'd never seen him so pale. If the machine to his left weren't beeping, I wouldn't think him alive.

My mother sat next to the bed, her face covered with a lacy black mantilla. I don't know why — she wasn't Catholic or Spanish. I could see her tears beneath the dark lace.

Beth sat next to her. In her arms she held my niece, Emilee, though instead of looking like Emilee she looked like Baby Ruby.

I stepped farther into the room when I saw Baby Ruby. "May I hold her?"

Beth clutched Baby Ruby tighter. "Since

when do you hold babies?"

"Since I went and stayed with the Amish. I learned a lot of things."

"Like what?"

"I learned to bake pie, how to hold babies, how to —"

"Be loyal to your family?" Beth's eyes narrowed. "You took care of their father, but you wouldn't go near your own."

"But I'm here now!" I said, pointing to the figure on the bed. "I'm not too late!"

"Yes, you are," she said, and when I turned back to look at the bed, I saw the sheet had been pulled over my father's face.

"Why did you do that? He's still alive. Move the sheet, or it'll get stuffy in there."

"He's dead."

I pulled the sheet back. "No, he's not! He's alive! I just saw him alive! The monitor was beeping!"

She put a cautioning hand on my shoulder. "It's not beeping anymore. You're too late."

"I'm not too late!" I swatted away her hand. "Dad? Wake up! It's Jayne! Tell them I'm not too late. I know you can hear me! Please wake up. I'm not too late! Not too late!"

"Jayne! Open your eyes!"

I didn't know where the voice was coming

232

from. Open my eyes? My eyes were already open. Someone was shaking my shoulders. Who was that? Beth had disappeared. My mother was gone.

But a person crouched next to me in the dark. The person was Levi. He released my shoulders. I realized I was awake and had been dreaming.

I frowned and pushed myself into a sitting position. "What are you doing? What time is it?"

"Late. Are you okay?"

I took stock. I was not okay. I released the knot of grief that had held itself captive inside my chest and shook my head. "No."

"Do you want to talk about it?"

"Did I wake you up?"

"You were crying out."

I winced. "S-sorry. Did I wake your mom or Sara?"

"No, don't worry about it. Were you dreaming?"

I nodded.

"That would explain the iguana."

"There was an iguana?"

"In the hospital room."

"Oh."

"I'm not crazy!"

Levi handed me the tissue box from under the end table. "Didn't say you were."

I wiped at my eyes. "I dreamed my dad was in the hospital. My mom and my sister were there. He was alive. I stopped to talk with my sister, and then he was . . ." A sob caught at my throat. "He was gone. I missed it. I wasn't there. And Beth was telling me about how I was there for your dad but not for mine and . . ." I shrugged. "She's right. *You* have been available to your dad, and he's all but denounced you."

"When did your dad pass away?"

"About four weeks ago." Had it been that long? Longer? Shorter? "I think."

"Do you mind if I sit on the couch? This is killing my knees."

"Okay."

He shifted himself up and onto the couch, sitting next to me.

"Do you . . . need to go spend time with your family?"

"I wasn't there. I don't know why they'd want me around."

"Who do you have left?"

"My mom. My sister."

"I'm sure they miss you."

I hugged my arms to myself. "I'm sure they don't."

"A daughter. A sister. They miss you."

"I don't know why."

Levi leaned back. "We're designed to want

234

a relationship with our families. Even if things are strained, there is the desire for things to be better."

I thought about it. Did I wish things were better? Of course I did. Of course I craved beauty instead of ugliness. But I didn't want to concede the things I would have to in order to receive acceptance from my mom and Beth. I told Levi as much.

"What do you have to concede?"

"I don't know. My independence."

"Can I ask you something?"

I yawned. Hmm. Those sleeping pills were still in my system. "Okey-dokey."

"What's so great about independence?"

"Well, it worked for the American Revolutionaries."

"Personal independence can be overrated. Consider the Amish. Their families and communities are completely dependent on each other, and it works for them. They take care of their friends, family, and neighbors, knowing they'll be taken care of too when the time comes."

"I don't know," I said with a shake of my head. If I were more awake, I might have been able to come up with a better argument. My eyelids felt heavy.

"Are you getting sleepy?"

I forced my eyes back open. "I don't want

235

to fall asleep again."

"Why not?"

"If I close my eyes again, the iguana might still be there."

Levi chuckled. "I think you're already falling asleep."

"Am not."

"You're worried about the iguana?"

"And my dad. Maybe he's haunting my dreams."

"I don't think so."

"He's angry with me."

"If he's in heaven, he's too happy to be angry."

I shook my head. "You don't know my dad."

"Are you sure you don't want to go back to sleep?"

"He'll be there. Angry with me."

Levi took my face between his hands. "If he's in heaven, looking at you the way I see you, it would be impossible for him to be angry with you."

A part of me registered that maybe I ought to enjoy that touch, or resent it, or something, but I was too fuzzy to pick one. "You think?"

"I know."

My eyelids felt like lead weights. Were they always so heavy? "You're nice."

"Thanks."

"It's too bad I can't fall in love with you."

I think he may have stroked my hair. "It is too bad. Why can't you?"

"You'd want to know."

"Know what?'

"Everything." I yawned. "I'm sleepy."

"I noticed."

"I don't want to sleep."

"The iguana again?"

"No." I sank back into the couch. "The puppies."

"I'm not going to ask."

"Fluffy puppies."

"I'm sure they were. Do you love Shane?"

"Probably not."

"Why can't we be together?" Was it the artificial sleep, or did he sound sad?"

I waved a hand. "I can't remember. What time is it?"

"Late. You should go to sleep."

"I don't want to close my eyes."

"Why don't you just rest your head on my shoulder?"

"Really?" I shifted so that his shoulder would be in range. He had a comfortable-looking shoulder.

"You don't even have to close your eyes."

"Okay."

The next thing I knew, I was curled up on

my side on the couch. It was morning, and I was all alone.

I began to reheat Gemma's breakfast casserole per the instructions taped to the casserole lid. Even as I went through the motions of placing it in the appropriately warmed oven, I tried to piece together the events from the night before.

I remembered the dream vividly. The scent of hospital hallways still clung to my nose, though my logical self reminded me of my recent trips to the hospital. Then there was the oddness of the, ah, animals that also inhabited my dreams. I chalked them up to a snack of cheese and crackers before bed.

But after the dream . . . I remembered Levi waking me. I remember talking with him, calming down. After that, things were a bit fuzzy. And that was bad. I had a tendency to react to tiredness as if it were truth serum and not remember things I said, a fact Joely and Kim had attempted to exploit more than once.

Not Gemma, though. Gemma was too nice.

The fact that I was medicated probably hadn't helped, either.

I whipped around when I heard footsteps, hoping it was Sara or Martha and not the person who had witnessed me at my most vulnerable.

Again.

Levi stood on the threshold of the kitchen. "Hey."

"Hey back."

"How are you this morning?"

My heart sank. If only he had the same memory issues I did.

"Fine," I answered.

"You didn't seem to have any other disturbing dreams."

I winced. "Not that I remember. Listen, about last night?"

"Yeah?"

I almost didn't continue. His eyes, occasionally guarded, were open and full of a hope I hated to shatter.

"I, um, I don't really remember much after you woke me up."

Levi smiled. "I'm not surprised."

Fine, but I was. I expected him to be upset, not smiley. "You're not?"

"You were pretty out of it."

"Oh. What did I say?"

He shrugged. "Stuff about iguanas."

"Iguanas? You're making that up."

"Surprisingly, no." He stretched his arms. "Where do you keep your coffee? I'll start a pot."

"Um . . . I don't actually have a coffee-maker."

Levi froze. "You don't have a coffee-maker?"

"No."

"French press?"

"Which I believe is a kind of coffee-maker . . ."

"Instant granules?"

"I have green tea."

From the look on Levi's face, you would have thought I'd told him to raise a glass of hemlock to his lips. "So tell me," he said after he recovered, "is there any decent coffee to be found in this town?"

"Somewhere, yes. This is Portland, after all. Who do you think Seattle sells it to?"

"Want to help me find some after breakfast? I haven't had any in over twenty-four hours."

"Can't have that," I said, realizing without disappointment that I'd just agreed to go.

CHAPTER 18

Martha stopped dead when she walked into the kitchen and found breakfast prepared. "I'm sorry," she said. "I must have overslept."

"That's perfectly fine." I reached for a serving spoon. "Would you like some?"

She nodded. I didn't imagine people made breakfast for her very often.

Sara followed shortly after. "Any news on Dad?"

Levi shook his head. "I'm about to call the nurse and check."

"Or you could talk to him yourself," I murmured in the softest of soft voices.

"Not over the phone," he muttered back.

I made a face at him.

He made a face back.

"I can call," Martha said, oblivious to our moment. "I would like to hear his voice."

We ate in silence as Martha borrowed my phone for the call.

She listened carefully to the person on the other line, but her face lit up when Gideon came on.

I smiled as I watched. "He must be awake."

"And upset that he's still in a hospital bed," Levi added.

Sara rolled her eyes. "He's probably going crazy."

Five minutes later, Martha held the phone out to me. "How do I hang up?"

I snapped the phone shut.

"Oh. That makes sense. I'd like to go to the hospital soon."

"Is Dad okay?" Sara asked.

"He says he is, and the nurse agrees. But he wants to get out of bed, and I need to be there to stop him."

Levi and Sara exchanged glances.

Levi looked to me. "Another time?"

Another time for . . . oh, right. Coffee. "Of course." Probably for the best anyway.

Levi took Sara and Martha to the hospital while I stayed behind to "work."

"Working" being code for figuring out what to do with my life.

I used to think that was what college was for.

Gemma was right. I either needed to make

things better with Shane or at least move on. Staying with him because I liked him as arm candy wasn't fair to him.

And as far as my family went . . . if my dream was any indication, the dissonance had gone on long enough. They either loved me or they didn't. I either loved them or I didn't. I had to choose one.

It struck me as ironic that, really, my situation surrounding my family and my boyfriend were so similar.

Basically, I needed to make up my mind.

I sighed, picked up my phone, and dialed Shane for the first time in a while.

"Jayne? Where are you? The connection is the clearest it's been since you left."

"I'm actually in my apartment."

"Finally had enough?"

"Not really . . ." I gave him the short and sweet version of Gideon's heart attack. "So Martha and Sara are staying with me while he's at OHSU."

I sort of edited out the fact that Levi was sleeping in my study.

"I miss you," he said.

"I miss you," I echoed back, although I wasn't certain that I did. Maybe I did. I probably did. "Anyway, I called because I think I'm going to cut my time in Albany

243

short and go to Lincoln City to see my family."

"Oh. That's nice."

"I was wondering . . ." I paused and then took a deep breath, "if you wanted to come with me."

"Why?"

"I thought . . . I thought you might want to meet my family."

"You want me to meet your family."

"Yes."

"You realize that would involve me talking to them."

"Yes."

"And you still want me to go?"

"Wait. Let me think about it . . ."

"Jayne!"

"Just kidding! Yes."

"And this isn't just because you're going and you need a buffer."

"No."

"No, you don't want me as a buffer?"

I couldn't lie. "Well, it's one of those side benefits. But not the only reason. At all." I released the breath I'd been holding. "This next weekend?"

"That's fine. I may need to bring some work with me."

"Bring whatever you need, as long as yourself is included."

"You're doing okay?"

"I'm . . ." I thought about it. Was I okay? I was conflicted. And confused. And not looking forward to the Lincoln City trip. Did that make me not okay?

I straightened my spine. "I'm fine."

I was alive and healthy. That made me okay enough.

I ran errands that afternoon, picking up a bag of Stumptown coffee for Levi as well as a coffeemaker, reasoning that at some point I might brew coffee at home.

It's also possible that I went to Powell's, because, well, I hadn't been to Powell's in more than a week and I was low on reading material.

The Martha who returned to the apartment seemed younger and, I don't know, lighter than the one who left. Not that she weighed less, but that there was less weighing her down.

"He's doing very well," she reported, her cheeks glowing. "The doctor said that if he continues to do so well, he can leave in two days. Two days!"

"That's good news!"

"I insist on making dinner," she said, tugging at her apron. "After a day of sitting

around at a hospital, I need to do something useful."

I couldn't stop her, not without feeling horribly guilty. "Knock yourself out."

She frowned at me. "Knock myself . . ."

"Er . . . go ahead. The kitchen is yours with my blessing."

"Is that a thread on your shirt?" Sara glued herself to my side and picked at the hem of my cowl-necked T-shirt.

"It is," she said, before I could reply. "The hem's coming out. This wasn't sewn together very well. Would you like me to fix it?"

I figured if I let her fix it, she'd let go.

"Can you take it off?"

I had to physically restrain my eyes from darting to Levi for his reaction. Instead, I schooled my features and said, "Why don't we go to my room? You can mend this shirt, and then you can look for other garments in need of your care. Does that sound like fun?"

She all but skipped down the short hallway. I followed.

In the short expanse of time that followed, Sara found six T-shirts, two blouses, and three pairs of pants in desperate need of her service. Then she looked at me. "Where's your needle and thread?"

Seriously. "Sara, I don't have a needle and thread."

She rolled her eyes in such a way as to make me a believer that teenager-dom is a reality that crosses cultures. "You probably don't have extra buttons either, do you." It was a statement more than a question.

"I save the buttons that come with my clothes," I said defensively, and it was true. I did save them. I didn't know how to attach them if and when the need arose, but I had them just the same.

She pointed to the pile of clothes on my bed. "I can't fix these without thread."

I chose not to suggest dental floss, instead opting to bundle up and make a trip to Fred Meyer's.

Freddy's has everything.

"Need company?" Levi asked when I returned to the living room.

I shook my head. "Just a quick trip. I'll be right back. Did you see the coffee?"

"Coffee?" The look in his eyes turned a bit desperate.

"I bought coffee for you. It's on the counter."

"You don't have a coffeemaker."

"The box next to the coffee that says 'Mr. Coffee' on it."

I could hear his grin as the door closed

behind me.

I found all sorts of things at Freddy's. Scissors made especially for fabric. Who knew such a thing existed? My mother, probably.

There were needles of all lengths and thicknesses, and a little more thread than I felt comfortable around. But I struck gold with what they called an "Emergency Mending Kit," which contained thread of assorted colors, needles, a miscellaneous button, a tiny measuring tape, tiny scissors, a tiny thimble, and two small safety pins.

I don't know what kind of emergency might necessitate this sort of kit, but I was pretty sure it had everything Sara might have asked for.

When I got back to the apartment, dinner simmered on the stove and the scent of brewed coffee filled the air. Martha bustled around the kitchen, putting the last touches on her meal. Levi sat on the couch, a book in one hand and a mug in the other, while Sara breezed in and out of the living room, putting away items that had managed to drift out (mostly by me) since morning.

The sense of family took my breath away. Was this what coming home to people was like?

I pulled the emergency kit from the plastic

Fred Meyer sack and waved it in the air. "Hope this works," I told Sara, "otherwise we'll have to improvise. Yank thread from my duvet, that sort of thing."

Sara's eyes narrowed. "What is that?"

"A kit."

"What kind?"

"Emergency mending, and you're the field medic."

Her eyebrows pitched forward in an expression of complete confusion.

"She means you're an emergency doctor," Levi said, looking up from his book.

"Oh."

He looked at me, his eyes twinkling.

Sara began to peel away the plastic covering. "This has everything I need," she said. "I should have your clothes done right away."

"But not until after dinner," Martha called from the kitchen. "Sara, would you set the table?"

Sara dropped her eyes and moved back toward the kitchen as if driven by an invisible force.

When we sat down to dinner, I found myself struck again by the sense of family. I couldn't remember the last time the idea of family was so appealing.

My mind wandered before I could stop

myself. I wondered what Martha would be like as a mother-in-law. Shane's mother was an interior designer (one of the reasons they'd never come to my place on a visit, since I had decorated the place in a post-college eclectic style she probably wouldn't approve of) and married to her career. I couldn't see her preparing and serving dinner, unless it involved a caterer with excellent presentational skills.

I shook my head. Not that it mattered. I didn't see myself getting married anytime soon — or at all — and certainly not to a carpenter from Albany.

Seriously.

Even if he was good looking, handy, and an all-around enjoyable person to be with. Didn't matter.

The next few days flew by. Gideon continued to steadily improve, and the Burkholders began to ready for departure. Levi and I never had a chance to go for coffee, which was fine with me. I was with Shane.

Sara and I never had a chance to paw through Gemma's closet, which was also just as well. As far as I knew, Sara hadn't yet made up her mind about her future with the Amish. Exposing her to Gemma's closet would just be unfair to her. I didn't know how the Amish could compete with a French and Italian wardrobe.

Levi never visited Gideon in the hospital. "I can't run the risk of upsetting him, not when he's like this," Levi told me when I pushed the issue for the last time. "I don't want to be responsible for killing him."

"At least there are health care professionals around, unlike at the farm," I reasoned halfheartedly.

Levi shrugged. "Another time."

His plan was to leave before I drove Martha and Sara to the hospital to pick up Levi. "I want to thank you," he said, his backpack slung over his shoulder.

I waved my hand. "It was nothing."

"You let the Amish take over your home for five days."

"They're good people."

"I noticed you have a lot of books."

"You're very perceptive."

"I thought I could make you a bookcase. As a thank-you gift."

I opened my mouth to protest but decided against it. "That would be nice."

"I was thinking a tall one, with short shelves to fit a lot of books, but two taller shelves in the middle."

"I could live with that."

"Light wood? Dark?"

"You're the carpenter."

"You're a special lady, Jayne."

He left, then, and I found myself wishing that maybe things could be different.

Gideon slept through most of the trip back to the Burkholder farm, but for that matter so did Martha. Sara sketched out a quilt pattern on her notebook.

I played Sixpence None the Richer softly over the car stereo; I knew the Amish weren't big music listeners — Sara had explained that recorded music was taboo — but I had to do something to avoid joining the communal nap.

The kids ran out into the driveway despite the downpour, and I understood how Levi felt about driving up to them. I managed to miss their toes but I did catch their hugs after I opened the door and stepped out.

I packed the rest of my things after Gideon was settled inside — my quilt squares, a pair of socks, and the dress Sara made me and insisted I keep.

Martha stepped inside the room just after I finished. She held a quilt in her arms.

"I would like to thank you for all of your help while Gideon was sick, Jayne. I — we — would like you to have this."

She held the quilt out to me.

It was exquisite. The shades of blues worked together to create a subtle three-dimensional effect that took my breath away. Black and purple pieces ran along the edges.

I ran my finger over the stitches. "Martha, it's beautiful."

"Take it."

I found myself hugging it close before pulling Martha into that hug. I didn't want to leave. "Thank you for letting me stay and be a part of your family."

Martha's body, stiff at first, relaxed. Her hand patted my back. "You're welcome."

I said my goodbyes to Gideon, Amos, and Elam, and hugged each of the younger children.

"Do you really have to go?" Elizabeth asked as she held onto my knees.

"I do," I said, stroking her braid one last time. "I need to be with my family before I go back to work."

"Will you write letters?"

I looked up to see Martha's encouraging nod. "If you want me to, I'll write."

Sara stood in the living room, her back straight as the ladder in the barn. "Take better care of your clothes," she said. "You really should learn to sew."

I gave her a knowing smile. "I'll miss you too."

CHAPTER 19

I thought about stopping by Levi's shop on the way out of town, but I decided against it. Saying goodbye to the Burkholders had already made me more emotional than I wanted to admit.

Besides, a part of me needed a clean break from Levi. I needed to focus on Shane if that relationship wasn't going to dissolve into Oprah-discussion material.

Clean break. Need space. Getting back to my life. I reminded myself of all the reasons why it was okay to go home to a quiet, empty apartment.

Quiet as it was, the walls still seemed to hold the memory of noise, people, and laughter. The sound of pots clanging echoed in the kitchen. Sara's disbelief over my wardrobe still resonated in my bedroom.

And Levi . . . truth be told, he was everywhere. He was everywhere but I ignored it, unpacked my belongings from Amish-land

and prepared for my trip to the Oregon Coast.

I couldn't sleep that night. My nights on the couch had been hit-and-miss, considering the mix of exhaustion and the fact that I wasn't used to sleeping on something with arms and a back, but this was different.

Every time I almost fell asleep, I heard something. A Harley roaring past. Skateboarder kids yelling. An emergency siren — no, two.

I hadn't heard a siren while I was sleeping since I'd left to stay with the Burkholders, and I couldn't believe how fast I'd accustomed myself to not hearing them. Now that I was hearing them, they annoyed me to no end. It was four in the morning! How much traffic could there be? Couldn't they flash their lights and make that *whoop whoop* noise when necessary, instead of waking up every resident within a one-mile radius?

Unfortunately for Shane, I woke up the next morning groggy and irritated. When he arrived, my things weren't packed, my hair was wet, and I had only just gotten dressed.

Who knew getting dressed could be so difficult? I'd spent more than a week without clothing options, and now pairing a shirt with jeans took mental calisthenics I'd never expected. Sara had made me twitchy about my clothes. I held up a shirt and wondered, *What would Sara say?*

It made the whole process rather time consuming.

"You're not ready?" Shane said, deciding, I supposed, that today was a good day to skate hard on thin ice.

I glared at him. "*No,* I'm not ready. And you're early. Why are you early?"

"No traffic. Why are you so defensive?"

"I told you! You're early and wonder why I'm not ready! Of course I'm not ready. If you'd been here on time, I might have been ready."

"Sorry, no traffic. Are your bags packed?"

"No. But they might have been if you'd gotten here when you were supposed to."

Shane checked his watch. "I'm ten minutes early. Would you have been packed and dried your hair in ten minutes?"

I crossed my arms. "Yes."

He just looked at me.

"Maybe," I amended. "At least I'm dressed."

"Congratulations." He sighed and took off his jacket. "Do you need help with anything?"

"No."

"Did you, um . . . not sleep well?"

"No."

"Ah. Take a deep breath. Go pack."

I did. Or I tried. In the end, I shoved most of my closet into my suitcase, then pulled it all back out. "I need to go shopping."

"What was that?" Shane called from the living room.

"I said I needed to go shopping."

"I didn't know you shopped."

"Everyone shops." I packed socks. You couldn't go wrong with socks. "Otherwise, we'd starve."

"I meant clothes shopping."

"I've got to get them somehow, and shoplifting seems out of the question."

"But you don't enjoy it."

"No." I tucked away a selection of underwear. "But it's like the dentist. Bad things happen if you don't go."

Especially according to Sara, a girl who made all her own clothes. I would have discredited her opinion, except that it sounded a lot like everything Gemma had ever said about my motley collection of garments.

"You got a coffeemaker." Shane, I guess, had moved from the living room to the kitchen. "Stumptown. That's good stuff. Need coffee? I'll make you a pot."

I winced. "No, I'm fine."

"Might help take the morning edge off."

"You want me cranky *and* caffeinated?"

"Never mind."

Thought so. I didn't need coffee in the air. It would remind me too much of a certain caffeine addict.

"Where exactly are we staying?"

I couldn't decide which jeans to take, so I brought them all. "The Sea Gypsy."

Shane grimaced. "Is it clean?"

"I'm going to forget you said that. Of course it is. It's pristine."

"Just asking."

"It's the coast, Shane, not the slums of Mumbai."

"Just checking."

"Stop checking," I said, dragging my bag down the hall. "Start loading. Please."

Shane eyed my bag in disbelief. "Tell me that's half empty."

"I like to think of it as half full."

"Jayne!"

"What? I'm an incurable optimist."

"It's two days! Unless I missed something . . ."

"No. Two days."

"You need all that for two days? And we're not scuba diving?"

"I hate scuba diving."

"What's wrong with scuba diving?"

I rolled my eyes. "The fact you're supposed to move away from the earth's main oxygen supply."

"You take air with you."

"Not the same. Why are we talking about this?"

"Because you have a suitcase you'd have to pay extra for to take on an airplane for two days on the Oregon Coast."

"It's not fifty pounds!"

"It's close!"

My voice hardened. "You haven't even touched it! Do you weigh things with your eyes now? How much do I weigh?"

"I —" He stopped. Took a deep breath. "I'm sorry. This morning started off wrong."

"You didn't answer my question."

"Which one?"

"How much do I weigh?"

"Hi, Jayne," he said, ignoring my question and taking my hand. "It's good to see you. I've missed you."

"I've . . . missed you too."

"Promise?"

I nodded. I really had.

"I'm sorry I was argumentative."

I shifted my feet. "I'm sorry I was irritable."

His other hand slipped around my back. "Can we make up?"

"Okay." I put my arms around his neck.

He leaned closer and kissed me.

I analyzed the kiss with a clinical detachment. Did I enjoy it? Was the chemistry the same? Had I imagined the chemistry before?

The kiss . . . well, it wasn't the best. Shane kissed with a great deal of precision. If he were being scored on technique, he'd be Olympian.

But I wasn't seeing rainbows, or feeling at the least as though I wanted the kiss to continue forever.

Another two or three seconds was perfectly fine. I could move on without much of a second thought.

Then the guilt hit. The reason I was rainbow-less was because I was being so pickin' analytical. Being analytical would kill any kiss. Even the one I shared with Levi.

Wait — I wasn't supposed to be thinking! I was supposed to be moving on, mending fences, revisiting my past in order to prepare for my future. I was doing everything Dr. Phil would want me to, dash it all, and thoughts about Levi wouldn't get in the way.

Shane pulled away. "You seem distracted."

"Oh?"

"You're really tired, aren't you."

"Yes."

"Let's get you in the car. You can sleep on the way."

I gave him a light hug. "You're sweet. Wait a minute!" I dashed back into my room, grabbing a small bag before returning to my behemoth suitcase.

"You forgot something?" I couldn't miss the irony in his voice.

I opened the bag and let him look inside. "My quilt squares are in here."

"Quilt squares?"

"Something I got into last week. It's very calming."

"You sew?"

I put my hands on my hips. "I cut."

"And then what?"

"Haven't gotten that far. I just like cutting them out."

Shane shook his head. He continued to shake his head even as he dragged my suitcase down the stairs to the car.

Shane's offer of travel time slumber was sweet, if impractical. If I couldn't sleep in my bed, logic followed that sleeping in a car while he griped about other drivers wasn't particularly likely.

I closed my eyes anyway.

He shook me "awake" once we entered the town of Rose Lodge. "Mind if we get something to eat when we get there? I'm starved."

"We're close to Otis Café, if they're not too busy."

Shane studied the sparse, rural buildings and lots littered with the occasional mobile home on cement blocks. "Busy?"

"There are only about eight tables and the café's been written up in a lot of national press — *USA Today* included. It's quite popular."

"What kind of food?"

"Farmer's breakfast-type fare. Man food. A lot of potatoes. The bread's really good." *The Burkholders would love it.*

Shane shrugged. "I'm game if you are. I thought you avoided carbs."

"I've been living with the Amish."

"Right. How close are we?"

"A mile or two."

We drove for a while.

"Is that it?" he asked.

"Does it have a large sign that says 'Café'?" I didn't open my eyes.

"Yes."

"Is it on the right?"

"Yes."

"Then pull in. We're here."

I sat up straight and opened my door, looking out my window at the familiar sight that was Otis Café.

My family came here every year for Beth's birthday, and often drove down for lunch after church.

It wasn't too busy inside — we managed to slide into a table before an onslaught of diners entered on our heels.

The waitress kept looking at me while she took our order. It probably had something to do with the fact that she graduated a year before I did, and we had geometry together.

She brought the food without saying anything about it, and that was fine with me.

As I ate my potatoes, I remembered all the reasons I'd stayed away.

I didn't like small towns. I didn't like being remembered. Trouble was, people in small towns remembered you because there was little else to do.

Not only did they remember you, but they had an opinion on you, or whatever you were doing. Or not doing. Living in a small town was like being followed by a Greek chorus who lamented your latest mishap. Maybe that was why God and I weren't close. He paid too much attention.

I didn't need a chorus. I didn't want a chorus. I wanted everyone to mind their own business. But I, of all people, knew that was simply too much to ask for.

"Looks like there's a nice view," Shane said, when we pulled up to the Sea Gypsy.

"And a close walk to the beach, if you don't mind the cold. Or the wind. Or the rain." Secretly, I didn't mind. But it hurt my anti-home image to say so.

Shane offered to carry my suitcase; I declined, choosing instead to lug it up the stairs myself. After sitting in the car for so long, the idea of physical exertion appealed to me.

"Reservation for Tate," I told the receptionist once we'd managed to schlep our belongings inside.

"First name?" the receptionist asked, looking to Shane.

"Last name," I corrected. "First name Jayne."

The receptionist bobbed her head and clicked her mouse. "Jayne Tate. Two double rooms." She left the computer to retrieve the keys from the back room.

"Two rooms?" Shane asked.

"Mm-hmm," I said, distracted by the one key on my keychain that refused to slide into the side pocket of my shoulder bag.

"I thought . . ."

"What was that?"

"I thought this was a getaway weekend."

"It is, kind of. We're seeing my family, but we're also away."

"I thought we'd be sharing a room."

"We'd be . . . oh." I stiffened. "But we've never . . ."

"I thought you might —"

"On a weekend to see my mother?"

"At the coast!"

"That's where she lives!"

"So who's paying?"

"What?"

"What if I wanted a different room?"

"I'm paying for it. I figured it was the least I could do for bringing you with me. If you want a different room, that's up to you. You just can't have mine."

"Shall I show you to your rooms?" The receptionist returned with our keys and either hadn't heard our conversation or should have been sent to Hollywood.

I grasped my suitcase. "Lead the way." I looked back to Shane. "What are you going to do? I can rent a car if I need to."

He frowned but shook his head. The receptionist started walking and he followed.

But he wouldn't look at me.

CHAPTER 20

Even after we found our rooms, Shane had no desire to speak with me. Maybe car rentals were in my future, not that I cared. I wasn't in the mood for one of Shane's tantrums.

Granted I'd thrown my own earlier . . . but if it's unflattering for a woman, it's worse for a man. Especially when it was about the subject of sex.

I hadn't slept with Shane. Ever. Even more, I had no intention of doing so unless we at least went through a legal civil ceremony first. Thing was, I'd spent the first eighteen years of my life living with my parents. And for better or for worse, my mother's voice resonated through my cranium whenever things became a bit . . . involved.

Why buy the cow when he can get the milk for free? If there's any sort of passion dampener, it's your mother comparing you to a cow. Until I was married, that voice wasn't going anywhere. Truthfully, I had concerns about it even then.

And here I was, back in Lincoln City, trying to make amends with the keeper of that voice.

I fished my phone out of my tote bag and dialed the home number.

No answer.

I tried her cell, bearing in mind that I had a fifty-fifty chance of her not hearing or noticing the ringing of her phone.

Nothing.

I hung up and chewed on my lip in frustration. Would Beth be around? I tried her number, which rang until a voice message announced that I could leave a message for Steve as long as I left my name and number.

Beth wasn't married to a Steve. She was married to a Gary.

Wow. I didn't even have my own sister's current number.

I didn't feel like sitting at the motel all day, and I had no deep desire to putter around and see the sights. I grew up here. The sights had been seen.

The reason I came was to see my mom. If I was serious, then I would do exactly that.

I got off the bed and left the room, walking down the corridor to Shane's door.

I knocked. He opened his door, still looking grumpy, his cell phone crunched between his ear and shoulder.

"I'll call you back," he said before hanging up.

"Hi."

"Hi." His voice sounded wary.

"I can't reach my mom or my sister over the phone. I don't want to sit around here all day. I'm just going to go to the house and see who's home."

"How are you getting there?"

"That's up to you. You can calm down and we can go together. Or you can go home and I'll rent a car."

"Harsh, Jayne."

"I don't think so," I said with a frown.

"Come inside. I don't want to argue in a breezeway."

I shrugged. "Up to you." I stepped inside and he closed the door.

"I've asked you this before." Shane pulled up a chair, sat, and leaned forward. "Are you serious about us?"

"I told you that I was. I asked you to come, to meet my family."

"I mean, are you wanting to take us to the next level?"

" 'The next level.' Makes us sound like Donkey Kong."

"You know what I mean."

"You're asking if I want to sleep with you."

"Well, yes."

"Haven't we already talked this to death?"

"I thought you were saying no because you weren't ready to commit to us."

"No, I was saying no because . . ." I sighed. "I was raised to believe in certain things, Shane. Even though I'm no longer that person, some of those concepts stuck."

"Concepts like . . ."

"Unmarried sex." The words came out in a whoosh. If he pressed any harder, I'd spill about my mother's voice and the whole thing could get very ugly.

His shoulders tightened. "Oh. You could have just said that."

"It makes me feel like Emily Brontë."

"And you won't change your mind?"

"Positive." My mother's voice could be very insistent.

"Do you want to get married?"

A vein of panic welled up inside me. "Ever?"

"In the nearer future."

"To you?"

"You think I'd ask you about someone else?"

I fought to keep Levi's face from my mind. "I don't know. I would like to get married, I think — someday. I haven't spent a whole lot of time thinking about it."

"We've been dating for six months!"

"I didn't know you were wife shopping!"

"I'm not —" he exhaled hard. "I'm not wife shopping."

"That's good, because I didn't mean for this trip to be an opportunity for you to offer my mother an assortment of goats for my hand in marriage."

A smile tugged at his lips. "Oh, I think you're worth at least a couple camels."

I may have kicked him.

"Stop checking your hair," Shane said, a minute after we pulled up in my mom's driveway.

"Her car is here."

"Good. That means she's home."

"And because she's here, she'll see me."

Shane's head quirked to the side. "Am I missing something?"

"She'll see me. She'll see if my hair is in place — or out of place. If I have excessive lint on my clothes or if I'm missing a button." I tugged on my blouse to inspect the front.

"You've got to relax, Jayne."

"This is my mother we're talking about!"

"Right. Your mother. She's not going to

throw anthrax in your face if you've got a scuff on your shoe."

"There's a scuff? Why didn't you say so earlier?"

"Your shoes are fine. That was just an example."

"*Why* would you say something like that?"

"You're really worried about this."

"Now that you mention it, yes, I am." I rolled my eyes.

"I've never seen you this dramatic."

"You've never met my mother." I gave my hair a final shove behind my ear and opened the car door, moving more on impulse than anything else.

I had decided this was the best course. I would move forward. Even if it was hard.

Even if it hurt.

I strode up to the front door, Shane trailing behind me. He reached for the doorbell but I slapped his hand back. "She doesn't like the doorbell being used."

"Then why is it still there?"

"Because it would look funny to not have a doorbell." I knocked on the door.

And waited. Nothing.

I knocked again.

Shane cleared his throat.

I folded my arms against my chest. "What?"

"Maybe you should ring the doorbell."

"She's home. She's somewhere."

"And you're going to knock until she hears you? Why wouldn't she have answered the phone?"

"Sometimes she doesn't hear it."

"But she hears knocking?"

"Not hearing her cell phone is because she leaves it in her purse and forgets about it. It's not like she carries it from room to room."

"But she has a landline, doesn't she?"

"If she's in the garage, she can't hear it."

Shane blinked. "So if she can't hear it, how will she hear you knocking on the door?"

"If she were in the garage, she wouldn't hear the doorbell, either. Do you need to go sit in the car?" I knocked a third time. Seriously. She had to be in there somewhere.

"Jayne —"

"Do you hear that? There's music playing. She's home."

And to prove it, I heard footsteps. The bolt creaked back and my mother unlocked the door.

"Jayne! This is a surprise," she said. "Have you been here long?"

She looked different since the last time I'd seen her. Grief still clung to the edges of

273

her eyes, but her hair was shorter now, and blond instead of gray. Had it been that way at the memorial and I hadn't noticed?

"We've just been a few minutes," I answered, hedging.

"I'm sorry I didn't hear you. I had the KitchenAid on. Come on in, both of you." She opened the door wide and extended her hand to Shane. "We haven't met — I'm Nora Tate."

Shane shook her hand, a bemused expression on his face. "Nice to meet you."

She patted his hand before leading us to the living room. "Sorry you were standing outside for so long — it's awfully drizzly out. You should have rung the doorbell."

"How long are you in town for?" Mom asked when she returned with tea and coffee.

I took the teacup she offered. "I have work on Monday, but I was hoping to stay until then."

"Do you have your bags with you? I can set you up upstairs."

"I, um, checked in down at the Sea Gypsy."

She froze, her gaze darting from me to Shane.

"In separate rooms." No use torturing her.

274

Mom tried a nonchalant shrug. "I didn't ask."

But she was thinking.

"It's up to you, but I have plenty of space for the both of you. If you'd like to stay here — it's entirely up to you."

I looked to Shane. He nodded. "That'd be really nice."

She beamed. "Excellent. Have you seen Beth yet?"

"No," I said, my face turning red. "I don't think I have her current number."

"She switched phone services. Why don't I give her a call? Do you have dinner plans?"

We said no, and I watched as my mother all but skipped to the phone to call Beth.

"What were you so worried about?" Shane set his coffee cup down. "Everything seems cool. Your mom even makes good coffee."

I smiled, thinking it was a comment Levi would have made. I forced myself back to the present. Standing, I walked around the living room and looked at the pictures sprinkled around the room.

Beth and me as little girls, dressed for Easter Sunday. Beth looking like a princess, me looking like a princess who would rather be the scullery maid. There was Beth's graduation photo, followed shortly by the wedding pictures, she and Gary smiling and looking so very young.

There were other photos I appeared in — my first day of kindergarten, that sort of thing. But after my graduation, there were no more photos.

I knew why. I had made it a point to not be available for photo ops.

There were other pictures I hadn't seen. Beth holding a newborn in her arms, a smiling Gary sitting on the edge of the hospital bed.

I knew I'd visited briefly weeks before the baby was born and sent a card shortly after. But there were moments I'd missed, moments I'd never get back. I always thought I was fine with that. Now . . . I wasn't so sure.

My mom came back to the room. "I just got off the phone with Beth. She and Gary are free tonight, so they'll be over soon. They'll bring little Emilee with them. I can't believe how fast she's growing up!"

"How old is she now?"

"Turning five next winter."

I think I might have sent her a birthday present. Once. I certainly wasn't in line for any "Auntie of the Year" awards.

"They'll be a little while, coming in from Neotsu," my mom continued. "If you like, you could check out of the motel and get settled in here."

A part of me hesitated. If things blew up over dinner, I wouldn't have anywhere to go.

However, it also meant that I would have to stay and sort out my problems.

Which was technically the reason for the trip.

"That sounds nice," I said.

"I'll go start dinner." She frowned. "You're not vegetarian, are you? Either of you?"

Shane emphatically shook his head.

"Excellent. When you get back, will you want your old room, Jayne?"

I shrugged. "Fine with me."

"And Shane, there's a bed in the sewing room."

"Sewing room?" I didn't know Mom sewed.

"Beth's old room." She sighed. "It'll be so nice to have everyone here. I just wish . . ."

Her voice trailed off, but I knew what she meant. She wished my father were there.

I didn't know if I could agree with her or not.

The receptionist gave us an odd look when we checked out. I imagine it looked a bit shady that we'd only checked in a little while ago, but we were in separate rooms, for Pete's sake. "My mom invited us to stay with her," I explained, trying to make the woman's expression go away.

"That's nice," she said, but the expression only slightly softened.

Back at my mom's house, she led us upstairs to the rooms, even though I'd grown up there. Maybe she thought I'd been gone so long I'd forgotten.

My room looked very little like I remembered. Granted, it had been eight years. My striped bedspread had left with me for university life. In its place was a floral-print quilt that coordinated with the soft green color of the walls. It was very soothing, very pretty. Made me think of my room at the Burkholders.

Speaking of the walls, they looked different than I remembered. Probably because ACDC no longer scowled down on anyone who walked in.

I went to check on Shane once I had put my bags down.

Beth's room really had been converted to a sewing room. Tubs of fabric lined a wall. Plastic sets of pull-out drawers held thread, scissors, and measuring tapes. A table against the wall held a massive sewing machine. Next to the machine sat a stack of . . .

"Quilt squares!" I rushed over to pick

them up. They looked so nice, so organized, their edges trimmed just so.

Shane came up behind me. "Explain to me what you'll do with them? Seeing as how you don't quilt . . ."

I narrowed my eyes at him. "Cut more squares so they'll be with friends."

"You just have stacks of quilt squares?"

"Aren't they nice?"

"Do you collect three-by-five cards too?"

"Shane —"

"Do you stack them as well? Or I guess you don't need to. They come out of the shrink-wrap that way."

"You're impossible."

"You like me that way."

I leaned over to give him a quick kiss. "Define like."

Shane deepened the kiss but pulled away when the doorbell rang. "That's probably your sister. *She* rang the doorbell."

I rolled my eyes and stepped away. "Seriously, the doorbell used to be very taboo in this house."

But it had changed. Obviously. I just wanted to know what other things — aside from our bedrooms — had changed as well.

CHAPTER 21

Shane and I headed downstairs, following the sound of people — chatter, the rustle of coats, Velcro, and zippers.

As we came into the entryway, I could see Beth, Gary, and Emilee. My little niece looked a lot larger than I'd imagined. I hadn't seen her at the memorial. Beth had elected to get a sitter rather than put a four-year-old through that.

Beth looked up. I smiled. Her chilly expression caused me to stop where I was. Shane nearly ran over me.

"Hi, Beth," I said, hoping that maybe her expression was an anomaly.

The corners of her mouth moved a fraction of an inch up. "Hi, Jayne."

"This is my boyfriend, Shane," I said, attempting to distract everyone. "Shane, this is Beth, my sister, and her husband, Gary." I flashed my most winning smile. "And Emilee is my niece."

Shane shook everyone's hand, charming as usual.

"Shane and Jayne?" Beth asked. "Do you date because you rhyme?"

I heard Gary chide his wife under his breath, but Shane jumped in before I could form a non-incendiary reply.

"More like, we date, therefore we are. I've always tried to be existential about my romantic relationships," he said, and because he's witty and charming, everyone but Beth laughed, even if they didn't understand.

Existentialistic humor not being for everyone.

"Dinner's going to be a little while," Mom said, taking coats to the hallway closet near the utility room. "Settle in and get comfortable."

"Do you need any help in the kitchen?" I asked. Sitting around in this crowd wasn't my idea of relaxing.

Mom stopped still. Beth stopped still. It's possible the earth froze in its orbit for a moment, at least until my mother caught her breath.

"I'd love help." My mom glanced at my brace. "Are you sure your wrist feels well enough?"

Beth snorted. I refused to look at her. "It's

nearly healed."

"I thought I'd put a pie together. Would you like to help with that?"

I could feel Beth's gaze shifting from me to Mom.

"I love pie."

"She can eat it, but she can't bake it," Beth mumbled, and I heard Gary mumble something back.

Shane squeezed my hand. I left for the kitchen.

"Do you have an apron I could borrow?" I asked, thinking for the first time that I might want an apron of my own. Not that I'd necessarily travel with it, but I kept going places and wanting one. At some point, I'd probably want one at home too.

My mom produced a flowered apron that triggered childhood memories of cookie frosting and postdinner dishes. I slipped it over my head and tied it behind my back

Something strange happened in that instant. Before the apron, a part of me felt out of place, like the object on Sesame Street that Big Bird would decide didn't belong. But after the apron — I felt more settled. More centered, as though I were back at the Burkholder farmhouse, with a garden in the back and a loose pig and children underfoot and everything in a state of rightness.

I measured out the flour the way Martha had taught me. I placed the measuring cup inside a slightly larger bowl, spooned the ingredient into the cup, then leveled off the top, all with my good arm.

I could feel my mom watching as I worked, but I didn't care. I was in my happy place. When Mom offered to help with the rolling, though, I didn't turn her down. Within minutes, the lower dough layer was in place in the bottom of the pie pan.

"What kind of pie are we making," I asked, fingering the edge of the crust.

"How does cherry sound?"

"I didn't know cherries were available," I said, thinking about how much more they would cost at the coast.

Mom raised a finger to her lips. "Don't tell Beth." She opened a cupboard and retrieved three cans of prepared cherry filling.

I stifled a laugh. I'd never known my mom to bake anything *not* from scratch. Even brownies never came from a box.

"I drain them, so there's less of the cherry syrup in the pie."

"Very clever." Feeling like a coconspirator, I helped open the cans and dumped their contents into the sieve in the sink. We gave the sieve a tiny shake, then emptied the ripe, sugar-coated cherries into the pie pan. I watched as my mom made a lattice top out of the remaining dough, cutting strips and laying them out just so.

When she finished, I went around and crimped the edges so that they waved in a perfect circle.

I let Mom put it in the oven.

She brushed the excess flour from her hands. "Do you bake often these days?"

"Not until recently."

"Oh?"

I ducked my head and smoothed my apron. "I, um, went to stay with an Amish family for a while."

"Really? What was that like?"

What was it like? How could I begin? "Hard to describe," I started, realizing I wasn't making any mental headway. "It's a society that makes so little sense to me. But there's something really beautiful about it."

"Will you go back to visit again?"

"I hope so."

And before I knew it, I was telling her about Martha and Sara, Gideon and the boys, about Leah and little Elizabeth. I told her about Ida, Naomi Zook, and her twins Mary Ellen and Becky, little Doyle and Baby Ruby.

Woven throughout their stories was the ever-present Levi, whose face had followed me ever since I left the farm.

I told her more than I had told anyone, even Gemma. I didn't know why, either. I had never been one of those girls who had been able to confide in her mother. When I was a teen, I thought she'd criticize me for what I said.

"Tell me more about this Levi," Mom said when I was through. She stood at the stove, stirring a sauce. "He sounds like an interesting fellow."

I listened for a quick moment for Shane and the others in the living room. Shane was saying something, Gary was laughing.

"Levi . . . is a puzzle. He left the Amish to use his mind, and then he left his corporate job to be back near them. He could befriend anyone."

"Like Shane?"

Shane would befriend, yes, but name-call later. "Yes. And no. They're different."

"How long have you and Shane been seeing each other?"

"Six months."

"Is he serious?"

"Yes."

"Are you?"

The chatter in the living room died down.

I shrugged, rather than incriminate myself audibly.

"The sauce is done, and I think the roast is too. The pie will bake through dinner. Shall we call everyone in?"

"How's the pie?" Shane asked when I returned to the living room.

"Cheery cherry."

"Cherry?" Beth's eyebrows lifted in surprise. "Where'd Mom get cherries this time of year?"

"She has her ways, I guess," I answered with a straight face. "Dinner's ready, if you'd all like to come in to eat."

"I don't think I heard," Beth started, pointing at my arm, "how you wound up with a brace."

I opted for the condensed version. "I fell down."

"Out of nowhere?"

The Beth I grew up with never pressed this hard. Somewhere along the line, she had become quite a pain. A pain with a backbone.

"There was a short trashcan involved."

"Was that at the Amish house?" Shane asked.

"No. It was . . . in town."

Gary chuckled. "There's a lawsuit waiting

to happen."

Hmm, I didn't like where this was going. I pointed to the dining room. "Dinner — hot — in there. Good stuff."

"Is the pie sanitary?" Beth asked innocently.

I saw Gary give her a dirty look.

"It should be," I said with a straight face. "At least, once the E. coli cooks out."

Shane snorted.

"Who's Ecoli?" little Emilee asked, the first time I'd heard her speak.

She had a sweet little voice. Reminded me of Naomi's twins. Come to think of it, they were about the same age.

"Don't worry about it, honey," Gary told his daughter. "E. coli is a kind of germ, but there won't be any in your pie. Your aunt was just joking."

"Where is everyone?" Mom called from the dining room. "Dinner won't be hot forever!"

"Coming!" I called, walking in her direction and willing everyone else to follow suit.

I could hear Beth and Gary arguing softly behind me, but their voices never seemed far away, which I took as a good sign. Shane came up beside me and squeezed my hand.

I squeezed it back.

"Shall we pray?" Mom asked, once we'd

287

all settled at the table. "Gary, would you like to pray for us?"

"We should check with Jayne first," Beth said.

My stomach sank.

"Is it all right if we pray?" she asked me, her voice heavy with sarcasm. "It won't disagree with your religion, will it?"

"Beth —" Mom warned.

"We don't know if it would offend her, Mother. We've seen so little of her. She could be Baha'i by now. Or Buddhist. Are you Buddhist, Jayne?"

"What is your problem, Beth?" I asked, crossing my arms. "I'm here. Need to get something off your chest? I don't want you to wear yourself out. Potshots can be exhausting."

"I can't believe you!"

"What can't you believe?"

Gary pulled Emilee's chair back out. "Honey, why don't you go play upstairs for a little while? The grown-ups need to talk."

Beth reached to still Emilee's chair. "She needs to eat, Gary."

"She doesn't need to hear you —"

"Hear me what? It's past her normal dinnertime."

Gary lifted Emilee from the chair. "There's a granola bar in your bag. That should tide her over."

With that, Gary and Emilee retreated to safety upstairs.

I knew exactly how they felt.

"I can't believe you'd not visit for three years, barely show up at Dad's memorial, and then waltz back here like nothing was wrong. Did you notice how Mom's lost twenty pounds in the last month? Who helped take care of Mom when Dad was in the hospital? Who brought her meals? Who organized the caterer for the memorial, made the phone calls, wrote the thank-you cards for the bouquets?"

"I'm sorry, Beth." I struggled to keep my voice steady. "You want to know why I came? I came because I didn't like the way things were. Because I wanted to try, *try,* to make things right."

"Why didn't you try five years ago? Did it occur to you that you might be five years too late?"

"Beth, that's enough!" Mom chided sharply. "If you can't be pleasant, you can leave."

"Let me answer, Mom." I looked back to Beth. "I did consider that it was probably *eight* years too late, but I wanted to try anyway."

"What if," she said, "I wanted a sister that

whole time?"

I sighed. "What if I did too?"

"I was here! We all were!"

"You didn't want a sister who was a reporter in Portland. You wanted a sister who could look through children's clothing catalogs with you. I couldn't do that."

"No. Instead, you ran away to the big city, doing big-city things so important that you didn't need us anymore."

The room at the Sea Gypsy called my name, but I remained in my seat. "I'm sorry, Beth. I don't know what to tell you. I'm trying. I'm doing what I can. The rest is up to you."

Beth closed her mouth, though she looked as though she had a lot of words still hanging around on the tip of her tongue. When she finally spoke, her voice was controlled.

"Would someone please pass the peas?"

"The pie was good," Shane said, settling himself on the floor next to the couch where I was stretched out.

"The cherries were canned."

"They were good."

"The crust wasn't as buttery as Martha's."

"Martha . . ."

"Burkholder."

"Right, the Amish lady. Just use more butter next time."

"You don't use butter in pie crust."

"Then how . . . never mind."

"My sister hates me."

"She doesn't hate you."

"Where's my mom?"

"Talking to Beth outside."

I groaned and buried my face in a throw pillow with an appliqué butterfly. "It's like we're six years old again."

"I can't understand you when you talk into pillows."

"Sorry." I lifted my face. "I said it's like we're six years old again, and we need Mommy and Daddy to help us get along. Never mind she's married with a kid and I'm a working professional. We're not adult enough to work this out."

"She's not adult enough. You were amazing in there. I just about took her out when she started choking on the pie."

"If the crust had come out like Martha's, she wouldn't have."

"The only way she wouldn't have is if Martha had made the pie. The pie had nothing to do with it. It was the fact that you made it."

"You're a whiz at making me feel better."

"Just saying."

I heard the front door close and a single

set of footsteps walking in our direction.

I was glad it was only one, that Mom hadn't made Beth come in and make an attempt at an apology.

"You all right there?" Mom took a seat in the chair next to me.

"I'm fine." I turned my face away from the pillow when I spoke. If Mom caught me accidentally drooling on that butterfly, that could have been the end of things.

"Jayne, well . . . give Beth time. She'll get over it."

I didn't believe her, but I chose not to argue.

"Heaven knows you're both too stubborn for your own good. You take after your father that way."

I masked my wince with a cough.

"I'm sorry the night went the way it did," Mom continued. "I was so glad you came. I just wanted it to be special."

I pushed myself up. "Beth's right. I've been gone, and I haven't been much of a daughter or sister for the past several years. I never expected to show up and have everyone welcome me with open arms."

"Well, you're welcome here anytime. Both you and Shane," she said, nodding in his direction. "Anytime."

I got up then, and gave her a hug. She

hugged me back. I shoved my hair from my face. "It's good to be home."

CHAPTER 22

Mom made smiley pancakes for breakfast, though they weren't served that way. The fruit had been rearranged into a more sophisticated arrangement in the middle — but the red juice from the strawberries and raspberries left their indelible mark on the surface.

She had started making me a smiley pancake and thought better of it. It made me a little sad; I think I would have enjoyed a breakfast that grinned back.

But it probably would have weirded Shane out if he too had received such a breakfast, and it would have been unfair if they didn't match.

Thus the rearranged fruit.

Mom sat down a few moments later.

"Do you both have plans for the day?" she asked, cutting into her own elegantly topped pancake.

Shane and I looked at each other. "Not

particularly," I answered. "Although I thought about taking Shane to Kyllo's for lunch."

"Oh," Mom said with a nod. "Kyllo's is nice."

I played with the edge of my black sweater for a moment before I asked the question I really wanted the answer to. "So . . . I saw some quilt squares in Beth's old room."

Shane snorted and covered it with a cough. Anyone under the age of five might have been fooled.

"Anyway," I continued, flashing a warning glare at my boyfriend, "I was wondering . . . do you quilt?"

"I do." Mom took a sip of her coffee. "I started a few years ago when I bought that sewing machine. Why?"

"I went to a quilting bee when I was staying at the Burkholders'."

"Really? An Amish quilting bee? What was that like?"

"Crazy. A lot of women and a lot of quilts." I though for a moment about Rachel, Levi's perfect ex-girlfriend. I wondered what she was doing.

Probably cleaning something.

"That must have been fascinating."

"It was. Sara — the teenager — taught me how to cut quilt squares. She wanted

295

me to do something useful."

"Good idea."

Shane choked again. I turned to him. "I hope you're not coming down with something. You seem to be having trouble swallowing. Airway closing up?"

Shane wisely returned to his breakfast.

"She taught me to cut quilt squares, and I kinda got hooked on it. Except I don't know what to do with them now."

"You just keep cutting squares?"

"Yes."

"How many do you have?"

In truth, I didn't know. After breakfast we went upstairs and counted through the bag I'd brought. Mom counted one-half, I counted the other. After several moments, I put my stack down. "I have fifty-two."

Mom fingered through the last of hers. "This is tricky . . . I should have gotten my reading glasses."

"You have reading glasses?"

"They're a part of life at my age."

"Oh. I don't think of you as being of the age that would need reading glasses."

She gave a soft smile. "That's very sweet of you."

Another few moments passed before Mom set her stack down. "I have forty-seven here. You've been busy."

"Ninety-nine? I cut ninety-nine squares?"

"You could have Shane count to check."

No, thank you. "I had no idea. I wasn't paying attention most of the time." I looked up at her. "What should I do with them?"

"First," she said, "I think you should cut one more so you have an even hundred."

"Oh. Is one hundred a better number to have in quilting?"

"No. I just thought you might like to be able to say you cut a hundred squares."

"True." I smiled. "I can do that. I have fabric in my room."

"You're welcome to mine. It's all going to be cut up, anyway."

"Oh. Thank you."

"After that, I think you should make a quilt."

"Really?" My mind reeled. Me? Make a quilt? "But there . . . there isn't enough, is there?"

"You don't have to make a full-sized quilt. You could make a lap quilt or a throw."

"Oh." I mulled it over in my head. "Hmm. I never thought of that."

"You won't know how large it'll be until you piece it together."

"Oh." I fingered the squares. "I have no idea how to do that."

Mom smiled. "I think I could pitch in a bit."

"My stomach's growling," Shane called from down the hall.

"I know, I heard." I pinned another square onto the fabric amoeba on the floor.

"I'm really hungry."

"That's nice."

"We should give the boy a break and get him some food, don't you think?" Mom said, pinning a square before straightening. I heard her spine crack.

"I guess." I put the straight pin I'd been holding back onto the metallic pin base.

"I might pass out," Shane's voice sounded fainter than before.

"You're such a drama queen!"

I try not to reward such behavior, but when he's that whiny, there's not much to do but feed him.

We invited Mom to join us and ended up driving her car, since the last time Shane sat in the backseat of my car there was a lot of sighing and comments about cramped toes.

A deluge of memories filled my brain as we pulled into the parking lot. "I don't know if I told you," I said to Shane, "but I used to waitress here."

"Oh, yeah?"

"Yeah. It's kind of a Lincoln City thing. About everyone under thirty has either worked here, at Salishan, or been in construction."

"As in plastic surgery?"

I swatted his arm. "Houses. Condos. You know what I mean."

"What's Salishan?"

"A spa and golf resort south of here."

The hostess who seated us did not look familiar, thank goodness. We settled into our cozy booth and eyed the menu.

Shane studied his. "I'm impressed."

"I thought you would be."

I had almost relaxed when our waitress arrived.

"Jayne?"

I looked up. My heart sank. "Gretchen! Wow."

We hadn't seen each other since graduation. We were best friends in middle school, slightly less so in high school. After graduation and my leaving for college, we lost track.

Or rather, I lost track. I think she had tried to email me a few times, but I was busy with school and not particularly desirous of maintaining a connection to home.

"How have you been?" she asked, her eyes

brimming with curiosity. She probably thought I'd run away with the circus.

"Jayne's been working as a reporter for the *Oregonian*," my mom answered.

I turned to look at her, surprised at the pride in her voice.

"Really?"

"She's written some terrific features in the last few months."

My mom read my work?

"That's so exciting!"

"This is my boyfriend, Shane," I said, collecting myself.

"Nice to meet you," Gretchen extended her hand. "Jayne and I went to high school together."

"What have you been up to?" I asked, feeling as though I had to return the question.

Gretchen shrugged. "This and that. I've been making jewelry lately, but this pays the bills. I'm so glad to run into you! I heard your dad passed away recently — I'm really sorry about that."

"Thanks." I didn't know what else to say.

"So cool to see you. Can I get you guys started with drinks?"

After lunch Shane and I dropped Mom off at the house, bundled up, and drove down to the beach for a walk.

"Why haven't you visited?" Shane asked, taking in the coastline. "The food's good, the people are friendly. You had friends here."

"I had to get away."

"Your mom is great. I wish my mom was as laid-back as yours."

"You never met my father."

"True, but how bad could he be?"

"I frankly have no memory of him telling me he loved me. As a child, as a teen, as an adult. Not that I gave him much opportunity later on, but maybe he could have left it as a voice mail message."

"Never?"

"Maybe when I was a toddler, but my memory doesn't stretch back that far."

"I'm sorry."

I sighed. "I am too."

Beth was not invited to dinner that night. "I hope everyone likes lasagna," Mom said when we returned.

"Mom makes a mean lasagna," I told Shane.

"I don't think there's a man alive who doesn't like lasagna." Shane clapped his hands together. "Sounds good."

"The lactose-intolerant ones are probably a bit leery."

"They probably are."

An hour later, Shane and I helped set the table. Mom brought the food out, and we sat down to a much quieter, drama-free dinner.

Until halfway through. Mom said, "Church is tomorrow. Were you two interested in coming along?"

I froze.

I had a million memories of sitting in that sanctuary and not being able to sit still enough. Not wearing the right clothes. Not paying close enough attention to the sermon to be able to answer the questions my father asked afterward.

"Miss Lynnie will be there. I'm sure she'd like to see you."

"Miss Lynnie's still alive?"

Shane asked, "Who's Miss Lynnie?"

"My kindergarten Sunday school teacher." I put my hand to my chest. "I can't believe she's still alive!"

"Ninety-six last December."

"Wow." I sat for a moment and basked in happy Miss Lynnie memories. I turned to Shane. "Imagine the sweetest, tiniest old lady in the world. I think half the reason we liked her was because she was about our height. She always told us that when she went to heaven, she wanted her job to be bathing the little babies."

"Babies in heaven get dirty?"

"Even if they weren't, I think God would let her wash them," I said. "I don't know that even He could deny her that."

I thought for a moment. Most of the time I didn't spend a lot of time thinking about God or believing in heaven, but I believed, with all my heart, that when Miss Lynnie passed away she would be in heaven bathing those babies. I didn't want to believe that someone like Miss Lynnie would simply cease to exist.

A part of me wanted to believe better, so that I could join Miss Lynnie and hand her the soap, if they use soap in heaven.

"I'd like to go. I haven't seen Miss Lynnie in ages." I turned to Shane. "Would you like to come too?"

"I'm probably due for a trip."

Mom gave the gentlest of smiles. "Attending church isn't like a dental cleaning."

"It's not? Could've fooled me," he said with a chuckle. "Pass the salad?"

I spent Sunday morning in a panic. What did people wear to church these days? I mean, I knew now what Amish people wore to Amish church, but I didn't think that counted.

303

"You know, it makes it tricky to get out of my room when quilt squares are every-where," I heard Shane grouse down the hall.

"The quilt is at a very delicate stage right now," I said. I didn't know if that was true or not, but his whining was annoying me and I decided he could take it.

In the end I decided on gray trousers and a soft, black wool wrap sweater. I paired it with a red, five-strand beaded necklace that Gemma gave me for Christmas the year before.

I even paid attention to my makeup that morning.

Shane whistled when he saw me. "You look nice."

"Thanks."

"You've been dressing snappier since you went to stay with the Amish."

"It's what happens when a teen in an apron critiques your wardrobe. And I don't think you're supposed to whistle at a woman before church."

"Probably not." He leaned over for a kiss. "Are you ready?"

"Did you smudge my lipstick?"

"You're wearing lipstick?" He rubbed at his lips. "Am I wearing lipstick?"

"There's a bit of shimmer, but it suits you."

"Gross!" He pulled an about-face and all but ran for the bathroom mirror.

"Hurry up!" I called, walking downstairs.

Mom stood in the living room, Bible in hand. "You look lovely," she said, looking up as Shane descended. "Both of you."

"Thanks." I gave her a hug.

The drive to the church was quiet. In truth, my heart pounded. "Will Beth be there?" I asked.

"She might be." Mom turned on the car's blinker. "We didn't discuss if they'd be there today or not."

I sighed, but I reasoned in my head that being in church would give Beth cause to at least keep her voice down while she ripped my head off.

She couldn't kill me during a sermon or worship. There would be witnesses.

The inside of the sanctuary was as beautiful as I remembered, the wood paneling glowing in the pale morning light.

I didn't see Beth or Gary. We followed Mom to where my family sat traditionally, four rows back on the right-hand side.

The worship music was in full swing, and I realized I had been gone so long I didn't know many of the songs.

I also realized Shane couldn't sing. His pitch was approximate rather than accurate, and if I didn't know better I'd wonder if his voice was still changing.

I'd never known that about him before.

We followed along with the projected PowerPoint slides as best we could. People weren't turning and staring the way I'd feared, only singing.

In Shane's case, singing badly.

Halfway through "Here I Am to Worship" I heard a rustling to our right as people slid into our row.

I turned to see Beth and Gary clutching their Bibles and rain gear. I waved a hand and smiled, hoping for the best.

Beth waved back. The expression in her eyes could only be described as hope.

CHAPTER 23

Or maybe her expression wasn't hope, but indigestion. You know, when you eat breakfast right before church, it can do funky things to you. I didn't want to get my hopes up. As much as I wanted things to be okay between me and Beth, I was a realist.

I'd never known my sister to make a decision or change her mind with anything resembling speed. She dated Gary for two years. The engagement lasted another year, partly because she couldn't pick a wedding date for the first six months. The likelihood of her deciding in thirty-six hours that I wasn't the cause of the breakdown of the American family and global warming was fairly low.

I said hello to her and Gary after the service. She didn't bite my head off. No barbs, no snarky comments.

So as not to test my luck, I spotted Miss Lynnie in the back and made a run for it before Beth could change her mind.

Miss Lynnie greeted me with the biggest smile I'd ever seen.

"Look at you, all grown up," she said, reaching up to pat my cheek. "Are you busy doing big things in the world?"

I gave her a careful hug. She smelled the way she always had — of lavender and Jean Nate bath powder. "I think so," I said.

"I thought you would. You were always a special girl. Are you loving your Lord and Savior with your work?"

My mouth opened and closed for a moment as I tried to figure out how to answer that. Was it possible to love God through reporting?

"I hope so," I said, feeling that answer was positive and yet vague enough not to get me into too much trouble.

She gave me a knowing look. "I hope so too. Now, tell me, who is that handsome young man? He looks like he knows you."

I turned to find Shane lurking a few feet away. "Miss Lynnie would like to meet you." I gestured for him to come closer.

Shane stepped forward and offered his hand to the tiny woman. She took it and gave it a pat. "What's your name, young man?"

"Shane Colvin."

"Do you love Jesus?"

"I . . ." Shane paused, clearly taken aback by Miss Lynnie's directness. I didn't remember her being so direct. Must have been old age. "I have a great deal of respect for Him," he said finally.

"That's very nice," she said, still patting his hand. "But so do the demons in hell."

Shane forced a polite smile. "It's very nice to meet you." He turned to me. "I'll be waiting in the car."

Miss Lynnie did not seem sad to see him go. "Mark my words, Jayne dear. Marry someone who loves the Lord."

I said goodbye to Miss Lynnie and headed out for the car. Shane was standing beside it, hugging his coat to protect himself from the fine, chilly drizzle.

"I realized I don't have a key."

"I'm sorry."

"Your Sunday school teacher just told me I'm condemned to eternity in the underworld."

"She's a ninety-six-year-old Sunday school teacher. What did you expect?"

"You just stood there!"

"What was I going to say? I didn't want to upset her — she's fragile. She could go at any moment."

"Can we leave, please?"

"I don't have a key either."

"We should have taken my car."

Mom emerged from the church moments later, followed by Beth, Gary, and Emilee.

"Beth's joining us for lunch," Mom said.

"Oh. Okay. Good."

"We can't stay long," Beth said. "Emilee needs her nap."

"No, I don't." Emilee twirled under her father's hand. "I don't need a nap."

"Yes, you do, little girl," Gary said, picking up his daughter. "We'll see you at the house?"

Mom unlocked the car; Shane all but leaped inside.

"Don't worry." Mom nodded to me after the doors were closed. "I talked to Beth. She said she'll be on her best behavior."

"I wasn't worried," I lied.

At lunch we rolled out leftovers from the previous two nights, the microwave buzzing away and bringing renewed life to the lasagna and pork roast.

I helped Emilee with her lunch while Beth talked to Mom and Shane chatted with Gary.

"Would you like potatoes?" I asked

Emilee nodded.

"Broccoli?"

Emilee shook her head.

"Would your mom like you to eat broccoli?" I said, turning to Beth.

Beth looked at Emilee. "Two pieces. Two baby trees."

I picked out two from the Rubbermaid container. "Two baby trees, coming right up."

Emilee wrinkled her nose. "I don't like baby trees."

"They're good for you. Broccoli helps your eyes to see well and helps prevent colon cancer."

She looked back at me, blankly.

"Broccoli will help you to stay healthy and maintain a svelte, princess-like figure."

"Broccoli will make me look like a princess?"

I chose my words carefully. "You already look like a princess," I said, "but eating broccoli will help you to keep looking like a princess, even when you're a grown-up." *When you're a grown-up, and your hormones are out to get you.*

She stood up on her tiptoes and examined the broccoli spears on her plate. "I want three."

Beth stepped in. "I want three, *please.*"

"Please!"

I placed another broccoli floret on her plate.

Lunch passed companionably. Emilee ate all of her broccoli. When she started getting a bit cranky, Beth asked Mom if she could take a nap in the sewing room.

"Maybe Jayne's old room would be better," Mom said. "Jayne and I have a quilt on the floor of the sewing room."

"A quilt?" Beth's eyebrow lifted. She turned to me. "You quilt?"

"I cut quilt squares. Haven't actually made a quilt yet."

"You will," Mom said before taking a sip of ice water.

"When are you coming back to visit?" Beth asked.

I paused. When was I planning on visiting again? I hadn't contemplated the possibility of a return; I didn't think anyone would want me to. "Um . . ." I stalled. "I'll have a lot of work to catch up on come Monday morning."

Mom's and Beth's faces fell.

"But," I continued, "I don't see any reason why I couldn't come out weekend after next."

They both brightened.

Mom took a satisfied bite of lasagna. "The guest room is always available for you."

"Unless Emilee's napping in it," Beth said drily, "but it wouldn't be longer than a two-hour delay."

Everyone laughed.

"Why is that funny?" Emilee asked, sending everyone in chuckles all over again.

After lunch Mom and I cleared the plates while Beth put Emilee down for a nap upstairs. Gary and Shane settled in the den in front of a baseball game.

When the kitchen was cleared, Mom and I went back to work on the quilt while Beth offered her two cents about the layout and design of the squares.

I packed up my things after Emilee woke, cranky and fuzzy, from her nap. Shane carried my suitcase down to the car with minimal grousing while I hugged everyone goodbye. My heart melted when Emilee wrapped her arms around my neck, kissed my cheek, and said, "Goodbye, Auntie Jayne!"

Mom promised to take good care of my quilt squares in my absence. Beth gave me a hug and didn't utter a single insult, even professing to be looking forward to seeing me next.

Shane and Gary exchanged man hugs, with a good deal of thumping on the back for extra measure.

I retreated to the car as my eyes grew damp; I didn't want to leave.

I sighed as Shane drove around the corner and the house completely left my sight. "That was wonderful."

Shane nodded. "Yeah. Gary's a cool guy. Things seemed like they went better with your sister today. And your mom . . . she makes a really good lasagna."

"What about little Emilee? She's so cute."

"Yeah. She's a great kid."

"You know, I never really thought I'd want to do the kid thing. I mean, kids, you know, they ooze, they smell, they're terrible communicators. Why would someone create them on purpose? But then I meet Naomi's kids and Baby Ruby, and now little Emilee. Even if they don't have a complete vocabulary, they're excellent at showing how they feel. They're better at body language than, I don't know, a mime."

"A mime?"

"Or something like that. They're very expressive." I turned to him. "I never thought I'd want kids. But now I think I do."

I almost missed how Shane's hands tightened on the steering wheel.

"We've never talked about kids before," he said.

"No, I don't think so."

"I like kids, don't get me wrong. I've just never wanted any of my own."

"Even a little girl like Emilee?"

"No."

His words started to sink in. "You really don't want children, do you?"

"I don't."

I turned to stare out the window.

We didn't speak again until we were nearly back to my apartment.

"Jayne, what do you think about us?"

I looked at him. "I . . . I like us. I like you."

"Where do you see us in the future?"

I tried to imagine us dating for another year — I could visualize that. After dating though . . .

"What I'm trying to say is, do you *want* to marry me?"

My eyes widened. "Are you proposing?"

"I'm asking. Sometime in the future, do you want to be married to me?"

"You don't want children? Not ever?"

"No."

Miss Lynnie's words floated back to me. *Marry someone who loves the Lord.* I couldn't begin to call myself a good Christian, although I had asked Jesus into my heart two decades ago. As much as I liked

Shane . . .

"I don't think I could marry you," I said, in sudden realization.

He sighed. "I didn't think so."

"It's not just the kids," I blurted out in a rush. "It's . . ."

He held up a hand. "I know. The church thing. I thought you were over that."

Believe me, I thought I was too. "Being with the Amish — it made me realize things about myself. About my life."

"I noticed. Quilting?"

I gave a half smile. "I know. Who saw that coming?"

"Not me."

"So . . . are we breaking up?"

"I think . . . yes."

"Huh." I ran a hand through my hair. "I feel like one of us should be yelling or something."

"You yelled a couple days ago."

"We didn't break up a couple days ago."

"I think we both saw this coming."

All I could think of was Levi. "Maybe."

Shane and I broke up so graciously, Nora Ephron would have been proud. He drove me to my apartment and helped me carry up my luggage. I found a couple of his books that had been lurking on my own shelves, as well as a jacket he'd left behind a few months prior.

He promised to bring over my copy of Ken Burns' *Jazz,* my volt meter (for my motorcycle battery), and the fleece blanket I'd loaned to his couch since his apartment ran so cold.

I gave him a hug. He leaned in for one last kiss and I couldn't turn away.

He rested his forehead against mine when the kiss ended. "I loved you, you know."

I laid a finger on his chin. "I know."

I just hadn't loved him back.

After Shane left, I lay down on my couch and stared at the ceiling.

Huh. I hadn't been single for so long, I'd forgotten what it was like.

For starters, Shane wouldn't be calling to make plans with me anymore. True, he had a few things he needed to bring by, but we weren't headed to dinner and a movie anytime soon.

Interesting.

I unpacked my bags, really and truly this time, taking care to check my garments for damage and wear. After starting a load of laundry, my stomach rumbled. I walked to the kitchen to investigate the food situation.

I shouldn't have been surprised. My

freezer was full of labeled leftovers from Martha. My pantry was more full than I'd ever seen it.

On a whim, I picked up the phone and called Gemma, Joely, and Kim. "I have tons of food," I said. "Come over and eat with me."

Somehow, everyone was available. Joely was the first to arrive. "Look at you with your all-weather wrist brace! You look great. And I've never seen your apartment this clean."

"Yeah, I decided the open sewage finally needed to be taken care of."

"You survived the Amish okay?"

"They were wonderful. Challenging, but wonderful."

"You called just in time. I just got off my shift and I'm starving."

"Did you break speed laws getting here?"

Joely had the grace to turn a bit pink. "I was really hungry."

Kim and Gemma showed up shortly after. "Where's this food I was hearing about?" Kim asked, seeing that I hadn't really taken anything out.

"I was waiting for you. It's in the freezer."

With Gemma's help, I had dinner on the table in fifteen minutes.

"I just can't believe how clean everything

is," Kim said between bites.

I rolled my eyes. "It's not like this place was a safety hazard or anything."

"But it wasn't this . . . this *spotless,*" Gemma said. "The backsplash of the sink is clean, and the ridge around your sink has been cleaned with a toothbrush."

I grimaced. "How can you tell?"

"That's the only way I know of to get the ridge to look that way, unless the Amish know something I don't. I'm assuming Martha — was that her name?"

"Yup."

"I'm assuming Martha was cleaning up. Unless you decided to hire someone."

"You don't think I'm capable of being this clean by myself?"

Gemma, Kim, and Joely broke out into simultaneous laughter.

I rolled my eyes. "Flattering. Thank you."

"It's just not your style," Gemma said. "You're more comfortable. Lived in. You've never been obsessive about tidiness."

"And that makes me a slob?"

"No," said Kim, "cluttered."

"We're only pointing it out," Joely said. "It's not like my place is all that clean. There are parts of my bathroom that will probably get up and walk away someday."

Gemma grimaced. "Gross. That's why I

never use the bathroom at your place."

I clapped my hands over my ears. "Too much information!"

"Changing the subject," Kim said, holding out her hand. "Have you seen Shane since you got back?"

I shifted in my seat. Now was as good a time as ever to tell them.

"I did. We actually went to visit my mom this weekend."

"That's nice. A little weekend getaway?" Kim asked.

"Something like that. But we, ah, we broke up."

Kim put her fork down. "You broke up at your mom's?"

"On the way back."

"So who dumped who?" Joely asked.

"Whom," Kim corrected.

"It was mutual." I swished the water around in my glass. "Anybody want anything else to drink?"

"I never liked Shane," Kim offered.

"Well, not dating him anymore."

"Any plans, now that you're free?" Gemma had a glint in her eye.

I knew exactly what she was referring to, even if she wasn't going to come out and say it.

"Oh, catch up on work." I kept my voice

light and vague. "I've been gone so long, things will be crazy."

Gemma's eyes danced with questions, but she didn't say a word.

Which was fine, because I wasn't about to tell.

CHAPTER 24

I actually made myself breakfast the next morning before work. Before I went to stay with the Burkholders, I seldom ate a morning meal.

Martha had spoiled me with biscuits and hash browns and bright yellow eggs. In her absence I fed on leftovers and cereal.

Since my little dinner party the night before, I'd made a decision. I was going to try to keep the apartment in its post-Amish state.

Along with that, I was going to learn to cook, bake, and quilt. If the Amish could do it, I could do it.

I had to stop myself from clapping my hands over my ears as I sat at my work computer. Since when was the newsroom so loud? People talking, people working. Brian typed loud. Laura, two cubicles away, was still complaining about her sunburn and the resulting peeling skin on her face.

I jumped when my phone rang. It was Sol, wanting to see me in his office.

In five.

The whole thing felt very familiar.

"Jayne," Sol said when I walked in. "You look good. Rested."

I sat down. "Thanks."

"How are things?"

"Broke up with my boyfriend."

He winced. "But you're fine?"

"It was mutual."

His face relaxed. "Good."

For a second there I think he was contemplating firing me. I mean, it's not like I was going to take two mental health breaks in one month. That's what unemployment was for.

"While I was gone," I said, "I stayed with an Amish family in Albany."

"Really." Sol leaned back in his chair. There are days I'm surprised he doesn't fall over altogether.

"I thought there might be a story there."

He shook his head. "I put you on mandatory leave and you went story chasing?"

Um, yeah.

"I should be surprised," he said with a sigh. "But I'm not. Go on. Did you get a story?"

I reached into my briefcase, retrieved the printout of the story I'd written, and plopped it on its desk.

The pages splayed with a satisfying *slap*.

Sol lifted them from his desk. "Did you pick up your flair for the dramatic from the Amish?"

"Just read it," I answered.

"I don't have my reading glasses."

I saw them at the corner of his desk and handed them over.

"Thanks." He settled them on the bridge of his nose and started reading.

He didn't talk while he read. When he finished, he flipped through the pages again before tapping them onto the desk to align the sheets.

"Aside from a split infinitive near the end, this is good." He tapped the pages against the desk once more. "Really good."

"Thank you."

"You've got your groove back, Tate."

I grinned. "I'd hoped you'd say that."

"We'll run it Saturday after next. Human interest. You changed the names, right?"

"I did."

"Good. Don't want any issues with Legal."

"There won't be."

"Until then, there's an urban garden southeast of town that's been vandalized several times despite security upgrades."

"Security at an urban garden? Aren't those things pretty open?"

"They are until people dig up plants and spray paint racial slurs on the fencing."

"I'm on it."

"Your piece looked good. Glad to see you're back."

"I'm glad too," I said before retreating to my cubicle.

I collapsed on my couch after work. The busyness of the day had sapped every last bit of energy from my body. I fought the urge to pull the afghan over my head.

Because that would just be silly.

Instead, I channel-flipped for a while until I realized I'd left my jacket, purse, and keys in the entryway, and if Martha had seen it, she would have cleaned it up by now.

I hoisted myself up from the couch, hung my jacket up in the hallway closet, and looked around for a place to put my purse.

There was the chair, and I could place it there to look artful, but then it might lead to other things being dumped on the chair.

I needed a hook or a shelf of some sort. Or a shelf with hooks under it. Maybe Levi could make me a shelf with hooks underneath. Nice, large hooks, suitable for wom-

en's motorcycle accessories.

After all, he'd promised to make me a bookcase. Maybe he could make me a shorter bookcase and a shelf.

With hooks. Couldn't forget the hooks. They were the most important part.

But until that day when such a shelf magically appeared (whether through Levi or Home Depot), I set my purse on the floor of the hallway closet, tucking my keys inside my jacket and removing my phone before I closed the closet door.

I flipped my phone open. One missed call. One new message. I lifted the phone to my ear to listen.

I almost dropped the phone when I heard Levi's voice.

"Jayne," he said, sounding (let's face it) devastatingly sexy in the process, "two things. I wanted to talk to you about the bookcase. It's almost done. Wondered if there was any way you'd be able to give it a once-over before I finish up. Or I could send pictures, I guess, so I'd need your email address. Secondly, Sara would like to write to you but realized she doesn't have your mailing address. I think I remember what street you're on, but not the apartment number. Give me a call if you have a moment and I'll pass that on to her. And your email address, if you want pictures. Or let me know when you can stop by, if that works out. I know it's a long drive. Just let me know."

I snapped my phone closed.

Levi had called.

I flipped it back open.

Closed.

Open.

Closed.

Open. Who was I to deny Sara my mailing address?

"Jayne? Thanks for calling me back!"

"You're, um, you're welcome. Anytime. I mean, I got your message. And I'd love it if Sara wrote to me. That'd be great. Really great."

Wow. When was I smacked with the idiot stick? Before I could say anything else that was completely inane, I recited my address while he wrote it down.

"Are you going to be able to see the bookcase anytime soon?"

"The bookcase? Sure. I can come down. That's no problem."

"Really?"

"Yeah. I, um, have some time this weekend."

"This Saturday?"

"Okay."

"What time?"

"Noon?"

"Great." He sounded unreasonably happy. I mean, I was just going down there to inspect his carpentry. Nothing to get excited about.

The week sped by. I called Gemma Saturday morning.

"I'm so glad you're back in town," she said after she picked up. "Things were much too quiet without you."

"Glad you thought so. What are you doing?"

"Right now? Working on a few freelance pieces."

"Little tired? Little cross-eyed? Need a break?"

"What's up?"

"I'm driving back to Albany."

"Oh. Are you doing some more Amish research?"

"Um . . ."

"You're not going to go see Levi, are you?"

"Maybe."

I held the phone away from my ear as Gemma squealed. "And you, all broken up with Shane, you're so available! Wait — Levi isn't a rebound, is he?"

"He's not an anything. I'm just going down there to look at a bookcase."

"A what?"

"He's been building me a bookcase as a thank-you for housing his family while his dad was in the hospital."

"Really."

"Yes, really. And he wanted to know if I could come by and take a look before he finishes it."

"He couldn't send pictures?"

"Pictures wouldn't do it justice."

"Your words or his?"

"Mine."

"So you're going to Albany. What's my part in this?"

"I don't know what to wear."

"Oh. And what's my part in this?"

"Gemma!"

"Just kidding. I'll be over in a few minutes. Do I need to bring anything?"

"You've seen my wardrobe. You tell me."

"I'll bring a few things."

"Thought you might."

Before I knew it I found myself driving to Levi's shop wearing my own jeans, a floral-print silk shell of Gemma's (I didn't know it was a shell — I would have called it a blouse, but she corrected me), and a coordinating black cardigan that was woolly enough to keep me warm.

I'd asked Gemma if she thought I looked as though I were trying too hard and didn't look like myself.

She assured me I looked casually beautiful, and she pointed out that Levi had only really known me a couple weeks and wasn't likely to have pinned down my personal style during that time.

She had a point.

Spencer whistled when I walked into the shop office. "Look at you, all nice and cleaned up."

"Yes. I traded in the apron," I said, before I got an eyeful of his ensemble. "You wore a Star Trek uniform? To work?"

"Hey," he said, smoothing the tunic or the shirt or whatever they call the part that covers your torso in space. "It's casual Saturday."

"I thought casual day was Friday."

"Saturday's casual too."

"And casual is code for being ready to uphold the Prime Directive?"

"I used to think you were nice."

"I am nice. Is your boss in?"

"He is, hard at work on a bookcase." He clucked his tongue. "It's nice."

I tucked a piece of hair behind my ear. "I'm sure it is."

"*Really* nice."

"Am I going to get a chance to see it?"

"I'll page him." Spencer lifted the phone, dialed a set of numbers, and set the receiver back down. "You been staying busy? Liked that piece about the urban garden."

"You read it?"

"I did."

"Did you get your copy of the paper from your onboard replicator?"

Scowling, he stood up, walked to the shop door, and threw it open. "Hurry up, man. She's killing me in here."

The sound of power tools drowned him out.

"I don't think he heard you."

"We have a connection, he and I. He heard."

"You're telepathic? What does that make you . . . Beta-something? Betatape, Beta-version . . ."

"Betazoid," he corrected through clenched teeth. "The Betazoids were telepathic."

"Right. Betazoid. Tip of my tongue."

Spencer opened his mouth for a comeback but found himself interrupted when Levi stepped through the door.

I'll admit my breath caught.

For just a teeny moment.

"Jayne," Levi said with the most beautiful smile. "I see you've met Number One."

331

Spence pantomimed stabbing himself with a knife. "Et tu, Brute?"

Levi gestured to me. "Wanna come see it? It's out here. I'll have the guys shut down the tools. They need to take lunch anyway."

He made some sort of signal and the noise ceased. We stepped into the shop, Levi leading the way.

"I went with cherry," he said as he walked. "I saw that you didn't get a lot of light in that room, so I figured a nice, bright wood with a sheer red stain would help to liven it up."

I looked ahead. "Is that it?"

He beamed. "It is."

I closed the distance in three more steps. "Wow," I said, running a hand over one shelf. "It's beautiful."

"Thank you."

The sides, rather than being plain, had carved rectangles the same height as the shelf. I remembered now what he'd described before he started, how it had shorter shelves at the top and bottom and taller shelves in the middle. The top had a carved crown molding, and a divot ran along the center of the shelves' edge as well as all the way around the front edge.

And the wood . . . the wood glowed. "It's perfect."

"Not quite perfect. I still need to do the finish."

"You haven't? It's so smooth and pretty now!"

Levi chuckled. "It'll be even smoother and prettier when it's done. I'm planning on a hand-rubbed oil finish. It will prevent dust and water rings."

"In case I set a drink down on a bookshelf in the office?"

"Or you have a vase of flowers and condensation leaks out."

"Ah, true." Not that I had a vase of flowers back there, either, but it was a pretty thought. Shane had never been much for flowers, and I never bought them for myself.

I crossed my arms, not knowing what to do with my hands anymore. "Well, it's absolutely perfect. And beautiful. I can't wait till it's done."

"Glad you like it."

All right. I'd done it. I'd looked at the bookcase. What next? I maintained eye contact with the bookcase and shoved another stray piece of hair behind my ear.

Levi checked his watch. "Wow. It's past lunchtime."

If he meant fifteen minutes past noon, then yes.

"Hungry?"

333

My head snapped to look at him. "Hungry? Me?"

"Want to grab something to eat? I know a good spot for lunch."

"I'm hungry."

"Yeah?"

"Starved."

He smiled. "Then let's get out of here."

CHAPTER 25

When Levi and I pulled up to Pastini in Corvallis I began to wonder. Was this a date? Like, a real date? I mean, I knew we were sharing a meal together, but lunch isn't necessarily the "date meal."

I changed my mind as we sat down. Levi held out my chair and pushed it in for me. Any lunch with chair assistance is a date.

All of a sudden, I wasn't hungry at all. In fact, I felt distinctly sick to my stomach.

"Are you all right?"

I looked up to face Levi, who had taken the chair opposite me. "Fine. Dandy. Why?"

"You started frowning and turned pale just now."

"Oh." I felt color rise to my cheeks, which was probably good. "I was just thinking about . . . work."

"What's it like being back?"

"Good. Weird." Almost as weird as my inability to form sentences. I put a little more thought into my next statement. "It's good to be back, but I definitely grew accustomed to a different pace." I sucked in a breath. "Busier and quieter at the same time."

"That is what it's like with the Amish, isn't it? More activity and less noise."

"Less random noise. More people noise. I like people better."

The waitress arrived at our table with a bright, if tired smile, asking for our drink orders. I asked for Sprite, Levi for coffee.

Big surprise.

He unrolled his silverware and placed his napkin in his lap after the waitress left. "You were talking about seeing your family. Did you?"

"I did."

"How did it go?"

"They hated me less than I thought." I unrolled my own silverware.

"Yeah?"

"My mom didn't hate me at all. My sister? I think she'll thaw. Things were . . ." I searched for the right word. "Satisfactory."

"Glad to hear that."

I shifted in my seat. "And I, um . . ." My mouth felt dry. I took a sip of my water. "Shane and I broke up."

"Oh." He ducked his head, rendering me unable to read his expression for a moment.

"Are you . . . ?"

I shrugged. "I'm fine with it. It was a mutual decision." Didn't talking about your ex break all sorts of dating rules? "Anyway, it's over. I'm glad. I'm making a lot of life changes right now."

"Like what?"

"I want a relationship with my family. I want . . . I want to like who I am."

"You don't right now?"

"I've let myself get lost. I want to start going to church again."

Levi gave a kind smile, his eyes crinkling at the edges. "You're always welcome to join me for church down here. I'm sure Spence's mom would be happy to have you for a weekend."

"That's sweet," I said, knowing I'd never take him up on it. Finding a church and attending was something I needed to do without a man. And who knew what the mother of Spencer would be like? "Have you heard anything from your family?"

"Ida drove Sara to the shop a couple days ago."

"Really?" Ida was such a rebel.

"She — Sara — said everyone's well. The boys have picked up the slack around the farm, making up for Dad. The younger girls are doing fine. Sara says they miss you."

"And Sara herself? How is she?"

"I think she'd like to leave, but Dad's health is stopping her. At least for the time being —"

I couldn't take it anymore. "Levi, are we on a date?"

"Technically, yes."

"Technically?"

"I asked you to lunch, you said yes." He spread his hands. "Ergo, date."

"But what if you'd asked Spence to lunch?"

"I wouldn't. He tends to talk with his mouth full."

"Or Grady. Or whomever. You get my point."

"*My* point is that I didn't ask anyone else. I asked you."

My shoulders sank. "Why?"

"You're good company."

"So is Grady."

"Jayne, you're funny, smart, and compassionate. I don't think I said it today, but you look," he paused, his eyes taking in my carefully chosen ensemble, "really, really good."

I felt my face flush. "Thanks."

"I asked you to lunch because I wanted to spend time with you. I want to keep getting to know you."

"I live in Portland."

"I know."

"Seventy miles away."

"Right now, we're eighteen inches away."

I sighed and sipped my water. "I'm not very good at dating."

"Me neither. I don't know what to do when a buggy is out of the picture."

I snorted. "And not climbing into girls' rooms through their windows?"

"Without windows and buggies, I'm out to sea."

"Sorry. I'm fresh out of buggies."

"What was that?" Just then, the waitress appeared at our table. "What did you say you were out of?"

I lifted my eyebrow, daring Levi to tell her "buggies."

He didn't take the bait. "We may need another couple minutes to order."

When she left, Levi reached across the table and took my hand. I almost yanked it back out of shock but thought better of it.

Having my hand held felt nice. Having Levi hold it — nearly divine.

"I think we should date."

"How old are you?"

"Does that make a difference?"

I feigned indifference, pulling my hand away to toy with my napkin. "Maybe."

"You tell me first."

"I'm twenty-six."

He lifted an eyebrow. "Awfully young for a reporter in your position."

I bristled. "It's not my fault I'm good. You haven't answered my question yet."

"Thirty-two."

"Wow." I sat back. "You're old."

He kicked my foot under the table. "Thanks."

"Okay. Maybe not *that* old."

"Do I pass? Will you go out with me?"

"I'm not in town anymore. I mean, I'm here now, Levi, but I can't be here every weekend. I don't know how —"

"Do you have to know?"

"Yes."

He leaned forward. "I don't. I'm perfectly capable taking things a day at a time."

"I'm a reporter. We're trained to think ahead of schedule."

"What would happen if you let someone else do the worrying for a change?" He nodded toward my menu. "What sounds good?"

"What are you having?" I hated choosing something before the guy, preferring instead to match my order to his. If he ordered a sandwich, I'd order a sandwich. If he ordered a steak, I'd check out the menu's pricier items.

He folded his menu. "Rigatoni with meat sauce Bolognese."

"Yeah?"

"Yeah. Do you like artichoke dip?"

"I do."

"Then we'll get artichoke dip. I got hooked on artichokes in college."

"Artichokes not figured into Amish cuisine?"

"Not often."

When the server came back, Levi recited his lunch order before gesturing to me.

I closed my menu. "I'll have the Rigatoni with chicken cacciatore."

"That's my favorite," the server said, as she scribbled on her order pad.

She probably said that to all her customers.

"So?" Levi said, bringing my attention back to the topic at hand.

As if I could think of much else.

"Do you want to be adventurous with me? Want to give it a shot?"

"Us dating?"

"No, us going deep-sea diving. Haven't you been paying attention?"

I gave him a playful smack on the arm. "You're high-maintenance. Fine. Let's give it a go."

■ ■ ■ ■

After lunch we walked around downtown Corvallis for a while. He didn't try to hold my hand, but he stayed close to my side as we walked and talked about his family, my family, our jobs, and whatever else came up. My feet were sore by the time we returned to the truck, but I didn't care. I couldn't remember the last time my heart felt so light.

"I need to get back to work after this," Levi said as the familiar form of the shop came into view. "When do I get to see you next?"

"I told my mom I'd visit her next week-end," I answered, already feeling the tension of a long-distance relationship.

"In Lincoln City?"

"Yes."

"I'd love to meet your family."

I frowned. "You're joking."

"It's only fair. You've lived with mine."

"But —"

"It's up to you. You can let me know later."

"I'll think about it."

"Thanks."

"Have a good rest of your weekend."

"Jayne," he laughed and shook his head.

"Relax!"

"I am relaxed!"

"That's why your shoulders are up to your ears. Just relax. We're having fun."

We were. And that was the problem.

To my eternal shame, I ducked away from the shop and back to my car before something along the lines of a goodbye kiss could be discussed.

Instead, I think I reached out and squeezed his elbow, fast, or something ridiculous like that. Can't be certain what, the whole thing was a blur.

Pretty sad, really.

On the drive home, I felt a strong urge to call my mother. Strange, because I don't believe I've ever had the desire to call her just to talk.

But there I was, dialing her number on Highway 20 anyway.

As the phone rang, I worried she wouldn't answer. As far as I knew, she had all sorts of activities lined up on Saturdays. As the phone continued to ring, I debated telling her I'd gone to Albany at all. Back in Lincoln City, I'd told her I couldn't come this weekend because of work. Well, work certainly hadn't stopped me from driving seventy miles to see my new . . . boyfriend?

Significant Male? Gentleman caller?

Before I could think better of the whole mother-calling action, I heard her voice. "Hello?"

"Hi," I said, sounding much more breathless than I'd meant to. I sounded like a bad Marilyn Monroe impersonator.

"Jayne?"

"Yeah, Mom, it's me."

"Oh. Good. How are you?"

"I, uh, I broke up with Shane."

"I'm sorry to hear that. Did it just happen?"

"No. Actually, it was on the way back from visiting you."

"I hope — I hope it wasn't anything that happened here?"

"Not really. It was just time."

"*Not really* sounds a lot like *partially yes*," she said drily.

"It became clear that we were going in different directions."

"You should run for political office."

"Thanks, Mom."

She sighed. "I'm not surprised. About you and Shane, that is."

"You're not?"

"You seemed like good friends, but there wasn't . . . chemistry. Not love chemistry, at any rate."

"Well, I'm glad you're not disappointed."

"He seemed like a nice man, but no."

"I'm also . . . seeing . . ." I exhaled hard. "Someone else."

"Oh? Was it that boy you met researching your Amish story?"

Wow. She was good. "Yeah. It's Levi."

"How do you feel about him?"

"I . . ." was it possible to know how I felt? I'd hardly known him a few weeks. Had it only been a few weeks? Crazy. "I like him a lot."

Which was code for, "I can't stop thinking about him."

Being new to the whole mom-talk thing, I kept that to myself. I didn't need her picking out baby names.

Come to think of it, I didn't know if she was the picking-out-baby-names type.

"I'm very excited for you," she said.

I licked my lips. "I know I said I'd visit next weekend."

"If you can't, we understand."

"What I'm asking is . . . can I bring him?"

"Of course!"

"Would that be too weird? What am I saying? Of course it would be too weird. That's two guys in two weeks."

"It's up to you."

Of course it was. "He wants to meet my family."

"You lived with his, didn't you?"

Naturally, she'd have to throw that back too. "I did."

"Bringing him or not bringing him is your decision. If he's fine sleeping in a room covered in quilt squares, then he's welcome to join you."

I brightened at the mention of quilt squares. "They're still on the floor?"

"They are. Waiting for you."

Such faithful quilt squares.

"I'll talk to Levi." Who knew? By next week we might have thrown in the towel. "Either way, you'll definitely have at least one guest next weekend." A stray thought stuck in my head. "Mom?"

"Yes?"

"Will Beth mock me if I bring over a different man?"

"She wants to see you happy. She really does."

That so didn't answer my question.

Or maybe it did.

I called Gemma when I got home. "You go to church, don't you?"

"Every week. Why?"

"Can I come with you?"

"Of course. You really want to?"

"You know I grew up in the church, right?"

"Jayne, you . . . you don't talk about yourself very often."

I ran a hand through my hair. "I know. I'm sorry. I don't want to be that person anymore. And that means going back to church. So can I meet you there?"

"You can meet me or I can pick you up."

"I need to be as independent about this as possible. I need to drive myself."

"You're independent, so you're letting me help you choose a church?"

"It's a springboard. And no woman is an island."

"Amen, sister."

"Save it for church, Gem."

"Touchy."

"Nervous. It's been a crazy day."

"Like how?"

I told her about my date with Levi.

"Really! Good thing you looked so nice. Are you guys an item now?"

"Working in that direction."

"Are you terrified?"

I sighed. "Petrified."

"It's good for you. Gosh, I can't remember the last time I felt that way about someone."

"You've had a bit of a dry spell, haven't you."

"Like the Sudan."

"You know," I said, "Levi has several employees. One of them is really into Star Trek. You guys might hit it off."

"You're cruel. Besides, dealing with my family isn't for the faint of heart."

"That's the flip side of growing up with so much great food."

"Very true. So tomorrow?"

"Tomorrow."

Heaven help us all.

CHAPTER 26

I took a nap Sunday afternoon. I'd forgotten how much I loved my postchurch naps. When I was growing up, my entire family napped after church. No one emerged before four forty-five.

Church with Gemma went well enough. The pastor was highly educated and highly able to make me uncomfortable with the probing nature of his scripturally based remarks.

But I wasn't attending church to stay in my comfort zone, so I stayed in my seat.

It's funny to me how many churches in the last ten years have made the swap from pews to interlocking chairs. While the chairs make it harder to slide into your seat, they are more comfortable and better delineate personal bubbles.

Not that personal bubbles matter much with Gemma's family. Her Italian father wrapped me in a hug while her French mother air-kissed me on each cheek.

Really, it's amazing Gemma's as normal as she is.

Being surrounded by Gemma's family and multiple siblings made me feel for the briefest moment as though I were back with the Burkholders.

Which made me think of Levi. Thinking of Levi, until recently, had only made me feel guilty.

Now it made me happy. Unabashedly happy.

Even as I lay down for my nap, I couldn't stop smiling.

My first letter from Sara arrived Monday.

Jayne,
We miss you very much. I had a very nice time at your apartment, although I regret that we could not go to see your friend's closet. Maybe another time?

Leah and Elizabeth say hello. Things are well here. Father is mending, although he complains about eating fish and not being able to work the farm as much. Mainly the fish. Mother has begun cooking with less butter and fat for the sake of Father's heart. I think he would rather have another heart attack than give up fat, but I don't say anything. The boys are complaining about so much fish, but only when Mother is out of the room. They haven't complained about going fishing more often.

Levi said you'll be writing an article about us. You aren't going to write about me thinking about leaving, are you?

I hope that you will visit us sometime. Are you still cutting quilt squares? Have you tried to piece them yet? I'm sure if you called my grandmother, she'd be able to tell you what to do.

It would be nice if you wrote back.

Sara

I smiled and refolded the letter. After a long day of writing and editing written material, hearing from Sara made me miss the Burkholders' farmhouse.

Things were simpler there. Of course, things were more complicated now that I was seeing Levi. I didn't know how Martha would feel about me dating, him, but I could guess that in her heart of hearts, she would want him to return to the community. Dating an outsider would hinder that.

I felt I knew Levi well enough to know he had no intention of ever returning, so I couldn't feel guilty for holding him back. Furthermore, I met him before I met his family.

What would drive me over the edge would be Sara. How do you know when to give the girl-power speech or encourage her to live the life of her ancestors?

I knew I wouldn't want to live that life. Here I was trying my own version, and already scuff marks had resurfaced on the tile and my shower was turning pink where water pooled. But there was something about knowing that somewhere everything was perfect, orderly, clean. Peace and simplicity reigned in that place, even if it wasn't here.

Not that I wasn't trying. I mopped my floor the other day for the first time in eighteen months, and that wouldn't have happened if I didn't find the Swiffer commercials so convincing.

I found paper and an envelope in the study.

Dear Sara,
I miss you all terribly. Sorry about all

the fish, but from what I hear it really is good for the heart. Don't worry. I didn't put anything about your thoughts of leaving into the article. Also, I changed everyone's names for your privacy.

I'm back at work and wishing I was still baking in your family's kitchen. However, I did help bake a pie at my mom's house and surprised everyone. I also started a quilt with my mother; we'll work on it again this weekend.

You told me about your dreams of designing clothes. That took a lot of trust. I don't know if Levi's mentioned it to you, but we've decided to try a relationship. I guess we're dating. I hope you're okay with that. Levi is a very, very special person. I don't know how serious we are — or not. We've agreed to see what happens. I just wanted you to know.

Give the children hugs for me. I miss all of you.

Jayne

P.S. Don't worry — I've been very careful with my clothes since you left. No missing buttons.

I addressed and stamped the letter, but decided against sealing it. Instead, I walked down the street to the convenience store and picked up a glossy magazine with a "Best Dressed" section before going back home.

Once I was behind closed doors, I perused the pages and found the parts I thought Sara would like most. I pried the staples from the magazine before cutting out the pages.

I folded the contraband to fit inside the letter, slapped on another stamp, and headed outside to the mail drop.

People don't usually whistle at me when I show up for work, but the next morning I received two before arriving at my cubicle.

Once I saw my desk, I understood why.

"Those are some serious flowers," said Laura, who apparently decided to make my reaction her next story.

Thing was, she wasn't exaggerating. On my desk sat a bouquet of a dozen light pink, long stemmed roses.

Upon closer examination, I realized it wasn't a dozen, but a baker's dozen. There was a card tucked among the blossoms. I opened it to find a printed message:

Because I couldn't climb through your window, the least I could do was send you flowers. Have a good day at work.

Levi

I smiled and put the card back into the envelope before sliding it into the top drawer of my desk and away from the prying eyes of my colleagues.

I worked with a roomful of investigative reporters. I knew the only thing stopping Laura from going through my desk was the threat of what I might find in hers if I returned the favor — rumor had it she kept quite the chocolate stash and the odd prescription medication in her left-hand drawer.

Calling Levi at that moment would have provided more fodder for the entertainment section of the office, so I opted to wait until lunchtime rolled around.

It wasn't raining at noon, so I stepped outside, taking my phone and my jacket with me.

"Did you see your surprise?"

I couldn't help but smile. "Yeah, me and every one of my coworkers."

"Hope it didn't bother you."

"Not too much. Hey, I hope you don't mind. I told your sister about us."

"She wrote you already?"

"She did."

"I don't mind. She'd have to find out eventually, and she likes you."

"Yeah?"

"Yeah."

"I talked to my mom the other day."

"Always a good way to continue the relationship."

"She said you're welcome to come with me this weekend."

"Only if you want me to."

A bitter breeze nipped at the edges of my jacket. I tucked my free hand deeper into my pocket. "Sure."

"You sound excited."

"It's the right thing to do."

"Your decision, Jayne."

"I mean, I'm feeling kinda pressured here."

"Whoa, whoa — where is this coming from?"

"You send me a dozen roses —"

"Thirteen. I wanted to be unique."

"Whatever. Thirteen. You send me this big statement in front of all my coworkers and you think that will smooth the way for you to insinuate yourself into my weekend and my life. What if I'm not ready?"

"Then you're not ready. And that's okay."

"You won't resent me?" I stepped aside as the door behind me opened and two women from archives emerged from the building, cigarettes in hand.

"Nope."

"Do you want the flowers back?"

"Jayne, the roses had nothing to do with me meeting your family. I don't see you often because we don't live in the same city. The roses were me trying to, I don't know, make up for that in my clumsy guy way. I told you. I'm not good at dating. I thought girls liked roses."

"I do like the roses!" I shouted into the phone. The archive ladies backed away even farther.

"The weekend thing is really bothering you, isn't it."

My shoulders slumped in defeat. "It feels too fast."

"And that's fine."

"I want you to meet my family."

"I'd like to. But only when you're comfortable."

"Then come with me this weekend."

"But you don't want me to."

"Yes, I do."

"Why?"

I ran a hand through my hair. "Because I won't get to see you this weekend otherwise.

Because I know it's the right thing to do. And I want to go to church on Sunday, and Miss Lynnie is getting old, and I know she'd like to meet you."

"Who's Miss Lynnie?"

"My Sunday school teacher."

"And you want me to go to the coast with you this weekend because she's old and you want me to meet her before she dies."

"Yes!"

"Okay."

"Okay?"

"Okay."

He was exhausting.

"Why don't I drive to your place on Friday and bring your bookcase?"

And then he'd go and do nice things like that. "That sounds good."

"Are you positive?"

"Yes."

"I didn't want you to feel about the bookcase the way you felt about the roses. This isn't a manipulative bookcase. It's a thank-you bookcase."

"I consider myself adequately thanked. And I like the roses."

"Miss me?"

I smiled. "Yeah."

"I miss you too."

Friday couldn't arrive soon enough.

I dreaded the arrival of Friday with all my heart.

In the meantime, I finished up part two of the urban garden story with the help of my police insider. Joely was more than willing (for the price of a coconut cupcake) to get me past the red tape and into the initial police reports and list of witnesses present when the crime was reported.

I interviewed community members, took pictures, and wrote up a nice yet haunting story of senseless vandalism to conclude the piece I had written earlier.

Wednesday, I readied my study for the arrival of the new bookcase. I tidied up the papers that managed to cover every flat surface and vacuumed into the corners of the room.

When I finished, the study was spotless. The rest of the apartment was not.

I don't know where all the clutter came from. Seriously. I was a professional, not a slob. Maybe little messy elves came out when I slept. I don't know how else my jackets found themselves stacked up on the chair by the door, and how I'd taken to playing a round of hide-and-seek every morning with my keys, finding them under banana peels or inside my laundry closet.

When did I last buy bananas, anyway?

Thursday I came up with the brilliant idea of cooking dinner for Levi before we left for the coast.

Martha cooked dinner every day after spending the day working — why couldn't I? I tracked down Gemma that afternoon at her desk.

"Got a minute?"

"Always." Gemma turned her chair around and folded her hands in her lap. "What's up?"

"I want to make dinner."

"Noble."

"Tomorrow. After work. For Levi."

"Oh." She thought for a moment. *"Oh."*

"Stop saying that."

"You're cooking for a *man*."

"Which means he'll eat anything in large quantities, right?"

"Usually. Not always. If he's related to me, yes, but I've never seen Levi eat."

"Do you have to observe someone eating before you can cook for them? Are there hidden cameras involved?"

She rolled her eyes. "You're funny. Does he like Italian?"

"Yes. He took me to Pastini in Corvallis."

"Last weekend?"

"Yes."

"So that's why you've avoided me all week."

I folded my arms. "I haven't avoided you."

"Returned any of my calls or emails lately? Or clothes, what about clothes?"

"You know, of all of us, people say you're the nice one."

"I am the nice one. So, you went on a date with Levi."

"I didn't say it was a date."

She tapped her pencil against her desk. "A man took you to an Italian restaurant in a town separate from the one he lives in. It's a date. And it was nice, otherwise you wouldn't be cooking for him." She tapped her hands on her desk. "Are you sure you don't want me to bring over some of the food from the restaurant? It'd be like having a catered dinner."

"That's sweet, but no. I want to cook."

"Okay." She thought for a moment. "He's a meat eater, right?"

"Yup."

She began scribbling notes on a piece of paper. "Good. That's good."

"What are you doing?"

"Writing out your recipe. That's why you came, right?"

"It's a simple recipe?"

"It is. Add a salad and a box of Rice-a-Roni, and you're done."

"You eat Rice-a-Roni?"

"Don't tell my mom. I'd be disowned."

"Your dad wouldn't care?"

"He doesn't believe in Rice-a-Roni the way adults don't believe in Santa Claus."

"Interesting. Family is complicated, isn't it."

"Kind of like men," Gemma said, sending me a significant glance. "But both are very, very worth it."

CHAPTER 27

I shopped for groceries Thursday night, following Gemma's list like a scavenger hunt guide.

Pork. If only she had been more specific! She did say boneless, but there was the thin cut pork that was light, and the thick cut pork that was dark. Most of the time, the thick cut was cheaper — did that make it lower quality?

I stood there in the meat section for five minutes, a package of light pork in one hand, dark in the other.

Not one of my prouder moments.

I called Gemma and explained the problem. She said, "Go with the pork sirloin — the darker one."

"You've decided on that?" I asked.

"I've listened to my parents debate about the finer points of recipes since I was in my mother's womb. Don't argue with me."

"Yes, ma'am." I hung up.

Cream. Pretty straightforward. I didn't see any difference between the store-brand cream and the name-brand cream, so I stuck with the store brand and figured the cows weren't stamped with a product name, so why should I care?

Unless they selected the cows differently . . .

I pushed my cart forward before I could talk myself out of the store-brand cream.

I checked the rest of the list — one lemon, one bunch parsley, one package hazelnuts, four red potatoes . . . for Pete's sake, I was going to be there all night.

Parsley — I found it in the produce section. Trouble was, there was Italian parsley and flat-leaf parsley.

I pulled out my phone again. "Gemma?"

"Tell me you're not still at the grocery store."

"I'm not at the grocery store."

"Are you lying?"

"Yes. It's the parsley."

"What's wrong with the parsley?" She sounded frustrated.

"Italian or flat-leaf?"

"They're both green, you know." Her voice grew practical again. "Use the Italian."

"Thanks!"

"Anything else you've got a question about?"

"I don't know yet. I don't grocery-shop that often."

"It builds character."

"And you really can't come down and help me?"

"I'm thirty-five-minutes away. By the time I'd get there, you'd be done."

"No, I wouldn't. I'd wait." Really. I meant it.

"You can do this."

"I am a skilled person."

"Very true."

"I can order off a Chinese menu with agility and accuracy."

"I don't know if I've ever ordered Chinese takeout."

It boggled the mind. "If you ever need help, you can call me. I'm great with Indian and Thai too."

"I will defer to your vindaloo knowledge. Until then — keep shopping."

I sighed and hung up.

That night I dreamed I cooked dinner for Levi. I put the pork chops in the oven. When I opened the oven to check on them, they'd turned into chickens. Whole, roasting chickens. I had to call Gemma to see if the recipe would turn out okay with chicken. She told me that it wouldn't work with chicken, but it might work with veal or lamb. So I closed the oven door for twenty minutes.

Twenty minutes pass, I check, and there's a rack of lamb in my oven.

Instead of marveling at my oven, I reasoned that all was well because Gemma said lamb would work. Then I went to start the salad and found that the whole thing had wilted overnight.

Then Levi showed up, and I had to explain to him that I didn't have salad. He stood up really straight, saying he couldn't eat dinner if there wasn't any salad.

That's when I woke up. Sweating.

I marched down the hall to the kitchen, flung open the refrigerator, pulled open the produce drawer, and retrieved the bag of salad.

Fresh and crisp and green. Just like I'd remembered.

Rolling my eyes, I went back to bed.

I looked at the clock. Five thirty. Levi had told me he planned on arriving at a quarter till.

Problem was, the pork chops were nowhere near done, and I had a horrible suspicion that I had overzested the lemons.

I'd remembered reading one of Gemma's articles once about the white stuff being bitter. Unfortunately, I didn't remember this until I'd dumped the lemon zest into the sauce mixture.

I jumped when my cell phone buzzed on the laminate countertop. "Hello?"

"Hi, Jayne, it's me," Levi said. "I'm running late. I had trouble closing up, but I should be there soon. Do you want to pick up some dinner on the way out? I was thinking something quick, like sandwiches."

My eyes darted to my still-pink-in-the-middle pork chops "No, we can't pick something up!"

"Why not?"

I bit my lip. "I just . . . don't want to."

"Do you want to eat something at your place and I'll pick something up for myself?"

"Can't you wait until you get here? How far out are you?"

"Thirty minutes."

Surely the pork chops would be done in thirty minutes. They'd been cooking for nearly an hour.

"Okay. I'll see you in thirty minutes."

"So what are we doing about food?"

"I'll think of something," I said and then hung up.

Thirty minutes. I looked at the pork

chops, picked my phone back up, and called Gemma. "They're not cooking!"

"Who they?"

"The pork chops! He's going to be here in thirty minutes, and the pork is still really pink."

"How long have they been on the stove?"

"An hour!"

"Um, Jayne, I don't mean to insult your intelligence, but is the correct burner *on*?"

"Of course it is!"

"And there's heat coming from it?"

"Yes!"

"Keep your pants on. Are the chops browning at all?"

"A little."

"What temperature do you have the burner on?"

I examined the little black dial. "How should I know?"

She sighed. "Okay. I think I told you to start with medium-high heat, brown both sides, and then cook covered on medium low."

"Oh." That would do it.

"Use your words, Jayne."

"Where on the dial would you call medium-low?"

"Between medium . . . and low." She cleared her throat. "Jayne —"

"Closer to the medium or the low?"

"Middle."

"Oh."

"Where is it?"

I yanked the black dial into the appropriate position. "In the middle."

"Right. Where was it before I asked."

"Um . . ." I winced. "Maybe . . . more low than medium?"

"Did you ever have them on medium-high?"

"Not so much?"

"Well, if they've been there for an hour they're at least making progress. Turn the heat up to just under medium."

"You speak words of confusion."

"You get odd when you're cooking. Turn the dial to not-quite medium. Cover them and ignore them for ten minutes or so."

"Or so?"

"Check in ten minutes. Call me back."

I would like to draw a veil over my memories of the food preparation and phone calls that ensued.

Twenty-six minutes later, my phone buzzed again.

"I'm really close," Levi said, "but there's an accident on I-84."

"Can you get off?" I asked as I set the table. "I can give you back-road directions."

"I'd get off if I could, but nothing's moving at the moment. I'll call you back when that changes, okay?"

"That's fine."

"Are you all packed?"

"Just about."

Kind of, sort of, not really. I had the clothes I wanted to bring in a pile. They were clean. This was progress.

"Okay. Let's try to leave pretty soon after I get there. How late does your mom stay up?"

"She'll be up if she knows we're running behind. I'll call her when we know what our actual estimated time of arrival will be."

"I miss you."

A smile broke out across my face. "Yeah?"

"And I hate being stuck in traffic when I'm so close to seeing you."

"I'll be praying it breaks up soon," I said and then hung up.

Then sat down.

Pray? I didn't pray. Not anymore, and not unless it was a life-threatening situation. But it had occurred to me, just the same.

I closed my eyes. God and I were doing better these days. I'd gone to church with my mom and Gemma. I'd sung the songs. Spontaneous prayer shouldn't be far behind.

Would God listen to a prayer like that?

Was He actively concerned with Portland's traffic troubles? More important, would He pay attention if I asked?

I knew the answer to that question even as it passed through my mind. Years of Sunday school had that effect on me.

He would pay attention. He just wouldn't necessarily answer the way I wanted to.

Did that mean I shouldn't ask?

Before I could talk myself out of it, I bowed my head and uttered the silliest prayer of my life, "Lord, please help the traffic to regulate."

That was all.

I let out the breath I'd been holding. My tense shoulder muscles relaxed.

My cell phone buzzed again.

"It's me," Levi said when I picked up. "I just wanted to tell you traffic's moving and I'm coming up to an exit."

I gave him directions to my apartment, all the while wondering if the traffic had cleared before or after I prayed.

When Levi arrived at the door, my eyes gravitated to the bag in his hand. "You got dinner."

"Just fries." He wrapped his arms around me in a hug, but I was too upset to enjoy the sensation.

371

"Are you still hungry?"

"Wha—" he stepped inside and saw the set table, the serving plates, and bowls covered in foil. "You made dinner."

"It was supposed to be a surprise. Are you still hungry?"

"Of course." He beat the bag with his hands into a wad. "Of course I'm hungry. It smells amazing in here."

Actually, it smelled like I spilled something on the burner, but it was sweet of him to say so. "There's pork chops and rice and salad. I even had time to run around the corner and get a loaf of bread."

"I'm sorry I'm late."

"That's okay. I called my mom. Everything's fine."

"I've got your bookcase in the bed of my truck."

"Shall we bring it in?"

"Sure." He planted a short kiss on my lips.

"How heavy is it?" I asked on our way down the stairs. "Can just the two of us handle it?"

"I was clever and designed the back to attach with pegs; we'll be fine. You look wiry."

Fifteen minutes and a lot of grunting later, we had all of the pieces up the stairs. Didn't tweak my wrist once. Levi dragged the parts into the study, where I had cleared a space for the new piece of furniture. "The pegs, see, go in like this."

I watched as he aligned the back with the body and connected the two. "It seems like it would be hard to design it to match perfectly."

"It was. I'm that good. Shall we get it into position?"

At that moment, my stomach growled. Loudly.

"Let's eat," he said, turning my shoulders toward the table.

I lifted the foil from the serving plates, checking to see if the food was still warm. "Let me get this for you." I began to scoop food onto his plate. "What do you want to drink? There's filtered water, Coke, and milk. I've been drinking milk ever since your mom was here."

"Hopefully not the same carton."

"I bought new milk. Even finished the last one before it got chunky. Do you want pepper? I think I have a pepper shaker around here somewhere."

"Sit down. Get yourself some dinner."

"I'm trying to do this right." I shoved my hair behind my ear. "I wanted it to be . . . you know . . ."

He smiled. "It's very special. I appreciate it a lot. May I?"

I nodded, and watched as he filled my own plate with food.

"When do you think you'll be able to be brace free?"

"I don't know. Another week, maybe. Maybe less."

"You've managed well."

"I improvise. How does it taste?"

"Wonderful. Really, really good."

"Really?" I took a bite, expecting the worst. "Hmm. You're right."

After a few moments Levi pushed his plate away. "I can't eat another bite. That was amazing."

My eyes narrowed. "You didn't eat very much."

"It was filling."

I looked at my plate. I'd already put away the same amount and wasn't yet near full. I put my fork down. "You filled up on fries."

"Jayne, I didn't know you were making dinner for us."

"I asked you not to get dinner!"

"I didn't get dinner."

"No, you got a giant deep-fried appetizer."

"I'm sorry. My hands were shaking on the road. And I didn't think you cooked."

"I'm broadening my horizons! I'm perfectly capable of cooking a single meal. Your mom makes meals in her sleep."

"That's because she's been doing it since she was eighteen."

"And I'm twenty-six, so I'm behind and it's time I started catching up."

"You're not seriously angry about this, are you?"

"No. Yes. No. I don't know."

"Finish your dinner."

"I'm not hungry anymore."

"Right. Just look at those juicy, perfectly cooked chops."

"You're not going to make me hungry."

Trouble was, they were really, really good. But I didn't particularly feel like giving him the satisfaction of being right.

I reached for my fork.

"It's Gemma's recipe. Of course they're perfect."

My resolve lasted for another thirty seconds. "These are really good."

He sat back in his chair. "You look pretty."

I smiled. "Thanks."

I knew I looked rumpled, and I had yet to take off my apron, but the way he looked at me made me believe him.

"Want to get the new bookcase settled?"

"Sure." I followed him down the hallway.

We pushed together until the bookcase was flush against the wall. I stepped back. "That looks really good." I hugged him

375

around his torso. "Thank you."

"You're welcome," he said, turning me so I faced him. "Always."

Under his gaze, I couldn't move. With a single smooth gesture, he cupped the back of my head with his hand and drew me close, his lips touching mine with infinite care.

So this was what it was like to kiss Levi on purpose. I ran my fingers through his hair and kissed him back.

Lincoln City could wait.

CHAPTER 28

Levi held my hand until we hit the Van Duzer corridor. By that time, the sky was black and the road slick with new rain. Levi kept two hands on the wheel; I rested my head against the seat back. I couldn't see the ocean in the dark, but I knew it was there, close by.

I didn't worry about my mom meeting Levi. I knew she'd love him.

The houselights were on when we pulled up in my mom's driveway. They cast dappled light patterns on a car to our left.

My sister's car.

"Beth wants to meet you."

"Oh?"

I nodded toward the Subaru Forester with the telltale booster seat in the second row. "She's here."

"Isn't it late for your niece?"

"With any luck, Beth came by herself."

"I'm not afraid of them."

"That's good. That's very good. Hang on to that. Beth can be a pain when she wants to be, but her meds seem to be kicking in lately."

"I'll stand up for you."

"I know." I clasped his hand. "Shall we go in?"

"Want to grab bags first?"

"If my sister's going to be here late at night to scope you out, she may as well help carry luggage."

"I don't have that much —"

"Yeah, but because of your sister, I do."

"How is your bag Sara's fault?"

"Have you met her? I'm barely qualified to wear my clothes, much less choose them and pack them with the care they deserve. So I bring everything these days. Sara's doing, all the way. When I went to stay with your parents, everything I needed fit into my motorcycle panniers."

"And then Sara."

"And then Sara."

"I think your clothes always look good."

"I've been letting Gemma pick out stuff for me lately."

He rolled his eyes. "Trying to compliment you here. Are we going to sit in the car and talk about your wardrobe or go inside?"

"I have a choice?"

"Jayne —"

"Because I can talk buttons."

"Let's go." He leaned over and pressed a quick kiss on my lips before opening his door and stepping out.

I sighed and opened my own door.

He held my hand on the way up the walk. When we arrived at the door, I knocked.

Loudly. Because I could.

Two footfalls and the door opened. I had to wonder if *someone* was peering out the kitchen window.

"Jayne!" My mother's face glowed. "Come in, both of you." She closed the door, shutting out the wisps of the damp night breeze.

Levi extended his hand. "I'm Levi. I'm very glad to meet you, Mrs. Tate."

"It's very nice to meet you, Levi." She clasped his hand. "May I take your coat?"

"Oh, thank you," Levi shrugged out of his jacket. When his back was turned, Mom winked and gave me a thumbs-up.

She liked him. I knew she would.

From the corner of my eye, I could see Beth and Gary in the living room.

Poor Emilee. With any luck, she was asleep upstairs, curled up with Beth's old stuffed dog, Sniffy.

The rundown of the following events:

Gary shakes Levi's hand. I admire Levi's

firm grip.

Beth eyes Levi, presumably checking him for, I don't know, suspicious rashes. When he turns to greet her, her face transforms into the smiling visage of the girl-next-door.

Emilee stumbles in, hair mussed, eyes half shut. She must have conked out on the couch.

Levi kneels and introduces himself. The women in the room not already in love with him are now.

Or at least, they ought to be.

"We should be going," Beth said. "We just stopped by because Mom said the car's brakes were making noise."

Yes. And what better time to check them out than eleven p.m. on a Friday night? She probably mentioned the car to Gary at least a week ago.

"I just need to replace the brake pads," said Gary. "I'm going to come back over and work on them tomorrow."

"Want a hand?" Levi asked. "I've spent some time under cars."

"I never turn down free help."

"I'll throw in lunch," Mom said. "I don't expect you to work on the car for free."

Beth pulled Emilee's coat from the closet and began the fastening process. Gary reached for his jacket.

"We'll walk out with you," I said innocently. "We need to get our luggage."

"We can help with that," Gary volunteered. "Come on, Beth."

Score.

The men left for the bags. I stayed inside with the warmth.

"Are you ready to go home and sleep, Miss Emilee?" I knelt and tugged on Emilee's left braid.

She shook her head. "I'm not sleepy."

"She'll fall asleep in the car." Beth pulled the hood to cover Emilee's head.

"No, I won't."

"Okay, you won't." Beth patted her back.

"If the guys are working on the car tomorrow," I started, wondering how such words could trip from my mouth, "would you all like to go shopping with me?"

"Of course," Mom answered right away. "I'd love to."

"Shopping?" Beth said the word as if I'd just suggested a skinny-dipping trip off a jetty.

"I could use some new items . . . and help picking them out."

Beth tilted her head and studied me.

I refused to flinch under her gaze.

"I can be there as long as Emilee holds out. She can be a pretty good shopper.

Can't you, Emilee?"

Emilee nodded absently.

Maybe she was right. She wouldn't fall asleep in the car, but on the way to the car.

I never felt like this with Shane. I scrubbed my face in my mom's guest bathroom, door closed, washing off the day's makeup and travel grime. The feeling of vulnerability was new to me. I didn't know how I felt about it. Would I be able to sleep knowing he was down the hall?

A knock sounded on the door. I cracked it open, mouth full of toothpaste foam.

"You okay in there?" Levi asked.

I wanted to smack the look of amusement right off his face, but it might have caused the toothpaste to splatter. I nodded instead.

"Can I brush my teeth at some point?"

I spat into the sink. "Sure. Of course. I'm about done."

"Really."

"You know, there are other bathrooms in this house."

"I didn't want to dirty up another sink. I thought you'd be done . . ." he checked his watch. "Twenty or so minutes ago."

"I'm done."

"Am I making you uncomfortable?"

I tucked my hair behind my ear, noting its

slight oiliness. "Why would you think that?"

"Because you've never struck me as the kind of girl to hold herself hostage in a bathroom."

"You think you're so funny."

"You're not answering my question."

"You grew up around girls who never spent any time hogging a bathroom. Your parents don't even have a mirror in there."

"You weren't like this when I stayed at your apartment."

I put my toothbrush down. "It's just kind of weird."

"My being here? How is that different?"

I shrugged.

"If you want me to leave, I will. I won't be mad."

"No — not at all. I'm sorry, Levi." I folded my arms across my chest. "We're just so . . . new. When you were at my apartment before, we weren't, you know, together. I mean, we had our first dating kiss just a few hours ago."

"Still doesn't make sense, but okay. What can I do to help you feel more comfortable?"

"Tell me something embarrassing about yourself."

"I used to have the same haircut as my brothers."

"That's not embarrassing. That's who you were."

"I found a toy in town and kept it hidden from my parents. I realized a couple years ago it was just a little McDonald's toy with a cartoon character."

"You don't have any embarrassing stories, do you?"

"Wanna go for a drive?"

"Right now?"

"Sure."

"It's almost midnight."

"You're all keyed up. I doubt you'll sleep anytime soon."

"My teeth are all brushed."

"The car won't change that, unless you find gummy bears under the seat."

"Mom's already in bed."

"Leave her a note. You're not seventeen."

"Not seventeen, Amish, and climbing out of windows with boys? I almost pulverized one of Sara's callers."

"He probably had it coming."

I forced my shoulders to relax. "Let me throw on my coat."

"You're okay working on the car tomorrow?" I asked, as we curved down Highway 101.

"I like to be helpful. I want to get to know

your family. It seemed like a good place to start."

"This whole night-drive in your pajamas is very comfortable. You should try it sometime."

He squeezed my hand.

The sky had grown even darker, but this time I could just make out the line of ocean foam against the sand as we drove down the coast. The rain had lessened and the sky had cleared. A couple of stars peeked out from behind black clouds.

I'd forgotten how dramatic the Oregon Coast could be. After moving to Portland, I'd spent much of my time reviling my roots. Now I found comfort in them.

We didn't talk during the drive. Before I knew it, I felt a gust of cold air and strong arms reaching around me. My eyes opened, which meant they must have been closed.

"Was I asleep?" I asked, except that I'd been sleeping, and I wasn't quite awake, so it came out "Wha ay as-eep."

With horror I realized I had a line of drool on the left side of my chin.

If Levi noticed, he didn't say anything. "You relaxed."

I nodded, and surreptitiously swiped at my chin.

Levi helped me the rest of the way out of

the car, borrowed my key, opened the front door, and gave me an arm up the stairs.

"Are you ready to go to bed? Anything else to do in the bathroom?"

To his credit, there was only the tiniest shred of irony in his voice. I shook my head.

He nudged my bedroom door open with his foot. I leaned into the doorframe while he turned my bedcovers down. When he finished, I shrugged out of my coat, sank into the bed, and nestled my head into the down feather pillow.

I think he may have brushed a kiss against my lips, but I could have been dreaming.

The next thing I knew, it was morning.

Morning, and someone was using tools. Loud tools. Either loud tools, or Mom was having it out with a cast-iron pan.

Against the wall.

What was so important that it had to make this much noise on a Saturday morning at . . . I checked my watch.

A quarter till eleven? I checked again.

Still quarter till. How did that happen? I never slept that late.

I pulled the covers back and sat up. Too fast — I laid back down. Sat up again, this time slower. Okay so far. Two feet on the ground . . . check. I stood with unsteady legs.

I checked the lower half of my face for drool. Negative.

The noise continued. It was lower than the sound of a cast-iron pan. It sounded like a hammer. A hammer being used by someone with a steady swing.

My mom didn't handle a hammer like that, unless her upper-body strength had suddenly increased overnight. Protein-enriched night cream, that sort of thing. Not likely. That left . . .

"Levi!" I called from the top of the stairs.

The racket stopped. "You're awake?"

"This relationship isn't going to work!"

"Oh?"

"What are you doing?"

"Fixing your mom's shelf."

"Why?"

"It was falling down. Do you want to come the rest of the way down the stairs?"

"If I come down, I might be angry with you for waking me up."

"It's almost eleven."

"You woke me up."

"I helped you go to sleep."

"Hammer!"

"Jayne —" my mother's voice floated up the stairs. "Would you like to come down

387

for some breakfast?"

"Hammer!" I ignored the petulant, four-year-old tone to my voice.

"I made caramel-pecan rolls."

Oh. I thought about it. Weighed my options.

Weighed my options until I was in the kitchen, smelling the rolls.

"Hi." Levi's face creased into a wide smile. "How'd you sleep?"

"Fine, until you woke me up."

"Eat a roll, Jayne." My mom handed me a plate with an oozy, gooey roll, a fork sticking out of the top.

"You knew I'd come down."

She patted my shoulder. "It's not rocket science."

I pulled the fork out and cut a bite. The caramel melted in my mouth the way I'd remembered. "Mm-mm-hm-mm-hmhm."

"I thought it was good too. Did you sleep all right until your boyfriend helped your mother with a shelf that nearly fell and crushed the rolls?"

I clutched my plate, horrified that my yummy, yummy caramel-pecan roll had nearly met with a certain, flattened end. I swallowed my bite and looked to Levi. "Boyfriend?"

"I'm sorry." Mom's forehead creased and

her face flushed. "Are you not . . ."

"We are," Levi interrupted. He snagged a pecan off the side of my plate.

I didn't look at him. "My boyfriend has courage." Boyfriend, boyfriend, boyfriend. The word rolled around my head. I tried it again, to see how it felt on my tongue. "Boyfriend."

"Want to sit with me?"

I nodded, hair falling in my face and dangerously close to the caramel residue on my lips. He reached over and tucked it behind my ear before kissing a bit of the caramel off.

I looked around. Mom had disappeared from the kitchen.

Sneaky.

"I didn't mean for you to wake up on the wrong side of the bed, but your mom said these were your favorites."

"They are."

"I didn't think it was that loud."

"Sound carries in this house."

"I'll remember that."

"If you're my boyfriend, does that make me . . ."

"My girlfriend? I think that's the way it works. I don't know. I never went to a traditional high school."

I wove my fingers through his. "I

really . . ." I sighed. "I want this to work."

"Me too."

Looking into his eyes I felt hope. "If this is going to work . . ." I locked eyes with him. "You have to keep away from my pecans."

Chapter 29

My sister was a shopping machine. I think even Gemma would have been impressed by her skills. My original intention for the trip to the outlet malls was to pick up some nice pieces that would allow me to create decent-looking outfits without much effort in the morning.

Beth created a "wardrobe scheme," finding me a pile of clothes that all seemed to coordinate and yet not look like a bad mix-and-match puzzle. She managed to do all that *and* keep me under budget.

"I do it for myself all the time," Beth said while we stopped for lunch in the deli section of Sip Wine & Bistro. "It's not like I can spend a lot of time figuring out what to wear these days." She glanced at Emilee. "The goal is that I can pick up four things from the floor, and at least two should go together."

I reached over and tugged on Emilee's

blond braid. "You're a very good shopper's assistant."

She pulled her thumb from her mouth. "I get two cookies when we get home."

"And you will have earned both of them."

Mom pointed at her bowl. "This potato salad is really good."

"Speaking of very good," Beth said, leaning toward me, "when are you going to talk to us about Levi?"

"What about?"

She pinched the bridge of her nose. "Jayne, the last time you came, you brought Shane. Now it's Levi. At some point we need to lean in, whisper, and giggle. Where did you guys meet?"

I didn't point out that Beth and I had never been whisper-and-giggle sisters. But in the interest of improving our relationship, I lowered my voice and answered. "His woodshop. He was a source for the Amish story I wrote."

"Were you instantly attracted to him?"

"No."

"Oh."

"Sorry. Trumpets weren't playing, and I didn't see an armed Cupid in my peripheral vision."

"Well, what changed? Something must have happened."

"I stayed with his family for a week and a half. I interviewed him a couple times. We just kept seeing each other. After a while . . ."

Let's face it. After a while, I was gone. Embarrassingly gone.

"After Shane and I broke up, we had an opportunity to explore things," I finished.

"Nothing happened while you were with Shane?"

Define nothing . . . I bit my lip.

Beth snapped her fingers and pointed at me. "You're doing it. You're hiding something."

I batted at her pointed finger. "Put that away."

"You get that look on your face when you don't want to tell. What did you do?"

Pined for Levi until Shane and I ended.

"We met. I really liked him, but we didn't start having a relationship until after Shane. Shane ended, and Levi and I got together."

"Just like that?"

"He took me out for a really nice lunch."

"You like him."

"He's my boyfriend. I'm supposed to."

"You really, really like him. You didn't look at Shane the way you look at Levi."

"Beth, you only saw me with Shane over one weekend. We were together for ages.

You don't know how we did or did not look at each other."

Mom patted Beth's arm. "Are you ready to get back to the shops? I'd like to hit Kitchen Collection."

Mom was distracting Beth. I knew it. Beth knew it, but no one except Emilee said anything, and Emilee only announced her need to use the ladies' room.

We returned home, arms full. I couldn't remember the last time I'd shopped and returned with so many logo-emblazoned bags. I felt like a character in a chick flick during the scene when she gets a makeover and goes on a shopping spree. Hadn't felt like that before. I was more likely to return with yoga clothes I'd wear to the gym for a week before using them mainly in front of the TV, utilitarian work pieces, pants I bought because they were long enough for my legs and didn't pucker oddly in the back.

Not inspiring stuff. But for the first time I was kind of excited about my purchases.

Gary and Levi were still working on the car when we returned. Emilee ran to her dad, but Gary lifted his hands out of the way. "Careful there, sweetie. Daddy's messy."

Beth closed the car door. "How'd you

both manage to get so greasy? I thought you were just changing out the brake pads."

"This is just brake dust," Gary answered.

I tilted my head, waiting for the full answer. There were undeniable grease spots on Levi's face.

"We decided to change the oil while we were at it," Levi said, his eyes charged with unreleased laughter. "I dropped the oil plug in the drain pan." He held his own hands out. "And I got brake dust."

I smiled. "See you inside?"

"Only if you agree to walk on the beach with me. It's dry right now."

"We'll see." I gave my best attempt at coyness. From Levi's expression, I guessed that it worked.

Thirty minutes later, Levi was grease free and we were walking along the beach at Road's End. The wind whipped at our clothes; Levi held my hand inside his jacket pocket.

"I like your family," he said, avoiding a crab shell in the sand. "They're very . . ."

"Defiant of classification?"

"Fun. Talkative. Protective of you."

"They are not."

"Gary threatened me with bodily injury if I didn't treat you right."

"Oh. Wow." Impressive, considering I'd seen him maybe four or five times since he and Beth married.

"He was pretty specific about his methodology."

"Sorry about that." I wondered if Shane had received that speech. But then, Shane had never participated in a one-on-one activity with Gary. Poor Levi. No good deed went unpunished, I guess.

"I don't mind." He squeezed my hand. "I'm glad you have people who care about you."

"They're different than I thought they were. I wish I hadn't missed out on so much time."

"You're here now."

I took a breath. "Your parents aren't going to be happy if we . . . stay together." I didn't think I should bring up marriage this soon, but I knew I had a point. "They want you to go home and marry Rachel." I hated myself as soon as I said the words, but the thoughts had been worrying me for too long.

Levi didn't seem perturbed. "I've been worshipping a personal, gracious God for too long. I can't go back. I like the drums in my church service too much."

"You don't miss Rachel?"

"How did you know about Rachel?"

"Ida."

He sighed. "No, I don't miss Rachel. She wanted the life her parents had. I didn't. In fact . . . now's as good a time as any to bring this up."

"What?"

"I'm thinking about selling the shop."

I pulled my hand away in shock. "Honestly? Why?"

"I bought it and built up the business to be near my family. Near my siblings if any of them wanted to be like me. Sara's the only one who's expressed any interest . . . I don't know. I worked so hard to leave and learn and do something different. Now I'm building furniture."

He ran his hand through his hair, an ineffective gesture since the wind restyled his hair moments later. "I've been looking around at some other jobs. I've even thought about maybe starting my own firm."

"Would you stay in Albany?"

"I . . . don't think so."

I felt my heart twinge. "Don't do this on account of me, Levi. What would Spencer and Grady do?"

"I'd offer to sell them the business first." He shrugged. "I haven't figured everything out yet. I just wanted you to know what I was thinking."

"What about Samuel? And Leah and Elizabeth?"

"If they need me, there is a phone on the farm. And they've got Grandma."

"You're okay not having contact with them?"

"I don't have contact with them as it is, Jayne. From what I hear from Sara, my dad's home all the time now. I couldn't visit if I wanted to."

There had to be something else. "Why would you voluntarily choose to return to corporate life?"

"I was never a workaholic corporate guy. I took vacations. Sure, I wasn't traveling up the ladder at the speed of sound, but I liked my job and felt good about what I did during the day."

"And you don't at the shop?"

"I feel like I've done my brain a disservice."

"You feel like that because of the shop, and not because you're overdosing on coffee?"

"Hey now!" He reached out to tickle me, but I was too fast. I sprinted ahead, my feet digging into the sand.

"What are you thinking?" Levi asked as we

were driving back to my mom's.

"Just woolgathering," I answered.

Truthfully, I couldn't get my mind past the conversation we'd had on the beach. I felt myself moving toward the ideals of the Amish: simplicity, family, faith. I craved the way I'd felt at the Burkholder farm — for the first time, I didn't feel my life was spinning out of control. Since then I'd restructured my own life, repairing my family relationships and reconciling with a God I'd ignored for too long. I was learning to quilt, bake, and make my apartment mold resistant.

Basically, I was moving from big-city life to the simple life.

And now Levi wanted to move in the opposite direction.

I knew he wasn't about to abandon his faith; he was stronger than that. The idea that we were otherwise moving in different directions scared me.

My mind took it one step further.

What if he did move to Portland? What stood in the way of us having a real, serious, adult relationship? The kind that led to "save the date" cards?

Nothing.

I was terrified.

■ ■ ■ ■

I remained terrified through dinner, and our family-sans-Emilee viewing of *Witness*, with Levi pointing out all of the inaccuracies.

"An Amish woman would never be so forward toward an English man," Levi said. "Ever. Even if she were in one of the least restrictive communities, she wouldn't speak like that with a man she'd just met."

"Sara would swoon for clothes so tailored," I added.

Levi chuckled.

"What was it like, growing up Amish?" Beth asked, not caring that the movie continued.

"I have a wonderful family. We were very close. I was raised to be a farmer, but I didn't want to be one."

He explained how he left, turning his back on everything he was raised to be, and how he returned to be near his family.

"Now you're leaving them all over again." Suddenly all eyes were on me. "Well, he is."

"Jayne —" Levi started.

"And it doesn't matter that they need you or that they're your family. You're outta there, because they weren't smart enough, or old enough, to follow you."

My mom stood. "Why don't I check on dessert?"

"I'll help you," Beth said. Gary joined her.

Outburst over, I took that moment to study my hands. In detail.

"Thanks, Jayne. Appreciated that."

"Sorry," I said, although I knew a part of me wasn't.

"Does it bother you that much that I want to leave Albany?"

I didn't know what to say.

"Your family has welcomed you with open arms." Levi's brow wrinkled. "You show up on the doorstep, and they let you in. I go home, and my brothers won't look at me. They won't look at me!"

"Your sisters look at you."

"My father pretends that I am dead. I don't exist to him."

"Your mother misses you."

"But I'm not welcome in her home."

"Sara talks about leaving."

"If she leaves, she'll be just like me. She'll never see her older sister again; Rebecca's husband will see to that. And why do you care if she leaves? You're mad at me for leaving a second time."

"I . . ." Anything I said made me look like a hypocrite.

"I need to take a walk."

"It's raining outside."

"I don't care."

He stood, crossed the room, and retrieved his jacket. In an instant, he was out the door.

I stood and walked to the kitchen.

"You can stop skulking now." I ran a hand through my hair.

"We didn't want to interrupt," Mom said.

"If you'd interrupted, I might have stopped talking, and that might have been for the best."

"Communication is the key to relationships," said Gary, his sage words punctuated by a swig from his root beer.

"We should take Emilee home," Beth said. To my amazement, she reached out and gave me a hug. I forced myself to relax. "Everything will be okay."

I was glad she thought so. I wasn't so sure.

Levi returned half an hour later. I was on the couch reading Mom's *Reader's Digest* when he came back, jacket soaked, hair dripping.

I studied his face. "I'm sorry."

He hung his jacket on the closet knob. I heard tiny pats of water hit the tile.

"Beth and Gary went home?"

I nodded. "And Mom's in bed."

"Do you really want to be with me, Jayne?

Or do you just like the idea of me? I'm not a quilt. I'm not your path to a more simplistic existence or whatever else you think you need."

"I'm just trying to figure things out."

"So am I. But you didn't answer my question."

Beth's words at the mall floated back through my head. I was crazy for Levi. I knew it. That scared me to death. What I didn't know, exactly, was *why* I was so crazy for him. Maybe he was right. Maybe he was the human version of my quilt squares.

That would be the easy answer. Life would be simple if I were crazy about him for all the wrong reasons.

Being with him for all the right reasons? That was serious.

He still waited for my answer.

"I couldn't stop thinking about you when I was with Shane. You, who you were. I don't know if how much of how I see you has to do with your job. I honestly don't know, Levi. All I know is that I couldn't get you out of my head."

He took a step closer. "You need to see me for who I am. I'm not my job."

"I . . . I want to see you for who you are. We just need time." I took a step closer to him.

His hand glanced over my hair and then caressed my face. I closed my eyes. "I hope so," he said.

I did too.

CHAPTER 30

I don't know anything about makeup sex, on account of my mother's voice in my head making me think about cows.

Makeup kissing on the other hand . . . hadn't really experienced that one either.

Until now.

We stood in my mother's living room, cradled in each other's arms. If I'd believed in ghosts, I might have worried about my father's disapproving glare. But Dad wasn't here. His body was in the urn on the mantle, and his spirit was in heaven.

My thoughts concerning Levi were wildly conflicting. I hated the idea of him selling the shop. I met him at the shop. I think I fell for him at the shop. I loved everything it stood for.

Without the shop, though, Levi was still Levi. He still smelled the same. His eyes still crinkled when he laughed. I knew he still cared about his family. I knew he still cared about me.

I knew this, because one of his hands was buried in my hair, the other nestled in the small of my back, holding me steady. His lips caressed mine, over and over.

We came up for air a couple moments later. His eyes burned into mine as he stroked my hair. "I love you," he said.

I froze. I knew I was crazy about him. I knew I didn't want to be without him. But love?

Love was a big deal.

Rather than answer, I kissed him.

Kissed him and hoped he didn't think too deeply about it.

Before church on Sunday, Mom and I worked on piecing my quilt. It didn't take us long to get the whole thing pinned into strips. Levi checked in from time to time.

"Are things all right with you two?" Mom asked after Levi offered to bring us refreshments.

I didn't know how to answer. "How did you know that you wanted to be with Dad?" The question was difficult to ask, but I had to know.

"He was everything I was looking for — a believer, a leader. Handsome. I loved him very much. When everything fits together like that, you know."

I wanted to ask a thousand questions. There were pictures of my dad smiling; I just hadn't been born yet to witness those smiles myself. Had he always been like that? What had happened — or who? Was there something about me that was so wrong?

"He loved you, you know," Mom said, using the mind reading abilities she'd picked up the second she gave birth.

For a moment, I was confused. Did she know about Levi? But then my mind reoriented itself, and I knew she was talking about my father. My stern, unyielding father.

"He . . . he had trouble showing it. I know that parts of your childhood . . ." she took a deep breath, "couldn't have been easy. I'm so sorry about that. He was proud of you, though. Proud of your going to the university, proud that you had your job at the paper. Whenever you wrote an article, it spent a week on the fridge. After that, he put it into a notebook. It's around here, somewhere."

"I didn't know."

We both knew that I might have known, had I bothered to return home for more than a few minutes around the occasional holiday. My mom was gracious enough not to point that out.

I looked over my shoulder, checking the hallway for listeners. "Levi . . . told me he loves me."

"Of course he does."

"Not helping."

"Do you love him?"

That's the question that frightened me. I didn't have a chance to even try to answer; as soon as I heard Levi's footfalls on the stairs, I turned my attention back to the prickly quilt.

After arriving at church, I received compliments on my flippy navy skirt, printed blouse, and tangerine cardigan, and reveled in the fact that I was the recipient of such comments. On my clothing, no less.

Sara would be so proud.

Miss Lynnie found me after the service. "Who is *this* young man?" she asked, not looking at all upset that I had a new husband candidate with me.

"This is Levi," I answered, performing introductions.

Levi shook her hand carefully and complimented her brooch. Miss Lynnie smiled, delighted. "I like this one," she said.

"Me too," I answered. "He's also a believer," I added, before she could ask.

"Of course he is," she said with a wave of the hand. "How else would he know all five verses of *Come, Thou Fount of Every Blessing*?"

She shuffled away after patting both of us on the cheek, her version, I think, of a blessing.

"She approves," I told my mom after Miss Lynnie was out of earshot.

"Of course she does," Mom answered, smiling at Levi. "Shall we all find something for lunch? Emilee's hungry."

We ended up voting for lunch locations, and Hawk Creek Café won unanimously. We started with a large Thai chicken pizza and ended with the crusts drizzled with honey. Near the fireplace in the back, I almost fell asleep.

Levi and I packed up after lunch, despite my yen for a nap. We gave final hugs to Mom, and began the drive back to Portland.

For the duration of the drive, we listened to Levi's Trace Bundy CD. Levi wasn't feeling talkative, clearly, and I certainly wasn't either. I closed my eyes and allowed myself to drift off.

I awoke to the feel of turning into a driveway. I opened my eyes. It was the driveway to the parking lot at my building. We were home. My home, anyway.

"Sorry," I said, trying to sit up. "I didn't mean to sleep the whole way."

"That's all right." The tone of his voice told me it probably wasn't. "Need help with your bags?"

"I . . . sure." I'd assumed he'd come in and we'd spend a little time together. Apparently I was wrong.

Levi carried my duffel bag. I carried my purse, windbreaker, and tennis shoes. I opened the door; he walked through it, took my bag down the hall, and deposited it in my bedroom doorway.

"Thanks," I said, dumping my things in the chair by the door and kicking off my shoes.

"You're welcome. I should get back."

"Oh — okay."

"Bye."

"Bye." I watched in confusion as he started to walk out the door. "So that's it?"

He stalled in the doorway but wouldn't look at me. "I don't know."

I crossed my arms. "You have to talk to me."

"What's there to talk about?" He closed the door, so at least my neighbors weren't getting their live *As the World Turns* installment from me. "I told you I loved you. You didn't say anything."

"I seem to remember kissing you. If I didn't like you at all, I probably wouldn't have engaged in any sort of physical contact with you."

"I don't know that."

"Levi!" I laid a hand on his shoulder. "You know I care about you. A lot. I just . . . didn't know what to say."

"Because you don't love me."

"You don't know that!"

"Don't I?"

I retracted my hand. "I told you, I care about you."

"But you don't love me."

"I want to be with you!"

"You don't love me."

For Pete's sake, he was slow. "We've been together such a short while. Love takes time."

"You're saying I don't love you?"

"No. I believe you. I just need more time."

"How much time?"

"I don't know."

"What about if I sold my carpentry business? Would you still love me? If I decided to think practically instead of allowing my life decisions to be made on the basis of wishful thinking and sentimentality, would you still be there?"

I hesitated, just the tiniest second.

"Thanks. That's all I need to know."

"Levi —"

He reached again for the doorknob. "Jayne, I love you. No matter what you do."

I pulled myself up. "Obviously not, if you're leaving like this."

"I love you." He shrugged. "I can't help but love you. I've loved you since you scheduled an interview with me on a day when you didn't have anything going but pretended you did and then rode away on your motorcycle. That was the first day I met you. You're not being honest with me, and you're not honest with yourself. You like the idea of me. If the idea shifts . . ." his voice broke. "It makes me sad. I wish you felt the same way about me that I do about you."

"You don't know I don't."

"Do you love me, Jayne?"

"Yes!"

The look in his eyes wrenched at my heart. "I wish you were telling the truth."

"It's not that easy —"

"Sometimes it is. Goodbye, Jayne."

He left, closing the door behind him.

I jumped to my feet and threw the door back open. "Levi! Wait!"

He kept walking down the stairs. I followed him, the damp soaking into my socks.

"Levi!" I could hear my voice shake, but I didn't care what anyone thought. "Please!"

His steps didn't slow. He didn't turn around, didn't do anything to acknowledge that he'd even heard my voice. Levi, the man I couldn't stop thinking about, climbed into his truck and drove away.

Just like that.

I spent the night in the living room next to my phone, in case he came back or called.

I left the door unlocked, so that if I fell asleep he'd still be able to come in, wrap his arms around me, and tell me everything was all right. I cried myself to sleep sometime around three.

Because I'm a creature of habit, I woke ninety minutes before I needed to leave for work. As usual.

I stumbled down the hall, but I locked the door before I did so. I didn't need a weirdo entering my apartment while I was in the shower. I peered at my reflection in the bathroom mirror.

I looked like a typhoid patient.

Thoughts of calling in sick shot through my mind. The idea of not dealing with people appealed, but staying at home and continuing to cry my eyes out appealed less. I went through the motions of washing my hair, drying my hair, dressing in my most comfortable, work-appropriate clothes, and finding my keys. I couldn't eat breakfast — the thought of food turned my stomach.

I managed to arrive at work without getting into an accident. Brian leaned over the joining cubicle wall after I sat down. "What happened to you?"

I didn't feel the need to look up. "Bad weekend."

"I've got a couple aspirin if you're hungover."

"I'm not hungover."

"Sick?"

"No."

"Woman's issues?"

I slammed my pencil down. "Since when is that any of your business?"

"Sorry. My eyes have been opened to the difficulties of being female ever since I got married."

Somehow, I doubted his increased sensitivity, and I guessed his wife would agree with me.

"I'm not sick, hungover, or experiencing untoward hormonal fluctuations."

"Are you sure? Because ovulation can cause mood swings too —"

"Brian!"

"Sorry."

But he wasn't sorry enough. When I got up to use the restroom, I came back to find Kim and Gemma at my desk, textbook concerned looks on their faces.

"Brian, you just couldn't help yourself." I looked to Kim. "Do I get my chair back?"

"What happened?"

"Bad weekend. I was out drinking."

"No, she wasn't!" Brian said from behind the cubicle wall.

"Your pupils aren't dilated. We don't believe you." Kim tossed her head.

Gemma lifted an eyebrow. "I'm impressed."

"Come on. Am I the only one who listens to Joely's cop talk?"

"She lost me at Miranda rights."

Seriously. "If I were hungover, you two would be giving me a headache. But I'm not. I'm just sad. Not hungover or hormonal or sick. Just sad."

Gemma reached for my arm. "What happened?"

"We broke up, okay? Levi and I broke up. And I'm sad. But I'm moving through it."

They went through the motions of trying to comfort me. It felt like rubbing a wool blanket over soft skin. "Don't worry about it, okay? I mean, I'm a breakup pro. Me and Shane, me and Levi. I'm old hat."

Gemma frowned. "I've never understood that phrase."

"It means I am weathered or experienced. I think. If I'm using it wrong, you certainly wouldn't know. Don't you both have jobs? Food to taste, politicians to expose?" My phone rang. "I've got a job to do. You guys can drown me in ice cream and *Love Story* later."

"Bleh," Kim said, sticking out her tongue. "I hate that movie."

Second ring. "Fine. *The Way We Were.* Bye!" I lifted the receiver and swiped at the dampness near my eye. "Tate."

"Tate? Sol. Come in for a visit, why don't you."

I stood and leaned to the right so I could see through his office window. "Can't we just chat about this over the phone?"

"Not while you've got a three-ring circus at your desk. Move."

So I moved.

"If you'd managed to check your email," Sol began as soon as I closed the door, "you would have seen that we've had a huge reader response from that Amish piece you wrote."

"Really?" My outlook on life almost brightened. Almost, because it reminded me of the family of the man who never wanted to see me again.

"What's going on? You look like — well, it would be ungentlemanly for me to say what you look like."

"Flatterer."

"Waiting."

"Boyfriend. Broke up."

He narrowed his eyes. "I thought you broke up with that architect boy last week. What's new?"

"Different boy. The family I stayed with?"

"You dated an Amish boy?"

"No, and he's hardly a boy. He's thirty-two. And he left the Amish, but they're still his family. And . . . he left."

"That's no good. I called you in here to ask you to do another installment on the Amish series."

"It's a series?"

"It is now. Are you up for it?"

"Yes." The word came out in a whoosh. "When?"

"Soon as you can. Might want to clean yourself up a bit. You'll frighten the Burkholders."

Knowing Martha, she'd probably feed me and wrap me in a warm blanket. The thought of being back at the farmhouse made me ache for the warmth of the kitchen and Elizabeth's gapped grin.

We went over the word count and angle he wanted. I jotted a few notes and stood to leave.

"And Tate —"

I stopped, my hand on the doorknob. "Sir?"

"Take better care of yourself. Can't afford to lose you."

"Thanks."

"New reporters annoy me."

"I'm sure they do."

I packed up later that morning, my emotions impossibly mixed. I longed to see Martha; I dreaded seeing Martha. In fact, I felt that way about the entire family. The last thing I wanted was to see Levi's resemblance to his brothers, his sense of humor in Sara . . .

I was pathetic.

If only I had been able to tell Levi I loved him.

If only I knew I was telling the truth.

If only my intense attraction and affection for him had been enough. I knew I'd screwed up that night at my mom's when I'd practically attacked him in front of the family. Not one of my prouder moments.

He didn't want any less than all of me. Less than that was unacceptable. So unacceptable that he walked out as if I'd never meant anything to him.

Rethinking that night and that week and every other encounter made me cringe, but my mind wouldn't stop the instant replays.

Was this part of God's plan? Now that I was going back to the faith of my childhood, was this His way of making sure He had my full attention?

"That's not playing fair, God," I said out loud to make sure He was listening.

I ripped apart the Velcro holding my wrist brace together and then wiggled it off.

My wrist felt naked and unprotected without it. I flexed my fingers and rotated my hand. So far, so good. Maybe it was . . .

I winced and replaced the brace. Okay, not yet. But soon. I missed my motorcycle, and this would have been a nice trip to take on it.

I stretched my back and neck and tried to recenter myself. I had to be stronger than this. I couldn't be the girl who fell apart when a guy left. I had to hold strong to what I believed.

So what did I believe?

CHAPTER 31

On the way back to the farm I took a detour and drove out to Silver Creek Falls. There were a few other cars in the parking area, but I couldn't see any people. With my hands shoved into my pockets, I hiked the short way down to the North Falls. The question I'd considered at the apartment had haunted me during the drive and stayed with me as I walked down the concrete path.

What did I believe?

I believed in God.

What was He like?

Was He someone I could trust? It was one thing to be told by a pastor that, yes, God was trustworthy, and entirely another to believe it for myself.

I could hear the falls as I approached. A fine mist filled the air.

The water was magnificent. I felt myself relax just watching.

I knew God was a father, and yet the only

father I'd ever personally experienced wasn't one I'd readily recommend. Did my feelings about God have anything to do with that?

Standing in front of the falls, I realized if I continued thinking along this vein I'd be here all day.

With a mixed-up heart I went back to my car and pulled onto I-5.

The moment I saw the farmhouse, I had a strange desire to get out of my car and race toward it, arms outstretched.

The breakup was making me crazy. I made a mental note to avoid romantically inclined relationships in the future. I wasn't a fan of the fallout.

Having decided not to run to the farm-house, I grinned at the sight of Leah and Elizabeth running toward me.

Then I started worrying about running them over. I remembered Levi complaining of the same thing — and the memory stung.

I stopped, yanked at the parking brake, retrieved my keys, and stepped from the car.

Leah and Elizabeth hugged my legs, asking so many questions I couldn't understand a single one.

"What are you two doing out of school?" I tried my best to pick them up, one arm per child, but I couldn't manage to get them two inches off the ground. "You've grown!"

"Teacher's sick today. I lost another tooth," said Elizabeth, pointing at a new hole in her mouth.

"Yes, you have. Is your mom inside?"

Leah nodded. "She's in the kitchen. We're going to have dried peach pie tonight!"

"Sounds yummy! Walk me in?"

The moment I stepped inside, I was embraced by warm, dry air filled with the scents of yeasty bread and roasting meat.

"Jayne!" Martha's smile when she saw me was welcome enough. "This is a surprise."

"I wish I could have written first, but my boss wanted me to write a follow-up piece for the paper."

"Would you like to help with the pie dough?"

"Of course." I took off my jacket, washed my hands, and picked up the rolling pin Martha had left on the counter. "I was planning on staying in town a few days."

Martha frowned. "Why in town?"

"I didn't want to be underfoot."

"You must stay here. I insist, and Gideon will too."

"How is he?"

Martha rolled her eyes. "He's in the fields with Elam and Amos."

"Not working too hard, I hope?"

She shrugged. "They're keeping an eye on him. He's stubborn."

Reminded me of someone else I knew.

A thought struck me — this time around, if my computer battery died, I'd have to go to a coffee shop. Levi wouldn't be opening his office electricity to me anytime soon.

"That looks thin enough," Martha said, glancing at the pie crust dough. "You can probably stop there."

"Oh." *Thin enough* was being kind. There were places where the dough was near translucent in its papery thinness.

That's what I got for thinking about Levi and trying to bake at the same time.

Sara chose that moment to swing around the corner. "Oh. It's you."

If I hadn't read her letter, I would have thought she was completely indifferent.

"Yes, it's me. What gave it away."

Sara shrugged. "I heard you from upstairs. You're really loud."

"Nice to see you too."

I turned my back, but I could feel Sara analyzing my outfit. Because she didn't depart immediately, I knew she approved.

Success!

"We are very pleased to have Jayne back,"

said Gideon at the dinner table that evening. "And very pleased that on the night she returns we are not eating fish."

"I hear fish is good for your heart," I said, mainly because I could get away with it.

"Good for your heart, but maybe too much is not good for your soul."

Interesting theology. "How have you been feeling?"

"I feel like I am young again."

Somehow I doubted that.

"Well, I'm just here to observe for a few days. I don't want to get in anyone's way."

I think I heard Elam snort.

Punk.

"Grandma is coming the day after tomorrow," Sara said. "We're going to quilt together."

"Really!" An idea popped into my head. "I've been working on my quilt. I'll have my mom send it down."

The shipping would cost an arm, leg, and a kidney, but I didn't want to miss out on quilting with Sara and Ida.

Everyone needs something to look forward to.

As far as the breakup was concerned, I think I'd moved from denial to anger. I lay under a stack of Amish quilts that night, stewing.

Levi knew I'd just come off a relationship with Shane. He knew I was going through a lot of major life changes. Who was he to give me a "love me or leave me" ultimatum?

I wondered briefly if he had a brain tumor. I spent a few minutes worrying about him before I reverted back to anger.

I broke a plate at breakfast that morning. I may have been thinking about Levi at the time.

"You're wearing your normal clothes," Sara commented as we washed the breakfast dishes.

"I can switch, but there weren't any other options in the guest room, and I forgot to ask."

She looked around, checking for little listeners. "Your clothes look better than before."

"Thank you. I went shopping."

"With Gemma?"

"My sister."

Sara gave an appreciative nod. "She did a good job."

"And I pulled out my debit card with exceptional skill."

"What's a debit card?"

I explained, realizing the Amish weren't

exactly regular bankers.

"How are you and Levi . . . you know."

"You mean are we still together?"

"Yes."

"We aren't." I sighed.

"Oh." She scrubbed another plate. "That was fast."

Too fast. "It happens."

"Was it you or him?"

"Meaning . . . ?"

"Which one of you did something to ruin it?"

"Sometimes, relationships don't work out. Not for things people did or didn't do, but just because those people don't work together."

"You find out that people don't work together by what they do or don't do," Sara pointed out.

"Stop being so smart."

"Am I right?"

"Sara, give me a break. I'm trying to be a good ex-girlfriend and not speak badly of he whom I dated. Can I get credit for that?"

"You still like him."

"We need to finish the dishes and start the laundry."

"You still like him."

"Be nice to me. I sent you contraband."

"Do you think he'll change his mind?"

I didn't want to cry, not in front of Sara. "No, I don't. What about you? Any boys sneaking through your window these days?"

Her eyes grew wide. "It's a secret!"

"Well, so was Levi. Spill."

"There's no one."

Was that because she planned on leaving? I didn't want to know. We dropped the subject of the opposite sex altogether and paid very close attention to the rest of the breakfast dishes.

My mom agreed to overnight my quilt strips. I didn't tell her about Levi. I couldn't get myself to explain that I had ended two relationships in one month.

When the package arrived the following morning, I saw that my mom had also included enough fabric to back the quilt, as well as some edging and batting.

Ida arrived shortly after, and we set to work. I asked Martha for assistance with the treadle sewing machine, but she deferred to Sara.

Sara instructed me to practice with scrap fabric until I got the hang of the treadle sewing machine. Then she showed me how to thread the needle and fill the bobbin, place the fabric, and then run a line of stitches.

I watched her do it first. She turned the wheel on the right-hand side, using it to start the rhythmic movement of the needle slowly before beginning the pedaling movement with her feet. "Don't push the treadle too fast," Sara advised. "You want to keep control of the stitches. When you pedal, put your right foot ahead of the left, like this —" she lifted her skirt out of the way so I could see her feet with an unobstructed view. "It keeps your ankles from getting tired. Your turn!"

"I think I should watch a bit longer," I said, not that she was listening. She'd already sprung from her seat and waited expectantly for me to replace her.

I sat. "Which direction do I turn this?" I asked, touching the wheel on the right.

"That's the balance wheel. You always turn it toward you."

"Toward me. Okay."

"Do you want to practice the treadle?"

"Sure." I pedaled a few times. Sara knelt, adjusted my feet, and had me do it again. "That's good. Now try it with fabric."

I tried a line of stitches. To my surprise, they didn't veer off and begin a trip to Jersey. "That's not bad."

Ida nodded. "You have good quilting hands."

I studied my hands. I hadn't thought of them that way before.

Sara began to rattle about the finer points of basting, reversing, and tension, and I just barely kept up. When she was talking about sewing and fabric, she came alive. I got the feeling she could talk for a week about hems.

If she stayed, those skills would translate into sewing for her family, likely with a quilting business on the side. Would that be enough for her?

I thought about Levi. Keeping his family's accounts wouldn't have been enough for him, and running the woodshop clearly wasn't either. Was I kidding myself to believe he would be happy there forever?

Sara, Martha, and Ida continued to quilt long after I begged off with sore calves. The sky was clear outside, and I resolved to take a walk around the farm to stretch the rest of my muscles. I stopped still when a familiar green pickup pulled into the drive. I saw the truck slow suddenly, as if the driver braked hard in surprise.

I couldn't move as Levi climbed from the cab. He looked to Ida's car, parked next to mine in the driveway. "You're back."

I nodded.

"My grandma's here?"

I nodded again.

"I'm looking for my dad."

"Oh."

He didn't ask why I was there.

Not that it mattered much to him.

I watched as he walked toward the barn. When he was sufficiently away, I took an alternate route to the same location. Every one of my reporter's instincts urged me to move faster, to think harder, to remember all of the details.

When it began to rain, I didn't care. There was a back entrance to the barn that would allow me to listen to any words spoken. Granted, the gas-powered generators were loud, but people had to shout over them anyway. The shouting I could hear. And knowing Levi and Gideon, the likelihood of shouting was present.

I don't know what farm equipment was in use, but some of it quieted.

"Do you have a minute, Dad?"

I didn't need to be in the room to see Gideon's scowl. I positioned myself just outside the back door.

"Don't call me 'Dad.' You are not my son."

"Did you know I left my job in the city to work in town, to be near my family?"

"You don't have a family."

"I'm sorry I had to leave. I'm sorry I

couldn't be the son you wanted me to be." I could hear the rising tension in Levi's voice.

"Don't upset him, please," said Amos' voice. "His health —"

"My health is *gut,*" Gideon snapped.

"I was never baptized, Dad. You don't have to shun me."

"I had a son. I had a son and he turned his back on his family and his God."

"God is still with me."

"Are you baptized?"

"Yes."

"Into an Anabaptist church?"

"No."

"Then I fear for your soul."

There was a pause. "You won't change your mind, will you."

"No."

"I love you, Dad."

Gideon grunted. There was quiet, and then I heard Gideon's voice telling Amos and Elam to get back to work.

I moved from my hiding place to see Levi walk back to his truck, his gaze steady ahead. I knew in an instant that he'd expected for the conversation to go the way it had, and yet he'd done it anyway.

The truck engine started up. I could see the women watching from inside the house.

I fought the urge to run up to Levi to

comfort him, to talk to him. He didn't want to talk to me.

He didn't look at me as he got back into his truck and started the ignition. I watched as the tires moved against the gravel drive and he drove away. Out of my life, and as far as I could tell, out of his family's lives.

I turned to go back to the house. My eyes caught Ida's as I neared the door. Her old eyes regarded me with an expression I hadn't seen before.

She met me at the door. "I need my sewing box. Would you mind helping me carry it from my car? My back ain't what it used to be."

I agreed, following her back out.

"He's in love with you, isn't he." She made the statement mere moments after the front door closed.

"We were together for a little while. He broke it off." I knew any attempt to hedge on the truth with Ida would be pointless.

"Do you still love him?"

"He left."

"He still loves you."

I shook my head. Ida opened her car door and pointed at the box. I leaned in and pulled it out, noticing that only a person with significant movement loss would have difficulty carrying it.

"He looks at you with love in his eyes. There is hurt, too, but Levi has never been good at hiding his thoughts from his face. Even as a boy. I knew he would leave. If only he could have been Mennonite, his family might have forgiven him. But once he grew his wings, he couldn't help flying far." She patted my cheek. "I don't know what happened between you. He loves you, though, Jayne. Don't worry."

She turned and walked back to the house with impressive speed. I followed her with the sewing box. All I could think of was the raw memory of Levi leaving my apartment and not coming back.

CHAPTER 32

Samuel, Leah, and Elizabeth returned home from school that afternoon, cheeks rosy and eyes bright. Ida, Martha, and Sara were all still in the throes of a large mending session, so Martha asked me if I'd mind helping the children.

"Your mom told me I'm helping you with your homework," I announced, trying to sound energized and pro-education.

They nodded.

"Where do you normally study?"

"The kitchen table," Leah answered.

"Okay." I clapped my hands together. "Do you eat a snack while you do homework?"

Three shaking heads.

"Okay. What kind of homework do you have?"

They each pulled their books out of their knapsacks. I picked one up.

The textbook would have looked at home in Punky Brewster's book bag. I flipped to the copyright page and checked the publication date — 1979.

The map in the social studies book showed the USSR covering half the world in bright red. Germany remained divided.

I forced a smile. "Let's get started."

I made a point of flipping through whatever books weren't in use as the children studied. "Do you ever study science?" I asked, trying to sound nonchalant.

Samuel shook his head. "We learn reading, 'riting, and 'rithmetic."

Which would explain my having to introduce Sara to the world of spores and molds several weeks before.

I wanted to talk to Levi. I wanted him to explain to me why the eight years of education these children were afforded were so poor.

He must have worked hard to get to where he was if his schooling was the same. I rubbed my forehead. I knew from some of my reading that it wasn't always like this, that some Amish children attended public school or studied under trained teachers.

I answered their questions about math figures as best I could. When they came to a point when they understood the material, such as it was, and the questions ceased for the foreseeable future, I wandered back to the sewing group and my own quilt strips.

"Did Sara tell you she's getting baptized next week?" Martha asked.

I nearly impaled my finger on one of the straight pins. "Really?" My head whipped around to where Sara sat. "That's . . . exciting."

Ida's eyes watched my every move. I could feel her gaze.

"Sara, tell Jayne about the baptism service," Martha said, encouraging Sara with a nod.

Sara cleared her throat. "It's part of the church service. Before the baptism, the bishop will ask applicants to leave the service, and then he asks if we're sure we want to be baptized. It's kind of silly, since we've all taken a class about it.

"We'll be asked a few questions before we return to the hymns and the sermon. Afterward, the bishop will have us go to the front. He'll remind us we're making a promise to God. Then he and the deacon — Mary Lapp's John — will take the bucket and cup. John pours water over the bishop's hands and then onto our heads three times in the name of the Father, the Son, and the Holy Ghost." She shrugged. "And then we're told to rise and such, and Mary, being the deacon's wife and all, will give me and the other girls the Holy Kiss."

"Of brotherhood," Martha added.

"Of brotherhood," Sara finished. "But shouldn't it be sisterhood?"

"It's family," Ida said, "whichever way you look at it."

I tried not to look confused. When we'd spoken over the breakfast dishes, Sara hadn't said a word.

"Don't baptisms usually precede weddings?" I asked, fishing.

"Often," Martha said, not looking up from her sewing. "But not always."

I smiled at Sara. "I'm glad for you." If that was the path she had truly chosen for herself, I really did wish her all the best.

The rest of the day was a blur. After helping the children with their homework, I finished sewing the front of my quilt together.

I should have felt better about it than I did. As a first quilt, it wasn't the shoddiest specimen.

But something wasn't right. It wasn't Amish enough.

My thoughts traveled back to Levi. I thought briefly of giving Shane a call, but I thought better of it. Shane and I were over, and I was okay with that. Levi and I on the other hand — we were over, but I *wasn't* okay with that.

Not that it mattered anymore. I tried to think of something else. I couldn't think of anything else. I tried harder.

At some point while trying harder, I fell asleep.

And dreamed about Levi.

I woke when the rooster crowed, horrified to hear several sets of feet moving throughout the house. I threw on my clothes and hurried out to join the others.

Leah met me in the hallway. "Today is Sara's birthday!"

"Really?" I gave her a hug as we walked toward the kitchen. "How old is she?"

"Eighteen!" Sara announced from behind us.

"I remember being eighteen," I said, smiling ruefully.

Of course, my eighteen and her eighteen were two different things entirely. If I remembered right, I celebrated by registering to vote, showing up at the elections office with my purple-streaked hair and Smashing Pumpkins T-shirt.

Sara, on the other hand, wouldn't be voting anytime soon, and her lovely brown hair was twisted up under her kapp.

"Will you celebrate today?" I asked.

Leah nodded and swung my hand from side to side. "We'll celebrate at dinner. *Mutter* will make a cake and roast a ham."

"Sounds delicious! Do you get presents?"

"Yes," Sara straightened her apron. "Probably some new shoes."

I stopped my sarcastic "Oh goody" comment from leaving my lips just in time.

"My sister Rebecca and her family might take a taxi from Washington and stay with Grandma," Sara added. "You haven't met Rebecca."

"Not yet, but it sounds like I will."

We ate a breakfast of dried apple muffins, eggs scrambled with peppers and bacon, fried potatoes, and sausage patties. After helping with the dishes, I made my excuses and drove into town, determined to find an appropriate birthday gift for Sara.

I may have driven past the shop. I wasn't *stalking* Levi, just checking to see if there was a sale or lease sign in front of the building. Just in case.

There wasn't. I proceeded to Fred Meyer's. What do you buy for an Amish teenager that you can give her in front of her family? If it were only between the two of us, and if she weren't being baptized, then I would go a little crazier, maybe find her a pair of sequined flip-flops for the summer. Or a bright scarf with fringe.

Probably should have checked with Martha first.

I wandered out of Fred Meyer's, got back into my car, and drove around until the red glowing sign of inspiration appeared: JoAnn Fabrics.

Inside, I chose several bolts of fabric I thought Sara might like and bought a yard each. I drove back to Freddie's for a gift bag, tissue paper, and a card.

I didn't know if the Amish did birthday cards, but I bought one anyway.

After wrapping the fabric in paper and stuffing it elegantly into the sack, I signed the card and drove back to the Burkholders'.

"Something's baking," I called as I stepped inside. I found Martha in the kitchen. "It smells wonderful, whatever it is."

"Sara doesn't have a single favorite cake, so I make a five-layer cake with every layer a different flavor."

"Oh!" That could either be very good or very bad. "What flavors?

"Pumpkin, coconut, chocolate, raspberry, and lemon poppy seed."

"Oh." The jury might remain out for a

while on that one. "Need a hand?"

"I'd appreciate it. Sara's birthday is the second most difficult of all my children's."

"Who's the first?"

"Elam. He doesn't like cake, so I make varieties of ice cream for him."

"From scratch?"

"Yes," Martha answered, but at that moment her gaze became shifty. "Well," she said with a lowered voice, "last year I was very busy with Rebecca's baby's quilt, so I . . ." her voice dropped still lower, "I *bought* ice cream."

"Martha!"

"And I made sure I got three flavors I hadn't made before so they wouldn't be able to compare."

I couldn't help but laugh. "Very sneaky. I would have done the exact same thing."

Actually, that wasn't true. I wouldn't have gotten conned into making three batches of ice cream in the first place. My mom used to make ice cream, and even with an electric ice-cream maker, it was labor-intensive. She would stand at the stove for ages, stirring the custard. Make three batches of heat-sensitive custard and then churn it? No, thank you.

"Do you make the same cake combination every year?"

"No. Last year it was carrot, yellow, ginger-pecan, chocolate chip, and Jell-O orange."

I couldn't even imagine, but a part of me wished I could. I wondered what it would be like to spend my days in a kitchen, cooking and baking for my family. To know what my children liked best for their birthdays.

The birthday party unfolded through dinner. Sara arrived at the table in her favorite dress — her favorite, I knew, because it was the brightest-colored one she owned. The rich brick red of her dress, covered by her black apron, accentuated the color in her cheeks and the green of her eyes.

Rebecca and her family arrived via taxi moments later. Out of all the siblings, she bore the strongest resemblance to Levi with her dark eyes and fair skin. She carried Baby Verna on her hip, while her husband, Karl, held young Henry.

Karl's genial smile faded the moment he saw me, dressed as I was in blue jeans and clearly not Amish. But Gideon jumped in and explained how I had called the ambulance for him when he'd had his heart attack and sang my praises about the way I'd cared for Martha and Sara while he was in the hospital, or, as he referred to it, "the clink."

He clearly didn't know that Levi had also been with us, but that was information for another day.

Ida appeared at the door, bearing a giant smile, and the gathering was complete. Complete except for Levi.

We crowded around the table and gazed at the beauty of the dinner provided. Martha had prepared — on top of the five-layer cake o' wonder — a ham crusted with brown sugar, creamy mashed potatoes, fresh green beans, buttery rolls, and homemade peach butter.

Everyone ate and laughed and told stories about Sara. When we'd all had our fill of dinner, we retired to the living room for a round of Parcheesi while we digested. Sara won, although I suspected everyone let her.

I came in second.

After the game, Martha called Rebecca and me to the dining room. Ida joined us. Within moments we had the dinner dishes cleared and cake plates out. Everyone else filed into the room, and Martha brought in the lit cake, all five layers of it.

I half expected the weight of it to send her toppling over, but after a lifetime of manual labor, Martha had untold brawn beneath her sleeves.

Applause broke out as she approached the

table. Elam and Rebecca teased Sara about the flavors, throwing out potential candidates, such as licorice, pork roast, twigs, and bark.

The latter two were suggested by Elizabeth.

As we sang Sara "Happy Birthday," my eye caught something through the kitchen window. I dismissed it as one of the animals on the farm. Sara opened her gifts one by one — fancy molded soaps from Rebecca, a new pair of shoes from Gideon and Martha, a set of thimbles from Elam, a new dress from Ida. Sara's face lit up when she lifted the fabrics from the gift bag I'd chosen.

"Do you like them?" I asked, although there wasn't much I could do if she didn't.

"Very much," she answered, hugging them to her slim body.

Something moving outside the window caught my attention again. For the briefest moment, I thought I saw Levi in the darkness.

I went to bed that night, warm from the time of family happiness and yet aching in my heart. I didn't want to leave the farm. Not ever.

With the weather just beginning to warm

up, Martha spent the majority of her day in the vegetable garden.

I watched from the window and spent a moment envying her ability to provide for her family through the work of her hands. I felt the familiar wrench in my chest at the calm in her life, the lack of distractions, how much purer things were in the shelter of the farmhouse.

Why couldn't I be like that? Why couldn't I keep my apartment clean? I didn't even have children, and clutter still accumulated. My quilt looked like a child's attempt, and I wasn't about to garden anytime soon.

This is not where I have called you.

I stepped back from the window as if I'd been zapped and looked around.

Are you sure? I asked back to the voice, so familiar and unfamiliar at the same time. *If I'm going to follow You, can't I follow You better here? Fewer distractions, no television, no internet — just You and me and the land?*

My questions were met with silence, but it didn't matter. I had already heard the voice.

I sighed and decided to take another walk.

The wind whipped my hair into my face; I kept brushing it away, even though I knew it would be back in the shortest of moments.

I wanted to stay at the farmhouse. It was that simple. But the more I thought about it, the more I realized the reason why I wanted to stay was because I liked myself better when I was with the Burkholders. I liked helping with the children. I liked being useful.

Could I still be useful in the outside world? Probably. Most likely. Yes. But it was so much more picturesque at the farm, with the bonnets and the buggies.

And yet, I knew the "picturesque" part wasn't entirely real. Levi's family was every bit as dysfunctional as my own. More, if you considered that at least my father acknowledged me as his child until the day he died. I had watched Gideon readily forgive a buggy thief but turn Levi away.

I knew the children were not receiving a quality education, so much more detrimental considering they only had eight years of it. Did it matter? I thought so. We were called to minister to the world, and it was hard to understand the world if you were unaware of the goings-on for the past thirty years.

Even though my return to the church was recent, I still knew in my heart that my God was a personal God, a gracious God, a God who cared less for our deeds than the quality of our hearts.

I didn't know what He was calling me to, or where, but I wanted the quality of my heart to matter. I wanted my actions to stem from love rather than tradition, guilt, or habit. Just because my life wasn't simple didn't make it insignificant. Owning a cell phone didn't make me a lesser person.

I sighed. It was time to go home.

CHAPTER 33

"Are you packing?"

I turned to see Sara in my doorway. "Hi there. Yes, I'm packing. It's time for me to leave."

"But — you only just got here."

"I need to get back to the paper." And to the rest of my life, such as it was. "It's time."

"Your quilt! You haven't finished your quilt!"

"I will."

"Do you have a sewing machine at your apartment?"

"No . . ."

"Then how?"

"My mom. I'll take it with me when I visit."

"Oh," Sara said, her rosy mouth stretching into a frown.

"You can still write me," I said, continuing to fold. "Although, I probably shouldn't include . . ." I let my voice drop, in case we had listeners. Little ones. "You're getting baptized soon, after all."

Sara shuffled her feet. "Yeah."

I wondered if she was really ready, but it wasn't my place to question.

"I'm looking forward to it. Getting baptized."

She said it with the enthusiasm most people show toward dental work.

"I'm glad," I said. "I don't suppose anyone's taking pictures."

Sara rolled her eyes. "We don't believe in posing for pictures."

"You wouldn't be posing. You're already there, getting baptized. Speaking of photos — would anyone mind if I took a couple shots before I left?"

"I don't know. Ask my mom."

"Good idea."

I tucked a few more items away and left to find Martha. I found her in the kitchen, scrubbing her hands free of soil. "I think I'll be leaving this evening," I said, not knowing how else to start.

Martha dried her hands on the checkered dishtowel by the sink. "We'll be sorry to lose you, but I'm sure you have work to get back to."

"I do. I was wondering . . . would you mind if I took a few pictures? Nothing intrusive, but it would be nice for the piece I'll be writing."

She shifted uncomfortably. "No faces, no posing, please." She gave a slight smile. "I trust you."

I returned her smile. "Thank you."

With Martha's blessing, I pulled my digital Canon SLR from its protective case, checked my battery and memory card, and set out on the farm.

I didn't profess to be a photographer of any skill, but it's one of those things that proves to be a useful skill when working for a paper in the day and age of media-downsizing.

And photographing the Amish. Seriously. As long as the photo was in focus, it looked amazing. Amish laundry was like that. To them it was just wet clothes drying — to us, mystical art.

The weather, while warmer, was still damp enough to mean there were dresses, pants, shirts, and aprons of various sizes drying inside on the rack. Not as picturesque as items flapping in the breeze on a sunny day, but they would do.

I took some shots of the buggy, some shots of the tidy white farmhouse from the road. Back inside, I watched as Martha puttered in the kitchen preparing lunch.

I kept my word. Every time I snapped the shutter, her features faced away from the lens.

Using a telephoto lens, I zoomed in on her hands as she worked, hoping I caught the lines and signs of labor on her skin. I snapped away as she immersed her hands in a bowl of bread dough.

"This ain't much interesting," Martha commented. I could hear the chuckle in her voice.

"Everyone's hands are interesting."

"You can see my hands?"

"With this lens, yes."

She brushed the flour residue away. "May I try?"

"Of course." I gave her the camera, telling her where to place her eye, where the digital sample showed up, and how to move the lens in and out.

"May I take a picture?"

I grinned. "Be my guest. The button is on the top."

She pushed it and then jumped when the shutter snapped. "I think I took a picture of the floor."

"Try again."

She pointed the camera out the window, snapped, and then peered at the tiny image at the back of the camera. "That's pretty." She tilted it toward me. "See? Oh. It disappeared. Is it gone?"

I shook my head. "It only shows for a moment after you've taken the picture." I pressed the right combination of buttons to bring the image back. "That is nice. You have a good eye."

Martha looked at the camera, looked outside, looked back at the camera, and then looked at me. "Are you done taking pictures?"

"Almost. Would you like to take some?"

"Such a fancy camera — I'd be afraid of a-breakin' it."

"Company camera. Have at it."

I made a point of returning to my packing, giving Martha the freedom to experiment how she wished. From the living room window, I could see her examining the mailbox, the barn, and the cows in the pasture. I watched as Sara walked out to meet her and said something — I couldn't hear what.

Not that I was spying or anything. Just watching out for the camera.

Martha nodded, Sara departed, Martha shot for a little while longer before returning to the house.

I busied myself folding the pile of dishcloths on the counter.

I didn't see Sara for the rest of the afternoon, and for that matter, I didn't see much
of Martha either. I was making sure I had
enough shots of the farm and checking
under the bed for stray socks.

The kids came home from school, rowdy
and energized. Martha sent them outside
for chores; when they finished, they began a
game of pickup volleyball in the field, using
the summer clothesline as the net.

Martha reappeared for the dinner prepara-
tions. But everything became clear after the
meal — as I stood in the entryway with my
bags packed, I realized what I'd forgotten.
"My quilt," I said, looking around. What
had happened to it? It hadn't been in my
room. "Sara, you haven't seen my quilt
around, have you?"

Her expression turned guilty. "I . . .
um . . . let me look."

We waited. When she returned, she was
carrying my quilt in her hands, but not the
way I'd remembered it. "Sara . . ."

"I finished it."

She had. The strips were all sewn together,
and it even had a back. And batting in the
middle. "You didn't have to —"

"Yes. You wouldn't have been able to fin-

453

ish it before summer."

Okay. Likely true. I gave her a hug. "Thank you, sweetie."

"I worked all afternoon on it."

I examined the quilt in closer detail. "It looks fantastic." I thought of her one-time hope to leave and become a fashion designer. Sara had such talent. I wished her all the best — and hoped that she'd be able to use her talent within the culture she'd chosen.

An expression passed over her face, but I didn't have long to decipher its meaning. Martha brought me a light cloth bag to carry my quilt in, and Elam offered to carry my luggage.

I thanked him and walked toward the door while Leah and Elizabeth clutched my good hand and begged me to write them too.

"Do you want your things in the car or the trunk?" Elam asked.

"Car is fine," I said, trying to twirl two little girls with one hand and nearly falling over in the process. Dusk had fallen. I had trouble seeing the keyhole for the car door. The Amish weren't much for outdoor lighting.

I said my goodbyes to everyone. Or was it everyone? "Where's Sara?"

Martha patted my arm. "Don't know

where she got off to. I think she's a mite sad you're goin'. She misses having Rebecca in the house. You've become like an older sister to her."

All the more reason to say goodbye. I thought about looking for her, but the farm was just too big, and I wanted to make it back to Portland early enough to unpack and sit for a while before bed.

I sighed, waved goodbye, and climbed into my car.

Time to go.

My heart still broke a little when I returned home. I would be alone, again. Maybe I should think about a roommate. I supposed I could rearrange things. I could move my office into my room, even if sleep specialists advised against working in the room you slept in. But after being with the Burkholders, living alone held little appeal.

I parked my car in at the base of the stairs, got out, and started removing bags.

That's when I heard it. Or did I?

I held very still and waited.

There it was. A thump. A thump from the back of my car. The trunk.

Why would there be a thump?

My mind raced over all the reasons for a thump in a not-running car.

There could be a serial killer in the trunk, waiting to kill me when I was stupid enough to lift the lid.

There could be a spare bowling ball in my trunk, and it was still rolling around after I parked. I dismissed that idea quickly, considering I didn't own a bowling ball.

A small animal could have jumped inside, but I couldn't remember when it was last open.

Another thump.

I sent up a short prayer for my safety and opened the trunk with my key.

"Hi, Jayne."

"Sara!" I exploded. "What are you doing there?"

She sat up. "I'm out!"

"No you're not, you're still in my trunk. What were you thinking? Is this why you disappeared earlier?"

She stretched her arms. "I'm *out*, you see?" She held out her hand — I thought she wanted help out, but I realized what she had in her fist. It was her kapp.

"You're . . . leaving?"

"Yes. Can I get out of your trunk?"

"Please." I stood back and watched her climb out. Naturally, once both of her feet touched asphalt, the heavens opened and a torrent of rain fell from the sky. To make things better, a nice, strong Columbia Gorge wind blew the water sideways.

I closed the trunk as quickly as I could, grabbed my things from the backseat, and raced up the stairs with Sara right behind me.

Once inside, I slammed the door behind us and plopped my things on the floor. "You're soaked through." Sara hadn't thought to bring a coat or cape of any kind; her cotton dress clung to her shoulders and dripped on the entryway tile. "You can't wear wet clothes. You didn't bring anything?"

"Why would I bring any of my Amish clothes? I want to stay here."

"Oh, I don't know. So you'd have something to wear?"

"We're about the same size."

If I wasn't careful, she might alter my things to fit her. "We'll find you something dry, and then we're going to talk."

"I'm not going back."

"I want you to tell me that when you're dry, not before."

In my bedroom, Sara took charge of the clothing situation, parsing through my little closet and choosing items for herself.

Incidentally, they were mostly items I'd picked up in Lincoln City.

When she was dried and dressed, and I had changed into thick, woolly socks, I steered her out to my dining room and sat her down at the table.

"First," I said, although so many thoughts clamored for the title of "first" that I hardly knew what to say, "it was very dangerous for you to ride in my trunk like that. What if I had gotten rear-ended? You wouldn't have had any protection."

"But we didn't."

"What if we had?"

She squinted at me. "But we didn't."

All right. Excellent progress. "Did you tell anyone you were planning on doing this?"

"No."

"Not even Ida or Levi?"

"No."

"You realize your mother thinks you're getting baptized on Sunday?"

Sara looked at her lap. "I know. I couldn't do it. I didn't want to live a lie no more."

"Sara —" I searched for words. "I left home at eighteen. I went to college, and I rarely went back. Things with my dad were never good, but I also never tried to meet with my mom or my sister. I never tried to make things better. It wasn't a priority, and I was hiding. I missed out on a lot. Lately, I've been able to go back and have a relationship with my family. They've forgiven me — things have been good. I'm still me, still a journalist, still living in the city, but I can visit them whenever I want. It won't be like that for you, not with your father. He may never be able to forgive you. I want to help you in whatever ways I can, but you need to know what you're giving up."

Her gaze was direct and calm. "I know what I'm giving up. I've thought much about this. I want to design clothes, wear lipstick, and meet a boy I haven't known since I was born."

"I'm sure your family visits relatives in other communities —"

"They're all the same. They're all Plain. They all want wives to cook and give them children. I cook, and I would like children, but maybe not eight. And maybe not cook every meal, every day. I look at my mother and wonder how her arms have not fallen off. I don't want that life." She reached into her pocket and said, "I've kept this with me so that when you left, I could go too."

I peered at the contents of her pocket — a fold of cash and a Social Security card with "Sara M. Burkholder" printed above the nine-digit ID number.

"I'm not a minor anymore," Sara continued. "I don't need my parents to sign for me. I have my card and the money I saved up."

"How much?"

"Three thousand six hundred fifty-three dollars."

My eyebrows flew upward. "Where did you get that kind of money?"

"I sold two of my more complicated quilts. Some babysitting. I saved up."

I couldn't save like that at eighteen, and I'd thought myself fairly motivated at the time.

I was about to ask if she had any specific plans, aside from the lipstick-wearing, when my phone buzzed in my purse. I almost ignored it, but a tiny thought encouraged me to take a look at the caller.

It was Levi.

CHAPTER 34

"Jayne, please tell me Sara is there with you." I could clearly hear the panic in Levi's voice. His alarm broke my heart.

"Levi . . . hold on." I pressed the mute button and looked to Sara. I almost asked if it would be all right for me to tell him, but thought better of it. I couldn't lie to Levi.

"She's here," I said, after reconnecting the call.

He exhaled into the receiver; it sounded like a windstorm. "That's good, because I'm halfway there."

A part of me bristled. The way he'd left before — I didn't know if I was ready for him to come back, much less uninvited.

He must have read my mind, or at least my silence. "I'm sorry. I know I should ask first, or be sensitive, but she's my sister, Jayne. You can drop her off at the corner if you want to."

"Drop her off at the corner? In this rain?

In the middle of Portland at night? Are you insane?"

"I'm sorry, really sorry. I was just trying to think of a way that you wouldn't have to be involved."

"She hitched a ride in the trunk of my car and is wearing a pair of my jeans. I'm already involved."

"I didn't — I didn't want it to be like this between us."

"I have no idea what to say to that."

"Can we talk about it?"

"*I* wanted to talk about it. You left."

"I was upset."

"And you're not now?"

"I never meant to hurt you."

"Too late," I said, and then I realized I'd revealed too much. I hung up before I could say anything more. "So," I turned back to Sara. "Maybe before your brother comes you should tell me how you got into my trunk in the first place. That was pretty slick. Have you been practicing?"

"I took your keys when you told me you were packing."

"Oh?"

Her eyes shifted downward. "And I opened the trunk. There was a little ridge on the inside, just enough for me to pull it closed."

"But I saw you right before I left. I had my keys in my pocket."

"I left after I gave you the quilt. I didn't close your trunk all the way earlier."

"What would you have done if I'd decided to put my things in the trunk? Your brother would have seen you!"

She shrugged. "When you came, I saw you had stuff on the seat of your car. I figured you would do the same when you left."

"For Pete's sake." I rubbed my head. "Have you ever thought about working for the CIA?"

"What's the CIA?"

"People who can sneak around almost as skillfully as you."

"People who sneak are called CIA?"

"Never mind. Did I tell you how dangerous it is to ride in a trunk like that?"

"Yes. What happened between you and Levi?"

"I don't want to talk about it. Want something to drink? Bear in mind I haven't grocery-shopped."

We passed the time over tea, a stale package of Oreos, and *I Love Lucy* until there was a knock at the door.

A knock I recognized. I opened the door and there he was — six feet, three inches of gorgeous heartbreak.

I wanted to hate him. He made it difficult. But my feet felt cold just remembering the night I ran after him. My back straightened. "Come on in."

"Thanks." The door closed behind him; he kicked off his shoes. I wish he'd kept them on. Being in stocking feet together felt much too intimate. "Sara . . . are you okay?"

I rolled my eyes. "Of course she's okay. She's had tea and cookies and is watching *I Love Lucy.*"

"Sara?" Levi persisted. "You didn't tell me about this. I wish you had."

"You don't have to baby me anymore," Sara said in a soft voice. "I'm eighteen now. Girls my age are getting married and starting their adult lives. I'm starting mine the way I want to. The way I've always wanted to."

I sat back down and gestured for Levi to follow. We formed a triangle: Sara and me on the sofa, Levi in the overstuffed chair by the door. I turned down the TV volume. The antics of Lucy and her cohorts cast flickering silver light on our awkward little gathering.

"I just want you to know what you're getting into." Levi tented his hands as he spoke. "Dad won't acknowledge me as his son. Mom has to obey him, but she'll be

464

conflicted. Amos and Elam never forgave me; Rebecca might talk to me if her husband allowed it. Grandma will support you. You know I will . . . I just want you to be prepared."

When Sara explained to him about her Social Security card and cash stash, Levi's eyes widened. "That's very good."

"Have you thought about what you want to do, specifically?" I asked.

"I want to get my GED and attend the Art Institute of Portland. I want to study apparel design." She reached into her other pocket, pulling out a much-folded school brochure. "I will apply for financial aid. I will get a job and earn money. If I need to, I will make quilts and take in mending to support myself."

"Why did you leave with Jayne?" Levi asked in a quiet voice. "What you did was dangerous. You could have come to me."

"You are too close. I could have changed my mind and walked home."

Levi gave a wry smile. "You can stay with me at my house. Get your GED at Linn Benton Community College. Come to Portland when you're ready."

"Too close." Sara shrugged. "Here, I can't go back."

■ ■ ■ ■

An hour later Sara's adrenaline began to fade and the fact that she'd been awake since five kicked in. Levi checked his watch and looked at me. "Let's go check on that bookcase I made for you."

I wasn't stupid. I knew that was code for "I want to talk to you without Sara hearing, and it probably wouldn't be appropriate to go to your bedroom, so let's hit the study."

I didn't mention how I'd had an urge to chuck the bookcase from the landing. The fact that I couldn't lift any of it — dismantled or not — without personal injury was the main factor stopping me. That, and the fact that I had too many books.

We both rose and walked down the hall. I turned to check on Sara just in time to watch her eyes close in sleep.

Sleep, or she was sneaky enough to pretend. I didn't care either way. The powwow was Levi's idea, not mine.

He closed the door behind us. Like that wasn't suspicious. "I'm so sorry about all of this," he said.

"Yeah, I'm sure you are." I ran a hand through my hair. After all, Sara being in my apartment meant that I was being dragged into the center of a complicated family issue — one I was sure I didn't fully understand the implications of. That, and it meant Levi's continued presence in my life.

I didn't know how I felt about that.

"Thing is," Levi continued, "unless you ask her to, I don't think she'll leave here."

"I was getting that."

"Are you okay with an eighteen-year-old roommate?"

"She's not a normal eighteen-year-old, Levi. You know that. She's been groomed since birth to be ready to run a household and raise a family. Most girls — women — her age can barely do their own laundry. Sara can do it without a connection to city power."

"She's my baby sister."

"No, Elizabeth is your baby sister. Sara's grown now, and you're her hero. She watched you leave and make a life for yourself. She wants to do the same."

"I made a life, and then I compromised that life."

I hated the bitter tone I heard in his voice. "You came back so you could be available to your family, available to Sara."

"And she hopped a ride in the trunk of your car."

"She wouldn't have done that if she didn't

have a goal. You gave her those brochures, didn't you?"

"I did."

"She's owning this, can't you see? She's not leaving because you pressured her into it. She strategized, planned — it's hers. You should be proud."

"You're okay with her moving in with you?"

"Sure. She's more qualified to live without adult supervision than I am."

"Trunk, Jayne. Trunk."

"Yeah, well, she probably won't let as much mold grow in the fridge as I do."

"True." He looked around the study. "Where would you put her?"

"Probably in here."

"I'll bring up a bed tomorrow from the shop."

"She left the Amish and you'll bring her an Amish-style bed?"

"If she's going to be a student, she needs to learn not to look a gift horse in the mouth."

A bed. One more object from Levi, one more arrival to be nervous about. I didn't want involvement with him. I couldn't take being hurt again.

"I'm sorry about earlier," he said.

I wanted to punch him for being considerate. "Oh?"

"I wish things didn't happen the way they did."

That was vague.

"Okay. Um . . . well, if she's going to stay here tonight, I need to make up a bed for her on the couch."

Levi opened his mouth as if to say something, but he must have thought better of it. "I'll be back tomorrow."

"If I'm not here, Sara will let you in."

"What hours are you working tomorrow?"

"Don't know."

"Guess?"

"Wouldn't want to say, in case I get a call."

"What kind of call?"

"The 'Jayne, there's a breaking story' kind of call." I didn't mention that since I'd been in features, a whole series of people would have to be extraordinarily unavailable for me to get that call. It could happen, I suppose. Gas leaks aren't an urban myth.

"I can always wait around for you here, if you're late getting home."

"What?"

"It's a long day for Sara to be home alone. I'll come up whenever and keep her company."

There was no getting around him. "Sure, whatever. Anything else?"

He took so long to answer that I lifted my hand. "While you think, I'm going to make a bed up for her."

In a matter of moments I had my spare bedding gathered, and this time Sara was truly asleep.

"She's a heavy sleeper," Levi commented.

"No kidding." I struggled to lift her head high enough to put a pillow underneath.

"Let me help." He reached under his sister and lifted her gently from the couch. While Sara was aloft, literally, I tucked a sheet under the back of the cushions and arranged the pillows. After he laid her back down, we both tucked a comforter over her sleeping form.

We stepped back, neither of us daring to look at the other. I'll admit that a part of me wanted to be next — I wanted to be tucked in too.

Cold feet. Cold feet.

"Have a safe drive," I said.

Levi took the hint and walked to the door. "Thanks. I'll see you tomorrow."

I thought about imploring him to leave me alone, to keep me out of things, to treat me as Sara's roommate, nothing more. Instead I said nothing as I watched Levi put on his shoes, thread his arms into his coat, and leave, pretending he hadn't broken my heart.

And pretending I hadn't broken his.

Sara woke up at her usual time, five a.m. I came to that realization shortly after deciding that my apartment hadn't been broken into, and the person making a loud breakfast for herself in my kitchen had in fact been invited.

I tried the traditional techniques; burying my head in my pillow, pulling the covers over my head. What no one ever tells you is that doing either of those things makes the air too warm to breathe.

Finally I swung my feet around to the floor, threw on my college sweats, and walked down the hall to the kitchen.

"Good morning!" Sara greeted me with a bright smile and a hug. "I woke up this morning when the sun streamed through the window over there. You get such very good light in here! I thought about staying in bed — I slept so well! But I decided to get up and make us some breakfast."

My brain really only caught the last bits of her speech. "Us?"

"I made pancakes and eggs, and I found some bacon in your freezer, so I scrambled it with the eggs and put cheese on top, hope you like that, I couldn't remember. Do you have potatoes? It's so nice to have potatoes around. Potatoes and onions. You never know when you'll need a good onion, and they go with every meal. Potatoes too —"

I held up a hand. "We'll shop for groceries later. Can breakfast wait until I've showered?"

Sara nodded.

"Okay. I'll be back." I turned and all but stumbled into the bathroom. I considered it a success to get into the shower without finding that I'd brought a sock in with me. Afterward I felt better, the sleep cleared from my eyes and some of the mental cobwebs cleared out of the way. I dusted on a bit of light makeup and went back to my room to dress, knowing all the while that Sara might find fault with my ensemble.

To my surprise, she didn't say a word about my clothes as she served our respective breakfasts onto two plates. Instead, she asked when we were leaving for work.

"We?" I asked, my fork hovering halfway between my mouth and the plate.

Sara nodded. "I thought I'd go with you this morning and then come home at lunch."

My first thought was, "I'd lose my parking spot." This was Portland, by the way. I had never parked illegally until I moved here. But my second thought was that it wasn't fair to leave her alone in my apartment all day. There wasn't a farm to run; she would be bored to tears. I could get her a visitor pass, especially considering that her family was the focus of the piece I'd be writing.

"If I bring you this morning, you'll need to bring a book or something to keep you busy." There was a computer bay, but throwing Sara into the internet would be like chucking her into the deep end of the swimming pool without arm floaties.

She nodded. "I'll just sit. I'll take my sketchbook. I can watch people and get ideas."

"Yeah, maybe I'll take you to the ad department for that. They're usually a little snappier than reporting and editorial."

"Can you take me shopping soon? I would like to buy some of my own clothes."

"What's wrong with my jeans?" I said, rolling my eyes before I smiled. "Sure. I'll see when Gemma's available. Or Kim — she can be good at finding sales."

"I like sales."

I knew Levi would have to figure into all of this at some point.

Which meant I would have to call him.

I mulled that over as Sara showered and readied herself for her first day as an English girl.

CHAPTER 35

Sara and I ran into Kim inside the foyer of the *Oregonian* offices.

Of all mornings.

"Jayne! You're back. Who's this?"

Thinking I could be saved by brevity, I smiled and kept it short. "This is Sara. She's my new roommate."

"Sara?" Kim looked at me, looked at Sara, and then looked back at me. "The Amish girl?"

I could see Sara wilt. "Look, she left and she moved in with me. She's hanging out with me this morning until lunch."

"It's 'take your Amish roommate to work' day? Wish I'd gotten the memo." She touched Sara's shoulder. "Sorry, great line, couldn't resist. Want to grab lunch with us? We'll make Gemma take us out."

I was going to protest, but Sara's face had taken on an almost unearthly glow of joy. "Lunch sounds good," I said. "But right now I need to get her a visitor's pass —"

"Wait." Kim held out her hand. "This isn't Levi's sister, is it?"

"Um, yeah, it is. So, we'll see you at lunch —"

"Any changes on that front?"

"Have a good morning!" I all but yanked Sara's arm as I tried to make a break for it.

"She asks a lot of questions, doesn't she," Sara said as we'd turned a corner and I'd determined a safety level that allowed us to walk at a normal pace.

"Occupational hazard."

Once Sara was processed and armed with a badge, I set her up on a couch not far from my cubicle. I left her with written instructions on how to find me, my phone extension, and an assortment of dollar bills if she wanted something from the vending machine.

At my desk I plugged my camera's memory card into the USB reader and took a look at the images I'd gathered. The buggy, the barn, the stone path up to the door of the farmhouse. My pictures were fairly straightforward. Then others began to load, and I realized they were Martha's.

Martha. Where was she in all of this? A mixture of guilt and grief clutched at my heart. Her daughter had left, and she used me to accomplish that. Martha had taken me into her home, treated me like family, and this is what had happened. I couldn't help but feel it was my fault.

Had Levi communicated back to Martha that Sara was safe, dry, and had a roof over her head? The thought worried me so much I picked up the phone to ask.

"Jayne? Is Sara okay?" Levi asked as soon as he answered.

"She is. She's at work with me. I was just wondering — did you tell your mom? Does she know Sara's with me?"

"I told her Sara is safe, but I didn't say where. I wouldn't put it past Elam and Amos — or my father — to try to bring her home."

"Drive all the way up in the buggy?"

"No, they'd take a taxi."

"Oh. But they're pacifists. The worst they would do is spend the night on the landing."

"You don't think that would be a little traumatic for Sara?"

"She's stronger than you realize. Your mother needs to know where her daughter is."

"Jayne, you don't understand —"

"I have a pretty good hunch that mothers, no matter where they live or what they believe, generally want to know where their children are, even if it's just a general idea. Your mother's been very kind to me. It's the least I can do."

He sighed. "It's your call. It's your apartment. Don't underestimate the mail brigade, though."

"The male brigade? Are we talking about your brothers again?"

"Mail, as in the post. Rebecca wrote me letter after letter telling me how Mom cried herself to sleep every night and how much my siblings missed me. I asked my grandma once. It wasn't *that* bad. Does anyone at the house have your mailing address?"

"Sara did. It's probably written down somewhere in her room."

"Mom will find it."

"I'm not afraid of Amish mail."

"Sara's doing okay with everything?"

"Honestly?" I looked all around, making sure she hadn't snuck up on me. "I don't think it's all sunk in yet. She's running on a lot of adrenaline. How was it for you when you first left?"

He exhaled. "It got harder as I realized what I'd done, but I didn't go back."

I sat up, feeling particularly mature. "How are things on the job front? You are looking, aren't you?"

"I have a couple interviews in Portland next week. Another in Seattle."

"Good luck."

"Thanks." I could hear a smile in his voice. I missed his smile, the way it made me feel like melted chocolate on the inside. Before I could think too much about missing him, I mentioned work to be attended to and hung up.

At least I was telling the truth — I had a lot of work to do. But before I got to it, I had to talk to Martha. I dialed and listened to the line ring. And ring. And ring. And ring. And that was okay. I didn't expect differently.

After what seemed like half an hour, a voice answered. "Who is this?"

The voice was young and male. Amos or Elam? "This is Jayne. I need to speak with your mother."

"Do you know where Sara is?"

"I need to talk to your mother."

"Do you?"

"Who is this, Amos or Elam?"

A pause. "Elam."

"Elam, please go get your mother." He sighed, and there was silence. I had the distinct impression that the receiver was dangling over the ground as he went to fetch his mom.

Moments later I heard commotion and voices. Then, "Jayne? Is that you?" Martha's voice held a note of panic that broke my heart.

"It's okay. Sara's in Portland with me."

"Oh, I'm so glad. Oh, goodness. Why did you take her? Her baptism is in three days!"

"I didn't take her, Martha. She left. She climbed into my car when no one was looking. I didn't discover her until I was home."

"She is in your apartment?"

"Yes."

"She's safe?"

"Yes, she is."

"She doesn't want to come back?"

I didn't know what to say. "Not . . . right now."

"Sara is stubborn. She's a lot like her brother."

And we both knew how *that* turned out. Levi wasn't about to go back, marry a nice Amish girl, and grow a moustache-less beard.

"Will you . . . watch over her?"

I nodded, not that she could see. "I will."

"Could you write to me about her?"

"Of course."

"Don't send it here — send it to my mother."

"Do you think Gideon will ever —"

"No."

"I'll take care of her," I said.

I could hear the tears in Martha's voice. "Thank you."

I worked straight until lunch without thinking twice about it or taking a coffee break. If Brian's wife hadn't sent him to work with curry-smelling leftovers, I might not have noticed the time.

I gathered my things in a rush and hurried down the hall to find Sara, half expecting her to be holding court with Kim and Gemma.

Instead, I found her chatting with a heavy-set, African-American man who looked an awful lot like my boss.

"Jayne!" Sol said when he saw me. "I was just talking to your new roommate here. Young Amish woman leaves home to pursue an education and career — story there?"

"Right now, she's my roommate, not a source."

Sol scowled. "You know, Jayne, I've heard rumors about reporters who listen to their editors."

"I think it's a good idea," Sara piped up.

I turned to her in surprise. "Are you sure?"

She shrugged. "Maybe having an article about me would help my chances at design

481

school."

Sol lifted a dark eyebrow. "Kid's got a point."

"We'll talk about it."

Sara crossed her arms. "I'm an adult. It's my decision. Besides, you've already written stories about my family. Why would this be different?"

"Uh, let's see, I changed all the names? Hey, if we're going to get lunch, we need to leave now."

"What about your friend Kim? And Gemma?"

So much for keeping a low profile. "I'll call them, we'll eat, I'll drop you back at the house."

Sol reached for Sara's hand. "I'm sure we'll talk later."

I rolled my eyes as we walked away. "Seriously. He may be an editor now, but the man's a diehard reporter at heart."

At Gemma's family's restaurant, DiGrassi & Elle, Gemma's father kept bringing us plate after plate of lunch specials until he came and found there was no room left on the table. Without room, he simply scraped the contents of the serving plate he was carrying onto our respective dishes. After that, Gemma waved a white flag — possibly her napkin — and the barrage of food ceased.

Until dessert.

To my surprise, Sara blended in with my friends seamlessly. Everyone asked her questions; she answered them openly. Gemma promised a shopping trip while Joely offered to teach her to drive. Kim volunteered to look into the area's GED programs and college financial aid options.

Sara moved differently away from her family, spoke differently. It was as if she was no longer looking over her shoulder, making sure no one guessed her secret.

I wished Levi could see her. Maybe he'd stop worrying.

The rest of the afternoon flew by. When I wasn't thinking about Levi, I managed to get an impressive amount of work done. But when I was thinking about Levi? Forget it. I may as well have stuck a Post-it Note on my head that read "Out to Lunch."

Eventually, however, the day ended and it was time to go back to the apartment and greet whomever I found there.

Because of my profound internal strength and fortitude, I did not step into the restroom for a hair check before getting in my car to drive home. I really wasn't that girl, though I impersonated her from time to time.

I saw Levi's truck even before I parked outside my apartment complex. Bracing myself, I walked up the stairs and tried the door handle.

Locked. I started with the bolt and then unlocked the door handle. But as I turned the key in the door handle, I heard the bolt scrape closed.

Okay. I unlocked the bolt again and tried to push the door open.

The knob was locked.

I banged on the door. "Hello? Sara? I'd kind of like to come in, please."

Nothing.

Fine. I unlocked the handle and turned it in my hand halfway; holding the knob, I unlocked the bolt. I felt the person on the other side try to lock the knob again, but it didn't catch since the knob was still turned. Before the bolt could be turned again, I turned the knob, shoved the door open, and just about knocked Spencer over.

"Spencer?" I put my purse down. "Pleasant to see you."

"Jayne?" Levi appeared down the hall. "Are you okay?"

"Spencer locked me out." I turned to the offender, who didn't look the least bit sorry.

"What are you, twelve?"

"He locked you out?" Levi rolled his eyes. "Sorry. I brought him so he could help haul the bed up the stairs. He has his own car and should be going home anytime now. Right, Spence?

"Come take a look at the office." Levi motioned for me to follow him down the hall. As I approached the doorway to the study, I could see what he'd done so far — the bed was flush against the far wall, but it wasn't what I'd expected. Instead of bringing a standard twin bed, Levi had brought a lofted bed and managed to fit a desk and a narrow dresser underneath.

My eyebrows lifted. "I'm impressed."

Levi put his hands on his hips. "Not bad, huh? With small spaces, the best thing to do is go up. I'm sure she'll need some additional closet space, but this way, moving her in takes over less of your life."

I nodded, still admiring his handiwork.

"I'm looking for an apartment in Portland," he said.

"Oh?" I turned to face him, surprised. "What about the shop?"

"Grady is buying it. He and Spence will keep it going, along with one of the shop guys who's got some brains. I'll be selling my house too. I know the market's not good, but I'm willing to sell it for less if it means getting out of it." He gave a sad smile. "Time to move on."

Move on. Did *I* want to move on? My life had undergone some huge changes, but there was one piece I couldn't let go of.

As I thought about it, I felt myself move toward him. "I hope things work out for you."

He stepped closer. "Thanks. I appreciate that."

I leaned closer to him. "You deserve to be happy."

"I don't know about that." His eyes studied mine, flickered to my lips, and returned.

I held my breath. His lips edged closer to mine until I could feel his breath against my face. He smelled like cinnamon. Our lips brushed together. I felt his hand glance over the ends of my hair.

"You guys hungry? I'm starved."

We jumped apart. Spencer stood with his hands braced against the doorjamb, eyes innocent. "Mexican? Italian? Pizza? What sounds good?"

In the end we chose sushi, partly because Spencer was against it. I thought about inviting Kim, Joely, and Gemma to dilute the amount of Spencer-ness in the dinner party, but decided against it. I wanted my friends to still be my friends afterward, and Spencer was in full loose cannon mode.

That, and Joely would probably kill him. With her police-issued shoelaces.

Levi and I didn't look at each other throughout dinner. At least, I didn't look at Levi. I suppose if he had been looking at me, I wouldn't have known.

CHAPTER 36

Levi and Spencer left after dinner. Sara sketched on the couch while I read a book in the chair. A movement caught my eye — Sara's shoulders shook, almost imperceptibly.

"Sara?" I put my book down. "What's wrong?"

Her shoulders stilled, but I could see her lips waver as she tried to regain control. I moved to sit beside her on the couch. "Talk to me."

She hugged a pillow cushion to herself. "I'm afraid I won't go to heaven now when I die. I thought I could forget about it, but I can't."

I frowned. "What are you talking about?"

"I left. I won't be baptized." She shrugged. "I don't have the hope of heaven anymore."

"What . . . what did your deacon teach about salvation?"

She shrugged. "It's boastful to think I can

know I'll go to heaven, I know that . . ."

"Sara," I took her hand. "It's not boastful." I took a deep breath. "I haven't been a model Christian for a really, really long time." Had I ever been? "Okay, never was," I admitted. "I should probably ask someone like Gemma to have this conversation with you. I've been kinda rude to God for a while. Thing is, I decided to make Jesus my Savior when I was a kid, and Jesus has been after me ever since. I know that, and I know that I want an active relationship with Him now. Scripture tells me I'll go to heaven, and I believe that."

Sara wiped at her eyes. "You think I can still go to heaven?"

"I do." I sighed. "Even if you're not Plain anymore, Jesus still loves you. He still wants to have a relationship with you. Do you want a relationship with Him?"

Sara nodded.

We prayed together. The words felt awkward on my tongue. I'm sure it wasn't the most eloquent, grammatically correct prayer of all time, or even this month, but it was a prayer, and it meant something.

Sara and I attended church together that Sunday with Gemma.

Throughout the week, Sara had taken in

her new surroundings with wide eyes, from Elephant's Deli to the Portland Art Museum, but nothing amazed her as much as the experience of a worship service. When the music started, she clapped her hands over her ears.

"Are you all right?" I asked.

She grinned and nodded.

It occurred to me that she hadn't likely heard much music, much less amplified by the sort of speakers this church had hanging from the ceiling.

Looking at her broad smile, I stopped trying to monitor Sara's every reaction and sang out, even if I didn't know all the words.

Sara sat with rapt attention throughout the sermon, which, appropriately enough, was about grace. She nodded when she agreed with the pastor, and tilted her head when she seemed to have trouble absorbing the words.

And me? I felt ashamed of having lost so much time being angry with God and angry with my family. Had I transferred that anger to Levi? Was I the sort of person who wasn't happy unless she was mad at someone? The thought troubled me.

"I have a job!"

"Really?" I steadied my phone headset to keep it from leaping out of my ear as I drove. "Sara, Levi has a job!"

Sara beamed from the passenger seat. "Is he moving back to Portland?"

I wondered that myself, but I asked the question that puzzled me most first. "They called you on a Sunday?"

"The corporate world doesn't take days off."

"Will they expect you to work seven days a week too?"

"No, but the person hiring wasn't an economist. He's just the head of the department."

"Crazy. Where's the position?"

"Portland."

"Oh, wow," I said, as my heart began to race. "So . . . you'll be moving?"

"As soon as I can. Job starts next week."

"Are you glad?"

He sighed. "Very."

"Then I'm happy for you. Truly." I shot a look at Sara. "What are you doing tonight?"

"Not much, why?"

"You could come up so we can celebrate. Knock back a few cups of coffee — I bought a machine. Besides, Sara would like to see you."

"I'd love to see her. I'll leave in a few

minutes."

I hung up and pulled off the cell phone earpiece. "He's coming up. He found a job here. We're going to party like it's 1999."

"He's moving to Portland?"

"He is." More cardiovascular palpitations at the thought. "The position starts next week. In the meantime, he'll be here this afternoon."

Watching Sara's smile, I felt myself grow glad on the inside.

By the time we returned home from church, the sun was out. We opened all the blinds and pulled back all the curtains, filling the apartment with warm, sunshiny light. After making a lunch of deli sandwiches full of tomatoes and avocados, Sara settled on the couch with a book.

Sunny day, and my wrist felt fine — I decided I was ready for a motorcycle ride.

That was the downside of the roommate thing. I had to work a little harder to have a moment to myself, as opposed to living in total seclusion all the time.

I supposed it was probably healthy for me.

I suited up and headed out. My bike took a moment to start; it hadn't been used in so long. But once I got it started, riding it felt incredible. The wind rushed through the vents in my jacket. The sun warmed the exposed spot on the back of my gloved hand.

Levi was coming. He was coming because I'd asked him to. I thought back to how we'd met, at the woodshop. The way he'd taken me to the emergency room when I hurt my wrist. How we towed the buggy back to the farm together. Our date at Pastini. The weekend at the coast when everything fell apart.

I lived a lot of my life expecting people to let me down, expect the worst of me, and shut me out. Had I expected that of Levi?

The root of our breakup was that I couldn't tell him I loved him. Sure, we hadn't known each other long. I'd needed time. Well, time had passed. Did I feel differently?

Or did the time not matter? Had I loved him all along but been afraid to admit it to myself?

I never wanted to live a life of fear, but I realized that I had done that anyway despite my best efforts. I had hesitated pursuing a relationship with my mom and sister because I was afraid they would hate me. Because of my fear, I'd missed out on so much. I didn't want to miss out on Levi, not if he loved me back.

I'd hurt him. I knew I had. Should I apologize? Beg his forgiveness? Not say anything and just add it to my feminine mystique? I felt confused. When I returned home, I found my phone and dialed my mom's number.

She picked up, sounding groggy. "Did I wake you?"

"It's Sunday," she answered, by way of explanation. "Is everything all right?"

I explained my situation.

"Well, dear, you fix it the way women have been fixing their man problems for hundreds of years."

"How's that?" I asked, ready to be horrified if somehow my mom had reversed her position in the milk/cow arena. If she had, I was back to square one.

"Easy, dear. You make him a pie."

CHAPTER 37

Pie. Pie. Pie. What did I have to make a pie with? "Sara, I need you!"

Sara got up from the couch and joined me in the kitchen. "What are you doing? What's wrong?"

"I need to make Levi a pie."

"Okay . . . what kind of pie?"

"Any kind of pie. We don't have time to go shopping."

"Oh." She joined me in fervent cupboard-checking. Then she moved on to the freezer, digging past boxes of frozen ravioli and grilled chicken strips. "What about these?"

"I'd forgotten about those." In her hand she held a bag of frozen peaches. "I was going through a smoothie phase for a while."

"Smoothie?"

"Blended fruit. Then I broke the blender. Sticking a fork in to loosen the fruit was a bad idea. I moved on to less dangerous cuisine." I winced as I heard myself babble.

Was I always like this under stress?

"You've got peaches, apricots, and . . ." she held the last bag close for examination. "Organic Oregon marionberries."

"Think there's enough for a pie?"

Sara shrugged. "Sure. Do you have shortening for the crust?"

"Levi bought it when you and your mom stayed here."

An expression of longing passed over Sara's features. I knew she missed her mom. I knew she wouldn't talk about it.

At her suggestion, we placed the fruit in a colander and ran it under warm water, just long enough for the fruit to lose most of its ice. I mixed and rolled out the piecrust, enjoying working gently with my hands without the brace, while Sara mixed the fruit with flour, sugar, cinnamon, nutmeg, and a little lemon juice.

Like an experienced team, we put the thing together — I put the bottom of the pie into the pie pan, Sara dumped the fruit inside, I put the top on, trimmed off the excess, and crimped the edges all nice and pretty. As a last thought, I carved LEVI into the top. We were congratulating him on the job, after all. Nothing says job congratulations like a pie.

Sara insisted we not put the pie in the

oven until it was fully preheated. So I stood, staring at the oven until the heating light blinked off. We placed strips of tinfoil around the edge before putting it in the oven.

"How long?" I asked, my fingers hovering over the timer function on the microwave.

"Forty minutes, remove the foil, and then another ten should do it."

I set the timer for forty minutes.

And waited.

By the time Levi knocked on the door, the apartment smelled almost as good as Martha's kitchen.

I opened the door. "Hi," I said, aware my voice sounded flight attendant perky. "Glad you could come up."

He smiled. "Me too."

I couldn't read the expression on his face. He seemed happy, but . . . guarded? Was that it? Hard to say.

Sara gave him a hug. He ruffled her hair; she made a face. He looked around. "Smells good in here."

I gave a careful smile. "We made pie."

"What kind?"

"Peach, apricot, and marionberry." Sara tugged on his sleeve. "Take off your coat."

He began to shrug out of his jacket. "I

don't think I've had that before."

"It's Jayne's specialty." Sara took the jacket and hung it up in the closet.

I began to panic. What was I thinking, that he would walk into the apartment and I'd suddenly know what to say? In front of Sara? It was one thing to try to make amends with the man who could very well be the love of your life, but another thing entirely to do it with his sister in the room.

Awkward.

I jumped when the microwave timer went off. The pie was really done this time — we'd removed the foil ten minutes ago. I walked to the kitchen and started to pick up every hot pad I could find.

"Sure you don't want me to do that for you?" Levi asked. I turned in time to see the glimmer in his eye. I knew he was remembering the time I'd set the hot pad on fire at the farmhouse.

I handed him my stash. "Be my guest."

He kept two and discarded the others. He beamed when he saw his name. "I don't think anyone's made me a pie with my name on it before."

I pulled out plates and forks. Sara frowned. "Doesn't it need to cool for a while?"

"I like my pie a bit runny," Levi said.

"Makes the fruit stand out."

He waited while I carved it into wedges; I handed him the first slice.

"What, no ice cream?" he teased.

"It's not a perfect world."

He didn't need to know that we'd essentially cleaned out my freezer with this pie.

We took our dessert to the living room and sat down while it cooled on the plates.

Sara ate hers with surprising speed before lifting a hand to her forehead. "Oh."

I frowned. "What's wrong?"

Her eyebrows furrowed. "I . . . I just got a headache all of a sudden."

"I'm sorry."

"It's like a throbbing behind my forehead. It's really bad."

Levi looked to me. "Jayne, do you have any painkillers?"

Sara held up a hand. "No, I don't want to take anything. I think I should just lie down."

With that, she got up, went into her bedroom, and closed the door.

Levi leaned back. "And then there were two. She's always been a terrible liar."

"What? How can you tell?"

"Her ears move when she lies. Always have." He looked out the front window. "It's a gorgeous day outside. Want to go for a walk?"

My hand itched to hold his. I dug it farther into my jacket pocket.

"The position is a good one," Levi said, as we walked under newly leafing trees. "I'll be doing what I love. Pay's all right. Certainly enough to where I can help pay for some of Sara's living expenses while she's starting out."

"I wouldn't tell her that just yet. I think she's liking independence."

"You think she's doing okay?"

"I do." I recounted to him the spiritual conversation Sara and I had had the other night.

Levi nodded. "I felt the way she did when I left. I'm glad she had you to talk to."

"Me?" I scoffed. "I'm the last person she should be talking to about spiritual matters."

"Why do you say that?"

"I've only recently gotten my life back on track. I spent too much time giving God the cold shoulder, pretending that if I didn't believe He existed, He might leave me alone."

"Did He?"

I snorted. "No."

"Glad to hear it."

Maybe this was my moment. I tucked my hair behind my ear. "Levi, I —"

He held up his hand. "Jayne, before you say anything, there's something I need to tell you."

"Okay."

"That night I left? I'm sorry. I handled things badly. I shouldn't have left like that."

"You had every reason to."

"No, I didn't."

"I hurt you. You told me you loved me and I . . . I was afraid. And here I was thinking I was going to stop living out of fear. Look," I said, trying to piece together a coherent thought. "I know I made a mess of things. Badly. Could you . . . forgive me?"

"Of course." His answer was immediate. He pointed to the right. "Let's go this way," he said, indicating a quiet alleyway.

Fine with me. I hated feeling as though I were having this conversation with an audience.

"What I'm trying to ask," I said, starting again, "is if you'd be willing to start over. With me."

"Start over?"

"Yes."

"All the way? Meet each other all over again?"

"Start over from where I screwed things up."

He stopped and turned to face me. "I want to, but I need to know you're not going to freak out on me again like that."

I shook my head. "I can't promise I'm not going to get scared again."

"Will you at least talk about it with me when you do?"

"Just don't leave."

"I won't." He cupped my face.

Not caring that we were standing in a Portland alleyway, Levi pulled me close and kissed me. Kissed me like a man who had lost his love and found her again.

He pulled me closer when the kiss ended, as if he were afraid I'd slip away.

"I missed you," I whispered.

"I missed *you*."

"You've driven me crazy for the longest time," I said with a sigh.

He stroked my hair. "Back at you. Ever since you rode away on your motorcycle."

"Yeah?"

"Yeah." He squeezed my hand. "Let's go back and tell Sara she doesn't need to have a headache anymore."

"Okay."

We walked back into the sunshine, hand in hand.

EPILOGUE

Six Months Later

Sara, Levi, and I watched from the window as the mail van parked to the side of the complex's mailbox unit.

"Can you see anything?" Sara asked.

Levi stretched to stand on his toes. I tried not to giggle. "No, he's behind the unit. I can't — wait."

"What?" I craned my neck.

"Sorry, wrong box. Yours is the one in the middle, right?"

"One of, yes."

"He stuffed something into one of the end ones."

I rolled my eyes. "Okay, guys, let's back away from the window and check the mail like normal people."

Levi kept his eyes on the mail van. "I'm not normal."

Moments passed in silence. Finally, Sara straightened. "He's gone. Let's go."

We hurried down the stairs, probably annoying the downstairs neighbors in the process. I carried the mailbox key; Sara plucked it from my fingers. When we got down to the boxes, she unlocked the door while Levi made an adept grab for the contents.

"Envelope from Portland Community College?" Levi fanned his face with the envelope in question.

Sara squealed and snatched the envelope from him before carefully tearing along the top fold to open it.

I crossed my arms. "The Apocalypse is ever nearer, Sara. Just open the thing."

"I don't want to tear anything that's inside."

I looked to Levi. "Just think. If today weren't Saturday, we would have missed this."

Sara awarded my sarcasm with an elbow to the ribs. In the time she'd spent living with me, she'd certainly learned to fend for herself.

She grinned. "I passed. I got it. I got my GED!"

Levi wrapped her in a bear hug. "I knew you could!"

"Let me see!" I managed to pry the letter from her fingers. "You scored well too."

She nodded. "It'll help with my entrance to the Art Institute."

I squeezed her shoulder. "You should set up that entrance interview."

"I'm going to go call Gemma!"

Levi and I watched as she ran back inside. "She did it."

I nodded. "I knew she could."

"And it's design school from here."

"Yup."

"Does she ever talk about the family with you?"

"Nope."

He exhaled. "I offered to take her to visit Grandma a couple weeks ago. She declined."

"Give her time. She's still Plain in her heart, as much as she doesn't want to be. I thought she'd cut her hair months ago." I hugged my arms to myself. "I lost out on time with my dad. I hate to think of what she'll miss."

"Not every story has a happy ending. I tried to make peace with him — it didn't work. You were there. I don't know that he'd treat her any different."

"God can change hearts."

"Yes, He can. My dad's is particularly stubborn, though."

I made a face.

"Until that time," Levi continued, rubbing his thumb over my diamond-and-garnet engagement ring, "we're her family."

I squeezed his hand. "People can change."

"Yes, they can."

"Sara passed."

"She did."

I looked up at him. "Let's make her a pie."

ACKNOWLEDGMENTS

Writing acknowledgments for a book is hard. At least I think so.

It takes a village to write a novel, and two villages to get it published.

I couldn't have written this book without my husband, Danny (who also took my fantastic author photo), whose calm suggestions helped me climb my way out of writer's block. He knew I was a writer and married me anyway — that's how great he is.

Exceptional thanks to the people in my life as I began my writing journey — my parents, Scott and Ruyle Manton, who filled my childhood with books and stories. Thanks to my brother, Geoff, who keeps me laughing, and my sister, Susannah, who reads my chapters every week.

Many huge thanks to my dear friend Kara

Christensen, for reading aloud chapters with me and asking critical questions.

Many thanks to Bobbie Christensen (mother of Kara), who took me to Oregon Christian Writers' conferences, advocated for me, and introduced me to wonderful people like Kara Christensen and Bonnie Leon.

Many thanks to Bonnie Leon, who read my manuscript when I was sixteen and told me I was "publishable," helped me with my book proposals, and answered my questions about publishing houses.

Many thanks to my parents-in-law, Ray and Denise Lodge, whose assistance with wood and coronary bypass knowledge proved invaluable.

Thank you to my draft readers: my mom, my sister, Aimee, Diane, Rachel, Kara, and Bobbie.

Many thanks to my agent, Sandra Bishop, for all of her help and encouragement, and to the Harvest House team as they've seen this project through. Kim and Carolyn — I couldn't ask for better editors!

Additional thanks to the mentors and encouragers I encountered throughout my journey to publication — Lorna Eskie, Esther Barton, Helen Kelts, and the rest of my extended family. I love and appreciate you all!

ABOUT THE AUTHOR

Hillary Manton Lodge graduated from the University of Oregon's School of Journalism. When not working on her next novel, Hillary enjoys photography, art films, and discovering new restaurants. She and her husband, Danny, reside in the Pacific Northwest.

Check out Hillary's website at hillarymantonlodge.com